A COMBAT OF DEVILS

A COMBAT OF DEVILS

KEITH DOVKANTS

Matador
9 Priory Business Park
Kibworth Beauchamp
Leicestershire LE8 0RX, UK
Tel: (+44) 116 279 2299
Fax: (+44) 116 279 2277
Email: books@troubador.co.uk
Web: www.troubador.co.uk/matador

ISBN 978 1780882 024

British Library Cataloguing in Publication Data.
A catalogue record for this book is available from the British Library.

Typeset by Troubador Publishing Ltd, Leicester, UK

Matador is an imprint of Troubador Publishing Ltd

Printed and bound in the UK by TJ International, Padstow, Cornwall

For Natalie, Dulcibella and Anthony.

CHAPTER ONE

They saw the smoke from about six miles. It seemed to hang in the still air, puffs of black tinged with yellow and blue, like a bruise on the pale sky. Below, pricking the smoothness of the sea, a single dark shape could be discerned.

'There she is,' Campbell said, lowering his binoculars. 'Alter starboard five degrees. Full speed.'

La Salle crossed from a wing of the bridge to the wheelhouse. The men inside glanced at him expectantly and Jenkins, the helmsman, visibly tightened his grip on the spokes.

'Shall we see some action, sir?'

La Salle smiled and looked at the compass.

'Possibly. Steer due west.'

The man flicked his tongue over his upper lip, staring hard at the binnacle.

'Due west it is, then.'

La Salle unhooked the voice tube.

'Chief, maximum revolutions if you will.'

The old ship gave a shudder as the engine room responded with more steam. The vibration in the deck turned to a throb they could feel through the soles of their boots and there was a sensation of climbing the lazy Atlantic swell, borne on a surging bow wave as she reached her speed. Campbell entered the wheelhouse.

'How long to close with her at this rate, do you reckon?'

Fisk, the navigating officer, looked up.

'If she's in the position given in the SOS, thirty to thirty-five minutes.'

Campbell nodded. 'Good. We'll go to action stations.'

La Salle leaned forward and pressed an electric button. Rattler gongs sounded throughout the ship, loud enough to be heard by everyone on board, but no more. A boy in his late teens appeared at the top of the companion ladder.

'Panic party to idle on deck,' La Salle said.

The lad paused. 'Shall I put my rig on, sir?'

La Salle narrowed his eyes. 'Yes. And make it so it would fool your own mother.'

'I'd be glad enough to fool the Hun, sir.'

'Let's hope you do, Dawson.'

La Salle suppressed a grin as he turned back to the forward end of the bridge. Of all the roles they could be expected to play in the coming action, if there was one, Dawson's was certainly the most strange.

Campbell was back on the bridge, training his binoculars on the ocean directly ahead.

'I can see her now,' he said. 'She's well down by the head. Afloat, but only just.'

La Salle raised his glasses. The stricken ship was clearly visible. Her deck forward was awash and the stern was clear of the water. The bridge was on fire. Two boats could be seen off her starboard side, the men aboard them waving wildly.

'Can you see anything of the submarine?' Campbell said, without lowering his glasses.

'Not so far.'

La Salle ran over the SOS message in his head: *Steamship Baronian 2,000 tons out of New Orleans with a cargo of mules attacked by U-boat in position 49. 45 N 10.05 W. Sinking. Abandoning ship.*

'You'd think a self-respecting U-boat commander would hang around to see who turns up,' Campbell said grumpily, feeling inside his reefer jacket for his pipe. 'Blowed if I can see him, though.'

La Salle steadied his glasses. 'Wait a second.'

'What?'

'I think I've got him. Two points off the starboard bow.'

'Got it,' Campbell murmured. 'About 2,000 yards from the boats.' He dropped his glasses on their lanyard and stuffed his pipe back in his pocket.

'Right. We do exactly what any merchant ship hearing an SOS would do. We must look as if our concern is for the survivors. We'll be on them in a few minutes. If that sub means to have a crack at us, he'll wait until we stop to pick up those men in the boats.'

Campbell walked into the wheelhouse and raised a speaking tube.

'This is the skipper. We have a periscope in sight. Gun crews stand by.' He unhooked the engine room voice pipe: 'Chief, Campbell here. Bring her down to quarter speed. Wait for my signal to stop engines.'

The ship slowed perceptibly, halting her climb up the face of the swell. As she lost way, a whaler from the sinking steamer pulled strongly towards them, less than a hundred yards away. Among the men aboard, some cheering, La Salle saw one in the stern sheets, cradling a limp figure across his knees. He swung his glasses back to the U-boat. It had vanished.

'The U-boat's dived!'

Campbell darted to the rail. He ran his binoculars over the sea. Nothing.

'Drat it!' he muttered. Then, in a reassuring voice: 'He can't have made our number. He's biding his time, that's all.'

At a distance of 300 yards from the sinking ship, La Salle signalled *STOP* to the engine room and watched as the boats came near. The man in the stern of the whaler had not moved. Neither had the man he was holding. The party on deck was rigging rope ladders, milling at the rail as the whaler bumped the topsides. La Salle ran down the bridge companion ladder with Fisk close behind. They joined the group on the deck. McGregor, the surgeon probationer, was looking over the side.

'There's at least one wounded man there,' La Salle said. 'You can put him in my cabin.'

McGregor nodded. At that moment the figure of a woman, dressed in a light topcoat, wavy dark hair loose around her shoulders, emerged from the break of the forecastle, turned and ascended the ladder to the bridge. La Salle smiled. *Very good*, he thought.

'Bear a hand! Wounded man coming aboard!'

Two men lowered an inert figure to the deck. He was a young man, unconscious and quite limp. Below his waist, La Salle saw, he was wrapped in a blanket dark with blood. Someone ran up with a stretcher and the casualty was taken below, with McGregor stooped over him, keeping pace.

'Take the boats in tow,' La Salle called to Fisk, then turned to a man just brought aboard. 'Is the master here?'

A heavily-built man of middle years stepped forward. La Salle recognised him as the figure in the boat, cradling the casualty. The bottom of one trouser leg was stiff with drying blood. He had lost his cap and his untidy hair gave him a wild look. He offered La Salle his hand.

'Captain Foster of the *Baronian*. I bless you for coming for us. Bless you!'

La Salle nodded and shook the man's hand. 'I'll take you to the skipper,' he said.

Foster glanced at the direction in which the casualty had been taken.

'He's in good hands now,' La Salle said.

'He's my son,' Foster murmured. He followed La Salle to the bridge where Campbell was studying *Baronian* through his glasses. She was showing little more than two thirds of her length, rudder and screw clear of the water. On deck there was havoc as the wooden stalls holding the

4

mules began to collapse. The animals were sliding down on top of each other, hundreds of them piling over the main hatch, crushed against the break in the forecastle. An awful wailing sound, almost like the screams of children, filled the air as the mules fought to stay upright, slashing at each other with savage kicks, trying to leap free of the panicked mass on the deck. Just then, with a loud cracking noise, the outer rails of the stalls gave way and the animals turned, bucking and clawing with their hooves to get a footing on the painted steel or their fellows crushed beneath them. One leapt clear over the side into the sea. It started a rush as others, some badly injured, thrashed forward in a struggle to jump the rail. Many caught their hind legs on the steelwork and hung upside down, writhing and helpless, trapped by broken limbs. The stanchions yielded and the mules, swept up in a crazed stampede, kicked and slithered their way off the deck into the sea. Only the dead and the disabled remained, heaped against the dipping forecastle, while all around the ship hundreds of bobbing heads searched this way and that for an escape from the water. Foster looked away, shaking his head. Campbell turned towards him, hand outstretched.

'Campbell. Master. Welcome to our ship. *Farnham.*'

Foster introduced himself, glanced around the ship. He noted the Danish flag. Neutral colours. It didn't mean anything, in those submarine-haunted waters. *Farnham* was not unlike his own vessel, although she was smaller and older. A tramp steamer of about 1,000 tons. Rather dirty and ill-kept. The men in her were shabby, too. Campbell wore a battered trilby hat. La Salle, by contrast, looked as if he'd have difficulty looking anything but elegant. He wore a cream silk stock at the open neck of his shirt. His trousers were tucked into a fine pair of sea boots, made of dimpled leather. As Foster took this in, a woman stepped out of the wheelhouse, crossed to the rail of the bridge. Foster noted her slim form and luxuriant dark hair. Under a smart coat she was wearing thick working trousers and a man's boots.

'How many casualties?' Campbell asked.

'One. First mate. Reggie Foster. My son. He needs the hospital urgently. Are you making for Milford Haven?'

Campbell ignored the question. 'Tell me precisely what happened,' he said.

Foster nodded. La Salle suspected he might be in shock. His eyes were dull, half-closed at times. He spoke haltingly, adding details here and there. The voyage from New Orleans, where they loaded, had been uneventful. They were bound for Milford Haven with wheat and a cargo of 500 mules consigned to the army for duty in Flanders. *Baronian* was British-owned but sailing under an American flag. As Foster talked, a muffled explosion came from the sinking ship. A hissing cloud of steam rose from her; the last exhalation of her ruptured boilers. There were shrieks from injured animals as jets of steam from broken pipes scalded them raw. Some tried to get up, to escape this new horror, but those able to stand succeeded only in sliding down the steep deck, slamming into the upperworks or tumbling into the sea. The hull swung close to vertical, kept afloat by the trapped buoyancy in her after sections. A number of mules had spotted *Farnham* and were swimming towards it. Despite the fine weather the water was still close to its winter temperature, a thought that occurred to La Salle as he watched the pitiable scene around the ship. The mules would not last long. Perhaps they were lucky. The Western Front might offer a far more grim prospect than drifting to a cold, sleepy death out here.

He turned to hear Foster say the submarine appeared around mid-morning. It surfaced off the port bow and signalled him to stop and send across the ship's papers.

'My boy took them in the whaler. When he came back he said the U-boat commander was keeping our papers and would sink the ship.'

6

'That's their usual method,' Campbell growled. 'The German Imperial Navy doesn't award prize money or decorations for tonnage sunk without proof. Your submarine skipper probably has his eye on an Iron Cross.'

Foster said they were instructed to take to the boats. They were given ten minutes to clear the ship. There were problems with the falls of the boats and it was taking longer. The U-boat commander became impatient.

'He fired a burst with his Maxim gun, across the foredeck. Reggie – the first mate – was hit.' Foster breathed deeply. 'I got him into the whaler. He passed out.'

'She's going,' La Salle said.

Campbell turned. *Baronian* was sliding downwards, strangely quiet, her steam exhausted. The fires out forever now. La Salle had never before seen a ship that size quit this world and he felt unsettled that such a huge event should be accomplished in silence. Suddenly there was a gasp and a fierce bubbling as a hatch on the poop blew open from the compression of the last remaining air. Then she was gone, with only a widening circle of ripples and a sea dotted with swimming mules to show she had ever existed.

'Well, that's that then,' Foster said. He was shaking. Campbell guided him to a narrow bench on the bridge.

'Sit down,' he said, his gruff Scottish voice more soft than La Salle had ever heard it.

'I don't want to sit down!' Foster cried, suddenly animated. 'What are you waiting for? Why aren't we making way? Do you want to be sunk too? For the love of God, get my boy to the hospital!'

Campbell glanced at La Salle, then turned to Foster.

'Steady on, old man,' he said gently. 'Things are not as they may seem.'

Foster looked at each man in turn, wide-eyed.

'What? What the devil do you mean?'

'We must give the submarine every opportunity to

attack us,' Campbell said, in a tone that implied utter reasonableness.

'What? Are you mad?' Foster thrust out his hands; imploring: 'My boy needs the hospital. My crew!'

'How did he sink your ship?' Campbell asked, unmoved. 'Was it a torpedo?'

Foster shook his head. He sank down on to the bench. 'No. He shot her up along the waterline, forward.'

'What sort of gun was it?'

'I don't know. Four inch maybe. Big enough.'

Campbell glanced at La Salle. Neither spoke. Foster raised his head, fixed his eye on Campbell.

'So you are a mystery ship,' he said flatly. 'I felt something was not right, from the moment I came aboard.'

'We are a man o' war in disguise, yes,' Campbell replied.

'Navy men?'

'Yes. Lieutenant commander. La Salle here is my first lieutenant.'

'What do you mean to do?'

Campbell turned to sweep his glasses over the middle distance. The sea was smooth and there was a polished look to the swell as it rolled in from the west, untroubled by the faint breeze.

'If I can,' he said, 'I shall sink your U-boat.'

Foster put his head into his hands. His shoulders swayed in a rocking movement.

'And my crew?'

'They will have to take their chances with us.'

La Salle felt distinctly uncomfortable. If they were to lure the U-boat into a trap they would have to act like a harmless merchant vessel picking up the complement of a sunken ship. The U-boat commander, if he was still there, would expect them to steam away as quickly as they could. That was what Foster wanted. But Campbell would not hurry. He would do everything, short of arousing suspicion, to make *Farnham* a sitting target. Meanwhile, the life of Foster's son was slipping away.

On the afterdeck, *Farnham's* men were making a hash of taking *Baronian's* boats in tow. They were as sharp and well-drilled a navy crew as it would be possible to find but their orders were to waste time and look like a bunch of grubby, pier-jumping merchant seamen. Like everyone else on the ship they had a part to play. A great fumbling and snagging of lines was what a U-boat might expect of the men in an undermanned tramp steamer, stripped of its experienced sailors by the war. But was it watching?

Foster stood stiffly, unsteadily. 'Can I go down and see my boy?' he said.

Campbell nodded. La Salle addressed the woman standing at the rail, staring out to sea.

'Dawson, take Captain Foster to my cabin.'

Dawson turned with a slight toss of his splendid wig. Foster looked appalled. An expression of helplessness crossed his face as La Salle led him to the companion ladder.

'The master's wife, as it were,' he whispered to Foster in a confidential tone. 'Everything must look correct … normal. Aboard this ship. We wish to be taken for a merchantman for reasons you'll understand.' He paused, held Foster by the shoulder in a comradely manner. 'By the way, Captain Foster, what you have learned here must not be passed on. *Farnham* is on His Majesty's Special Service and secrecy is essential. You do see that, don't you? Even ashore, you must not speak of what you have seen and heard.'

Foster nodded. La Salle let Dawson guide him down to the deck.

'Are those boats made fast?' Campbell asked. La Salle called down to the deck.

'All ready for towing,' came the reply.

Campbell grunted, squinted at the chart. 'Right. Let's see if we can get ourselves shot at.'

Farnham steamed in a lazy arc, turning slowly from the westward until her bow pointed to the north east. The sun was climbing towards its highest point and Fisk stood on the wing of the bridge to take a sight with the sextant. Campbell had given orders for *Baronian's* crew to remain on deck. They lounged, smoked and talked in small groups. La Salle posted *Farnham* men at strategic points in case the *Baronians* became inquisitive. The gunlayers, hidden from view, remained in their secret places in complete silence. It was warm and the sky and the sea fused at the horizon in a balmy haze. Dawson was back on the bridge, playing to perfection the part of a merchant captain's wife enjoying a spell outside in the fine weather. They had had no sight of the submarine since they came up with *Baronian*. That did not mean it was not there and they all knew if it was there it would be watching, calculating.

When La Salle checked on the casualty he found Captain Foster leaning against a bulkhead staring at his son, lying quite still on the bunk. The young man was deeply unconscious and Surgeon McGregor said he had lost a lot of blood. A round had passed straight through his thigh, although it had missed the femoral artery.

'He might have a chance,' McGregor said in a voice laden with pessimism. 'If we can get him to surgery.'

La Salle saw no reason to convey that opinion to Campbell. Only one thing mattered as far as the skipper was concerned. The loss or otherwise of an unfortunate merchant officer would not affect that. La Salle returned to the bridge and called the mate to discuss feeding the *Baronians* a dinner. It was decided they could mess below in the saloon, in shifts, but not with *Farnham* crew. La Salle did not want the men being asked questions they would be unable truthfully to answer. The mate was halfway down the ladder heading for the galley when the lookout shouted.

'Periscope! Off the starboard bow!'

Campbell and La Salle ranged over the sea with their

glasses. It was oily smooth and the shimmering haze created a blur at any distance, obscuring a clear view.

'Where-away?' Campbell cried.

'Four points off the bow. Looks like he's surfacing.'

As one, La Salle and Campbell trained their binoculars along a line forty-five degrees off the ship's course.

'I've got him,' La Salle said. 'He's coming up all right.'

'By God, so he is!' Campbell cried. 'How far? What's the range?'

'About 3,000 yards.'

Campbell pulled the other's arm. 'Don't let him see we've spotted him. Not yet.'

They steamed on. At 2,000 yards the U-boat's deck broke the surface.

'Right! Turn hard a'port. Make it look like we're making a run for it!' Campbell crossed to the voice pipes. 'Chief, increase speed but not much. I don't want to go over nine knots. We've got a sub in sight. Stand by.'

The ship began a tight turn to port. The submarine, just over a mile away, seemed to follow. As the ship's stern swung through the line of their previous course, La Salle saw men coming out of the conning tower hatch. Three were heading for the gun position forward while two figures in officers' headgear stood in the tower training binoculars on *Farnham.*

'Looks like a 3 ½ inch,' La Salle said as the U-boat crew raised the gun from its lowered position. La Salle identified it as a Ubts L/30, 88 millimetre. Somewhat less powerful than the newer 4.1 inch version, but frightening enough. They called it the *Schnelladekanone* – quick loader. The name was well-deserved. A sharp crew could fire a dozen rounds a minute. That translated into a delivery of more than two hundredweight of high explosive in sixty seconds. Rather more than their twelve pounder could manage.

'They're getting ready to fire,' he said, almost under his breath.

'They probably think we're not worth a torpedo,' Campbell said brightly.

'Not very flattering, is it?'

'Well, they do cost the Kaiser a thousand guineas apiece!'

'So however highly we think of ourselves, we're actually worth less than that. Quite upsetting, isn't it?'

Campbell emitted a short bark, a peculiar noise that, La Salle had learned, was as close as he ever came to laughing.

'Never forget it, my boy!'

La Salle chuckled, mostly at the thought of how their mood had changed. Suddenly, in the face of mortal danger, they were exhilarated. Day after day of criss-crossing the same stretch of ocean, seeing nothing, depressed them mightily. They worked at remaining optimistic and each man had his own way of dealing with the monotony, but the thought of the war pursuing its course without them crushed the spirit. Every man in the ship was a volunteer. They thirsted for action. Now, with the prospect at hand, they were like excited schoolboys. This was the game they longed to play.

La Salle saw a flash at the muzzle of the U-boat's gun. Before he could utter a word the air was filled with a high-pitched moan and then an explosion as a shell landed just off their bow.

'He's hoisting a signal,' he said, aware of a drumming in his chest, a dryness in his throat.

'Can you make it out?'

'*ML. STOP.*'

'Happy to oblige.'

Campbell called the engine room, ordered *STOP* then picked up the adjacent speaking tube: 'Campbell here. The sub has ordered us to stop. I want the panic party on deck with the *Baronian* crew. Await my orders.' He turned to Fisk, the navigator: 'Is the position up to date?'

'Yes, sir.'

'Right. Let's swap rig then.' Campbell shucked off his reefer jacket and passed it to Fisk. Then he handed over his old trilby. As Fisk put them on, Campbell nodded with satisfaction. 'You'll do,' he said.

La Salle joined them in the wheelhouse and traded jackets with Jenkins.

'You'd better have this too,' La Salle said, loosening the silk scarf around his neck, adding with a smile: 'Oh, Jenkins. I want it back.'

Jenkins grinned. 'If all goes well I'll be able to buy myself one,' he said cheekily.

'Cut the chat now,' Campbell snapped. 'And I don't like talk about prize money.'

'Yes, sir.'

Jenkins joined Fisk on the bridge. La Salle and Campbell crouched down, hiding themselves from view below the wheelhouse glazing. Campbell had his trench periscope in one hand.

'Can you hear me, Fisk?'

'Yes, sir.'

'Where is he?'

'Coming up on the port quarter.'

'Fully surfaced?'

'Yes. Hang on. He's hoisting another signal: *T.A.F.*'

'Bring-Me-Your-Papers,' Campbell intoned. 'Well, Fisk you'd better do as he says. Now remember, you must be the last off the ship. Direct the boats to go clear of the bow. The *Baronian* crew should do the same. Take the tender to make a show of giving him our papers. Jenkins, can you hear me?'

'Yes, sir.'

'You know the drill. Make sure the boats are not in my line of fire.'

'Yes, sir.'

'Good luck to you.'

La Salle heard the sound of boots on the companion ladder and shouts coming from the deck. Campbell put his trench periscope up to the glazing, turned, then lowered it.

'Nothing yet,' he said. 'He must be abaft the beam.' Campbell picked up the voice pipe linked to the hidden guns. The firing positions had peepholes and were better placed to see what was happening astern. 'Campbell here. See anything?'

A distant voice said something like 'abeam – port side.'

'How far?'

'About 600 yards.'

'Stand by. Good luck.'

Campbell slid on his stomach to the port wing of the bridge and raised his head to a spyhole drilled into the woodwork below the rail.

'Good God, Julian,' he exclaimed. 'Those idiots from *Baronian* are all over the bloody ocean!'

La Salle wriggled over to the spyhole. Fisk had got the *Baronian* crew away first in their boats, but instead of pulling clear towards the bow they were hanging off, apparently unsure of which direction to head in.

'They are between us and the U-boat,' he said.

'Damn them!' Campbell hissed. 'If they don't shift I shall fire anyway.'

'They're moving now,' La Salle said. He saw one of *Farnham's* boats pulling hard away from the ship with Jenkins in the bow, wearing his clothes. Fisk, with Campbell's jacket and trilby, was in the other boat. Would they fool a U-boat commander into thinking the master and his crew had abandoned ship in a panic? It was vital the submarine had no inkling that the true skipper and his gunners were hidden aboard, waiting for the moment to spring their trap. The *Farnham* boats were being rowed awkwardly, as if by inexperienced and frightened men. *A perfect panic party*, thought La Salle. But the U-boat

14

commander had had enough of time-wasting. They heard the report of a gun and almost simultaneously the ship shivered along its length as a shell crashed into the hull amidships. Splinters of steel shot past the wheelhouse with an angry whine and a great cloud of choking smoke enveloped the bridge.

'See anything?' Campbell asked, suppressing a cough. Before La Salle could reply the scream of another shell split the air above their heads.

'He's aiming at the bridge!'

They scrambled towards the hatch in the floor of the wheelhouse. La Salle threw it open and Campbell signalled him to go first. Halfway down the ladder, La Salle felt giant invisible hands take hold of his head and squeeze until he thought it would burst. The pressure wave from the blast of a shell sent him tumbling down, dazed and deafened. He was aware of Campbell's full weight striking him on the shoulders as everything went silent and dark. Slowly, the unseen giant crushing his skull relented. The pressure eased. Campbell lay beside him, his upper lip moving soundlessly over a bloodied chasm where his mouth had been. Most of his jaw was missing. Instinctively, La Salle raised a hand to his own face, felt it gingerly, rubbed his fingers over his skull. It seemed to be as he had always known it. He felt his head begin to clear, he even made out a dull sound as the ship shook from the impact of another round from the submarine. Campbell was trying to say something. La Salle couldn't hear properly and Campbell's face was like a lump on a butcher's block, although something moved in what remained of his mouth. Did he say "engage"? La Salle reached out for the bottom rungs of the steel ladder and pulled himself to his knees. He raised Campbell to a sitting position but his head lolled and he seemed distressed. The only light came through a deck prism but La Salle could see Campbell's tongue was shredded, his jawbone gone. He laid him out flat on the sole of the small passageway. Campbell vomited, convulsed violently and La Salle turned his head sideways. 'Please, please,' he murmured aloud. 'Don't let him choke.' His eye caught something behind Campbell's left ear. A shell splinter, jagged and shiny was sticking out of his skull. It had burned the hair around the wound and La Salle found himself wondering, almost as a matter of idle interest, how far it had penetrated. His hearing was beginning to return. The ship was being struck below the waterline now. Someone would have to command the gunlayers. The shell that hit the bridge would have destroyed the voice pipes. No question of that.

Campbell stirred, trying to lift his arm. The hatch in the wheelhouse had slammed shut as they fell, but there was a strong smell of smoke. Fire! Terror rose in La Salle's throat. The ship was taking a hammering. Who knows? Perhaps the gun crews weren't even there anymore. He was seized by an urge to escape. It would be possible, by following the passageway, to emerge on deck, slip to the starboard side and dive into the sea. One of the boats would pick him up, surely. He was aware of a searing heat from above. Anything would be better than being roasted alive in a blazing steel oven.

La Salle shook his head, as if trying to banish a bad dream. He pulled off his jersey, rolled it up and tenderly placed it under Campbell's head. He hauled himself upright, hand over hand up the rungs of the ladder; steadied himself. The ship was taking a heavy list to port. There was thick smoke in the air now. He felt his way to the door, opened it carefully. The bridge was on fire. Black smoke hid the forepart of *Farnham* from him, but he could see the dummy deckhouse that housed the twelve pounder. It was intact. Further aft, the mock lifeboat that concealed the six pounder was still there. The U-boat put another shell into the ship's waterline. La Salle could see nothing of the boats but the exploding rounds were drawing a hail of splinters like a white-hot curtain of metal around the ship. He slid aft on his belly with the zinging sound of shrapnel so close even his muffled ears could hear it. At the deckhouse he raised his head slightly. He could see the submarine now, clearly visible over the bulwark as the ship leaned groggily to port. La Salle crawled round to the starboard side of the house, putting it between him and the U-boat. He hammered on the false side panels with his fist.

'Roberts! It's La Salle.'

Someone spoke through a spyhole: 'What the bugger's going on? No bloody orders, the ship feels as if she's sinking. Where's the skipper?'

'He's wounded. I'm in command.' Uttering the words took La Salle aback. Yes, it was true. He was in command. 'The submarine is a few hundred yards off the port side, but the ship's listing about ten degrees. You'll have to get your elevation right pretty smartish.'

'All right,' Roberts said. His voice had gone strangely calm.

'Are you in touch with Edwards?'

Edwards was manning the six pounder under the dummy lifeboat. Roberts said he still had voice pipe communication with him.

'Good. Tell him to stand by. Get one of your men to pass on my order when I give it.'

'Right. We're ready.'

La Salle smiled. Roberts and his men had been in their tiny enclosure, without being able to move, not knowing what was happening, for almost two hours. "Ready" hardly did it justice. La Salle glanced at the mast. It was still standing, flying the Danish colours. He took a deep breath, clambered to his feet, sprinted towards the cleat holding the flag halyard. A white ensign was furled in a piece of small stuff at the base of the mast. He undid the halyard, tugged down the Danish flag.

'Stand by!' he shouted at the deckhouse. 'Let go!'

He pulled on the halyard, sending the Royal Navy's white ensign aloft. In the same instant the sides of the false deckhouse flew outboard with a clatter. Roberts and his men already had the twelve pound gun swinging towards the port side. One man was on the rangefinder calling out as his mate wound the elevating wheel furiously. Another had a new charge in his hands. Despite himself, La Salle jumped as the gun fired. He ran down the sloping deck. A geyser of water was tumbling into the sea fifty yards from the submarine.

'Short! Elevation! Elevation!'

He looked back at the U-boat. Two figures in officers' headgear stood in the conning tower, training their binoculars on *Farnham's* gun. La Salle glanced at *Farnham's* dummy lifeboat. It had folded open like a cracked walnut to reveal the six-pounder and its crew. The gun fired. La Salle whirled around to see a shell explode just over the U-boat. The U-boat's gun crew had just put another shot into the ship's waterline, forward of the beam. *Good*, La Salle thought. *The engine room is well aft of there*. One of the German officers was gesticulating at his gunners, pointing wildly at *Farnham*. Now they were shifting their aim, from *Farnham's* waterline to her decks and the men at the guns. The U-boat crew raced to reload. La Salle counted in his head. It took five seconds to load and fire the *Schnelladekanone*. Two … three … four. On five, *Farnham's* twelve pounder spoke again. This time the shell exploded only feet from the U-boat, in line with its gun. The German gunners were knocked over by the blast. As one man staggered to his feet the officers disappeared from the conning tower. *They're getting ready to dive*, La Salle thought. *They'll finish us with a torpedo.*

For the first time, he thought about the men in the boats. When the U-boat had dispatched *Farnham* it would resurface. Then, La Salle knew, the submarine commander would machine-gun the boats. The Kaiserliche Marine had declared Britain's mystery ships "pirates". Anyone on board one could expect to be shot. He thought fleetingly of Fisk, Jenkins, Captain Foster and his son. Well, young Foster was probably already dead. He caught sight of Roberts behind the twelve pounder. The gunlayer's face was eerily expressionless. Roberts was barely twenty, a thin, intense Welshman whom the others treated with care. As a gunner, few could equal him. La Salle saw something in his eyes; a cold eagerness. Roberts seemed entirely unafraid. La Salle envied him.

They had re-loaded. Roberts pulled the firing cord. To La Salle's immense joy he saw the round strike in precisely the position in which he would have placed it if he had had the power to drop it on the U-boat himself. It hit the submarine's hull high up, square on the turn of the deck. When the smoke cleared he could see buckled plating. The U-boat's gun had tilted to a strange angle. Two of the gun crew had disappeared completely. The third was lying under the gun. As he took this in, Edwards fired the six pounder. This time, the shell struck the base of the conning tower. It appeared to have little effect. La Salle felt a sickening sensation in the pit of his stomach. It was notoriously hard to penetrate the pressure hull of a U-boat, especially with a relatively light charge. He felt suddenly impotent, angry that everything they were doing was right, but not enough. The bully was too big for them. The U-boat was making way, angling forward slightly. He was diving. No one came out of the conning hatch for the gunner lying on the deck. They were getting away.

'Keep firing!'

Roberts did not need to be told. His next shot hit almost the same spot as his previous round and this time they were rewarded with a glimpse of jagged metal. Within seconds the damaged area was below water as the submarine crash dived. Edwards fired into the conning tower as the U-boat disappeared, a good hit, but then there was no target to aim at.

La Salle jumped up on to the gun platform.

'What do you think, Roberts? I thought I saw a hole in her.'

The gunlayers nodded.

'That last round got through,' Roberts said. 'I'm sure of it.'

There was a sudden lurch as *Farnham* slipped sideways. Below deck, metal was grinding on metal. *A bulkhead has gone*, La Salle thought. The ship was listing close to fifteen degrees.

'She's going down,' one of the gunlayers muttered. 'If he doesn't torpedo her, she'll find her own way to the bottom.'

There was one serviceable lifeboat on the deck. It looked more or less unscathed. They could put Campbell in it and tie it alongside, ready to board if the old ship went. But La Salle felt a resistance to the idea of abandoning their ship. There was a hotness in his blood. All cowardly thought was gone. He wanted to carry on fighting.

'We're not done yet!' he cried. 'Stand by the gun. I'm going down to the engine-room.'

Farnham was carrying a cargo of pit props. It was not genuine freight, but part of an experiment Lieutenant Commander Campbell had persuaded the admiralty to try. Campbell argued that a ship filled with wood would float even if badly holed by a torpedo or gunfire. It would give them an extra chance to fight back, he had said. To an extent, he had been proved right. *Without the wood in her holds Farnham would probably have sunk by now,* La Salle thought. But would it continue to keep her afloat?

He ran to the hatch over the boilerhouse and slid down the steel ladder. There was two feet of water at the bottom and the watertight door to the engine room was shut tight. He kicked at it with his boots.

'Chief! Chief! It's La Salle. There's water out here but you can open up. Chief! Can you hear me?'

There was a sound of sliding metal as the dogs on the watertight door moved. It swung open. The water was above the sill and it streamed through. Chief Dilkes seemed unperturbed. La Salle looked around the engine room. Two stokers stared back at him blankly. The engine space had not been hit. La Salle could have cried with relief.

'Chief, you're all right?'

'Yes. But I don't want too much water in here. I still have the fires going.'

'Can you make steam? Can we get the pumps started?'

'We can try. What's happening out there?'

'The skipper's wounded. I've taken charge. We hit the submarine. It's dived. We must try to make way. I don't want to be a sitting duck for a torpedo.'

Dilkes nodded, as if this was all the information he would ever need. He turned to his stokers, issued a brief command and walked to the controls.

'I'll try the pumps now,' he said.

La Salle clapped him on the back and splashed out of the engine-room. On deck he found Roberts scanning the sea to port. *Farnham's* boats were pulling hard back to the ship, but Roberts' attention was focused on a patch of sea somewhat farther away.

'There's something over there,' Roberts said, pointing into the middle distance. He handed his binoculars to La Salle. There was a disturbance on the water, a furious bubbling.

'He's blowing his tanks,' La Salle shouted. 'He's coming up! You did get him, Roberts. You did!'

The submarine began to surface at an odd angle, the stern slightly higher than the bow. 'That's why he couldn't get off a torpedo,' La Salle murmured to himself. He became aware of movement at the twelve pounder. The gun fired.

'Roberts! He might be surrendering!'

He threw out an arm, pulled at Robert's shoulder. Roberts did not shift his attention from the breech of the twelve pounder. He shrugged off La Salle's hand. The gun fired again. In the numbing split-second that followed the crash of the big gun, La Salle saw the afterpart of the U-boat fly into pieces like a joke cigar. Almost immediately he heard a double thump of two explosions, the second much more powerful than the first.

'His stern torpedo!' One of Roberts's gunlayers was shouting, throwing his cap on to the deck. 'His bloody stern torpedo!'

The U-boat seemed to hang suspended over the sea, then it rolled slightly, swung like a pendulum and, with the bow pointing skyward, slid vertically out of sight. No one moved. They all stared at the same bubbling patch of sea.

'Did you see anyone? Did you see anyone coming out of her?' La Salle asked at last.

'I think the hits on the conning tower probably jammed the hatch,' Roberts said, in a voice that could have been commenting on a good ball at a village cricket match. 'Nicely bottled up in there, they are.'

The word "are" struck La Salle like a slap. Of course. They were still alive. Most of the thirty or so men in the submarine would have survived the explosion of the torpedo. Now they were sealed in a steel coffin heading for the bottom in 500 feet of water. His mind flashed over the scene. Dark inside, probably. Plenty of air for now. But not for long.

'They might have been surrendering,' he said quietly.

Roberts stepped away from the gun, looked him squarely in the face.

'I heard your order to let go,' he said. 'I did not hear an order to cease fire.'

La Salle felt the eyes of the other men on him. He was

in command, but he experienced a shrinking sensation. Suddenly, he was small in their presence. Roberts was right. Their job was to sink submarines. Every one of them had volunteered for it. They yearned to succeed. Success meant killing men.

'You did well, Roberts,' he said. 'You all did.'

The deck was awash with water gushing from the pumps. Heads began to appear at the port rail. Men were climbing aboard. Fisk, still in Campbell's clothes, strode across the deck and grabbed Roberts by the hand, pumping it furiously.

'Bloody good shooting! I thought we'd lost him, but you got him all right!'

La Salle saw McGregor coming over the rail.

'Come with me. The skipper's wounded,' he said. He led McGregor to the passageway where they found Campbell as he had left him. 'There's a splinter in the back of his head,' La Salle murmured.

McGregor bent over the inert figure and pressed his ear to Campbell's chest.

'He's breathing well enough,' he said. 'Was there any other injury? Internal, perhaps?'

'I don't think so.'

'Let's get him below. I can't see properly in here.'

A fleeting image of the inside of a darkened submarine flashed into La Salle's head. He dismissed it instantly.

'How is Foster's son?' he asked.

McGregor shook his head, looking down at Campbell. 'I'll get a stretcher,' he said.

La Salle returned to the deck where Fisk was directing *Baronian's* boats to come back alongside.

'I need a damage report,' La Salle said. 'The chief thinks he can get up steam.'

Fisk disappeared with the boatswain to check the holds. La Salle climbed the twisted remnant of the bridge ladder as far as he could. The wheelhouse was still burning, but the fire did not seem likely to spread. He dropped down to the deck and ordered the hoses to be rigged. Could they save her? The wireless was gone and there was no possibility of working the helm, but could she be steered with chain and tackles? The weather, for now, was on their side. A breeze had filled in from the south west, but the sea was still smooth. Fisk came up on deck. He reported *Farnham's* hull free to the water from the forward hold to amidships. The wood packed inside her was keeping her afloat, but two bulkheads had collapsed and water was finding its way through the ship. It was making on the pumps, but if at least one bulkhead could be shored up and the pumps held out they might gain on it. La Salle ordered the carpenter to take a party into the hold with jacking equipment to work on the bulkheads while chains were rigged directly to the rudder arm for steering. The men from *Baronian* huddled in small groups on the high side of the deck as *Farnham's* crew hurried about their tasks.

Fisk lowered his voice confidentially: 'Will the old man live, Julian?'

La Salle winced slightly at the use of his Christian name. Fisk was a chum and in the Special Service they were under orders never to use or refer to naval rank aboard ships that took extravagant measures to pass themselves off as sloppy merchantmen. Saluting was strictly forbidden. They all learned and adopted the easygoing ways of the merchant marine as part of the mystery ship deception. But La Salle was secretly uneasy. The business with Roberts had unsettled him. What did he know, after all, of commanding one of His Majesty's ships of war, especially in those dire circumstances? He had tried to construct a bubble of authority around himself. Fisk's familiarity had punctured it.

'McGregor says he's in coma. We have to get him ashore. In the ship, if we can.'

'Will she swim?'

'The pumps are working, but she feels like she's starting to settle. Have you got a chart?'

Fisk took a folded chart from his jacket pocket and spread it on a hatch cover. He pointed to an empty stretch of sea in the Western Approaches.

'This was where we were when we took to the boats. Since then the tidal stream will have carried us about a mile and half to the north east. So I reckon we're about here.'

He marked a spot with his pencil, over the Cockburn Bank, almost due west of the Scillies. Their home port, Queenstown, lay just over 100 miles away, on the Irish coast to the north. It was closer than Milford Haven or Falmouth.

'Queenstown it is,' La Salle said.

As darkness fell, *Farnham* steamed slowly towards Queenstown harbour. The breeze freshened in the night to about twenty knots from the south-south west. A soldier's wind, the navy men joked; a fair breeze to blow them home. Just before dawn, with the Irish coast stretching ahead like a long dark ribbon between the sea and the sky, surgeon probationer McGregor came on deck to find La Salle conning the ship from a hatch forward of the burned-out bridge. McGregor climbed on the hatch, stretched and yawned mightily.

'Lieutenant Commander Campbell is dead,' he said.

CHAPTER TWO

The Old Head of Kinsale was abeam just before noon and at the top of the tide they shaped a course for the entrance to The Cove, Queenstown's harbour. In the approaches a naval vessel signalled: *"WHAT SHIP?"* La Salle sent up the secret code that identified her as a man o' war in disguise and she was waved through the narrows, below the watchful shore batteries, into the outer harbour.

'Are you sinking?' a pilot called out cheerfully, as his boat bumped along one of the few sound patches of hull on the port side. 'You ought to be!'

'Can you find me a spot where I can take the bottom at low water?' La Salle shouted back.

The pilot nodded and jumped for the rope ladder, swinging his wiry frame up to the scarred deck.

'A target ship, are you?' he said merrily. He ran the back of his hand over his eyes, wiping away dampness brought on by the keen breeze and, La Salle guessed, a morning tot. The pilot glanced around the deckworks then paused at the twisted and charred metal of the bridge. 'Casualties?'

'Yes,' La Salle replied, in a tone that did not invite further inquiry on the topic.

'Oh, that's sad. Very sad. What are you carrying?'

'Timber.'

'Lucky for you!' He turned to La Salle and seemed about to speak when the young man cut him off, smiling.

'I need a spot where I can take the ground.'

The pilot, who La Salle guessed was probably at least seventy, grinned to himself.

'What do you draw?'

'With this much water in her, fifteen feet, probably.'

The pilot pointed to a spot beyond Haulbowline Island.

'You'll have to be smart,' he said. 'The ebb's away now and you'll need to get there sharp to reach the clear bit of beach.'

Fisk directed the men on the steering tackles as the pilot took over the con of the ship. A customs launch came out, but when the officers aboard saw the condition of *Farnham*, and the sullen faces of the *Baronian* crew who had spent the night on the starboard side deck to help trim her, they agreed to complete formalities ashore. Less accommodating was the naval picket boat guarding the boom defence. The rather officious lieutenant in charge appeared to want La Salle to account for himself and his ship there and then and started interrogating him through a loudhailer. The pilot came to his rescue.

'If you don't let this vessel pass now you'll have a sunken ship in the fairway!' he cried out. 'I have to get her into shallow water right away!'

The lieutenant quickly saw the desirability of not being held responsible for impeding the harbour approach and ordered *Farnham* through.

'Don't you hate the navy?' the pilot said to La Salle slyly, a wicked grin on his leathery face. 'They think they own this place.'

So he had guessed their real identity, La Salle thought.

'They do own it,' he said pleasantly.

The old Irishman became suddenly serious.

'I suppose you're right. For now.'

He brought *Farnham* to anchor in a depth La Salle judged to be perfect, at that state of the tide. In a few hours she would take the bottom and she'd be safe. He sent along to the galley for some tea.

'How do you like it?' he asked the pilot.

'Very sweet,' the old man replied.

La Salle instructed the rating to make sure the pilot's

27

tea was sweetened with a large measure of rum. Then: 'Tell me, pilot, what is it about this ship you find not quite right?'

The Irishman shuffled slightly, fiddled with the muffler tucked inside his coat.

'You don't mind my little joke, do you?'

'Not at all. But since you seem to have guessed our true purpose I should like to know what gives us away. This ship can only be effective if our appearance is correct, as I'm sure you know.'

The pilot relaxed, tapped his nose.

'Instinct, mostly. She looks good enough, I suppose. That – ' he pointed to the dummy deckhouse concealing the twelve pounder '- might set someone to wondering as to what it's there for, but they've done a reasonable job in her get-up. From another vessel you'd probably take her for an old tramp. No, it's just a feeling. And, if you'll allow me, you're not a merchant officer.'

'I hold a master's ticket,' La Salle replied evenly.

'Skippering a fancy yacht, I'd guess.'

La Salle coloured. The perspicacious pilot was beginning to annoy him. The tea arrived and the old Irishman sipped his appreciatively. His waspishness began to fade.

'Did you get one? A U-boat?'

'You know I can't discuss that sort of thing.' La Salle waved to a rating. 'Signal for the pilot's boat,' he said.

'Your crew seem happy enough. Maybe expecting some prize money.'

La Salle rolled his tea mug between his hands. Queenstown was full of spies. Republicans were known to be collecting information for the Germans and this man had already said enough to betray his own sympathies.

'Are you a spy, pilot?'

The Irishman chuckled.

'I was six years old when my mother and two sisters

were taken in the Great Hunger. I know the value of a good position.'

He probably knows hatred, too, La Salle thought. He smiled.

'Well spoken, pilot. It would be a pity to hang a man who knows his business as well as you do.' He called to the rating. 'Some more tea for the pilot before he goes. Extra sweet.'

La Salle caught sight of Captain Foster talking to his officers near the break of the poop. He excused himself to the pilot and walked down the deck to join them.

'I am sorry about your son, captain.'

The *Baronian* officers fell silent and looked away. Foster nodded, examining the expanse of deck on which he was standing. La Salle paused. No one spoke.

'I shall have to have your details for my report,' he said finally. Foster nodded again, but said nothing. La Salle turned and walked forward. Fatigue suddenly hit him like an axe blow. He sagged slightly, gripped the rail. He was sorry about Foster's son. But what could anyone have done? He felt seized by an urge to turn back and reason with Foster. The country was at war with a cruel enemy. The U-boats had to be tackled by whatever means possible. Surely he could see that? Yes, it might have been possible to have saved young Foster if they had steamed full speed to the nearest port and escaped the submarine. But what of the U-boat? It would still be out there. Watching. Waiting. How many more lives would have been lost if it had been allowed to continue its mission?

'Are you going ashore?' Fisk interrupted his thoughts.

'What? Oh, yes. I have to make my report. Can you arrange something for Campbell?' He added wearily: 'And Foster's son.'

Fisk nodded, moved to go then turned, grabbing La Salle by the shoulders.

'You did it, Julian. You jolly well did it! And you brought the ship home!'

'We did it. All of us. And Campbell.'

The pilot was climbing over the side. He paused to offer a mock salute; La Salle put a finger to his lips. The pilot, chuckling, grabbed at the rope ladder and vanished.

'What was that about?' Fisk asked, peering over the side to catch a glimpse of the pilot's cutter.

'Oh, nothing. Let's get ashore.'

It was a hard pull to the landing place. The wind had shifted and the ebb was against them. La Salle could see the men were close to exhaustion. They had abandoned their watches so the work to keep *Farnham* from sinking could continue through the night. Jenkins was nodding over his oars, although young Dawson, back in his usual rig of dungarees, seemed full of vim. His eyes were bright and he laid on his pull with enthusiasm. Exhilaration, La Salle thought. And why not? They had accounted for a U-boat. Every man had a right to consider himself a hero. When his report reached the Admiralty Board there would be prize money – or a grant as they preferred to call it – a promotion or two and perhaps even decorations. He would make sure there was recognition of Campbell's courage, not least in pushing him first through the hatch when the bridge came under fire. *That certainly saved my life*, La Salle thought, glancing at the still figure swathed in blankets stretched out in the bottom of the whaler. Campbell was unmarried, he knew, but he seemed to recall him talking affectionately of his widowed mother back home in Greenock. A medal would probably be a comfort to her. La Salle felt a surge of gloom. So now he was defining comfort as the exchange of a few ounces of cheap metal for a man's life. Certainly, the war carried them into illogical situations, but perhaps there was danger, too, in the way it lured them into accepting alien and dangerous values. War was a cunning mistress.

La Salle felt inside his breast pocket for a pencil and the small notebook he always carried. He turned pages filled with handwritten snatches of sonnets, rhyming couplets, notes and workings of blank verse. He wrote: *War as mistress – seduction – loss of self – harlot … betrayal.* He closed the notebook and returned it to his pocket.

He rubbed his face. When he lowered his hand he caught Dawson looking at him. The boy immediately turned away but La Salle saw something in his eyes that prompted a stab of panic. Had the gunlayers talked? Yes, of course they had. His accursed attempt to give the U-boat time to surrender would have been all over the ship by the middle watch. Roberts would probably not say much but the other men in the twelve pounder crew had heard and seen everything. La Salle experienced a churning sensation in his belly. He imagined the chatter in the forecastle: *'The Lieutenant wanted to have the Huns round for tea, give them a nice slice of cake. But Roberts thought he'd better sink them!'*

Campbell would not have hesitated. He knew that. And the men knew that, too. But what they could not know, for he barely understood it himself, was that in his secret heart he had wanted the U-boat to surrender. Why? It would have been a better prize, certainly, if a vanquished example of the spiteful enemy had been captured, paraded even. A unique trophy. He drew a hand through his hair wearily. That was not the reason. Even in the heat of the action, roused to a pitch he had never before experienced and with his blood a-boil, he had hoped not to murder. The thought shook him wide awake. He looked anxiously over the faces of the men in the boat, as if such a monstrous idea could be communicated by its sheer immensity. The men rowed, the bundle that had been Campbell remained still. La Salle glanced astern. The patrol vessel *Heron* was in the fairway, shaping for the entrance. A ship full of men who would never baulk at the idea of killing Germans, La Salle thought, especially those Germans in the U-boats who doled out death to innocents. Yet he had hesitated.

Some impulse. What was it? Not pity. No. His concern was less about what mass murder did to the enemy and more about what committing it might do to him. Now it was done. It was irrevocable. He shook his head irritably. He had to clear his mind on this. He wanted a part in the war, of course he did. He wanted more than anything the chance to prove himself, to gain honour. Every man did. The war was necessary. The world had become dirty, chaotic and decadent. Now the cleansing was underway and in the future only those who had been a part of it could hold their head high. He had to learn this lesson and teach himself to live with the indelible fact that he had killed. And he had to cultivate a hunger to do more of it.

The tiredness struck again. Where was his cap? He caught sight of Jenkins hunched over his oar. He was still wearing the silk scarf La Salle had loaned him. It was a good scarf and La Salle had wanted it back. But at the thought of Jenkins laughing with the hands in the forecastle at how he had dithered over dispatching the submarine, La Salle knew he could never ask him for it.

The tender bumped the stone steps. He rose stiffly and the men made way for him to disembark. He climbed to the quay. Fisk took charge of the shore party and the duty with regard to Campbell. That, at least, was a relief. La Salle knew the admiral would want him to report immediately and in person. At the top of the steps he made an effort to straighten his back, square his shoulders. Shrug off the fatigue. He took leave of Fisk and strode across the harbourside.

Vice Admiral Sir Gerald Pettigrew had his headquarters at Admiralty House, a fine old mansion at the top of the hill overlooking the Cove. Sir Gerald, a baronet, was always called "Jelly" by officers speaking out of his presence, an affectionate sobriquet La Salle found strange because the admiral was the least wobbly of men. It dated back to his time as a midshipman in ironclads, apparently, although no one seemed to know precisely how he earned the name.

La Salle carried a small leather case in which he had folded the sheaves of paper and chart that made up his report. He had described the elements of the *Baronian* sinking, the encounter with the U-boat and the subsequent action. There were a few rough sketches and he had included a brief note from McGregor on his opinion of the wounds suffered by Lieutenant Commander Campbell. The report could be enlarged later, if necessary, although there would be no more inquiry into Campbell's death. Inquests were not considered necessary for men killed aboard armed ships.

As he climbed the hill, La Salle allowed his mind to range over recalled images of previous visits to Admiralty House and, in particular, Miss Vaizey, the admiral's niece. She had moved to Queenstown with her uncle when he took up his appointment as Commander-in-Chief of Patrol Area 21; the Irish Sea and Western Approaches. She was devoted to the old boy and the young officers at the Club would shake their heads sadly at the thought of such an attractive young woman heading, no doubt, for spinsterhood.

The admiral received him in the hall then directed him to his office. It was a large house and Sir Gerald had partitioned off the ground floor reception rooms into two parts; two thirds of the space became his working area while the rest was used as a dining room, drawing room and small salon. The billiard table was boarded over to create a vast expanse for charts. This was where he asked La Salle to spread his own chart and make his report. He listened quietly as La Salle explained how Campbell had been fatally wounded during the U-boat's attack. Sir Gerald nodded, and was about to say something, then appeared to think better of it.

'Carry on,' he said.

As he related the course of the action, La Salle became aware of the other's growing excitement.

'Did you, by Jove!' the admiral exclaimed at intervals.

La Salle finished his account of the action and the sinking. Then he said: 'When he re-surfaced I thought he might be surrendering.'

'What?'

'It was a moment's fancy, Sir. I wondered whether we might see a white flag.'

Sir Gerald eyed him over the top of his spectacles. 'Go on,' he said.

'But the gunners had his range and they put a shot into the afterpart. It seemed the round struck his stern torpedo, or other munitions aboard. There was a very big bang.'

'Did you give the order to cease fire?'

La Salle felt his face redden. 'No, Sir.'

'Jolly good!' The admiral seemed relieved. La Salle breathed a little more easily. He had offered an account of what happened, honestly, for the admiral's examination and it seemed the Commander-in-Chief deemed it unworthy of pursuit. Indeed, his next words confirmed it.

'The Kaiser's U-boat commanders can be tricky customers, La Salle. We have already seen some of their ruses; letting off oil, firing debris out of the torpedo tubes. Anything to fool us. Even the white flag has been used to pull tricks.'

He lowered his voice. 'It's not official, of course, but you know there's a recommendation to ignore white flags offered by the U-boats?'

La Salle nodded. The admiral sighed deeply.

'It depresses me to think how those devils have made warfare even more vile than it needs to be. The white flag was one of its more noble elements. Now I tell my officers not to trust it.'

He shook his head, as if dismissing a mental image; looked up and fixed La Salle with a benign eye.

'You did well. Be sure the Board will hear of that.'

'The gunners were the heroes of the action, Sir, if I may say so. I have stressed it in my report.'

'Good. Have you slept?'

'I'm all right, Sir.'

'When will you be ready for sea?'

La Salle smiled inwardly. Jelly was renowned for this question. At the Club they said an officer could step ashore from a sinking ship, bleeding through his dressings and the admiral would always ask when he was ready to go again. As La Salle well knew, there was only one answer:

'Ready now, Sir.'

'Good man. First, perhaps you will come and have some supper with Miss Vaizey and me? Tonight?'

'I should like that very much, Sir.'

'Come a little early, at seven. There are a few things I'd like to discuss with you. Just the two of us. Boring for Miss Vaizey, you understand.'

La Salle did understand. The admiral would not talk about the innermost workings of the Special Service at a gathering attended by his niece, although few doubted she shared his confidence utterly. And like almost everyone else in Queenstown she knew about the mystery ships. Indeed, the secrecy they tried to construct around vessels sent out to lure U-boats into a trap was pathetically transparent, something that worried La Salle. Queenstown was a hive of spies and if a photograph or even a good description of a mystery ship were circulated to U-boat commanders the vessel would be destroyed out of hand, before it could strike a blow. He determined to raise the issue with the admiral if the opportunity arose.

'I'll come at seven.'

'Good man. I shall signal to London and get this –' he

held up La Salle's handwritten report '– typed and on the next ship.' Sir Gerald seized his shoulder in a firm grip. 'Well done, my boy. You did well.'

Despite himself, an image of a still, dark submarine on the sea floor entered La Salle's head. He resisted an urge to salute. He was still in his merchant officer's civilian clothes. Sir Gerald's flag officer, Lieutenant Davis, appeared and led him back to the hall. At the door, La Salle turned to exchange a word with Davis and as he did so he caught sight of Miss Vaizey descending the staircase.

'Is that you, Lieutenant La Salle?' she called out.

'It is.' He nodded to Davis and re-entered the hall. She stood at the bottom of the stairs, a slender figure in a high-collared dress. La Salle remembered a discussion at the Club among some of the Sub Lieutenants about whether Miss Vaizey was truly beautiful. The conclusion was that she was not, but no one could deny she had a loveliness that was most appealing. Especially in her smile. Even if he had known nothing about Miss Vaizey, her smile would tell him much, La Salle thought. It seemed to declare of its owner an inner warmth and goodness of heart, as if promising a ready affection for the world and everyone in it. *Yes*, La Salle thought as he crossed the chequered floor to the foot of the staircase, *Miss Vaizey's smile is a delight.*

'I'm glad to see you again, Lieutenant La Salle,' she said, offering her hand.

He took it and bowed slightly.

'I hope all is well with you, Miss Vaizey?'

'Very well, but I wish there were better news from France. Have you come back from a patrol?'

'Yes.' La Salle pointed to his civilian dress, as if apologising for it. 'I have just got back.' A devil in his head was goading him to add: '*And I bagged a U-boat!*' He resisted and instead informed her that the admiral had invited him to supper.

'Excellent! I shall see if we can find something nice for you.'

When he turned to leave he concentrated hard on holding in his memory the image of her, eyes lit, bidding him goodbye. Annoyingly, it refused to remain sharp and by the time he reached the bottom of the hill Miss Vaizey's countenance was a blur, although a highly gratifying one.

He had first seen her some weeks previously, when the admiral gave one of his garden tea parties. Gordon Fisk had some sort of family connection and said Miss Vaizey's parents had died of fever out east – Batavia, he thought he said – while she was at school in England. The admiral, her mother's only brother and a bachelor, stepped in and Miss Vaizey became like a beloved daughter to him. La Salle reflected on how similar was his own personal history, apart from one detail. A rather important one, as it happened, but nonetheless there was a likeness in their early lives. When the admiral raised his flag in the new *HMS Marlborough* the previous summer, Miss Vaizey was taken aboard for the king's review of the fleet at Spithead. Indeed, she became something of a mascot in the fleet. When Jelly was at Scapa Flow she heard the young sailors were suffering homesickness and lacked means to communicate with their families. Miss Vaizey, at home in Eaton Terrace, went to the Army and Navy stores and purchased their entire stock of postcards. There were hundreds of them, Fisk said, and she had them packaged and sent by train. Everyone – stoker, rating, admiral – was invited to help themselves. La Salle had been tempted to inquire how she managed the expense of such an operation, but hesitated at inviting a discussion about money. In any event, in Queenstown Miss Vaizey had established an organisation to help survivors of the U-boat attacks and it was well known she paid for its activities from her own funds.

La Salle crossed the road at the bottom of the hill and walked into the naval office. Fisk was engaged in conversation with the Constructor who had already been out to look over *Farnham*.

'What do you think?' La Salle asked.

Barnes, the Constructor, was a well-regarded man among officers on the Queenstown station. He was in late middle-age, a shipbuilder of the old school who could handle the most complex of drawings as easily as he could swing a riveting hammer. Barnes did not share the failing of many of his kind who appeared to take delight in declaring a job impossible.

'It's a miracle she stayed afloat,' he said. 'When Commander Campbell told me about his idea for stuffing the holds with timber I thought he was in need of a bit of shore leave. But by God it worked!'

'Commander Campbell was killed in the action,' La Salle said quietly.

'Yes. Lieutenant Fisk has just told me.' Barnes laid a hand on La Salle's arm. 'I was sorry to hear it, Lieutenant. He was your first skipper in the Special Service, wasn't he?'

'Yes.'

'And a damn fine one. I'll make sure his ship goes to sea again. We'll get her over to the yard on Haulbowline Island, into the dry dock. When we get all the water out of her I'll know what's what. She's an old ship, but most of the machinery seems all right. I'd be surprised if we can't get her right again. Are you to have her? Bit soon to say, I suppose?'

La Salle smiled. Some might have thought the Constructor's question impertinent but La Salle was rarely piqued by people he liked.

'I don't think I have the seniority,' he said.

Barnes nodded. He remembered La Salle was in the Royal Naval Volunteer Reserve and had gone on active service at the outbreak of war, opting immediately for mystery ship duty. Barnes had an affection for sail, having spent his apprentice years building grain-carrying barques, and he knew that in peacetime La Salle had been sailing master aboard a schooner owned by some lord or another. They had often chatted about whether sail had a future and always concluded it probably did, while each hid his personal and deeply regretted view that the opposite was almost certainly the case. Barnes knew La Salle lacked sea-time as a naval officer, but the Constructor's knowledge of ships and men told him the young lieutenant wanted for little when it came to seamanship.

'Will you move ashore?' Barnes asked.

The question prompted a moment of confusion. It hadn't occurred to La Salle that home, his cabin aboard *Farnham*, would not be available for now at least.

'I'll have to,' he said slowly, then, turning to Fisk: 'What do you think, Gordon? Can we get rooms at Kimberley House?'

Kimberley House was a dark old warren set in a small park beyond the harbour. The admiralty leased it to provide shoreside accommodation for officers. There was usually a room to be had.

'I'll send for the chests and get them over there,' Fisk said. 'Are you going back to the ship?'

'Yes. I want to have another look when she takes the bottom. And pick up a few personal things. I'll pack my chest myself.'

Barnes offered them use of his motor launch to save time crossing the harbour. When they reached *Farnham* she had settled on the sand in about ten feet of water. She was close to an even keel, a tribute to the old pilot's knowledge of the waters of the Cove. Once aboard, La Salle climbed into the hold but there was nothing much to see, so he went up to the remains of the bridge and the wheelshelter. The structure was little more than a blackened, jagged stump on the deck of the ship. The smell of burned metal and paint stuck in his throat. He glanced at the hatch through which Campbell had pushed him, consigned a humble thought to God and returned to the main deck. A rating had brought up Fisk's chest and La Salle went below to pack his own things. There was blood on his bunk and his mind's eye flashed over an image of Captain Foster's dying son. Try as he might, a nagging sense of guilt refused to be quit of him. As he reached for his shaving kit something caught his eye. It was the silk stock he had loaned to Jenkins, folded neatly on the small desk. La Salle lifted his sea chest over the wooden fiddle screwed to the cabin sole and pulled it from under the bunk. He paused, struck by an idea. Had he worried more than necessary about the men's reaction to his willingness to give the U-boat a chance? Was it just the morbid effect of fatigue? He straightened and dropped on to the bunk. Fatigue. He felt mortally tired. Yet there was an energy, too, in the thought that they had triumphed. They had struck a blow against the enemy, something every man in England craved. What a feeling! He leapt up. With luck there was time for a hot bath and a couple of hours sleep before returning to Admiralty House. But first, he thought with a pleasurable pang, he had to find some splendid roses.

The ringing started somewhere far away, bearable at first, but then it came on in an irresistible jangling rush that filled his head painfully. La Salle felt a jab of shock. He jerked upright, stared around the darkened room. *Clock. Damned alarm clock.* He reached out, turned off the bell and sank back, eyes closed. In that same moment a wave of recollection struck. Submarine – explosions – guns – flooded ship – mad-eyed animals in the sea – a man's shattered face – body in the whaler. He ran his fingers through his hair and shook his head. It was just after six. He had allowed himself an hour to get ready and walk the hill to Admiralty House, more time than was strictly necessary, but the meeting that lay ahead was one to which he did not care to hurry. He rose stiffly, crossed to the window. They had given him a large room at Kimberley House, sombrely furnished but comfortable. He drew back the curtains. There was still some sun and he gazed for a while at the pleasant gardens, bathed in the last of the warm light of early May. He would not need a topcoat and in any case most of his wardrobe was at Combe Hall, the house of his guardian, Lord Burnage. Mystery ship officers continued their merchant marine pretence even ashore and although his uniform was in the chest he knew he would be expected to wear civilian clothes. He had at least one clean shirt and a presentable suit. It was a dark blue worsted, single-breasted. He would wear it with one of the Sulka ties he kept rolled up in the chest. The maroon – no, the salmon with the fine blue weave. His buff linen waistcoat was also presentable. He had a pair of spats in the chest but the words of a recent government poster stuck in his mind: "To dress extravagantly in wartime is worse than bad form. It is unpatriotic." Well, he did not wish to appear unpatriotic. Happily, there was a change of undergarments. One of the advantages of serving on a mystery ship, La Salle discovered, was that the men were not allowed naval issue flannels. Since laundered underclothes were usually dried around the deck on the kind of sloppy vessel they pretended to be, it was argued that a U-boat commander would quickly identify the distinctive service underwear and their merchant ship disguise would be penetrated. So he was able to avoid, with an easy conscience, scratchy naval flannels in favour of Jap silk ordered from Merryweather in Jermyn Street. The admiralty even granted them a special allowance to buy civilian clothes, although the money they were given to kit themselves out entirely would hardly cover Merryweather's bill for vests and drawers. Thoughts about money led him to wonder about *Farnham's* prize, the admiralty grant. The award for sinking a U-boat was £1,000, shared between the officers and crew with the greater parts awarded for seniority. As first lieutenant he could expect close to £200. The thought made him suddenly irritable. *Blood money*. Yet if the U-boat men who killed Campbell had survived they would be claiming their own reward from the Kaiser. La Salle tried to shake off dark thoughts. Sometimes he felt the only thing worse than fighting in the war was not fighting in it. He dressed carefully, picked up the bouquet for Miss Vaizey and set off for Admiralty House.

The streets around the harbour were pleasantly quiet. He passed two young women swinging their parasols and made a slight bow of his head. They acknowledged the courtesy with a nod. Here, at least, a young man in civilian clothes was safe from the horror of being presented with a white feather. Indeed, the situation in Ireland was too complicated, politically and socially, for anyone to assume a fit man not wearing a uniform was a coward, afraid to do his duty. Even Sinn Feiners had volunteered to fight for the king. There had been agreeable surprise at the large numbers of Irishmen who had rushed to join up. Yet were they inspired by loyalty, La Salle thought? Or had they also fallen, like young Englishmen, for the siren call of the vile seductress? In any case, no one could doubt they were brave. *Brave*. The word lingered in his head. He had picked up a couple of newspapers on his way to Kimberley House and read them in his bath. They were full of bravery. It seemed there was hardly an item of news that did not contain examples of heroism and the headlines seemed to be arranged according to a story's courage quotient. In France, British and German troops were locked in a duel at Hill 60, near Ypres. Using poison gas, the Germans took some ground. The artillery cut them to pieces. Others took their place. There was more grim news from the Dardanelles. In the House of Commons someone asked about Canadian losses. Over 6,000 men and 250 officers, came the reply. All brave men. Yes, La Salle thought, courage was the currency of the age. He had been amused to read a piece about a Harley Street physician who had written in *The Lancet*. The eminent medical man warned that people of a nervous character were far more susceptible to illness than those – and La Salle recalled the exact phrase – "whose courage is at a high level." La Salle chuckled inwardly. Why not an article on the beautifying effect of courage? Or perhaps something on how bravery can make you rich. Why, a plucky officer in the Special Service could be nicely set up with prize money if he sank enough U-boats.

The thought triggered one of those nagging sensations of guilt to which La Salle was particularly susceptible. Were Special Service men truly brave, in the context of the times? How would he be valued in the coin of courage? On a fine day at sea, without sight of a U-boat for days, weeks, it was impossible not to think of the men in the trenches. While he might be leaning over the rail of the bridge, watching a sea bird skim the waves or perhaps a pod of porpoise playing in the bow wave, what would his counterparts in the army be doing? Blowing a whistle and scrambling over a trench-top, leading a band of terrified men straight into a near-solid wall of machine-gun bullets? Charging over ground erupting with explosions and scything metal tearing off limbs and heads that mingled with the stretch of muck they were trying to deny the enemy?

La Salle shuddered. A ship under shellfire was no soft option, to be sure. Even if he weren't maimed or blown to pieces, a sailor's death, trapped in a sinking vessel or adrift until his life ebbed away, could be a miserable one.

And the Special Service carried its own risks. In mystery ships they deliberately set out to attract the enemy's fire. They invited destruction, to gain an opportunity to destroy. La Salle recalled what Campbell told him when he first joined *Farnham*: 'We are the bait, my boy. The tethered goat!'

There was another uncomfortable truth. Unlike soldiers at the front, they could expect no quarter. Mystery ships were pirates, the Kriegsmarine declared, and if a U-boat commander got the better of one he was unlikely to take prisoners. The admiralty acknowledged the risks and paid Special Service men hard-lying money. For most it meant double pay and even the lowliest rating pocketed an extra ten shillings a week. The money was said to attract volunteers, although it meant little to La Salle.

As he reached the drive at Admiralty House he thought of *Baronian's* mules, wild-eyed and terrified, swimming in the sea around a ship that puzzlingly would not save them and then watching it steam away as they grew weaker and colder. An ugly death, yes, but perhaps better than the fate that might have awaited them in Flanders. Did the same apply to men? *Probably*, he thought.

The maid took the roses, repeated the two syllables of his unfamiliar name with difficulty, then led him to the office. The admiral rose from an old leather armchair, holding the same edition of the *Daily Telegraph* La Salle had read earlier. Sir Gerald waved the paper distractedly.

'Can't say the news is much cop,' he said. 'Have you seen it?'

'Yes, Sir.' The admiral pointed to a sofa. La Salle remembered, with faint regret, that Jelly ran a dry ship at Admiralty House.

'Rested well?'

La Salle nodded. 'Thank you, Sir.'

'Good man. Now. I received a signal from the admiralty this afternoon. Your action in *Farnham* has gone down very well. Very well indeed. You know I was sent here to deal with the U-boats. And you know how blessed difficult it is. Tricky foe. Very tricky. But every one we account for lifts a little of the threat we face. I can tell you, La Salle, German submarine attacks are destroying hundreds of thousands of tons of shipping a month. The Kaiser's strategy is clear – starve us into submission. They know they won't beat us on the ground, but we are islands and we cannot live without sea trade. Admiral Von Tirpitz has persuaded the Kaiser that only unrestricted submarine warfare can bring Britain to its knees. So they attack our ships and any other vessel that so much as looks as if it is entering or leaving our waters. Your U-boat commander was a rare bird, La Salle. He preferred to empty his targets of men before sinking them. He probably knows we're already drawing up a list of war criminals. More and more we are seeing ships torpedoed without warning and their people left to the mercy of the sea. It's Satan's work, La Salle. If we can't stop it we shall die. As a nation, we shall succumb for want of food, fuel and everything else that comes by sea.'

He made an impatient gesture: 'Oh, I know our soldiers are doing more than any man should be asked to do. But the army is helping to save France. It has fallen to us to save Britain.'

He peered closely at La Salle, as if wanting to be sure this point had not been lost on him.

'Only we can stop the U-boat devils.' He paused. 'Should you like to smoke? Do so, by all means.'

La Salle shook his head.

'Well, as I was saying. We are in the front line here when it comes to the U-boats. The approaches to England from the west are our vital sea routes. We must keep them open. The cruisers, destroyers and armed trawlers are all doing a good job. But I believe the mystery ship is a trump in our pack.' He turned and looked away briefly. 'You

45

know there are those at the admiralty opposed to the decoy vessels?'

La Salle nodded. 'I had heard that.'

'They think they are a stunt. Expensive. Not very effective. Play acting. They call us the Gilbert and Sullivan navy. Bah! Your action wasn't play acting, was it? Sank a U-boat, saved goodness knows how many tons of shipping and who knows how many lives. What?'

'Yes, Sir.'

'That's the way forward, La Salle. I want to build a flotilla. Mostly based here, perhaps with a few ships at Falmouth. I want to persuade the admiralty to let me buy ships, arm them and disguise them and put aboard some of the bravest men in the service. Men like you, La Salle.'

La Salle flushed. 'Thank you, Sir.'

'Mr Churchill's on our side. Met him in London. Strange cove. He sees the danger in not hitting hard at the damned – excuse me – U-boats. Mr Churchill suggested the mystery ship campaign, you know. Right at the beginning. Jolly good on his history, Mr Churchill. He said the German has a terrible fear of fighting men out of uniform. Dates back to the Franco-Prussian war, you know. The French franc tireurs inflicted big losses. If the Prussians caught one, they shot him immediately. There and then. Not even a firing squad, often.'

Precisely the treatment I expect in the same circumstances, La Salle thought.

Churchill's enthusiasm for mystery ships was well-known, but La Salle wondered how much power the First Lord of the Admiralty really had now. The Dardanelles campaign, which Churchill had personally promoted, was turning into a disaster and Jackie Fisher – Lord Fisher, the First Sea Lord – was in open opposition to him. Churchill was without doubt a friend to the Special Service, but there might well be questions over whether he would, in the future, have influence to exercise.

'Is there support for the flotilla idea, apart from Mr Churchill?' La Salle asked.

'Oh yes. I hate to say it, but every ship that goes down strengthens our case. I've already been given permission to purchase a number of small vessels and we're negotiating on two or three now. But I want a fleet of them, La Salle, all over the sea lanes. I want those U-boat commanders to fear them. I want those … those devils to be afraid and shy of shelling and torpedoing every merchant vessel they come across.'

The admiral rubbed his chin. 'What do you think we should call the ships in our little fleet? I've been trying to think of a name. Queenstown Flotilla seems a bit long-winded.'

'Well, Queenstown is our base. Q-Ships, perhaps?' La Salle ventured.

'By Jove! That's good, La Salle. It's got that Special Service ring to it. I'll think on that.' He took out his pocket watch. 'Time for supper, I think. Shall we go in?'

As they walked to the dining room, the admiral confided in a low voice that he had just received signals reporting the presence of another U-boat in the Western Approaches, south of the Fastnet Rock. It was on the surface, steaming north east but before it could be engaged, it dived and contact was lost.

'Up to no good, I'll warrant,' he growled.

Miss Vaizey was already at table. La Salle noted, with an unreasonable prick of disappointment, that Lieutenant Davis, the admiral's flag officer and aide was also there. La Salle was placed next to the admiral who was at the head of the table. Miss Vaizey was on her uncle's left, thus facing the two guests.

'We don't need introductions, do we?' Sir Gerald asked, answering his own question by taking his seat.

La Salle nodded to Miss Vaizey and Davis in turn. The flag officer was a few years older than he, La Salle thought.

He had met him only a few times and always at Admiralty House. Davis seemed decent enough, but La Salle knew some officers felt he tended to clothe himself in the admiral's cloak of authority more enthusiastically than was justified. For his own part, La Salle thought he detected in Davis an interest in Miss Vaizey.

'Thank you for the flowers, Lieutenant,' Miss Vaizey said. 'It was kind indeed to have such a thought after everything that has been happening to you.'

La Salle thought Davis, sitting next to him, twitched slightly.

'I'm glad you like them. I was lucky to find them, so early in the year. But everything grows so well over here.'

'It's a rich island. We must never lose it,' the admiral grunted.

'The Sinn Feiners are getting bolder by the day,' Davis said. 'They see an opportunity, with the war taking virtually every effort we can make.'

The soup arrived and La Salle wondered whether this was a good moment to raise his concerns about spies.

'If *Farnham* is to go back to sea,' he said, 'I feel it would be worth re-arranging her away from here. Altering her appearance; new name and so on. Perhaps at Portmadoc.'

La Salle favoured Portmadoc for discreet fitting-out. The Welsh port had fewer facilities than Queenstown, but enough to give a small steamer a new disguise. And the risk of being spied upon was small compared to an Irish port.

The admiral laid down his spoon.

'There's a lot in what you say,' he said. 'Surprise is the most powerful shot in the mystery ship's locker.' He turned to Davis: 'Can you make a note of that? If a ship's been bowled out we should either drop it or completely change her. Devonport might serve better, though. Look into it.'

Davis mumbled a 'Yes, Sir,' and continued taking his soup. Miss Vaizey looked up at La Salle.

'What will you do now? You have some leave, surely?'

La Salle glanced at the admiral.

'Well, we were near the end of our ten day patrol. But …'

'Of course you must take some leave,' Sir Gerald said. 'You've got your four days shore leave, anyway.'

'Well, I should like to visit my guardian. In Devon.'

'Lord Burnage, isn't he?' the admiral said.

'Yes, Sir.'

'Never met him. Got a fine yacht, they say. Gave her to the admiralty, didn't he? I think they're fitting her out for the Lowestoft patrol.'

'That's right, Sir. She's being re-fitted in Plymouth now. I was sailing master in her. Before the war.'

'What is she? Schooner?'

'Yes, Sir. Topsail schooner. Some squaresail. Little over 200 tons. She's got an oil motor. About a hundred horsepower. First class ship. We took her to the Mediterranean in 1913.'

'Where does "La Salle" come from?' Davis asked suddenly. 'French, is it?'

'Yes.'

'So are you French?' Davis went on. La Salle felt a surge of colour warm his face. He had handled these questions many times before, but the presence of Miss Vaizey and the admiral added difficulty.

'I was born in London,' he said evenly. 'My mother was governess to Lord Burnage's children. After my birth we moved to Paris.'

'Is she still there?' Davis asked pleasantly.

'My mother died when I was ten,' La Salle said quietly. 'I have no other family. Lord Burnage sent for me.' He waited for Davis's next question. The inevitable one, about his father. It never came.

'I see,' Davis said.

Yes, La Salle thought without real bitterness, *I suspect you do*. He glanced up at Miss Vaizey. She was looking directly at him. There was something in her eyes La Salle found unsettling and not entirely gratifying. It was compassion.

'I wish the French would do a bit more to keep the U-boats in check,' Davis said. 'They seem to have the run of the waters around Ushant.'

'That's where a lot of our problems start,' Sir Gerald agreed. 'But while the French are concentrating their fleet in the Mediterranean there's little they can do.' He paused over his plate. 'Actually, I think the admiralty is quite happy for the French to be down there in the Med. There's still a sentiment, y'know, that the Channel is ours. In time of war we take care of our own.'

Davis concurred. To La Salle's relief Miss Vaizey dropped her gaze. A fine joint of lamb arrived and the admiral set to carving.

'Y'know Campbell – God rest his soul – had a good thought when he stuffed *Farnham* with timber,' Sir Gerald said. 'Saved the ship, didn't it, La Salle?'

'I believe so, Sir. It's something I'd be keen to do in the future. Commander Campbell once saw a Finnish barque loaded with deals stay afloat after she'd been shelled. He told me it gave him the idea for loading wood into *Farnham.*'

'We'd be lucky to get the wood now,' Davis put in. 'Every spare piece of timber is going to France for the trenches and the tunnels. There's hardly a pit prop to be had over here.'

'There's plenty of timber in Canada,' the admiral rejoined. 'I've a mind to send our new Q-Ships there to fill up with it. Make a note.'

Davis nodded, his mouth full of lamb.

'So when will you go back to sea, Lieutenant?' Miss Vaizey asked.

La Salle shot a look at the admiral.

'Oh, we'll find you a ship,' Sir Gerald said.

La Salle turned back to her. 'Soon, I hope.'

'And you wish to stay in the Special Service?'

'Very much. Yes.'

'My uncle calls the U-boat commanders "Satans",' she mused. 'I understand that's also what the Germans call the men in our mystery ships.'

La Salle smiled. 'They think our tactics are evil, I'm afraid.' His voice became earnest: 'I suppose we are both wicked, in our way. They use deceitful methods; so do we. But when they launched the U-boat campaign everything changed. Before the war none of us, I'm sure, would have dreamed of circumstances in which submerged vessels would sneak up on merchant ships and sink them, often without warning.'

He shook his head, as if perplexed. 'Innocent people killed. You may feel anything necessary to fight that is justified.' He relaxed and smiled again.

'Even if it means being condemned as "Satans".'

'Satans against Satans,' Miss Vaizey murmured. 'A combat of devils.' Then: 'But I don't think of you in that way.'

La Salle had an inkling of Davis twitching again.

'The Hun cannot expect us to handle him with kid gloves when he behaves as he does,' the admiral growled. 'Look at what he did in Belgium. Civilians. Atrocities. Now we've got it here. Not just the U-boats. Scarborough. Zeppelins. Murdering children. How can the Hun do that and still ask for fair play? What?'

La Salle pictured a recent recruiting poster, urging men to enlist under the words "Remember Scarborough!" The German surprise attacks on the town – and Whitby and Hartlepool – had enraged the nation. Just before Christmas German battleships shelled the towns with big guns, killing more than 150 civilians, including schoolchildren and a fourteen month old baby. Last week, while he was patrolling in *Farnham*, they had picked up wireless traffic about Zeppelin airships bombing East Anglia in an early morning raid, killing people as they slept. La Salle found the German strategy mystifying.

'It's incomprehensible,' he said, almost to himself.

'Of course it is!' the admiral thundered. 'The whole thing is irrational. None of it makes sense, unless you look into the Kaiser's character. What do you see? You see a man deformed physically and mentally.'

There was a view, to which La Salle felt unable to contribute, that the war was forced by the Kaiser because he blamed Britain, and the British obstetrician who delivered him, for his withered left arm. The deformity was caused, it was said, by excessive force applied during his breech birth.

'The Kaiser has always hated us,' the admiral said. 'I remember when I was in *Indomitable*, in Portsmouth. It would have been '95, I reckon. The Prince of Wales, the old king, invited a few officers out for a day's sport at the Cowes Regatta, aboard *Britannia*.' He paused. 'You're a sailing man, La Salle. Ever see *Britannia*?'

'Yes, Sir. She's a very fast yacht.'

'I'll say. Well, old Bertie wouldn't let us touch her, of course. He had his crack crew aboard, most of them Brightlingsea men. The Kaiser was aboard his *Meteor*. Anyway, *Britannia* gave *Meteor* a hiding and the Kaiser couldn't stand it. When they rowed him ashore he stood on the steps at the Royal Yacht Squadron and waited for Bertie. Something happened between them. There was some foolish talk about blows being exchanged. I never believed it. It was all hushed up, anyway. Whatever happened the Kaiser never went back to Cowes.'

'Is it possible personal hatred could lead to war and all that is happening now?' Miss Vaizey asked incredulously.

'Yes, if you think of it in terms of a family feud, prompted by envy,' Davis offered. 'The Kaiser calls himself an emperor, but his empire is very small compared to the one his cousins have across the Channel. I can see a seed of jealousy growing until it's out of control. After all, a plague can be started by a tiny germ.' A thought occurred to him: 'Or a very big Germ – an!'

La Salle and Miss Vaizey smiled politely. The admiral snorted.

'The quicker we finish it the better,' he said.

All agreed heartily. The meal ended with coffee in the drawing room and conversation turned away from the war. They discussed the controversy over Mr Lloyd George's plan to introduce new taxes on alcohol, a move Sir Gerald, a lifelong teetotaller, thought an excellent idea. Miss Vaizey talked about the garden at Admiralty House and her plan to replant the flower beds on the lower slopes. She sees her future here, then, La Salle thought. With her uncle. He found the idea faintly depressing.

It was dark when he left and pleasantly warm. He walked down the hill with a springy step, all tiredness gone. He thought he'd go back to Kimberley House via the harbour, to see what ships were in. He had considered popping into the Club for a nightcap, but he didn't want to see anyone he knew, or talk even. Miss Vaizey had left him with a strange sense of wanting to preserve his mood exactly as it was. He didn't want the intrusion of company.

He crossed the harbour road and strolled across the stone flags on the quay. The admiral's cruiser was on her buoy and a few smaller vessels were tied up alongside the wall. La Salle could see lights burning in the Cunard office. *Strange*, he thought, *to be working so late*. Then he remembered. The admiral said a U-boat had been sighted heading towards the southern entrance to St George's Channel and he planned to divert any major vessel into Queenstown until the threat passed. La Salle turned towards Kimberley House. The *Lusitania* was due tomorrow.

CHAPTER THREE

Merrick Olsen stretched indulgently, almost the full length of the bunk, rolled over and faced inboard. After five days at sea he knew every detail of the plain, white-painted cabin, but it amused him to lie there and let his eye wander over the simple panelling, the metal washstand and the rivets in the huge steel beam overhead. He imagined the men who had put together that space, just a tiny corner of the huge ship. They were shipwrights, joiners, plumbers; ordinary, honest tradesmen living normal lives. They went home to families, enjoyed companionship, friendships and respect. Reputation. Things he hoped to find on this side of the Atlantic.

Lusitania's foghorn boomed again, a mournful deep moan. It had started at dawn and Olsen saw through the single portlight that the ship was enveloped in fog. He reached over to the catch-all above the washstand and checked his watch. Ten to six. He had slept well, the best rest he'd had for weeks. He swung his legs over the side of the bunk, gripped the steel tubing at the head and slid to the floor. It was a four berth cabin, third class on the main deck, forward. He had had his pick of the berths because, the steward told him, third class was less than a quarter full. First class, with the likes of Mr Alfred Vanderbilt aboard, was well-booked and so was second-class. But, the steward said, poorer folk didn't travel much in wartime. No offence. Olsen took none. He revelled in the luxury of his solitary space. By the standards of other ships the third-class accommodations were sumptuous. The bunks were covered with elegant spreads embroidered with the gold lion crest of the Cunard line, an unexpected touch of luxury upon which he remarked to the steward. 'Yes,' said the man. 'It's to stop people stealing them.'

The days at sea had passed pleasantly in fine weather, although Olsen chose to spend much of the time below in his cabin. It was a big ship and it was impossible to know whom one might encounter. The foghorn boomed again. He took off his sleeping suit, rolled it up and stuffed it into his bag. There was a clean shirt he'd been saving for arrival in Liverpool and he put it on, dressing quickly. He carried his pea-jacket because he suspected it would be cold on deck. In that fog. He opened the door and glanced down the passageway. Before he could dart back inside, Mrs Madden spotted him.

'Mr Olsen! Mr Olsen!' She hurried towards him, waving her parasol.

'Good morning, Mrs Madden.'

'It seems the most horrible morning to me, Mr Olsen. I haven't slept, you know. Not a wink. How can one? Mr Burgess and his talk of submarines. Did you hear him last night? "We'll be in submarine waters by morning," he said. Are we, do you think?'

Olsen frowned. 'Can't say, Ma'am. I'm going out to take a look.' He raised his cap to her and walked smartly down the passageway.

'I'll come with you,' she said.

Olsen groaned to himself. Mrs Madden had been recently widowed, as she announced as soon as the ship turned its bow down the Hudson River. She told one and all of her plan to return to England with the intention of re-settling there. Her talkative manner was not unpleasant, however, and the other passengers liked her for her bright giggle and kindly spirit. She had taken to playing the piano in the third class saloon in the evenings, an entertainment very much enjoyed. Olsen overheard a group of men in the smoking saloon talking about her. They called her "The Merry Widow" and laughed coarsely.

She was certainly attractive, and still young. Olsen had a feeling she had been determined to make friends with him since the first day of sailing and he had found it hard to escape her insistent probing of his situation. It was hard to know how to put her off without appearing to be discourteous. Sometimes, he thought, it would be an advantage to have some idea of how women worked. Could they be understood, like complex machinery?

They emerged on to the main deck to find a world made entirely grey. Beyond the ship's rail, where an ocean, horizon and a sky had been, there was now mere vapour, as if the ship had exchanged the material world for a cloud. Everything dripped. Droplets ran everywhere, from the boat deck above, from the portlights, the door handles. All were covered in a dank mist. Mrs Madden shivered.

'Goodness, it's cold!'

Olsen peered into the fog. He guessed the visibility was down to a few hundred feet, at most. It was impossible to make out the bow, although they were standing well forward of amidships. There was a ghostly glimpse of the foremast rigging, but then it vanished as the greyness darkened around them.

'Would the submarines see us? In this?' Mrs Madden asked.

'I doubt that,' Olsen replied.

'Then why doesn't Captain Turner stop making that hooting sound? If they can't see us why advertise our presence with that awful noise?'

'Hitting another ship would be about as bad as coming up with a U-boat, I guess. Besides, it's regulations.'

Mrs Madden tilted her head.

'Are you a mariner, Mr Olsen?'

He winced. She had prised his name out of him but he had no desire to tell her – or anyone else – more than necessary.

'I shouldn't worry about submarines,' he said, smiling.

'I reckon we'll be safely tied up in Liverpool this afternoon.'

'I suppose you're right. The Germans would never attack a ship like this, would they? I mean, a civilian ship, carrying women and children? Even they would scruple at that, wouldn't they?'

Olsen smiled reassuringly, although his mind ran over an advertisement he'd seen in one of the New York papers just before they sailed. It had been placed by the German embassy and warned passengers against making the Atlantic crossing because the waters around Great Britain had been declared a war zone. It did not alarm him. He did not fear death. The traps sprung by life held greater horror. Yet he had no wish to be sent to the bottom by a U-boat and he certainly did not want Mrs Madden, importunate as she was, to worry herself into a state about it.

'The ship has made the crossing many times,' he said. 'I'm sure this will be no different.'

She looked at him and smiled weakly, but her eyes betrayed a deep anxiety. Olsen summoned his own nerve. An act of generosity was needed. He extended an arm.

'Mrs Madden. Would you do me the honour of accompanying me on a stroll through the fog?' He lifted his cap and made a bow, brushing back his wavy blonde hair as it fell untidily around his face.

She laughed lightly and raised her parasol with a girly flourish. They set off along the deserted main deck, walking forward below the bridge where the moan of the horn seemed even louder, more forlorn, and the swirling grey wisps swept by at precisely the quickness of the speeding ship.

The fog cleared late in the morning to reveal a sparkling ocean, a blue sky and, faraway on the bow, the shadow of land. Mrs Madden had fallen strangely silent on their walk around the deck and when Olsen returned her to her cabin he felt an untypically gloomy mood had overtaken her. She murmured something about perhaps seeing each other at luncheon. The dearth of third class passengers meant there was only one sitting for meals and the long tables set for ten had been convivial meeting places during the voyage, although Olsen had taken care not to attach himself to any one group. He did not tell Mrs Madden, but he had decided not to take lunch. There would be a gay mood in the dining saloon, with land in sight, and he preferred not to join in. In his cabin he read a little, tidied the clothes in his bag and went over his papers once more. Everything was there: his certificates, engineer officer's log, passport and close to 500 dollars. He took out his box of brushes and paints, checked the clasp top to make sure it was closed, put it back in the bag. He leafed through a few sketches he had made of seabirds on the crossing, folded them carefully into his copy of Elliot's *North American Shore Birds* and sat on a lower bunk. That was it. Everything he owned, everything he was. All in the bag. The rest was in his head, some of it buried less deep than he would like.

There was a sound like the slamming of a giant door. The noise, accompanied by a tremor, seemed to be below him, further forward. Just as he started from the bunk a second explosion shook the cabin, far more powerful than the first, jerking him sideways like a puppet. The whole space seemed to vibrate with sound. It attacked him like a physical force; a deep, gut-thumping and – so it felt – solid noise. Then there was stillness. Everything was as it had been, there in that small space. But the ship seemed to stagger, leaning. He threw open the door. People were rushing from cabins, milling in the passageway. Olsen walked with deliberate calm; along the corridors, up the stairs, out on to the deck on the starboard side. A small group stood at the rail. A man was pointing.

'I saw it! I saw it!' he shouted. 'A torpedo. It came straight for us!'

The ship had taken a list to starboard. Olsen felt she was slightly down by the bow. Already! Her speed seemed unchecked. *He'll sail her under if he doesn't get way off pretty damn quick,* he thought. Mrs Madden ran out on to the deck, eyes wide, her long fair hair falling about her shoulders as if she had been interrupted in the act of pinning it. She had changed from the black she had worn throughout the voyage and was now wearing a white dress, not unlike a wedding gown. She looked rather beautiful, Olsen thought abstractly.

'What was it?' she cried. Olsen patted her arm.

'Looks like we've been hit,' he said quietly. 'Better get your lifevest.' He smiled. 'Just in case.'

At that moment the deck dropped away as the ship heeled sharply. Mrs Madden half fell, screamed and held on to him with both hands. There was a crowd on the main deck now and Olsen saw two officers approaching.

'Lifebelts, everyone,' one called out. 'Please make your way to the muster stations. Lifebelts now!'

Olsen pulled away Mrs Madden's arms gently.

'Stay here,' he said. 'Do not move from here. I'll be back with a lifevest.'

'But my things!'

'You can get them later. Promise me you'll stay here?'

She nodded. Olsen ran into the passageway. There were four lifebelts on a rack in his cabin. The ship took another heavy list to starboard and he had to pull himself along the handrail to make progress up the steep incline. In the lobby a small group was entering the lift.

'What are you doing?' he cried at a man ushering a woman and three small children into the lift car. 'Get out of there! The ship's going down!'

'We're going to the boat deck,' the man replied calmly. A sudden lurch slammed the lift gates closed. Olsen tried to wrench them open, his feet slithering on the sloping floor.

'Get out of there! Get out!' he shouted. The inner doors closed and there was a whirring sound. The lights in the lobby flickered, then went out. Olsen sank to his knees. The lift machinery fell silent. The sound of a woman's screams could be heard, coming from the liftshaft. Then a man's voice, shouting. The voices were loud, very close, as if they were just at hand, there in the blackness somewhere. Olsen struggled nearly upright, feeling for the steel bars of the lift gate. He seized something, shook it violently. It would not move. The gates were locked shut by the mechanism which, without electricity, would not now open them. Olsen experienced a surge of nausea. The noise from the lift was louder, mingling with the sobs of a child, then another. Olsen kicked and slammed the gates with his fists. They rattled, but stayed firmly closed. He felt for the control panel, pushed the buttons wildly. The floor seemed to be giving way beneath his feet, slowly but perceptibly as the ship pitched forward. Two shapes tumbled into the darkness of the lobby.

'Which way? Which way?'

It was a woman's voice, shrill and terrified. Olsen shook his head, tried to block out the sounds from the lift, the images they conjured.

'Follow me,' he said, abandoning any idea of making it back to his cabin and out again. The idea of being trapped there as the ship sank could not be contemplated. He put out a hand towards the voice. He felt a shoulder, ran his hand down an arm, found a hand. It gripped him with a ferocity he found startling.

'How many?'

'Two.'

'Hold on to each other and hold on to me.'

'Yes.'

Olsen knew the way out. It was downhill, towards the

sinking starboard side. The stairs were close. The handrail
kept them from falling headlong, but they could not move
quickly. They reached the end of the last corridor at last
and Olsen threw open the door and looked out, blinking.
His guts lurched. The sea was only a few feet below the
level of the deck. Glancing forward he saw the bow was
under water and he knew it could only be a matter of
minutes before she went. Some people were pulling
themselves along the rail, heading aft, away from the
rising sea. There was no sign of Mrs Madden. Olsen turned
to the woman gripping his hand.

'All right?' he said. She nodded, biting her lip. A boy
of about ten was holding her other hand. Neither of them
had lifebelts. 'Follow me, then.'

They made it to some steps and climbed up to the boat
deck. There was a mass of people, but no panic. A smiling
officer walked through the crowd checking lifebelts.

'Nothing to worry about,' he called out cheerily. 'We'll
be landing in rather smaller vessels, that's all.'

A man in a tweed suit tried to hold on to the officer.
He seemed to want to deliver a dressing down. Olsen
heard the words "absolute disgrace," and "I'll be writing
to the chairman" before the officer, still smiling, pulled
himself free and continued his walk among the passengers.
Somewhere above them the band was playing *Tiperary*.
There was a lot of movement around the lifeboats. Olsen
did not like what he saw. On the voyage he had witnessed
a lifeboat drill. It consisted of nothing more than seamen
climbing into a boat, raising their oars and then, at the
signal from a whistle, climbing out again. Now he saw
men fumbling with unfamiliar lines, trying to swing out
the davits jammed by the steep list, the tackles stubbornly
resisting unpractised hands.

'There's a boat going there!' the woman at his side
cried.

A lifeboat, filled with women and children, maybe

61

fifty or more, was being lowered. It hung precariously over the steeply heeled ship's side and its progress was jerky, but it seemed it would launch successfully. Immediately aft of it, another boat was being swung out. A seaman knocked out the pin holding the boat to the deck and Olsen saw the bow dip. It started to assume a crazy angle, its stern high in the air as the after fall jammed, while the forward lines ran freely. People in the boat started screaming, trying to stop themselves falling down into the bow. The deckhand on the stern falls was struggling with the ropes. Olsen saw him take a line off the cleat that was holding it. The rope shot through his hands, the stern of the lifeboat fell and the whole thing swung forward, still tethered by the bow. Passengers dropped into the sea, some fell among those in the first boat which was having difficulty escaping the side of the ship. Then the line holding the hanging boat parted. It fell, stern first, on top of the crowded lifeboat below. There was a dreadful crunching noise, then silence. Almost immediately the air became filled with the cries of people in the boat, people in the sea, people on the deck. Below the ship's side there was a mad thrashing in the water as those who had escaped the falling boat tried to flee the carnage. Some struck out alone, others tried to help badly hurt children, clambering on to the wreckage of the two boats. Broken bodies bobbed against the ship's side, some thrashed pointlessly with a still functioning arm or leg.

Further aft a boat was properly launched, then another. Passengers began climbing up the inclined deck of the ship. All calm vanished. People swept past the smiling officer who had resorted to using a megaphone. Men climbed into the boats. One was imploring his fellows to make way for women and children first, but he was ignored, pushed aside in the scramble for a lifeboat. A number of women with babies had gathered in a group. No one was helping them.

'Best get into the first boat you can,' Olsen said to the woman and the boy.

She shook her head and tightened her grip on his hand.

'It's your best chance,' he said. She did not move. The boy was watching them intently. Olsen shot a desperate glance around the deck, seething now with milling people. Three seamen were trying to lift a collapsible boat over the rail. There were a number of these rafts with canvas sides stowed below the lifeboats. Olsen turned to some men clinging to the handrail near the Grand Entrance.

'Quick!' he called. 'Help with this.'

He wrenched himself free of the woman and half rolled, half ran to a liferaft. It was still securely tied to eyebolts in the deck. Olsen pulled out his clasp knife. The lashings on the liferaft yielded quickly to the knife's wickedly sharp blade. The men lifted the cumbersome rectangle of canvas and wood to try to throw it over the side. Olsen stopped them.

'Find the painter!'

They uncovered a long rope coiled in a canvas flap and Olsen made it fast to the rail.

'Now – heave!'

They pushed the raft over the rail. It wobbled unsteadily, but floated. The boat deck was now about fifteen feet above the water. Olsen turned to the woman and the boy.

'You'll have to jump for it,' he said.

The woman shook her head. The boy was staring at Olsen.

'It's the only way. Jump, then swim to the raft. Can you swim?'

She nodded. Olsen looked at the boy. He nodded his head.

'Go then!'

Dumbly, the woman gathered her skirts, heavily

layered and of thick material. Olsen, still holding the clasp knife, seized her shoulder, turned her around and slit the gown down the back. He ripped it open the rest of the way.

'Sorry, ma'am. You can't swim in that. Now go!'

She shucked off the tatters of her dress and, without a word, led the boy to the rail.

'Go!' Olsen shouted again.

They jumped into the sea and he saw them swim to the raft. A number of people in the water had already climbed aboard. Others clung to its edge, unable to lift themselves up the sheer sides.

'Let's get another over the side,' Olsen called to the men. They worked on launching a second raft as the officer with the megaphone succeeded in putting the women and babies into a lifeboat. The seamen had learned how to manage the falls now and the lifeboat began a more or less steady descent. Then, just as it was lowered below deck level, a rush of passengers, mostly men, threw themselves into it, causing it to swing wildly from side to side. The seamen on the falls lost control and the boat plunged downwards, capsizing the moment it hit the water and turning upside down. Olsen resisted an urge to dive in, then and there, to try to save whom he could. One woman was treading water, trying to hold her baby's head above the sea. Another child, a little older, had climbed on to his mother's shoulders as she tried to swim towards a raft. Olsen muttered something through clenched teeth. He turned back to the collapsible boat on the deck, the only hope now for many of those in the water.

'Let's get it over. Lively now!'

A few men had stuck with him and they launched the raft, taking care, as before, to secure the painter so it didn't float away. They were close to the stern now and there were no more boats, no more rafts. A couple in the group moved away to climb over the superstructure to try their luck on the port side, riding high out of the water. The ship lurched forward, dipping and turning.

'She's going!' a man shouted. He ran to the deck edge and jumped. Others followed him. Olsen could still see people on the upper levels. A few had gathered on the second class deckhouse. He looked over the side. There was a clear patch of sea below. He jumped.

Silence. No clamour, no sound. Above him, Olsen glimpsed a pale sky through the water. He kicked off his shoes, scissored his legs and broke the surface. As his ears cleared they were immediately assailed by shouts and screams. Some boats were pulling clear of the ship, there were rafts nearby and a number of people were holding on to an upturned lifeboat. Everywhere names were being called. Olsen turned, looked back aft. There were hundreds of people in boats, in the water, some holding on to pieces of wrecked lifeboats. He guessed they were less than half those who had been aboard the *Lusitania*. He dipped his head and struck out towards a raft. As he reached it, he saw an elderly man try to climb its side. Olsen put his left hand on the raft, his right under the man's crotch and heaved him aboard. There was no more space and some men were trying to rig the collapsible sides that turned it into a kind of rectangular boat with a suggestion of a prow and a stern. It occurred to Olsen that if they succeeded in raising the sides he'd never make it aboard. He thought, in a more or less relaxed way, that perhaps this was his time. But did it have to be? The sea was no colder than the waters of Boston where, as a child, he had spent long summer days fishing and swimming. He would probably last, at least, the rest of that day, if he kept his trousers and sweater on. Land was in sight. Someone would turn up.

Two men on the raft were trying to rig oars. Olsen had a sense the raft was being drawn back towards the ship. The giant shape was exerting a pull as it settled deeper, turning slowly to starboard as its stern lifted higher and higher presenting, to his engineer's eye, the glorious spectacle of four giant propellers, possibly the largest ever made, their bronze still pristine and unsullied by the sea. There was a collective gasp aboard the raft. Olsen looked up, saw *Lusitania's* funnels looming almost overhead, falling towards them. The raft was just out of range, he thought, but many were not. The forward funnel dipped into the sea, smashing bodies trapped below it, cutting a lifeboat in two, throwing its occupants into the water. Among them, Olsen saw, was Mrs Madden. He recognised her quite clearly, less than a hundred feet away. She was swimming now, disorientated. Towards the ship. The funnel seemed to hover at the surface as the ship paused again in its dive. Olsen felt a kind of paralysis seize him. Mrs Madden, her long blonde hair streaming over the shoulders of her white dress, was sucked headlong into the slowly sinking funnel. The gaping hole closed up with water and Olsen wished he did not know what would happen next. The funnel slipped below the sea and, almost immediately, there was a deep wheezing noise as the cold water hit the steam boiler. Then soot and steam erupted in a volcanic explosion and Mrs Madden was blown out of the submerged funnel, high above the water. She had turned completely black, twisting almost gracefully in the air then falling limp among the bodies in the sea.

The people in the smashed lifeboat tried to swim away from the falling superstructure as it collapsed like a toppled building. Many were caught by the steelwork as it crashed down. The funnels went under, one by one, each emitting a blast of black water and steam.

Olsen's raft was in line with the after mast and it seemed raised over them like a giant stick about to deliver a blow. The deckworks tottered, threatened to plunge down but the ship's reserves of buoyancy held her even then. Olsen reckoned this was a brief respite and he thought it better to strike away from the raft before the mast came down. He turned to push himself away then caught sight of a group from the wrecked lifeboat. They were struggling in the water, trying to free a child, a red-haired girl of about six or seven, caught in a tangle of radio aerial wires. As he watched, a man submerged as the girl dipped just below the surface, but he quickly came up again, trying to hold the child's head above the sea. The ship had paused in its descent and Olsen kicked his legs, struck powerfully towards the trapped girl. They were keeping her alive by pulling her up against the slack in the wire, but it seemed firmly twisted around her feet.

Olsen dived, found the cable and felt his way along it to where it held the girl by the ankle. He reached carefully in his pocket for the knife with his free hand, gripped the blade in his teeth and opened it. As he reached to slash at the wire he sensed a gentle tug, downwards. He jerked his head around. The light was fading overhead. They were some feet below the surface now and going down, darker and deeper. *Lusitania* was on her way to the bottom. Olsen fought an urge – an instinct – that told him to let go and strike out for the disappearing light. He let a little air bubble out through his mouth. He hacked at the wire, cutting once, twice, three times. The cable was thin copper radio wire but it would not yield. He turned the knife, put the blade under the cable and pulled upwards with all his strength. Something gave. He snatched at the wire, it slipped then came free. He held on to the child's ankle. He could see some paleness above. He pushed her towards it. She was spluttering, trying to breathe water. He was aware of a huge shape to his right, moving quickly like a shadowy headland gliding past in the night. There was a current, a suction following the ship down. He kicked hard with his legs, stroking upwards with his free arm. Something brushed past, more wire snaking out like a tentacle, but there was blue over their heads now. Olsen knew he would make it all right. He and his brother would check their lobster pots by diving on them. He'd gone deeper than this. He would be fine. But the child seemed lifeless and as they broke the surface he looped an arm around her and swam on his back, towards a raft, holding her head up. The people on the raft made space for him and helped drag the girl out of the sea. He turned her on her side and pumped. It seemed an age before the water started, then it came in a gush. She was alive. He pinched her nose and breathed into her mouth. She coughed, then spluttered. She began retching, shuddering. Olsen turned to the people on the raft. They were watching him with a kind of wonderment. In the midst of death he had restored life. From a sea bobbing with the newly dead he had snatched back one of the taken. They were in awe of him. Olsen spoke to a woman crouching nearby.

'This kid needs warmth. Can you hug her, ma'am?'

The woman held out her arms. Olsen, kneeling, lifted the child and passed her across. The girl was sobbing quietly, her thin shoulders shaking. She was a snub-nose ginger-top with freckles. A bit of a tomboy, Olsen guessed. He smiled at her as the woman cradled her gently. The girl stared back, sniffing, her face blank. She had no idea who he was. Olsen glanced around. There was no one in sight he recognised as being among those who had been trying to free her from the cable. Her family, he guessed. Well, if they lived they would find her later. He sat on the edge of the raft, too tired to try to raise its sides or even suggest it to the others. There was little breeze and no sea running. *Thank the Lord. Just wait for someone to turn up. It couldn't be long. Rest awhile.* The land was close, tantalisingly close. He felt they were still staring at him so he shifted slightly, looked out across a clear expanse of ocean from which the largest moveable object created by man had just vanished.

The dining room at Kimberley House was almost empty

and Fisk had picked a table near the window, overlooking the garden. He was reading the newspaper when La Salle entered, then set it aside as his friend joined him.

'Did you see the Constructor?' Fisk asked.

'Yes. It'll be some time before *Farnham* goes to sea again.' La Salle pulled out a chair. 'We'll have to find another ship.'

Fisk leaned forward, his jaw jutting earnestly.

'But we'll stay in the Special Service, won't we? They'll give us another mystery ship?'

La Salle sat down and glanced at the luncheon card. Boiled ham. Would an omelette, lightly done, be too much to ask, he wondered? Perhaps a green salad? Last time he was here he'd shown the cook – what was his name? Berry? – how to make a passable vinaigrette.

'Do you know if Berry, the cook is still here?'

'Who?'

'Oh. Never mind.' La Salle looked out of the open window. It was a perfect early summer's day. The garden seemed to throb with new life in the white and pink of the blossoms and a vivid, luxuriant green. Even the greenness of his adored Devon could not compare with the colour here, La Salle thought. He took a deep breath. For once, he was not especially anxious to get back to sea.

'I said do you think we'll get a mystery ship?' Fisk insisted.

'What? Well, I hope so. I don't see why not. It seems the admiral intends to build up a fleet of them.' La Salle paused. 'Actually, Gordon, you'd better forget I said that. I'm not sure how widely known his plans are.'

Fisk pulled some folded paper from his pocket.

'Take a look at that, Julian. What do you think?' He handed over a sales catalogue for the Rudge Multi motorcycle. 'Well?' he asked.

'I'm not very good on motors, Gordon. You know that.'

'Yes, but look at the testimonials. Marvellous service

on the Western Front. Despatch riders use them, you know. Very reliable. Multiple gears.'

La Salle smiled and handed back the catalogue which Fisk folded carefully and put into the breast pocket of his jacket.

'I'm going to order one when we get the prize money.'

La Salle wondered privately whether that was a wise move, investing money gained from the taking of life into a potentially lethal machine. Would that offend some moral equilibrium? The thought reminded him it was Friday. He'd go to Mass later.

'Have you ordered? It's getting late.'

Fisk picked up the lunch card. There was a loud banging outside, at the front door. The two men looked at each other, puzzled. They heard voices then a boy burst into the dining room.

'All officers to report to the dockyard!' He was out of breath and swallowed hard. 'It's the *Lusitania!*'

'What? What about it?' an officer sitting near the door asked curtly.

'She's been hit!'

The boy ran from the room. La Salle rose from his chair and Fisk followed him to the door. They joined the group of men running towards the harbour road. When they reached the quay they saw the admiralty paddle steamer, *Flying Fish,* sailing at high speed towards the narrows. The tugs *Stormcock* and *Julia* were tied up alongside, belching black smoke as their engineers hurried to get up steam. At the naval pier La Salle was ordered into *Heron*, a patrol craft under the command of a Lieutenant Smith, whom he did not know. Smith told him *Lusitania* sent an SOS, confirmed by her call sign *MFA*, saying she had a heavy list, ten miles off the Old Head of Kinsale.

'Was it a U-boat?' La Salle asked.

'Must have been,' Smith replied. 'There shouldn't be any mines out there.'

Heron moved quickly into the fairway, past the island and soon overtook *Flying Fish*. As they left the land behind they found themselves part of a flotilla of patrol craft, trawlers and tugs. La Salle swept the horizon with Smith's binoculars.

'Sailing vessels to the south west,' he said.

'That'll be the fishing fleet. Can you see *Lusitania*?'

'No.'

Smith glanced at the chart and checked his watch.

'We should be seeing her by now. In this visibility.'

La Salle handed him the binoculars. Their eyes met briefly. Neither wished to voice the thought they knew they shared.

'We'll hold this course,' Smith said.

They made out the lifeboats and rafts at a considerable distance and *Heron* was closing with them when they spotted a fishing vessel on a reciprocal course. The boat, a steam trawler, was low in the water. She approached sluggishly and La Salle could see why. She was crowded with people from stem to stern. He tried counting, but gave up at fifty. They slowed as the trawler came alongside. She was pulling a lifeboat which yawed precariously on the end of the tow line. It, too, was packed with people, a quiet crowd, many of whom were looking back, as if seeking something. A man raised an arm in greeting. He was not among those whose eyes searched the sea astern. The trawler skipper said he was making for Kinsale. Smith asked him if he'd seen the ship.

'No,' the man said. 'And she'll not be seen again.'

As the trawler drew away, La Salle saw rows of inert figures laid out on the well deck, some covered with a tarpaulin, others with a piece of clothing over their faces. Then they began to see bodies in the water. There were more than La Salle could have imagined, floating on the gentle swell, bumping here and there into pieces of wrecked boats, riding *Heron's* bow wave then falling back, face down, arms outstretched, as if their last act was to embrace the sea itself.

'We'll attend to the survivors first,' Smith said, his face ashen. .

They brought a half-sunken lifeboat alongside and rigged a scrambling net. Many of those inside were too weak to climb, so La Salle took two ratings down with bosun's chairs. The bottom of the lifeboat was awash and as La Salle moved among the people to be lifted he tripped on something in the water; he looked down and saw a baby, almost naked, its eyes half-closed. He lifted it gently and held it the way he supposed babies were meant to be held, although he had never actually done it and this one, a few months old perhaps, was quite dead.

'Where is the mother?' he called out, still cradling the pale bundle in his arms. The people in the boat watched him dumbly.

'Where is this child's mother?' La Salle repeated, aware his voice had changed.

'She jumped,' one said. 'When it died.'

They found an old man and a middle-aged woman dead among the people in the boat and all were taken aboard *Heron*. They worked through the late afternoon and took on more than ninety survivors and eighteen bodies before turning towards Kinsale. When they returned to where the *Lusitania* had been all the rafts and lifeboats had been emptied or taken in tow by the rescue flotilla. As darkness fell, *Heron* and the other vessels began a systematic sweep of the sea, recovering bodies with boathooks and looking among the scattered pieces of debris for anyone who had managed to cling to life. They came upon a fragment of a shattered boat, floating like an upturned shell and just big enough to carry one person. Inside, a woman, asleep or unconscious, was still alive but a man next to her was not. It seemed he had lashed his wrist to the wreckage with his necktie while in the water, anxious, no doubt, not to be separated from the woman. As they brought the woman and her dead husband, brother or suitor aboard, La Salle thought about love and its ability to heap cruelty on the heavy burden of loss. He thought of his mother and her painful illness and death, while still young. The anger he had felt, the rage against God. Then, as he grew older, the quiet acceptance. But there was no reason why the bereaved of the *Lusitania* should ever accept what had happened to those they loved. The baby, the dead children and women they had pulled from the sea, the man with the woman in the wreckage. Were they victims of the war, the war of which he was a part? Perhaps. But to La Salle it seemed this was something else, something even more frightening.

By midnight there was nothing to be seen and *Heron* set course for Queenstown. La Salle stood at the rail, plagued by gloom, a tightness in his throat. The breeze had freshened a little and the ebb had started. He stared out to sea, not really seeing anything. But there was something. On the starboard bow, just a few hundred yards away he saw a shape sticking up out of the dark swell. He called for a rating to get binoculars. With the glasses he saw what looked like a chair, being propelled slowly through the water. La Salle climbed quickly to the bridge and pointed out the object to Smith. *Heron* slowed and altered to starboard. It was a chair, a cane chair of a kind used on the deck of a liner. Its back and part of the seat were out of the water while its legs, La Salle saw, were being held by a swimming figure. As they drew alongside, the swimmer turned on his back and waved with one arm. It was a young man, La Salle saw, dressed in trousers and jersey. He was grinning, his teeth glowing in the darkness. They lowered a rope with a bowline in it and he tucked one foot in the bight so they could haul him aboard. He sat on the deck, his hands on his knees, head down, breathing deeply.

'Are you all right?' La Salle asked.

The swimmer looked up. He shook his head like a wet dog, smoothed down his wavy blond hair.

'Has the tide turned?' he asked. It was an American voice.

'Just,' La Salle replied.

'Thought so. I was doing OK when I had the stream with me but I could feel it turning. It did occur to me I might not make it.'

'You were trying to swim ashore?'

'I guess I was. I was on a raft but it got kind of crowded. I saw the chair and thought I'd take my chances. It kept me afloat so I could rest for a spell.'

'Good God!' La Salle exclaimed. He suddenly felt his mood lift. He held out his hand.

'Julian La Salle.'

The swimmer reached up from the deck.

'Pleased to meet you,' was all he said.

La Salle worked most of the night, helping to identify and catalogue the bodies brought ashore. They were taken to the Cunard warehouse and laid on the floor, covered with sheets. Others were placed in a temporary mortuary in the town hall then, when that was full, the barracks of the Royal Garrison Artillery. One of the Cunard clerks darted between the rows of corpses, some of them badly disfigured by injuries and one, a woman, burned black. The clerk carried sheaves of paper on a board and whenever a body was identified he ruled a line through a name with a pencil. At every turn he asked if anyone had seen Mr Alfred Vanderbilt. 'It is imperative,' he kept saying, 'that I find Mr Vanderbilt.' So far as La Salle could see he never did.

He returned to Kimberley House to sleep for a couple of hours then went back to the dockyard. The army and civilian authorities had taken over and soldiers were digging mass graves at Clonmel Cemetery. Men of the 4th Irish Regiment had been briefed to carry out the first burials later that day. At the dockyard office, La Salle found a message ordering him to report to Admiralty House that afternoon. There was nothing for him to do so he walked, without real purpose, into the town. He didn't want breakfast, but he thought of taking some coffee at the Imperial Hotel. He bought a bundle of newspapers, opened them to the news pages, glanced at the headlines and tucked them under his arm. The streets were unusually crowded, full of *Lusitania's* survivors, people with a dazed, bemused look. Police officers were directing them to the aid centre. Those who had already collected a few bits of clothing and some food wandered aimlessly in small knots, looking about them, holding their children very close.

At the Imperial, La Salle brushed past a family group on the pavement as he made his way inside. The mother was bending down, trying to arrange a hand-me-down coat around the shoulders of a redheaded little girl. As La Salle entered the hotel he became aware of the mother pointing to someone in the street and shouting.

'It's him! That's him!'

La Salle paused and turned in the doorway. The man he took to be the girl's father broke away from the group and seized a young man who was walking past. The man was barefoot. La Salle stepped outside. It was a curious scene. The father was half-hugging, half trying to drag the blond man back towards his family, but the other resisted. He shook off the older man and sprinted away. La Salle saw him turn a corner and disappear. It was the swimmer.

'No good, mother. He wouldn't take our thanks,' the father said, shaking his head.

'Do you know that man?' La Salle asked.

'No. But he saved our little girl. She was caught in the wires. He saved her.' He picked up the redheaded child.

'We wanted to thank him with all our heart.' He looked down the street, the way the swimmer had disappeared. 'Shy, I suppose,' the father said, pulling the girl in closer to his chest.

For reasons that were not entirely clear to him, La Salle found himself walking in the direction taken by the swimmer, turning the same corner. He came upon him in a small park opposite some shops. He was sitting on a bench, staring at the ground ahead. He did not appear to see La Salle.

'Hello.'

The American turned his head.

'I saw you last night. We picked you up. *HMS Heron.*'

'Howdy,' the swimmer said.

La Salle gestured toward the bench with his newspapers. The blond man moved, making space.

'How are you getting along? Have you registered at the Cunard office?'

'Nope.'

He was still staring at the pathway directly in front of him. La Salle felt a pang of awkwardness.

'Lieutenant La Salle,' he offered.

'Hi,' was the reply.

La Salle felt a stirring of exasperation.

'Look, old man. I'd like to help you,' he said. The other turned to face him, a faint smile on his lips. His hair was dry now, a wild mass of tow-coloured waves. He looked other-worldly, almost angelic.

'How?'

'Well, I think we should get you some shoes, for a start,' La Salle said lightly. 'You look as if you're about the same size as me. I've got a spare pair you can have. You could probably do with some breakfast, too. Have you eaten?'

The fair-haired man seemed to relax a little. 'No,' he said.

'What's your name?' La Salle asked.

'Merrick.' The young man paused, glanced away across the road to some shops, and then back again, looking La Salle squarely in the eye. 'Merrick Granger.'

La Salle established he was an engineer officer of the United States merchant marine, who had made the Atlantic crossing with the intention of volunteering for the Royal Navy. Everything he had, money, documents, clothes; all had gone down with *Lusitania*.

'So what you see is all there is,' Granger said.

A bit like being re-born, La Salle thought. He nodded at Granger's bare feet.

'My lodgings are about half a mile away. All right to walk?'

'Fine,' he said.

Granger became brighter, less suspicious. He told La Salle he was in his cabin when the torpedo struck and then, when it seemed sure the ship would sink, he jumped overboard. He said nothing about saving a child. They crossed the road, walked past the shops. One, La Salle noticed, was an ironmongery with a sign over it that read Granger's, like the name of his companion. It was a time of coincidences, he thought. The mystery of colliding circumstances.

At Kimberley House he gave Granger socks, shoes and a jacket. He offered a complete change of clean clothes but Granger declined, saying with a grin the garments he was wearing had never been so thoroughly washed.

'I imagine you're out of funds,' La Salle said. 'Take this for now.'

He held out a bundle of the new Treasury notes. Granger looked at the paper money.

'It's as good as gold, apparently,' La Salle laughed. 'Please take it. You can pay me back later. When you get fixed. If you like, we can talk about your joining up. If it's the navy you want I can probably help.'

Granger took the banknotes and stuffed them carefully into a pocket. It was too late for breakfast so they walked out to the Queen's Hotel and ordered coffee and sandwiches. La Salle decided against raising the subject of rescue, or the family outside the Imperial. It was clear Granger did not want to say much about himself and the most La Salle could get out of him about *Lusitania* was an idea for re-designing the way the lifeboats were launched. La Salle imagined his reticence was reserve, a quality he admired. Indeed, Granger was an intriguing character. He was courteous and softly-spoken, although he responded rather sharply when La Salle asked if he'd like something restorative with his coffee.

'I don't drink,' he said, a touch fiercely.

La Salle's jacket was a tight fit on the swimmer's broad-shouldered frame and his trousers had dried shapelessly, but his bearing transcended the strangeness of the clothes. La Salle found himself liking the American. They talked about ships, although Granger said little about his own experience in the merchant marine. At one point, as La Salle jokingly recounted an unfortunate episode in his own early career, he saw Granger looking at him intently, as if trying to divine something. His expression was faintly disturbing, almost a look of pain. Then he broke into a wide smile that seemed to light up their corner of the dreary hotel lounge. It occurred to La Salle that if Granger was a shipmate they would become friends. *And God knows*, he thought, *the navy needs engineers.*

When they parted it was time for La Salle to keep his appointment at Admiralty House. He shook Granger's hand and urged him to keep in touch, scribbling out his name and the postal address on a scrap of paper. Granger turned towards the harbour. La Salle imagined he was planning to join the survivors registering at the Cunard office, although, curiously perhaps, he'd said nothing about this.

The admiral was engaged when La Salle arrived. He was shown into a small sitting room where he unfolded his newspapers. The *Irish Independent* had responded swiftly to the *Lusitania* sinking and seemed to be especially well-informed. Its main news page carried a number of pieces including a dispatch from Queenstown filed by its reporter at 3 am. It said the ship sank in twenty-one minutes and spoke luridly of the "mangled and the dying" landed in the harbour. The paper put the number at 650, but La Salle thought the figure was probably higher than that. When he left the dockyard in the early hours, close to a thousand people had been brought ashore there and at other ports including Kinsale. Most of these had survived. The paper said 1,978 passengers and crew had been aboard *Lusitania*. La Salle made a swift calculation. From what he had seen that would suggest the number of those dead and still missing would be about 1,000. He leaned back in his chair. A thousand civilians. The rush of anger he had felt when *Heron* steamed into the sea of corpses returned briefly. He imagined a U-boat commander shadowing the great liner, taking her range and bearing before coolly giving the order to fire and watching the destruction from a safe distance. He tried to put himself inside that man's head, but could not. Was it possible, he thought, that they were different men? He dismissed the idea instantly. U-boat captains were naval officers, like him. No, if there was a difference it was in their orders. Someone in the German high command had decided their war plan should include the murder of civilians, women and children. Like the victims of Scarborough and the other coast towns shelled from the sea without warning. Or those killed in the Zeppelin raids. Someone, possibly even the Kaiser himself, had calculated that Britain would be more easily beaten if the weapons of war were turned on those who could not fight back, or even properly defend themselves. It was a departure, La Salle thought. A lever had been pulled, a button pushed. A terrible mechanism had been set working without anyone knowing how it could be stopped or where it would take humanity.

'You've seen the newspapers, then.'

Lieutenant Davis had entered without La Salle noticing. He stood up.

'Yes.'

'You went out, didn't you?'

'In *Heron*. We picked up quite a few. Survivors.' He paused. 'And others.'

'Well, you'd better come in and see the old man.'

Admiral Pettigrew seemed to have aged, La Salle thought. His cheeks were hollow and his eyes dark from lack of sleep. He looked up from the expanse of chart on his boarded-over billiard table.

'La Salle. Come over here. Sit down.'

They sat together on a large settee. The admiral swept a hand towards the charts.

'This changes everything,' he said. He fell silent, then in an outburst La Salle found shocking he smashed his fist into the arm of the sofa.

'They must be stopped! There isn't an officer in the Royal Navy who would turn his weapons on women and children. We must stop these murdering swines, La Salle. Kill them! Send them to the bottom where they belong.'

The admiral leaned back, he seemed to shrink inside his uniform. It had probably been the most difficult night of his life, La Salle thought.

'I'm giving all Special Service officers new orders. From today,' Sir Gerald said at last. 'Patrols will be doubled. When the ships are ready. And we will be seeking out the U-boats like never before. We will go after them. They will learn to fear my Q-Ships. Even if we don't sink every one of them, they will be harried, chased and the fear of God put into them!' He rose and crossed to the chart table.

'Look at this, La Salle.' He ranged an arm over the chart, covering the area of his command, taking in all the western approaches to Britain as far as Ushant and the French coast. 'This is the size of our task. We have to make this a zone of fear for the U-boats. The Q-Ships are our secret weapon.'

'I understand, Sir,' was all La Salle could think of saying.

'I want you to take your outstanding leave now. I know you probably want to get stuck in, especially at this time, but I need to get your leave out of the way because my plans for you will make it difficult to keep to the duty you've been used to. Your action in *Farnham* – and Campbell's, God rest his soul – has helped me get what I want. Ships, La Salle. And guns to fit them with. You can take four days. Where will you go?'

'To my guardian's house, Sir. It's near Dartmouth.'

'Good. Be sure the messengers have the address and so on.'

'Yes, Sir.'

Sir Gerald made a visible effort to straighten his shoulders. He offered La Salle his hand, something he'd never done before.

'We shall win, you know,' he said.

'Yes, Sir. I believe we shall.'

Davis told him Miss Vaizey was at the harbour with her volunteers, although La Salle had not inquired. He walked quickly down the hill towards Kimberley House. If he hurried, he'd be in time to catch the ferry. With luck he would be at Combe Hall the following afternoon.

CHAPTER FOUR

A light rain fell as the train drew into Kingswear. La Salle pulled his topcoat over his shoulders and walked out of the station on to the steep hill leading from the village. He crossed to the edge of the road and looked down towards the river. Mist filled the valley and although he could make out a number of vessels in the anchorage, the visibility was too poor to properly identify them. Even the vast bulk of the new naval college dominating the slopes over on the Dartmouth side was barely visible. He shivered slightly, put on the coat, pulled the belt tightly and shifted his grip on the small bag he had brought. He walked back down the hill. When the rain started he had thought about calling in at The Ship and engaging a horse and trap, but now he was here the weather didn't seem much of a nuisance. He'd walk the two miles to Combe Hall.

The village was strangely hushed, almost deserted and there was a sense of the vaporous air muffling all sound, because there was none. He passed a middle-aged woman and touched his cap to her and a boy careered down the hill on a bicycle, but there was no one else. No men, certainly. A detachment of marines was billeted nearby but they were rarely seen.

La Salle turned left at the crossroads and climbed the narrow lane heading east, towards the high ground behind the cliffs. He thought of the last time he had been at Combe Hall. It was early spring, usually a time of frantic work to sow the wheat. But there were not enough men to plough and seed all the fields on Home Farm and Lord Burnage decided to let some of the land lie fallow.

'Just for this year,' he said. 'Things will be back to normal next spring. When the boys are back home.'

La Salle hoped with all his heart they would be, but the progress of the war suggested otherwise. The German advance had been stopped, but the news from the Western Front held out little hope of an end to matters there. Defeat or stalemate in Turkey seemed possible and in his own part of the war the U-boats, at least for now, held the upper hand.

At the top of the hill some cows swayed towards him, driven by an ancient character accompanied by a lively dog. He stepped aside to let the animals pass and nodded as the old herdsman creaked by, tapping a stick on the backs of the hindmost beasts. He had a clay pipe in his mouth and his bow legs moved stiffly. He raised the stick in greeting and moved slowly on down the hill. La Salle did not recognise him, but the cows were from a neighbouring farm. The old man, like many others, had probably been dragged away from his fireside to replace a farmhand pursuing a quite different kind of husbandry at the front, he guessed. He wondered how things would be at Combe Hall.

The house had been built by Lord Burnage just before the turn of the century on the site of an old manor and was more modern than those on most of the estates in the county. It had electricity and central heating; plumbing. Even so, in peacetime the staff for the house, stables and garden alone had numbered nearly twenty. La Salle ran over names in his head, people he had known since he first arrived at Combe Hall nearly fifteen years earlier. Some, including most of the stable hands, had already gone to France. Mr Johnson, the gamekeeper, had volunteered despite being close to forty. His son Matthew went as soon as the recruiting stations opened. La Salle murmured a prayer for them all.

He turned from the road on to the lane that led to the

Hall. The entrance was flanked by two stone pillars, remains of an ancient gateway. He remembered his first glimpse of those mossy stones and a ten-year-old boy's terror as he entered the portal of a future life. He had been collected at the station by a small trap and driven in silence towards his new home.

Lord Burnage had visited them in Paris just before his mother died. At first he did not like the tall, severe-looking Englishman. He came to their apartment in the Rue de Seine a number of times during that desperate week and sat with his mother alone. La Salle thought of him as an intruder then, a day or two before the end, his mother had called him in. Lord Burnage was to be his guardian, she said. He was to go to live at his house in England. La Salle remembered crying that night, sobbing and praying on his knees for God to make it all different. But God, apparently, had better things to do. His mother died and Maitre Villepin, the notaire, made the arrangements. Then he was alone in the small carriage on the avenue leading to the Hall, his heart thumping, and his stomach knotted with the fear of being sick or worse.

Mrs Elmore, the housekeeper, took charge of him and La Salle experienced a rush of warmth at the thought of her. Her husband was alive then and he came to think of their quarters as a place of refuge, somewhere he could go with his book and be safe from the torments of Margaret, Lord Burnage's daughter. Margaret was just back from school in those days and already assuming the role of mistress. Lady Burnage, whom La Salle never met, was still in the sanatorium where she had been for many years and where, in due course, she would die. Godfrey, Lord Burnage's son, was at school and when La Salle eventually met him he was terrified he would be another version of his cruel sister, but stronger. Yet Godfrey treated him with cheerful disinterest. Later, when La Salle came home from *HMS Conway*, the school ship, he and Godfrey fell into a casual friendship and when La Salle was made second to Captain Lamont, the old sailing master on *Adela*, Lord Burnage's yacht, Godfrey would come aboard with his friends and treat him like a chum. To La Salle's immense relief, Margaret hated the sea and rarely went near her father's ship. When La Salle succeeded Captain Lamont and they took *Adela* to the Mediterranean in 1913, Margaret stayed in England.

Godfrey was running the family firm by then and spent most of his time in London where the Burnage bleach manufacturing company had a large factory on the Thames near Limehouse. It was never suggested that La Salle should become involved in the business and when he became older he was mightily grateful for it. Since his first days as a schoolboy cadet in *Conway*, all he had ever wanted was to go to sea and when he qualified as a merchant officer he worked for his master's ticket on a number of ships. Then Lord Burnage asked him to second Captain Lamont with a view to taking over *Adela*. It was all he could have wished for. La Salle thought fondly of Lamont. The old boy had sailed before the mast as a youngster and gained rank aboard vessels bringing wool and wheat from Australia. Lamont remembered the clippers and although he had never been in the tea trade he talked thrillingly of ships that could make seventeen knots in a fresh breeze and never falter at six points off the wind. La Salle resolved to call on Captain Lamont at his house in Brixham, if time allowed.

The drive turned around a stand of venerable chestnuts and the park in front of the house opened up before him. Beyond the green stood Combe Hall. It was a handsome thing, built of bright red brick with tall chimneys and slate roofs. Despite its name it was some way from the combe that led down between the cliffs to the sea. A motor stood outside the front door. La Salle did not recognise it and wondered who might be calling. He walked quickly across the grass, around the car and up the steps. The door was always unlocked at that time of day but, as was his custom, he rang the bell. The door was answered by a young woman wearing a maid's clothes. She seemed to be new.

'I'll call madam,' she said.

'Don't worry,' La Salle said, grinning pleasantly. 'I live here.'

He gently pushed open the door and brushed past her. Margaret Burnage appeared in the library doorway.

'Oh, it's you.'

She walked into the hall and gestured at the maid. 'It's all right, Lucy.' Margaret waited for the girl to withdraw, then turned to La Salle with a thin smile. 'So, Pierre. Have you won the war yet?'

La Salle flinched. Margaret had called him "Pierre" since the day he arrived from Paris, with his French clothes and imperfect English.

'Hello Margaret.'

She was wearing riding breeches and boots, although she hated horses almost as much as she hated ships. Her hair was coiled in a bun at the back, a style he had not noticed before. *God*, he thought. *She looks thin.*

She pretended to scan his chest.

'Any medals?' her eyes widened quizzically, simultaneously conveying a sense of hopefulness. 'Wounds?'

La Salle couldn't help himself.

'Well, we did sink a submarine.'

'Was it a German one?'

'It was attacking our ships, so I hope it was.'

'So do I!' she said, as if she lived in dread of him sinking one of the Royal Navy's own submarines. Then: 'How long are you here for?'

'Just a few days. Is your father here?'

'Coming tomorrow.'

'I saw a motor outside. Is someone visiting?'

She affected a look of weary disdain, suggesting graceful indulgence of an unloved child.

'Pierre, please. Anyone likely to be visiting by motor car has long since departed for the front. There is a war in France, you know.' She tossed her head slightly. 'The car is mine.'

'Congratulations,' he said, in a rather flat tone. 'I'll just pop in to see Mrs Elmore before I go upstairs.'

'She's in the kitchen,' Margaret said, over her shoulder as she walked back to the library.

He crossed the hall to the passage leading to the kitchen at the back of the house. Mrs Elmore and Dora, the cook, were leaning over a table on which they had spread that day's newspaper. La Salle saw they were going through the casualty lists.

'Hello,' he said.

Peggy Elmore looked up. Her face took on an expression of intense concentration, as if she wanted to be sure the scene she beheld really was as it seemed. She straightened, made a sign with her hand, beckoning him towards her. She started crying softly. La Salle crossed the floor and put his arms around her.

'Hello,' he said again. She seemed frail, smaller than he remembered. He held her shoulders and affected a hurt smile. 'Am I such a disappointing sight?'

She pulled a tiny handkerchief from her sleeve.

'Never a more welcome sight,' she whispered.

'Is that because you know I've got a present for you?'

She shook her head, crying again. He led her to a chair, pulled one round for himself and sat at the table looking at her.

'Is the news bad?'

She nodded, the handkerchief firmly pressed to her lips.

'Eric Johnson. And Matthew. Both of them. Father and son.' She lifted her head. 'Killed at Ypres.'

She pronounced it 'Wypers'. La Salle felt something creep upwards inside him, lodge in his throat. Mr Johnson and Matthew. The gamekeeper and his only son. Both dead.

'When?'

'She got the telegram yesterday.'

La Salle imagined Mrs Johnson, opening the door of her cottage to a boy on a bicycle, a lad too young to go and kill but old enough to carry life-destroying news.

'How is she?'

'Very quiet.' Mrs Elmore raised her head and looked at him. 'Thank God you're all right, Julian.'

He smiled. 'Oh, I'm a lucky dog. Never worry.'

He patted her hand. Most of the space in his small bag was taken up with an exceptionally fine piece of Irish lace he had bought in Queenstown. He had been looking forward to giving it to her, but now was not the time.

'I'm going up,' he said at last. 'We'll talk properly later.'

'You'll pay a call, won't you? Mrs Johnson?'

'Of course. When you tell me the time is right.'

'Have you eaten?'

'Yes,' he lied.

He stood, squeezed her shoulder and walked out into the passageway. Anger rose like hot blood from a wound. He strode across the hall, the library door was closed. He threw it open. Margaret was lounging on a couch, reading an illustrated paper.

'Why didn't you tell me about the Johnsons?'

She looked up. 'Do come in, Pierre.'

'I said, why didn't you tell me?'

She sat up and fixed him with a fierce look.

'Why didn't I tell you about Massey and Phillips and all the others! We've lost eight since you've been away.' She softened slightly, but her eyes still glittered in a way that always made him feel afraid. 'I didn't want to greet you with dreadful news. Was that so wrong?'

La Salle felt for the back of a chair. He sank into it.

Massey was a gardener. Phillips he didn't know. *Who were the others?*

'All killed?'

'I'm afraid so.' Margaret laid aside her paper. 'This Ypres business is shocking, Julian. You must have heard.'

'Yes. Yes, of course. It's just … People one knows.'

'You must have lost friends. By now.'

La Salle thought of Campbell. But no, he had not, so far, lost anyone close to him. How could he? Apart from a few chums in the service he had no intimate friends. Peggy Elmore and Lord Burnage were the people he cared most about in the world. And, in a strange way, Margaret. They, at least, were safe from the carnage in France. And so was he. The old guilt returned. He had chosen the navy because he was a mariner. There was no sense then that he would come to see his service as somehow second-rate in terms of sacrifice. What gave him the right to be sitting in that large pleasant room instead of being rat fodder in the Flanders mud? He was struck by a gloomy thought: would men who had served but had never seen the trenches be condemned to the lower slopes of the nation's esteem? That would be unjust, surely. Or would it?

Margaret stood, then moved towards him. He glanced up and was instantly struck by something in her face. Her mouth was more full, her lips seemed to have relaxed their scathing twist. There was a warmth in her look he had rarely, if ever, seen. He sat up in his chair. She gestured towards him, held out a hand.

'You don't know what it's like,' she said urgently. 'Every day. Waiting to hear. If someone … ' She broke off, seemed to stiffen. 'Damned telegrams!'

La Salle stared at her. This was a Margaret he did not know. Did she have a lover? In the trenches? *Impossible,* he thought. Without his having some inkling of it. She was going back towards the sofa and he caught a glimpse of her face as she turned. She looked ashamed.

'Well, at least you're all right,' she said at last in her usual voice, picking up her paper.

'I'm going to my room.'

He turned without another word and went quickly to the staircase, climbing two steps at a time. As he ran up the wide stairs he found it impossible to banish a notion that she had been talking about him. Dreading bad news about him. There had been times, over the years, when he felt they were drawing close. He remembered moments, some as vivid as if they had just happened, when an inflection of her voice, a movement of her hand, a tilting of her shoulder launched a surge of love in him. How he longed for her love! In lonely childhood hours he had ached for a sisterly presence. Yet he could not even call her "sister". In his last conversation with his mother that was made clear. Just as he was told never to think of Lord Burnage as his father. The Englishman was his guardian, to be addressed as "sir". One day, she had said, you will understand.

His room was on the second landing, overlooking the gardens at the back. He laid down his bag and crossed to the window. The rain had stopped and the mist was lifting. The sea lay like a blade of dull metal beyond the cliffs. A fishing craft, a Brixham trawler, was making slow progress to the east. Not much wind. Heading home on the flood, he guessed. The room felt damp. His bed had been stripped and he should have liked a fire, but he hesitated to call anyone. He fell into an armchair near the window, too low down to look out on anything but the sky. He pulled his coat more tightly around his shoulders and watched as the pale and deep greys shifted across the heavens like ashes in a breeze.

He took some dinner alone in his room then sat at the desk with his notebook. He had wanted to compose something about the war as seductress, a siren who drew men in with a promise of experience to transcend anything they had known. He thought he could capture that intoxicating sensation he had felt when he had first lusted to join the war, the joyful giddiness that seemed to bubble up from deep inside as mysterious and uncontrollable as love. Was that it? Were men created with a desire for war, the way they desired a woman? Certainly, the impulses did not seem to be governed by logic. There may have been some inner debate in which the arguments for embracing an ultimate opportunity for honour and the need to do one's duty were weighed against some dimly imagined horror, but mostly it was a visceral thing. He and many others, he suspected, hungered for it. Now he had tasted war.

Since childhood he had been tormented by a recurring dream in which he committed some unspeakable act, murder possibly. The guilt was torture but worse was the ever-present sense that what had happened was irreversible. He was a destroyed soul until the moment he woke, gratefully seizing the thought that it had just been in his mind. Now it was no longer a dream. He had been party to murder. And he was pledged to do more of it.

He glanced at the page. His pencil had been idly sketching out a shape. It looked like the letter "J". *Johnson.* Had Mr Johnson and his son been lured into a deadly trap by the foul seductress? He began scribbling some lines. In due course he stopped, circumvented the changes and deletions and read:

Now is the spring tide rising, past the shadow line
Scorning counter current, reckless in its flood
War draws high water mark and calls the time
For ebb to be returning, brimming dark with blood

He scribbled *"torrent of men"*, then crossed it out, closed the notebook and pushed his chair away from the desk. It was late. Tomorrow he would call on Mrs Johnson.

Shooting parties were seldom given at Combe Hall. Lord Burnage preferred to go out with his gun and springer spaniel, walking up whatever game he found and enjoying his land alone. Occasionally he would be accompanied by Eric Johnson. The gamekeeper managed a small shoot of partridge and pheasant and he also looked after the estate's herd of deer which, unlike their wild fellows elsewhere in the county, never suffered the attentions of dogs and riders.

The Johnsons lived in a cottage on the path that led to the combe. Mrs Johnson kept a kitchen garden and as La Salle approached, he breathed in the heady scent of sage, moistened by the late rain and now warmed by the sun. He pushed open the small gate, walked to the front door and knocked gently. There was a ferocious barking within, followed by scolding. The door opened and a woman he did not recognise stood at the threshold, holding back Johnson's Labrador.

'It's all right,' La Salle said, extending a hand towards the dog's muzzle. 'He knows me.'

The woman was unwilling to release the dog, although it now appeared to be delighted.

'Is Mrs Johnson here? I live at the Hall.'

She moved aside to let him enter.

'I'm Jenny's sister,' she whispered. She pointed to a door. 'In there.'

La Salle entered the small parlour. Mrs Johnson occupied a chair at the fireplace and she started to get up as he walked in. He quickly gestured her to sit.

'I am most desperately sorry, Mrs Johnson,' he said.

She nodded.

La Salle paused, wishing he'd rehearsed something. What could he say? That her husband and son were fine men? That they'd died in a noble cause? Their sacrifice would never be forgotten? He was not entirely sure he believed that. And what right did anyone have to offer an opinion on something that, effectively, had just robbed this woman of her own life?

'Is there anything you need?'

He regretted the words the moment they left his lips. Of course there was something she needed. She needed the people she loved with all her heart, her man and their child. She shook her head. She seemed to be rocking in her chair, clasping a small bundle in her lap. It looked like a collection of envelopes.

He thought he'd wait for a moment, to see if she wished to say anything. He glanced around the room. On the mantelpiece stood two framed photographs of men in uniform, posing stiffly in the manner dictated by the photographers who specialised in the two shilling military portraits. Even a stranger would recognise them as father and son.

'Please accept my sincere sympathy, Mrs Johnson,' La Salle said at last.

She nodded again. He smiled and turned to leave. The Labrador had watched the scene and now walked with him to the front door. La Salle patted the dog's head absently and the animal reached up, pushing affectionately against the pressure of his hand, then it turned its head and La Salle was struck by what seemed to be an expression of bewilderment in the animal's eyes.

'She hasn't said a word. Struck dumb,' the sister whispered, opening the door. 'I'm taking her home with me.'

'If there is anything, anything at all ...' La Salle heard his own voice fade away. He shook the woman's hand and walked down the path. The Labrador stopped at the gate and watched him go, head cocked to one side; wrapt in its own puzzlement.

The motor left at three to collect Lord Burnage from the afternoon train at Totnes. Margaret had gone off somewhere driving herself in her new car and La Salle waited alone in the library. When he heard the motor draw up he walked into the hall. Lord Burnage entered, beamed at him, strode across the floor and seized him by the shoulders.

'So you bagged a U-boat!'

La Salle experienced a jolt of irritation. Margaret had cheated him of his surprise by telephoning to her father with his news.

'Yes, sir.'

'Come on. Let's hear all about it.'

He led La Salle to the library, calling for some tea. They sat opposite each other at the hearth as La Salle told the story of *Farnham's* action. Burnage held a finger to his temple as he listened, as if better to concentrate. He was wearing a formal suit, his usual London dress, and La Salle couldn't help remarking to himself how wonderfully made it was. It fitted perfectly Burnage's tall, slim figure and enhanced a rather austere elegance which, in his seventh decade, he had retained. When the tea arrived, Burnage insisted on pouring it himself and settled back on the settee with his cup, impatient for more of La Salle's tale.

'You liked Campbell, didn't you?' he asked when it ended.

'Very much, sir. He was a first class commander.'

La Salle revealed then how Campbell had pushed him through the trap-hatch when the U-boat began shelling *Farnham's* bridge.

'I thank God for it, Julian,' Burnage said quietly.

They talked about *Lusitania* and La Salle told him the strange story of Merrick Granger.

'I should like him in my crew if ever I get a ship,' he said and they speculated on his chances of getting his own command. Burnage told him about the men from the estate who had been killed and the way attitudes to the war were changing.

'Oh, it was all very jolly when it started,' he said. 'Home by Christmas. Remember that? Now people are seeing what war in this modern age really means. The weapons we have now have never been used like this and it has come as a shock.' Burnage lowered his voice. 'We have been asked to take on war work. At the factory.' He paused. 'It's secret work, but you can probably guess what it is.'

La Salle could guess. The Burnage Bleach Manufacturing was ideally equipped to produce the new gas weapons being prepared for the Western Front.

'I can't say I like it, Julian. But God knows, the Hun used it first!'

Burnage was leaning forward, his eyes strangely aglow. It was a look La Salle had seen many times, in Margaret.

'You saw what they did at Ypres?' Burnage went on earnestly.

La Salle had been at sea when the Germans launched their chlorine attack at Ypres, but the newspapers continued to run reports about the effects of the gas on French, British and Canadian troops holding the salient.

'I just hope that's not how they murdered Eric Johnson and the others,' Burnage said. 'Burning up their lungs.'

It was clear he did not care to be involved in lung-burning, even if the intended targets were German. He did not say so, but La Salle knew he had taken on this government work because it was something he could not decline. Burnage had been a remote figure during his childhood; always benign but distant. After school, however, La Salle was gratified – no, he was thrilled – to remark a developing interest. Burnage encouraged him in his early career; he clearly cherished a hope that the young merchant officer, part of his family as it were, would take over as sailing master on his ship. That was where La Salle came to know the man he was forbidden to call "father". Burnage was happy aboard his yacht. He revelled in his own, not inconsiderable, seamanship and pilotage skills, teaching La Salle many things he had never learned in *Conway*. The long hours and days of sea passages aboard a small vessel encouraged intimacy and Burnage revealed himself a man of warmth and scrupulous rectitude. A phrase he used often *"do the right thing"* found its way into La Salle's own vocabulary until he became self-conscious about it and deliberately excised it. Nevertheless, he admired Burnage for his honourable code and he recognised his unwanted role in helping in the manufacture of loathsome poisons offended it. *How the war chips away at us,* La Salle thought, *and our sense of self.*

Burnage poured more tea and, as always, conversation turned to *Adela*, being re-fitted for the Lowestoft Patrol. Burnage said the admiralty had invited him to see the work and he suggested they take the motor over to Plymouth in the morning. La Salle agreed readily. In peacetime *Adela* was at the centre of his life. Yet so much had happened and now his old command felt almost like just another ship. No. He still nursed a special affection for her and it would be good to go aboard her again. *After all*, he thought in a sudden stab of bleakness, *we'd be lucky to both survive the war.*

Their conversation was interrupted by Margaret's arrival. La Salle watched with a mixture of emotions as she threw herself on her father's neck, although it was barely a week since she had last seen him. He suspected some of that may have been for his benefit.

They dined together pleasantly, agreeing at the start of the meal to say nothing about the war. Inevitably, it intruded. Margaret said Mrs Johnson wanted to leave the cottage as soon as possible, to go to Kingsbridge to her sister's house.

'There's an opportunity for you there, Julian,' she said (she never called him Pierre in her father's presence). 'You could have that little house all to yourself.'

He mumbled something about being very happy where he was, but she persisted. She had plans for the second floor of the Hall, she said. And anyway, it was time he had a place of his own. The next gamekeeper (if they ever found one) could easily be accommodated somewhere on the estate.

'Julian can have the cottage, can't he, father?' she pleaded, as if it were some great gift.

'If he wants it,' Burnage replied, a touch perplexed by the discussion and clearly anxious not to pursue it.

La Salle bade them goodnight and went up to his room. What was wrong with Margaret? She seemed to be more waspish, more brittle than ever. There had been moments over the years when, detecting a deep sadness about her, he had felt a warm brotherliness. But in time he learned not to invite a sharp rebuff and they remained at a distance. Yet he couldn't despise her. The war had probably destroyed any hope she might have had of escaping spinsterhood. He didn't want her to be unhappy. But every time he sensed she wanted to embrace him, in the emotional sense as a sibling, her iciness returned. Now she wanted to get him out of the house. A feeling not unlike the one he'd known on his first day at Combe Hall overtook him, a sickening of the spirit, a lowness of heart. It would be impossible to stay now, he thought, with Margaret clearly dedicated to removing him from the family home. Well, he would move. He'd take a cottage in Kingswear or perhaps Dittisham. *What does something like that cost,* he wondered? Money would not be a problem. Burnage had always been generous with his mother and she had invested wisely. He had inherited the apartment in the Rue de Seine which Maitre Villepin, the notaire, managed for him. There was also a considerable capital sum, he seemed to remember. And his earnings were hardly touched, except to buy clothes and books. Yes, he'd take a lease on his own place and engage a housekeeper to look after it when he was away. Mrs Elmore could come round for tea. Miss Vaizey too, perhaps. One day.

They found *Adela* among a collection of disparate vessels in a remote corner of the dockyard. Lord Burnage was waved through the sentry posts without fuss and the admiralty superintendent escorted him personally to his ship. La Salle glanced over her with a twinge of sadness. Her yards had been removed and most of the running rigging had gone.

'We'll hang on to the fore and aft sails,' the superintendent said, 'but it's the engine that will do the work.'

La Salle followed Burnage aboard and they went towards the bow, where men were installing a gun mount forward of the foremast. He winced when he saw the amount of bracing they were putting under the deck, tied in to the frames on each side of *Adela's* wooden hull. The steel beams were fastened with heavy bolts and La Salle privately mourned the number of holes they were making in the ship's innards. *They must be fitting a twelve pounder*, he thought. Patrol yachts were not heavily armed but they had to be able to give a good account of themselves, if necessary. A new Marconi set had already been fitted and Burnage was fascinated to hear the superintendent describe its capabilities. Further aft, the supports for a Maxim gun had intruded into Burnage's stateroom and La Salle doubted the walnut panelling would ever recover. But it was clear the navy shipwrights and armourers were treating the ship with respect. Burnage noted the fact in his discussion with the superintendent, who seemed rather gratified. It occurred to La Salle that the superintendent had probably suffered harsh treatment at the hands of wealthy owners who had seen their beloved yachts hacked about, probably irreversibly. Yet Burnage treated him gently. La Salle knew he wanted the man to be comfortable in his dealings with him. Making her fit for service was the navy man's duty. Giving her up without complaint was what Burnage held to be his own duty.

La Salle exchanged a few words with the superintendent about *Adela's* handling and especially her ability to motor into a head sea. They were hoping to have her on station by the end of June, the superintendent told him.

Burnage suggested they take luncheon at a hotel near the Hoe. It was an old-fashioned sort of place La Salle had never visited, but the rather shabby dining room had a splendid view of Plymouth Sound. Apart from an elderly woman snuffling over some soup alone at a corner table, they had the room to themselves. A pretty girl in a jaunty maid's cap took their order and as she withdrew La Salle couldn't help noticing Burnage's gaze follow her to the door. He seemed more relaxed than he had been the night before and he chatted enthusiastically about *Adela's* conversion to a ship of war.

'Shouldn't you like to have command of her yourself?' he asked.

La Salle thought about the dreary duty of the North Sea patrol. Day after day, watching and waiting for enemy ships that seemed determined to remain safely in harbour. At least the Special Service offered the chance of action.

'I'm happy where I am, sir,' he said.

'Quite right,' Burnage replied. 'You have already distinguished yourself, in my view.' He sniffed. 'Shouldn't be surprised if you get something, you know.' He raised his eyebrows with this, as if waiting for La Salle to assure him there would be a decoration for the *Farnham* action.

'I have suggested something for Campbell.'

'But you sank the U-boat! Surely that entitles you to some recognition?'

'Perhaps.' La Salle felt uncomfortable. Burnage was obviously very keen for him to be declared a hero. 'We shall see.'

The older man grunted. 'At least you're not in the trenches.'

La Salle smiled. Would he come to regret that, one day, he wondered?

Burnage talked about how well Godfrey was doing with the company. His work would exempt him from service, he almost whispered, especially since most of the Burnage Manufacturing production was now to be for the war effort.

They ate some good skate, with new potatoes La Salle found surprisingly well done. Probably steamed. Perhaps Lord Burnage had been there before, he thought. Burnage excused himself, left the room and La Salle watched as a destroyer sailed swiftly past the breakwater, out to sea, towards the Eddystone, perhaps. Had there been a report of a U-boat? He thought of the excitement aboard the ship, the hunger in every man aboard to engage the enemy.

'Has your father gone?'

The waitress stood there, her face framing the question rather charmingly.

La Salle felt colour rise in his cheeks. 'That gentleman is Lord Burnage,' he said gently.

The girl widened her eyes. 'I'm sorry … I thought …'

Of course she did. He was in every way a younger version of Burnage; the high forehead, longish nose, prominent jaw. La Salle stood, fumbled in his pocket, found a large amount of silver and put it on the table.

'Splendid lunch. Thank you,' he said and gave her arm a friendly pat. Just then Burnage entered. His eyes went from them to the conspicuous mound of coins.

'I'll be in the car,' he said roguishly, giving La Salle a look that needed only a wink to confirm its meaning.

They sat together in the back as the motor hummed along the Devonshire lanes and La Salle thought of how much he loved this part of England. The gentle undulations, richness of colour and sense of burgeoning new life on such a day in early summer enchanted the spirit. *Yes, it is worth fighting for*, he thought.

'Ever hear from that girl? What's her name – Georgiana? Does she write?' Burnage asked suddenly.

La Salle thought of Georgiana Bathwell, daughter of Sir Robert and Lady Bathwell, over at Torbay. The memory was unexpectedly painful, even now. He thought he might have been in love, but after some insistent probing by Lady Bathwell about his family and antecedents, invitations to their house ceased. Georgiana had written a rather formal note wishing him well when he was posted to Queenstown, but that was all.

'No,' he said. 'Not any more.' Then, brightly: 'I fear Lady Bathwell thought I was a shower!'

Burnage chuckled, suppressing a flicker of sadness. He should have guessed Lady Bathwell's veto would fall upon any suitor not equipped with transparent, not to say exalted, lineage.

'Pity about that chap Brooke,' he said, seeking a change of topic.

'What?'

'Brooke. You know, the poetry chap. Copped it in Turkey. Didn't you know?'

'No.'

'There was something in *The Times*. About two weeks ago.'

'I was on patrol then.'

'Yes. Of course. Not sure what happened. Buried him out there, apparently.'

La Salle sank deeper into his seat. So Rupert Brooke was dead. How strange that he should hear the news just as he was quietly rejoicing in the England Brooke loved and evoked so well. He thought of his own efforts at poetry, his groping for the words that could capture the emotions and anxieties stirred by the war. His failure. The sonnet he had sent to the *Westminster Gazette* in the hope of being published was returned with a reply he found grimly amusing:

"The editor regrets to inform you that our poetry section is currently oversubscribed and we cannot entertain further contributions. We will, however, continue to consider work submitted posthumously."

Like him, Brooke had been a naval reserve volunteer. His most successful work was not a sea poem, however and La Salle thought there should be more space in the vast canon of war poetry for a sailor's scribbling. He had read an admirable piece written by a chap on a minesweeper, about being a "fisherman of death" but otherwise it seemed the gore of the trenches nourished a harvest that was hard for the sailor to match, in his less fertilised element. He resolved to return to his theme of war as wicked seductress. If nothing else, there was something inside himself he would like to try to deal with.

A telegram awaited him at Combe Hall ordering his immediate return to Queenstown. Margaret had signed for it and seemed to guess its contents.

'I'll drive you to the station,' she said.

Cars did not interest La Salle much, but he was intrigued to see Margaret's car did not need to be cranked. It was a Model 30 Cadillac, imported from the United States, and it had its own electric starting mechanism. She noted his mild surprise with withering disdain.

'It's an age of engineering progress,' she said blithely. 'Hasn't the navy been making technological advances?'

Oh yes, La Salle thought. *Mostly in the field of mass murder.*

She drove fast, putting the car into curves recklessly. The motor swayed violently on one bend and he gripped the top of the door. She noted this with evident satisfaction.

'Not afraid, are you?' she cried hopefully.

'Frankly, yes,' he shouted back over the noise of the

wind rushing past. She giggled, patted his knee with her gloved hand and slowed a little.

There was a crowd outside the station, small groups engaged in painful farewells. Two men in uniform were trying to console a middle-aged woman who wept openly, her matronly shoulders rising and falling with each sob. Margaret stopped the car a little beyond the station, up the hill.

'Well,' she said brightly. 'You'd better get back to your war.'

La Salle climbed down and pulled his bag from the back seat.

'Oh,' he said. 'I almost forgot.'

He put the bag on the running board, opened it and took out a package, gift wrapped with a ribbon. Margaret looked at it, then him as he held it out to her.

'It's some lace,' he said. 'For Mrs Elmore.'

A shadow of hurt crossed her face. La Salle groaned inwardly. She thought it was for her.

'I'll see she gets it,' she said crisply, dropping the package on to the passenger seat. Then: 'Goodbye, Pierre.'

He said goodbye but she could not have heard it over the racing engine of her car as she sped away. He turned towards the station, a nagging feeling in his guts. He had wounded her. Through crass stupidity. He pushed gently through the throng in the street, a sickness in his heart. Why was it impossible for them to be at peace with each other?

He climbed on to the train as it hiccoughed smoke and steam, impatient to be off. There was an empty compartment at the end of the carriage and he threw his bag on to the rack, then settled on the bench near the window. The platform was crowded. He watched as tight little knots of people lingered over their goodbyes, the women dabbing handkerchiefs like signal flags. A young man in new khaki and shiny brown leather seemed keen to extricate himself, glancing about him as the woman La Salle took to be his mother pleaded, seeking some kind of reassurance. *You will be careful*, La Salle imagined her saying. The boy had the ruddy cheeks of a Devon lad and his cap was a touch too big, flattening the top of his ears. La Salle turned away. His head was suddenly filled with a scene in which the woman on the platform sat in a small parlour, rocking to and fro in her chair, twisting a wad of envelopes in her lap. He shook his head, tried to clear his thoughts. He remembered the look in Margaret's eyes when he asked her to give the package to Mrs Elmore. Damn! Damn! He brought the heel of his hand down hard on his knee. God seemed to have decided he was to be denied a loving goodbye like just about everyone else heading for the war. He resisted a surge of self-pity, more or less successfully.

Margaret bewildered him. Like that time at the bathing pool. There was a tiny strip of sand at the bottom of the combe and Lord Burnage had a rectangle of stone built on it, about three feet tall and twenty feet long. At high water the walls filled up and when the tide ebbed they held a pool of clear seawater that soon warmed in the sun. It must have been his second summer at Combe Hall, he thought. Margaret was on holiday from school. They went to the pool most days and on that particular day it was unbearably hot. They had flung themselves into the water gratefully, swimming up and down a little, but mostly just floating or crouching so the water covered everything but their heads. His English was perfectly fluent by then, but they didn't talk much. Margaret had a habit of saying 'Don't be silly, Pierre!' to almost everything he said. So they just swam and splashed and then sat under the trees that reached nearly to the shoreline, eating the lunch Mrs Elmore had given them.

A sharp hiss of steam startled him. He sighed and pushed his head against the back of the seat.

Margaret was lying on the grass, on a towel. Still

wearing her bathing togs. She called to him and he remembered that her voice was gentle, but hoarse. He rolled to her towel and she looked at him strangely, took his hand and slid it up the leg of her bathing dress. He tried to draw away but she pulled at his hand, her head lolling back, eyes half-closed, the tip of her tongue between her lips. Suddenly she snatched his hand away and shouted something he didn't hear, or understand. Then she spat at him and called him a "filthy Frenchie", jumped to her feet and stalked towards the path that climbed out of the combe. Miserably, he picked up the towels and the basket and followed her, some way behind. Then, before they reached the top, she stopped, turned and waited for him. She had her hands on her hips.

'If you ever do that again,' she breathed hard, 'or mention it to anyone.' Her lips were pursed. Thin. 'I shall tell my father!'

He nodded dumbly, vaguely aware of having done something unforgiveable, but not entirely sure what. Later – years later – he took it for what it was; a childish game, one of those harmless episodes that are part of growing up. Yet whenever things were strained between him and the woman he dearly wanted as a sister, he thought of it and it troubled him.

'All right then?'

La Salle looked up. It was the boy from the platform, announcing his presence a little uncertainly.

'Oh. Hello.' He smiled absently and turned to the window. The train shuddered then began to move. Handkerchief semaphore flashed all the way along the platform. No mistaking that message. The boy put his pack on the rack and settled into the seat opposite. La Salle caught him staring. *Probably wondering why I'm not in uniform*, he thought. There was a sting of discomfort. He didn't want this young man, who was almost certainly on his way to the trenches, to think he was a shirker.

'I'm in the navy,' he said, embarrassed by his own frailty.

'Infantry,' the boy said, relaxing and taking a packet of Woodbines out of his tunic. Then, with a brightness in his eyes. 'Off to France.'

La Salle nodded. He glimpsed the river between the trees as the train gathered speed. The boy lit his cigarette. La Salle felt engulfed by a tide of sadness. Would that boy see again the loveliness of the River Dart in early summer? He closed his eyes, strangely overcome by weariness. Would he?

CHAPTER FIVE

La Salle walked out of Admiralty House with a sense of being not entirely attached to his own physical self. He took the road down to the harbour with a feeling of being afloat and piloting his limbs rather than ambulating in the usual way. It would have been an upsetting experience indeed if he had not been so elated. The admiral had given him a ship. Better than that, it was a sailing ship. He was to have command of her right away, fit her out for Special Service and put together a crew. He was being made up to Lieutenant Commander (subject to confirmation) and Sir Gerald said, almost as an after-thought, he was to be recommended for a Conspicuous Service Cross. La Salle thanked him, although he had an inkling the CSC had just been renamed the Distinguished Service Cross. No matter. A mention would have been enough. He thought of Lord Burnage and Mrs Elmore. Margaret also crossed his mind fleetingly as did Miss Vaizey. He gripped even more tightly the manila envelope containing documents relating to the ship, running over the details in his head. Her name was *Freya*, a three-masted schooner bought out of the china clay trade. Her papers described her as 160 gross tons with an overall length of 120 feet and twenty-two feet in the beam. She had been launched in 1908 from William Thomas's yard at Amlwch on Anglesey, strongly built in steel, with steel deck beams and hatch coamings. Her merchant crew was delivering her to Haulbowline Island from Charlestown in Cornwall and she was due that day. La Salle felt his equilibrium return. He would go over to the island dockyard right away and wait for her. Where was Fisk? He'd leave a message at Kimberley House. Should he send a telegram to Combe Hall, with his news? No time now.

He turned left on to the harbour road and glanced at the sky to the westward. The weather was fine, settled with only a faint south westerly breeze. *Freya* would be motoring, he thought. The admiral made a special point of saying she had a good oil engine. La Salle thought of Merrick Granger. He would need an engineer. Was he still in Queenstown?

He called at the naval office and asked for Barnes, the Constructor. It seemed they were taking an age to find him, but eventually he came in.

'I've got a ship,' La Salle said, surprised by his own breathlessness.

'Well done!' Barnes beamed. 'What is she?'

La Salle gave him a brief description of *Freya* and asked if he could borrow a motor launch to get out to the island as soon as possible. Barnes called through to an adjoining office and received word that a boat would be available within the half-hour. La Salle nodded. He did not care to wait for the ferry service.

'What motor does she have?' Barnes asked.

La Salle opened his envelope and pulled out *Freya's* specifications.

'Bolinder.' He looked up. 'Swedish, isn't it?'

'First class,' Barnes said. 'Size?'

La Salle scanned the documents. 'Here it is. Eighty horsepower. Is that good?'

'For a ship like that, pretty good. I'd have to see it but it's probably a hot bulb semi-diesel.' Barnes stroked his chin. 'You'll need a good engineer, you know. No good signing on a chief who's been used to steam. These new engines can be difficult unless you have had a bit of experience with them.'

La Salle remembered that Merrick Granger had told him he specialised in oil engines.

'There was an American. We picked him up ... after the *Lusitania*. Granger. Decent chap.' La Salle brushed his hand over his head. 'Very wavy blond hair. He said he was keen to join up.'

'Well, I'll be blowed!' Barnes exclaimed. 'I know that man. Merrick. The missus took him in with two English stokers. From *Lusitania*. The English boys have gone now but he's still with us. He's working in my shop. Waiting for his papers to arrive from New York. Blessed good at his trade. He's a merchant officer, I think.'

'That's him,' La Salle said. 'Could I get him? If he wants it?'

Barnes sucked in his cheeks. 'I'd hate to lose him, lieutenant. I can hardly staff my workshops as it is. Men like him are hard to find.' He lowered his voice. 'The service is shipping men not up to the job, you know. Just to fill the berths.'

La Salle did know that. But the admiral had given him exceptional powers to equip and man his ship. The urgency and nature of putting together the Q-Ship fleet bestowed on its captains freedom of choice not enjoyed by other commanders. He did not want to go over Barnes's head and rob him of a valued worker if he could avoid it, but he was determined to recruit Merrick Granger.

'He told me he wanted to join the navy,' he said. 'If that's what he wants it would be a pity to stand in his way. And it seems he is an officer. Why don't we ask him?'

Barnes smiled. 'Come on, then,' he said.

They found Granger leaning over a collection of parts from a centrifugal pump, laid out on newspaper spread over a bench. He looked up, saw La Salle, glanced at Barnes and broke into a grin. La Salle turned to Barnes.

'May I make my case to this man, Constructor?'

'By all means,' Barnes said.

'Well, Granger. I remember you told me you wanted to join the navy. I think I can give you that chance.'

'I'm listening.'

'I am fitting out and manning a ship. I need an engineer with a good knowledge of diesel. Are you interested?'

Granger studied Barnes' impassive expression briefly then turned to La Salle.

'I'm very interested,' he said.

La Salle described *Freya* and, lowering his voice, hinted at the work she would undertake.

'Do you have any papers?' he asked. 'I seem to remember you said you'd lost everything on *Lusitania*.'

'That's right. My engineering officer's log went down on the ship. With my other stuff. That was the only copy. You'd have to take my service on trust.'

'I'll vouch for his ability,' Barnes said. 'I've seen enough to do that.'

La Salle faced Granger and gave him an earnest look.

'If I can arrange it, are you in?' He paused. 'I have to tell you our branch of the service is sometimes thought of as a little unusual. You'd have to volunteer.'

'Unusual? Do you mean unusually risky?'

'Well, yes. Perhaps. You'd be paid hard-lying money.' La Salle glanced around the workshop, leaned forward slightly. 'And there's a chance of an admiralty grant for success.'

Granger ran his eye over the neatly arranged machine parts on the bench.

'I'd like to think about it,' he said slowly. 'Finish this job first.'

La Salle frowned. 'I'd need an answer by tomorrow.'

'Sure,' Granger said. 'This time tomorrow.'

They left him with his dismantled pump and walked back to Barnes's office.

'What do you think?' La Salle asked the Constructor. 'Do you think he'll accept?' He felt a nagging sense of disappointment that Granger had not jumped at the opportunity he was offering him.

Barnes shrugged. 'He's been talking of trying for a destroyer,' he said. 'He's a very keen lad. My missus has grown very fond of him in the few days he's been with us.'

There was something in the older man's voice that told La Salle he, too, had grown to like their shipwrecked lodger.

'He'd get a commission, wouldn't he?' La Salle asked, a touch uncertainly. Merchant marine officers were generally given commissions on volunteering for active service but Granger's lack of documents might create a problem. It would be a pity if he were only able to offer him an artificer's rank. Barnes seemed relaxed about the missing papers. There was, after all, a perfectly valid reason for it. Barnes asked his clerk what the procedure might be and he had a ready answer. In wartime, the clerk said, the admiralty was prepared to accept a sworn affidavit and the results of an examination as proof of fitness to serve in a particular role. La Salle left Barnes in a positive frame of mind. He would press for Granger to be made Engineer Sub-Lieutenant if the American agreed to join his ship.

On the crossing to Haulbowline Island, La Salle felt the stirring of an old anxiety. The naval yard was a well-established ship works long before the war and like many of the admiralty establishments in the Cove, it was a part of the community. And the community was becoming more and more inclined to support the Republican cause. The Germans had been keen to exploit nationalist elements, even before the war. Now, few doubted they had a network of agents spying on ships and naval movements. The risks were recognised, but no one so far had been able to think of a way of eliminating them. If a man working on naval vessels was also secretly working for the enemy, there was little to prevent him passing on valuable information. The service's intelligence people were active, of course, but

111

unless a man gave himself away there was little they could do.

La Salle thought again of Portmadoc, a harbour where one could feel fairly safe from inquisitive Irish eyes. But the admiral said he wanted *Freya* in action as soon as possible. There was no time now to undo and re-make arrangements. La Salle pushed his concerns to the back of his mind, recognising in a distant way that his own impatience to get his command to sea made this rather more easy to accomplish than it might otherwise have been.

The motor boat dropped him at the jetty near the office and he was informed *Freya* was already in and had been warped on to her fitting-out berth. He hurried along the quay, faintly embarrassed by a feeling of boyish excitement he thought it better to disguise.

His first sight of her stopped him stock still. Her bowsprit, a full thirty feet long, rose from a clipper stem in a line as sweet as anything he'd seen. Below the sprit, a carved figurehead of the goddess of love and beauty, after whom she was named, reached out with slender arms. The sheer, dropping down from the bow, ran aft in a curve that beguiled the eye, rising at the stern to a perfect pitch accented by a teakwood capping rail on the bulwark, scrubbed to near-white. La Salle glanced aloft and swiftly took in the three-masted schooner rig, the mainmast just a little taller than foremast and mizzen. All three spars carried topmasts. A yard on her foremast was squared-off and stripped of canvas. He walked on, noting the fairness of her steel hull, painted a half-gloss black with *"Freya"* in bright yellow picked out just forward of the cathead. Level with the mainmast he paused, letting his eye run over her deckworks. She had two hatches to the hold, boarded over and covered with tarpaulin. On the foredeck he saw a small house and companion he guessed led to the crew quarters. Abaft the mizzen there was a larger structure and, forward of the wheel, a whaleback store or companion. Two boats were lashed down inboard, between the hatches. Two men were adjusting a spring line from the stern. They straightened at La Salle's approach and stood rather stiffly, as if to attention.

'Good day to you,' he called amiably.

The men nodded. 'It'll be the skipper you're after,' one said. 'He's below with the clerk. I'll fetch him.'

The man scrambled up a ladder on to *Freya's* deck. His companion, a grizzled fellow La Salle guessed was too old for military service, walked over.

'Pretty ship, ain't she?' the man said, his voice rich with a West Country drawl.

'Indeed she is,' La Salle replied.

'Well, if they look right they usually are right,' the other said.

La Salle smiled. The old seafarers' adage could rarely be faulted, in his view.

'You'll be taking her over, then,' the greybeard said quietly.

La Salle smiled again, but did not respond.

'I've been mate aboard her since she was launched. Seven years. I'd like to stay with her.'

La Salle turned to face him. 'Do you mean you want to join up?'

'Yes. If I can stay with this ship.'

La Salle paused. There was a streamlined procedure for merchant marine personnel to be recruited into the Royal Navy but this man was clearly too old. Another thought struck him. Men formed attachments to ships not unlike human relationships. It would be unwise to ship aboard a man with a sentimental feeling about a vessel he must deliberately put into harm's way.

'That won't be possible, I'm afraid,' La Salle said, giving his voice an edge that discouraged further discussion. The man shrugged, just as two figures emerged

113

from the whaleback companionway on *Freya's* deck. One walked over to the bulwark.

'I'm Captain Hughes,' he called. 'Want to come aboard?'

La Salle climbed the rope ladder and stepped on to the deck. The mate followed him, downcast. The man with Hughes introduced himself as the naval clerk. La Salle arranged to call on him later and he withdrew.

'What do you think of her?' Hughes asked.

'From what I can see she is a fine ship,' La Salle replied. They walked the deck together and Hughes pointed out the hatches over the hold, both about twenty feet in length.

'You've got fifty feet between the bulkheads,' Hughes said, gesturing at the hold. 'We've had over 100 tons in there.'

Hughes was also too old to serve, La Salle guessed. The papers showed he was a part owner, but he was rather brusque, businesslike and displayed none of the warmth for the vessel that was obvious in the mate. The owners were probably paid a good price by the admiralty, La Salle thought, and Hughes is doubtless happy about no longer having to run the gauntlet of the Kaiser's U-boats.

The skipper's cabin was a pleasant affair, located below the galley. There was a small sleeping space right aft and then a spacious saloon, prettily finished in white-painted panelling.

'We all mess in here,' Hughes said. 'You'll find there's plenty of room for you and your officers.'

La Salle agreed, although he thought extra cabins would have to be built somewhere, probably in a part of the hold. Hughes showed him the engine space and the tall, formidable looking Bolinder motor.

'Runs like a dream,' Hughes said, then, almost under his breath: 'Once you get it started.'

La Salle thought of Granger. Would he be able to manage the Bolinder? Something told him he would. After a short inspection of the forecastle and galley they stood at the wheel and Hughes talked about *Freya's* sailing abilities. The war had left him shorthanded, he said, and they did not use the squaresail, but she didn't suffer much for it, in the coastal trade. She would carry all fore and aft sail up to about a force five on Admiral Beaufort's scale. If the breeze became uncomfortably fresh, they'd reef down, hand the jib and the outer fore-staysail.

'She'll heave-to quiet as a lamb under backed staysail and reefed mizzen,' Hughes said.

La Salle listened carefully. Nothing Hughes said surprised him, although he murmured an appreciative 'Really?' when Hughes said she footed well at four points off the wind in a reasonably flat sea. He looked aloft and his eye followed the mainmast shrouds down to the chains. *Freya* was not an especially beamy vessel and it did indeed look as if she would sail well close-hauled. They discussed her performance under power and Hughes was frank about the Bolinder's limitations.

'It won't get you home against a gale of wind,' he said cheerfully.

Hughes made a half-hearted attempt to discover what the navy planned for his former ship, but abandoned the subject when he saw La Salle would not add anything to what he already knew, which was very little. They parted with a handshake and Hughes said he and his crew would clear the vessel that night.

The last of the late spring blossom still clung to the cherry trees on the pretty avenue that led to the Barnes's house. Granger liked this street. On his first day at the workshops he'd walked along it with Harold Barnes possessed of a sense of quiet joy. The horror of the *Lusitania* was behind him; he had survived and there might yet be a future. Indeed, he had emerged from the shipwreck with more than he could have wished for – a new beginning.

Everything had gone; his tracks had been erased. He had been reincarnated. A new life, even a new name. He thought over what La Salle had said. Was volunteering for Q-Ship service what he really wanted? He had come to Europe to make a new start and joining the British navy seemed to offer precisely that. But he had imagined himself aboard a big ship where he would be just another face among a thousand men. He would know none of them and, more importantly, none of them would know him. What La Salle proposed was different. The intimacy of a small vessel. Yet he felt drawn to the elegant English officer. He had been a friend in need. Granger flinched slightly. More than that. If La Salle had not spotted him in the sea that night he would likely be out there right now with the gulls picking at his bloated carcase. And La Salle had acted like the best of buddies. He had emptied his pockets for him and the jacket and shoes he was wearing were given in the same open-handed way. It had been a long time since anyone had treated him like that. That first morning, when they drank coffee and ate sandwiches at the hotel, they had talked, about ships mostly and their ability to make men look foolish. He had laughed at La Salle's self-deprecating story of an anchoring evolution aboard a merchant vessel, in which he succeeded in letting go the hook and chain without making sure the bitter end was fast, sending the whole lot to the bottom. La Salle had extended a hand of friendship and now he was offering a berth and a chance to join the war on the right side. Granger felt a soaring elation. Wasn't that what he crossed the Atlantic for? When he first heard La Salle's proposition he had been inclined to refuse. It was not what he was looking for. Yet the more he thought about it, the more perfect it seemed. From what La Salle had said the Special Service and its added risks held out a unique chance to prove himself. And that was what he wanted most of all.

Granger let himself in, although not without knocking,

a touch self-consciously. Mrs Barnes called out from the kitchen.

'The tea's nearly ready,' she said.

He smiled as he climbed the narrow staircase. When the English stokers told him tea was the main meal, he had experienced a schoolboy disappointment. He was very hungry. Yet the meal Mrs Barnes served up surpassed its name in every way. There was meat, gravy, potatoes, a magnificent pudding they called "duff" and, if you could manage it, bread and jam.

He entered his room at the back of the house and set down the small knapsack Mr Barnes had given him. Inside was the tin for his sandwiches and his mug. He took off the borrowed jacket, folded it carefully, laid it on the bed and reached under the mattress. He withdrew a child's exercise book, took it to the window and leafed through a couple of blank pages to a fine drawing of a heron, standing impassively patient, in the shallows at a shoreside. He had spotted the bird on a walk around the Cove and drew it from memory. Now, taking a soft pencil, he added a little texture to the bird's plumage, his hand moving swiftly over the page, leaving barely discernible traces that did, nevertheless, add remarkable depth to the image. He tilted his head, frowned, took the pencil to the bird's glittering eye, paused and returned to its feathers.

Mrs Barnes's voice called from the bottom of the stairs. He closed the book, slipped it out of sight under the mattress, picked up his mug and ran downstairs to the scullery. He rinsed the mug under the tap and put it upside down on the side.

'Everything all right at the shop, Merrick?' Mrs Barnes said from the adjoining kitchen.

'Oh, fine.' He walked through. There was a wonderful smell of roasted meat.

'I got an offer to join up,' he said. Granger surprised

himself with this. Since childhood he had learned to keep things to himself. Yet sometimes – just lately – the need for normal human contact had been overpowering.

Mrs Barnes turned from a pan on the stovetop. 'Did you?'

'Yes. It was the officer who picked me up. After the sinking.'

She turned back to the stove. 'And what did you say?'

'I said I'd think it over.'

'I see.'

Granger felt awkward. Mrs Barnes seemed troubled by his news. He had become fond of her and her bluff, amiable husband. They had welcomed him, not just as a shipwreck survivor, but almost as if they had known he had no family of his own. Oh, his family was still there, of course. But the letter he'd received in prison made it clear they wanted nothing more to do with him. Even Anders, his brother.

He heard Harold Barnes at the front door.

'Wash your hands now. There's a good lad,' Mrs Barnes said. 'It'll be ready in a minute.'

Granger rinsed his hands at the scullery sink and went into the small dining room off the passageway. Barnes always took off his jacket and waistcoat before tea and he walked into the dining room in an old cardigan and slippers, chewing an unlit pipe.

'Bit of a turn up, wasn't it?' he said, sitting at the head of the table.

Granger took his usual place. 'I've been thinking about it,' he replied. 'I'm minded to do it.'

Barnes nodded. He tapped his pipe thoughtfully.

'If it's what you want,' he said.

Mrs Barnes came in bearing a laden tray. She set the food on the table and took her place. Her husband picked up the two-pronged fork and carving knife and began cutting the meat.

'Merrick's got an opportunity to get in the navy,' Barnes said.

'I know. He told me,' his wife said quietly.

They fell silent as the plates were passed around. Granger experienced a gnawing discomfort. There were a lot of voids in his life and this good couple had helped to fill one.

'What will your mother say?' Mrs Barnes asked.

'Oh, I don't know,' Granger replied, rather defensively.

'Are any of your family in the services?' Barnes asked. 'Your father? Brothers?'

'No,' Granger said. There was a strained silence. He looked up from his plate. He owed these people more than a monosyllable.

'I lost touch with my family,' he said. 'My father is pastor at a Swedish church. Near Boston. He's kind of strict.' Granger would have liked to add his father was a firebreathing Lutheran zealot, who built his church by terrifying Boston's Swedish community into giving him the funds on pain of eternal damnation. He still remembered the Swedish shipbuilder immigrants his father had rounded up at the docks to do the labour. But that was all in a past over which the sea itself had closed.

Mr and Mrs Barnes exchanged a glance.

'Well, there's a chance for you to get a commission,' Barnes said. 'That's not to be taken lightly.' He explained the navy was desperate for skilled men and La Salle would try to secure him the rank of Engineer Sub-Lieutenant.

'An officer,' Mrs Barnes breathed, realising he was already lost to them.

'They'd expect you to move into admiralty accommodation,' Barnes went on.

Granger paused over his food. It hadn't occurred to him that he would be unable to stay there. Well, he would not be far away. When he was ashore.

'So. Do you think you'll take it?' Barnes said.

'Yes, sir. I think I will.' Granger looked at them in turn, smiling.

'I'll get the pudding,' Mrs Barnes said.

A week passed and La Salle was still unable to feel he had actually taken charge of his ship. *Freya* was officially the responsibility of the naval dockyard and the Shipping Office had been frustratingly slow in organising a plan for her modifications and armament. He decided to concentrate on putting together his crew. Gordon Fisk agreed to go as navigating officer, although La Salle noted in him a faint disappointment over the fact *Freya* was a sailing vessel and a rather small one at that. The crew was to be split into two watches and he needed another deck officer. Davis, the admiral's flag officer, said he would make some inquiries, but he cautioned against optimism, telling La Salle there was no surplus of volunteers for Special Service, especially among officers who were quite literally queuing for more promising berths on destroyers. The Naval Barracks did produce a handful of willing new ratings and one, a market gardener called Greene, who had never been afloat on any kind of vessel, turned out to be an amateur wireless enthusiast. La Salle quickly signed him up for a Marconi course. Fitting a wireless set into *Freya* would be a priority.

Granger was gratefully accepted by the admiralty and his commission as Engineer Sub-Lieutenant was processed swiftly. La Salle found him a room at Kimberley House and showed it to him.

'Will this do?' he asked.

Granger glanced around, noted the plump bed, a comfortable-looking armchair, a small table, a pair of chairs, dresser and a wardrobe with a key in the lock. He pulled back one side of the heavy curtains and looked outside. He had been reluctant to leave the Barnes's house but La Salle had obviously made an effort to get him a swell room. He would not appear ungrateful.

'With quarters like this it seems a pity to have to go to sea,' he drawled, grinning.

La Salle laughed. 'I'm glad you like it.' He saw Granger was still wearing the shoes and jacket he had given him. 'We'll have to get you kitted out,' he said.

Granger seemed shy about getting new clothes, but La Salle pointed out he would have to have a naval uniform and civilian clothes of a kind suited to the role of merchant officer. He detected in the American an awkwardness about accepting what some might perceive as charity.

'I can sub you until you're in funds again,' he said.

'I still owe you,' Granger muttered.

'My dear Granger,' La Salle said, holding out his hands as if to remonstrate. 'Would you deny me the pleasure of helping out a brother officer?'

Granger shifted and glanced around the room again.

'I should be able to pay you back.'

'You will. Don't worry.' La Salle took out his watch. 'Look, there's time to get into town. Gieves have a man there. I have an account.' He tilted his head. 'Shall we go?'

On his first appearance in the dining room at Kimberley House, Granger wore his new and rather stiff uniform. La Salle had advised him to wear it once to establish his presence, as it were. As Granger strode towards La Salle's table he attracted the attention of the room, not least because La Salle had also suggested he leave his hair uncut since they were soon to pose as merchant officers, whose appearance was infinitely more casual than that of their naval counterparts. So Granger let his wavy blond hair fall over his starched collar, creating the effect of a head from a classical statue transposed on to the shoulders of a modern British naval officer. Granger sensed he had made a stir.

'Something funny about my outfit?' he asked, sitting down and shrugging self-consciously.

La Salle smiled. 'You look absolutely splendid,' he said. 'You're new, that's all.'

Granger glanced around the room. There were a dozen or so officers of various rank, most of them awaiting a new posting.

'What do I say if people ask me questions?'

'As little as possible,' La Salle replied. He leaned forward over the table and lowered his voice. 'All the officers here are aware of the Special Service and its work, but we never talk about it.'

Granger nodded. 'Fine,' he said.

After the meal they walked down to the harbour for no better reason than the simple pleasure of looking at ships, which La Salle found they both enjoyed. He was secretly proud of his new companion. He had felt like an elder brother in the tailor's shop, gently advising on this and that and steering Granger away from the cheaper stuff. It had been rewarding because Granger wore clothes well. His athleticism gave him shape and line, the natural allies of good tailoring, La Salle felt. They paused at the harbour wall. He had been telling Granger about *Adela*, his peacetime command, and he mused aloud about her fine sailing qualities.

'I was in a Canadian fishing schooner,' Granger said. 'Three seasons. She sailed like a witch.'

La Salle felt a slight jolt of surprise. It was the first time Granger had volunteered anything about his past.

'They have a wonderful reputation, those schooners,' La Salle said. 'What are they like to sail?'

'Hard work!' Granger laughed. 'But a lot of fun. The ship I was in went to weather as if by magic.' He faltered. 'She still does, I hope.'

La Salle established he had sailed out of Marystown in Newfoundland and the schooner was owned and mostly crewed by French Canadians.

'*Alors, vous parlez Français*?' he said playfully, slipping easily into the language of his childhood.

'Yes, I do,' Granger answered, in English. Then, grinning: 'But not as well as I guess you do.'

They walked towards the quay. La Salle found himself wanting to tell Granger about his earliest memories, at home in Paris with his mother. The taste of bread, the sound of her voice; the city and the miracles it seemed to hold for a young boy. But he held back. Instead they fell to talking about books.

'Mr Conrad has a new one out,' La Salle said. '*Victory*. Nothing to do with the war. You can borrow it, if you like.'

Granger had read nothing by Joseph Conrad and La Salle said he thought Mr Conrad was yet to be fully appreciated on the other side of the Atlantic.

Granger mourned the loss of his books on *Lusitania*, especially a copy of Walt Whitman's poetry, now at the bottom of the sea.

They strolled back to Kimberley House as the daylight gave way to a soft paleness framed by dark shadows. La Salle noted a freshening of the breeze. He was struck by a sense of the hurrying wind carrying in the night from the sea, although why it should be darker beyond the unlit shore he could not say.

Word came at last of approval for *Freya's* fitting-out plan. La Salle and Granger took the service ferry to Haulbowline Island, both wearing civilian clothes. From now on they would assume the appearance of merchant officers when walking out. The admiralty clerk was a nervous little man who seemed to read everything at least twice, as if he were not quite prepared to believe it the first time.

'It seems you're to have two twelve pounders,' he said, scanning the papers pinned to his board. 'God knows where they're coming from.'

La Salle exchanged a glance with Granger. Two twelve pounders. That would indeed give the little ship some muscle. The clerk was muttering something to himself.

'Depth bombs,' he said. Then: 'Do either of you gentlemen know anything about depth bombs?'

Granger shrugged. La Salle made a face. He had heard of these new weapons but so far no one he knew had seen them. *Farnham* had not been equipped with them. They were a novelty; experimental.

'They go off at a pre-determined depth,' the clerk said. 'But you have to keep an eye on the cordite lists to make sure they don't go past their date.' He smiled amiably. 'Or they're liable to go off on your deck.'

The cordite list was posted at naval offices to show which munitions were approaching an age at which they might become unstable. Older explosives were marked for "destruction or return". The clerk muttered a few more discouraging details about the bombs and La Salle concluded their design was still being refined and only a few ships were being armed with them as part of the development work.

'How big are these depth bombs?' he asked.

'About the size of an ash bin,' the clerk said. 'You're down for six. About one hundred pounds each.'

'That's a lot of explosives,' La Salle said.

'It sounds like a lot,' the clerk said, 'but you'd have to drop them within twenty feet of a submarine to hurt the beggar. Your gunlayers will be briefed on how they work. The fuses, that sort of thing.'

La Salle nodded. The clerk went through his papers again.

'Nothing here about torpedoes,' he muttered, then, looking up: 'Did you want torpedoes?'

La Salle thought of *Freya's* deck. Some mystery ships had started carrying torpedoes in troughs on the deck, hidden behind detachable screens. He couldn't see how *Freya*, with her narrow beam, could accommodate such an arrangement. 'No,' he said.

'I've got you down for a Maxim gun and four belts of

ammunition.' He studied his board. 'Rifles. How many crew?' It was a question La Salle had been asking himself. He offered his best guess:

'Sixteen. And four officers including myself and Lieutenant Granger.'

'Right,' the clerk said. 'All we have to do now is find your twelve pounders.'

La Salle knew there was a shortage of guns. The twelve pounder, in a slightly different form, was used by the army and there seemed to be an insatiable appetite for them in France.

'I'm very keen to get to sea,' he said.

The clerk twitched. 'I know, I know. We'll do what we can.' He flicked through his paperwork yet again. Something caught his eye. 'Oh yes,' he said. 'And we've to get you five tons of concrete.'

'What?' La Salle said sharply.

'Five tons of concrete. For the bow. It's a new idea from the top brass. All armed trawlers and the like are to have concrete poured into the bow so they can ram a U-boat.'

La Salle had heard that ramming submarines had proved highly effective when practised by destroyers and cruisers, but *Freya* was a sailing vessel and her motor was unlikely to provide the speed needed for a successful ramming operation.

'Is the concrete absolutely necessary?' he asked.

'Yes,' said the clerk. 'Ramming is the navy's favourite stunt at the moment.'

La Salle saw Granger shift uneasily.

'Very well,' he said.

'Don't worry about your trim,' the clerk said. 'You'll have one gun right aft and you can stow your ammunition and depth bombs in the after end.'

La Salle nodded doubtfully. The clerk seemed satisfied he had finally done his papers justice. He said the dockyard foreman would be along to draw up plans for the gun mountings and disguises. La Salle and Granger walked to Freya's berth, climbed aboard and sat on a hatch tarpaulin.

'Well, I'm pleased we're getting two twelve pounders,' La Salle said brightly.

Granger stroked his chin.

'Even putting weight astern won't help much,' he said.

'What?' La Salle knew he was worrying about the concrete.

'Seems to me the last thing you want in a sailing ship is a lot of weight way forward.'

'I know.' La Salle stood up and held out his hands expressively. 'Hang it all, Merrick, we've got no choice. When the admiralty gets a bee in its bonnet there's nothing to be done about it.'

He opened the lunch bag from Kimberley House and peered inside.

'Looks like some of that pie they always do,' he murmured, then pulled out a packet. 'Some sandwiches here.' He unwrapped the greaseproof paper. 'Ham or cheese?'

Granger shrugged. 'Don't mind.'

'I'll have the cheese, then.' He held out a large tomato. 'Do you want that? I can't eat them raw.'

Granger took the tomato and sank his teeth into it. They ate in silence, quickly, like boys. La Salle suddenly remembered something and fished in the pocket of his jacket.

'Here,' he said. 'I found this at a shop in the town.'

Granger slipped the last of the sandwich into his mouth, wiped his hand on his new jersey and took the book La Salle held out.

'Walt Whitman,' he read aloud. 'Leaves of Grass.' He opened the book, read a few lines to himself and closed it.

'That's mighty handsome of you, Julian,' he said, rather softly.

La Salle was absorbed in extracting a sliver of rind from his last piece of cheese.

'Oh, it's nothing,' he said.

When the foreman arrived they went through the options for mounting and hiding the guns. The foreman, Mr Sitters, had worked on *Farnham* and he knew precisely what was required. They agreed the house abaft the mainmast was the best place for the forward gun. The structure already contained the galley and the crew heads, and there was a question about whether it could be extended. Sitters ran his folding rule over the deck immediately aft and found there would be enough room to accommodate the gun if the hatch into the hold was foreshortened by about five feet.

'The trick,' he said, 'is to make the new house look as if it was there when the ship was built.'

'Can you do that?' La Salle asked.

Sitters looked hurt.

'Of course we can! Every time we re-fit a ship we keep all the useable wood we take out of her. I've got some teak that will match this vessel perfectly, by the time it's had a few coats of varnish. We'll strip and re-varnish the original deck joinery to get a uniform finish.' Sitters adopted a conspiratorial tone: 'They say every German U-boat ships a man who's been a North Sea pilot. Hard to fool those fellows, but we do.'

'I'm glad to hear it,' La Salle said.

Sitters sketched out a design for collapsible sides on the gun house, hinged at half height. As in *Farnham*, these shutters were connected to a wire strop fastened inside with a slip. When the order to fire was given the slip was knocked away and the sides fell outwards, exposing the gun.

Sitters' men started work on the new deckhouse that day and he and La Salle moved aft to devise a way of concealing the second gun. Sitters suggested constructing a dummy hen coop which La Salle thought at first was a rather barmy idea. But Sitters persuaded him that many vessels in the coastal and Channel trade carried hen coops on board to provide the crew with fresh eggs. His men put together a rough shape with packing case lumber to see how it would look. La Salle had to agree it was, after all, an excellent solution. A place for the Maxim gun was found forward of the mainmast in a deck locker. Sitters said he would construct a steel mount that could be lifted clear of the locker then, when the gun was not needed, it would fold down inside with the lid closed over it. The depth charges could be placed in fake barrels lashed to the bulwarks on the after deck.

Welders arrived on the second day to fit the steel beams that would carry the gun mounts. Granger watched the work closely.

'How much weight do you think we'll be adding, on deck?' he asked La Salle.

'I don't know. Why?'

'Well,' Granger said, 'the two big guns make about 2,000 pounds apiece. The mountings … let's say half that. The new deckworks … a lot less, but some extra weight just the same. I make that somewhere around three tons. That's a lot to carry, that high above the waterline.'

'You're right,' La Salle said. 'What can we do about it?'

'Nothing, I guess. But we should try to get as much weight low down in the ship as we can.'

La Salle agreed. They had been promised a cargo of old railway sleepers to pack the hold, providing ballast and floatation of the kind that had saved *Farnham*. Would the tonnage of the wood make up for the extra deck weight? He put the question to Granger.

'I shall be interested to find out,' his friend replied.

La Salle found a message waiting for him at Kimberley House. Davis had turned up an officer to be his first lieutenant. His name was Higgins, a highly-experienced man, Davis said, who had spent his entire career in the service. He would call that evening. La Salle read the note again as he climbed the stairs to his room. Of course, nothing could be interpreted from the scant detail Davis had provided. And yet something troubled him. *Entire career in the service*. La Salle walked into his room and dropped the message on the desk. That would make Higgins the only real naval officer aboard *Freya*, he thought. Both he and Fisk were RNVR and Granger was, well, Granger. How would a man with Higgins's background respond to his command, he wondered? He glanced at his watch. He had arranged to dine with Granger at the Imperial Hotel. He'd been rather looking forward to dressing properly. He'd picked up a smart silk waistcoat at Gieve and it would need at least a trip to the Imperial to justify wearing it. Now he'd have to wait for Higgins. He slipped out and walked down the hallway to Granger's room.

'Come in!' Granger called out to his knock.

La Salle found him sitting at a small table by the window. He was sketching with a pencil in an unlined exercise book. He did not look around, but pointed his pencil into the garden.

'See him? In that tree right there?'

For some reason La Salle thought he ought to approach the window stealthily. He crept up and looked out. A woodpecker was clearly visible in an upper branch. He glanced down at Granger's drawing. He had captured perfectly, even in pencil, the vibrancy of the bird's black and white plumage.

'That's very good,' La Salle said, slightly self-conscious about the fact he had whispered.

'It's amazing,' Granger murmured.

'What?'

'Woodpeckers are like snakes in Ireland. There aren't supposed to be any.'

'Really?' La Salle looked again. It certainly looked like a woodpecker.

'They don't like crossing water,' Granger said. 'And – darn it!' He laid down his pencil. The woodpecker had flown. He looked up. 'I think he'll be back tomorrow. He seems to like that tree.'

La Salle studied the drawing. It was meticulously detailed, uncannily lifelike.

'Where did you learn to do that?' he asked.

Granger turned in his chair, frowning.

'In the woods back home, mostly.' He closed the book and laid it on the table. 'It's not much.'

He seemed unwilling to say any more so La Salle explained about Higgins. His friend said they could wait together and suggested some chess in the sitting room. La Salle agreed readily. Their chess games – after a cautious start on Granger's part – were becoming exciting duels and, if he remembered correctly, he was presently one game ahead. As he walked back to his own room he thought about Granger's drawing and what was clearly a significant talent. It occurred to him, with a feeling of pleasure, that for once his reticent friend had not hidden it from him.

The Kimberley House boy intercepted him at the top of the stairs.

'Two gentlemen to see you, sir,' he said.

'Two gentlemen?' La Salle gave the boy a questioning look. 'I was expecting one.'

'My 'rithmetic ain't perfect, sir, but they looked like two to me.'

He made a playful swipe at the lad's ear and the boy clattered off down the stairs. La Salle picked up his jacket and went down. In the hall he saw Roberts and Edwards, gunlayers from *Farnham*. Roberts, holding his cap, stepped forward.

'Sir,' he said.

'Roberts. How are you? And you, Edwards. All well?'

'Yes, sir,' Roberts said. 'That is, we heard you have a ship, sir.'

'Yes,' La Salle said carefully. The scene aboard *Farnham*, when he tried to hold Roberts back from delivering the death blow to the U-boat, began re-playing in his mind's eye.

'We want to stay in the Special Service, sir.'

La Salle cocked his head slightly, inviting him to go on.

'We'd like to ship aboard, sir. Your command.'

La Salle felt a frisson of joy. Despite the admiral's confidence in him and the thrill of taking up his own ship, self-doubt persisted. The prospect of Higgins, a real navy man, as his second had revived it. Yet now, Roberts, the gunlayer whose quiet intensity and acknowledged brilliance set him apart, wanted to serve with him.

'I should very much like to have you.' La Salle gestured towards Edwards, who had remained silent. 'And you, too, Edwards.'

They told him they had asked to stay in the Special Service after the *Farnham* incident and had been awaiting orders when word reached them about *Freya*. La Salle felt a twinge of misgiving about the fact his ship was being gossiped about but he knew in his heart it was inevitable. Sharing facilities with the rest of the service grossly compromised their secret role but the admiralty seemed to take the view that what happened within the confines of naval property was safe from the enemy. But was it?

He told the two gunlayers a little about *Freya* and they arranged a signing-on for the next day. The other gunners from Farnham had dispersed among ships in the regular service, they said. La Salle thought privately that a man who has been obliged to lie still and wait while being shelled by a U-boat could be forgiven if he did not care to repeat the experience. He took his leave of Roberts and

131

Edwards in the hall at Kimberley House and was about to climb the stairs when Higgins arrived.

Lieutenant Frederick Higgins RN, La Salle noted as he turned to greet him, was a man of mature years with iron-grey hair, cut short around a severe side parting. There was a stiffness in his bearing that struck La Salle instantly, a ramrod-up-the-back posture often seen among officers who had served during the last queen's reign. As they shook hands Higgins seemed to attempt a smile, but his facial muscles appeared to have ideas of their own and the expression that emerged resembled a grimace of pain. La Salle led him to the sitting room where Higgins shot a glance into every corner and crevice, as if wanting to weigh up every detail as to its possible value or, La Salle thought, its ability to conceal a nasty surprise. Higgins perched on the edge of a sofa, his cap held primly in his right hand.

'Lieutenant Davis said you might be interested in joining my ship,' La Salle began.

'Yes, sir.'

La Salle suppressed an inner jolt. Higgins's response implied a deference he found unsettling. Although his acting rank put him over Higgins there was something about the man that made La Salle feel disturbingly junior.

'You've been told the basics, I gather?'

'Yes, sir. You were made up after the *Farnham* action. Congratulations, sir.'

La Salle squirmed slightly. 'I meant about the ship,' he said.

'Oh. Yes, sir. Sailing vessel out of the Channel trade. Being re-fitted now, I understand.'

'That's right.' La Salle paused. 'You've come out of a cruiser, haven't you? May I ask why you volunteered for mystery ship duty?'

Higgins shifted on the edge of the sofa.

'I thought it would offer opportunity, sir.'

'Opportunity?'

'Yes, sir.' Seeing that La Salle wished him to go on, Higgins frowned. 'For action,' he added.

La Salle smiled. 'Well, yes. Possibly. It can also be frustrating. There's nothing to say we shall even see a U-boat.'

Higgins leaned forward. 'Yes. But if we do! And if we get one! There's opportunity there, sir. I'd say.'

La Salle thought he was beginning to understand. Higgins was making a last desperate attempt to move his paralysed career along before it was too late. Well, the nature of the incentive probably mattered less than the weight it added to the effort. He told Higgins about his plans for *Freya's* complement. The men would be split into two watches, one under Gordon Fisk, the other under him as first lieutenant, if he were happy to join on that basis. Naval discipline, including divisions and prayers, would be observed but outwardly the ship and her people would appear to be in the merchant service. He told Higgins he would be given an allowance of three pounds to buy civilian clothes to wear aboard and ashore, in the manner of a merchant officer. Higgins asked about hard-lying money and La Salle confirmed he would receive extra pay.

'There's an admiralty grant, too, isn't there? For sinking a U-boat?' Higgins asked.

La Salle confirmed there would be prize money for success, but he didn't mention the £1,000 figure. Something told him Higgins knew all about that.

They parted with a cordial handshake and Higgins said he would join the ship as soon as his berth was ready. As he left, La Salle glanced at the clock in the hall. With luck there would still be time for dinner at the Imperial. He took the stairs two at a time and rapped on Granger's door. Granger opened it, the Walt Whitman held open in his hand.

'Ready?'

'Sure. I'll get my coat.' Granger closed the book and laid it on the small table. He reached for his new reefer jacket, slung across the back of the chair. La Salle gestured towards the book.

'May I?' he said. Granger nodded, La Salle picked up the book, leafed through, found a page and began reading aloud:

'I understand the large hearts of heroes
The courage of present times and all times.'

He looked up, returned to the page, skipped a few lines, then:

'How he saved the drifting company at last
How the lank loose-gowned women looked when boated
from the side of their prepared graves,
How the silent old-faced infants, and the lifted sick,
and the sharp-lipped unshaven men;
All this I swallow and it tastes good ... I like it well
and it becomes mine,
I am the man ... I suffered ... I was there.'

He closed the book, placed it gently on the table, moved to catch the other's eye.

'What happened when *Lusitania* went down, Merrick?'

Their gaze locked for a moment. Granger turned away, pulled on his coat.

'You seem to know your way around that book pretty well,' he said.

'When I found that' – La Salle pointed at the Whitman – 'I bought myself a copy, too. I have to say I admire your taste.'

Granger smiled. He was holding open the door. La Salle shook his head, gave it up. They walked downstairs, out into warm-damp air of the evening.

They were given their usual table in the dining room at the Imperial hotel and, with barely a glance at the menu, Granger ordered the beef.

'Don't you want to try something different?' La Salle asked, a touch petulantly. Granger always chose the Imperial's roast beef.

'Why?' Granger seemed mystified. 'It's fine.'

La Salle shook his head sadly, returned to his own menu. The salmon fillet with tarragon looked intriguing, but the Dublin Bay prawns were a treat not to be missed. He ordered them with a bottle of Chablis which, if he didn't finish, he'd take back to Kimberley House. He was mildly annoyed with Granger. They had settled into an easy friendship that had established itself without effort. They had become comrades almost by instinct, a notion that gratified him enormously and appealed to his sense of a poetic ideal. But Granger had this off-putting way of retreating into his own mysterious hinterland. He would not talk about *Lusitania* or himself and although he, La Salle, had not revealed his own family background he had at least conveyed a few spare details. Granger could have landed from Mars, for all he said about his past.

'I was really impressed by that drawing of the bird, Merrick,' he said amiably. 'I envy you that talent.'

Granger coloured slightly. 'Oh, it's nothing,' he said.

'No, really. Did you go to an artists' school? Or get lessons?'

Granger smiled, appearing to weigh up something before he spoke.

'I got one lesson,' he said.

La Salle raised his eyebrows.

'Just one?'

Granger eyed his friend across the table. He sensed La Salle was put out over his uncooperative response to questions about *Lusitania*. But he just wasn't ready to talk about it. The children crying in the lift, the sight of Mrs

135

Madden scorched black and all the others he couldn't help. But there were things he wanted La Salle to know, if only he could find a way of expressing them.

La Salle urged him on: 'Just one lesson?'

'I got a drawing lesson from my old man when I was maybe four or five years old. I painted a boat on a blue sea with a pale blue sky and I showed it to him. I guess he must have known I was kind of proud of it.' Granger smiled. 'My pa's pretty old-fashioned. He doesn't hold with people getting proud. So he pointed to the space I'd left between the sea and the sky. He told me to do it again. Join up the sea and the sky, he said. I wouldn't do it. I knew there was a gap between the sea and the sky. It was, well, the air. So he larruped me pretty good, because I was too proud to listen.' Granger's features darkened. 'Of course, he was right. The sky and the sea join at the horizon. I'd never seen a horizon, is all.'

Almost as soon as the words were out Granger regretted them. This newly found compulsion to reveal, to share, was inimical. Yet irresistible.

'My dear chap –' La Salle began, then paused. He would not ask his friend a question he himself would abhor. About his father. So they fell to discussing their new ship, speaking in low voices and leaning towards each other as if to exclude all else.

Freya's guns arrived in the first week of June. It took three days to fit them and as the work progressed, La Salle took stock of his newly-created mystery ship. Part of the forward hold had been re-built as an extension of the forecastle to accommodate the gunlayers. Roberts and Edwards had been joined by four men of varying experience, but all knew how to manage a twelve pounder and its ammunition. La Salle had recruited a dozen ratings to sail and fight the ship, and four of them were placed in Roberts's charge to step in at the guns if necessary. Greene, the gardener who had never been afloat, was settled in a tiny space at the foot of the main deck companionway where the Marconi set was installed. When Greene was shown his quarters he thought at first a joke was being played upon him. He had been given a bunk, rather than a hammock, fitted precisely between two bulkheads. He thought it was a bookshelf, until he was shown how to spread his sleeping roll on it. As it finally sank in that this kennel-sized room was his home for the foreseeable future he swallowed hard, and grinned amiably. From then on he acquired the name "Sparks" and his unfortunate past as a man firmly wedded to the land was forgotten.

The wireless had given La Salle a problem. Vessels like *Freya* were rarely equipped with such expensive and difficult devices and there was a question over how to arrange the aerial. A wireless aerial rigged in the normal way would arouse suspicion, not least in the mind of a U-boat commander. Higgins suggested a solution La Salle found admirable. He directed the riggers to paint the aerial cable the colour of an old wire stay and link it between the main and mizzen topmasts. The lower section was painted to look like manilla rope and led down to the deck like a spare signal halyard. La Salle took the tender out into the harbour to view *Freya* from a distance. The disguise was perfect, even when seen through binoculars.

He came to respect Higgins during those days of fitting out. The lieutenant had never served in a sailing ship, as far as he knew, but his great experience and seaman's sense gave him an instinct for what was right. When the foreman, Mr Sitters and his gang were drawing up plans for officers' cabins for Higgins, Fisk and Granger, Higgins queried a plan to fit them with sliding doors. Sitters had proposed taking some space from the after end of the hold and the compartment doors were to be arranged athwartships in a bulkhead that would span the beam. Sliding doors, Sitters said, were an excellent device for saving space, since they did not require a clear area behind them for opening. But Higgins argued that sliding doors in a sailing vessel were a nuisance since they would constantly try to close or open themselves when the ship was heeled. When La Salle was brought into the discussion he readily agreed and it was decided the cabins, too small for conventional doors, would be closed off with heavy curtains, tagged at the foot.

Under her previous captain, Freya's charts were spread on the table in the saloon and Fisk, the navigator, was given a decent-sized working space in a corner of this cabin, now the officers' mess. Meanwhile, La Salle had moved into his own small suite in the stern. Sitters' men built two bookshelves into his sleeping space and he had them extend the small desk so it was big enough to take his papers and charts. They scraped some of the mahogany panelling where damp had brought off the varnish and they gave the whole cabin a fresh coat. La Salle was delighted with his tiny domain. The wood glowed with the brightness from the skylight overhead and although it could not compare with his airy and rather lavishly furnished cabin on *Adela*, it seemed to him a perfect place. Less perfect was the engine room. Granger had spent days working in the cramped area below deck and at one point La Salle was astonished to see he had cut away the top of the fuel tank.

'Is that necessary?' he asked.

'Yes it is,' Granger replied. 'They have been keeping the tank less than half full most of the time. So water has condensed under the top and corroded the metal.' He scooped a few flakes of rusty steel from the bottom of the tank.

'See this? Blocks the whole works. It's a miracle the darn thing ever ran at all.'

After Sitters' men had welded on a new tank top, with a removable hatch designed by Granger, La Salle was invited down to see the Bolinder run. He watched with concealed amusement as Granger fussed over the motor, priming the intake and setting up the compressed air tank that turned the flywheel. He thought he heard Granger whispering to the machine as he heated a sausage-like excrescence on the cylinder head with a blow lamp.

'Now,' he said.

There was a whooshing sound as the compressed air started to turn the engine, then something that sounded like a dry bark. Silence.

'Aha!' Granger exclaimed. He fiddled with a small hand pump and gave the compressed air lever another pull. The Bolinder turned, fired and ran, unsteadily at first, then with a rhythmic beat La Salle found rather reassuring. Granger cocked an ear to the motor.

'That is sweet!' he said. 'Julian. Is that sweet?'

La Salle grinned. 'It sounds very good to me.'

'You bet it is! Hughes didn't run it much because he couldn't get it to go properly. That's good for us because it's still tight and the compression is as good as it was when it left the factory. Lots of life left in her.'

Granger eyed the bobbing motor with a look of affection La Salle found quite touching.

'How long before you're happy to go to sea?' he asked.

Granger pulled a face. 'The motor's fine. The shaft, propeller; all good. The steering gear is OK, but I'd like to replace the connections at some point. Maybe not now. The pumps have all been overhauled.' He straightened, holding out his hands expressively. 'From an engineer's point of view this ship is ready to go, captain!'

La Salle clapped him on the back, left him with his motor and went up on deck. Higgins was having a discussion with Mr Oliver, from the Naval Store Department. Neither man seemed happy.

'Is everything all right?' he asked.

'No, it isn't,' Higgins said.

'Not my fault,' Oliver cut in. 'Regulations.'

139

Higgins explained that some of the men had learned a large consignment of gifts had arrived for the fleet. They were sent by people at home and, according to dockyard scuttlebutt, a warehouse had been virtually filled with items including gramophones, books, clothing, footwear and illustrated papers. But, Higgins said, none of this Aladdin's cave of treasure would be available to *Freya's* crew or officers because the vessel was not shown anywhere as one of His Majesty's ships.

'The regulations clearly state that these gifts are for men aboard His Majesty's ships,' Oliver said. 'Officially, that isn't you.'

La Salle frowned. Oliver was right. *Freya* was still on Lloyds List as a merchant vessel and would remain there for as long as she performed her mystery ship role. He took Higgins aside.

'Don't worry. We'll overcome this our own way,' he said. Then, turning to Oliver: 'I thank you Mr Oliver. I understand perfectly the situation.'

Oliver went through lists of stores and checked off items already delivered aboard and circled those still awaited.

'By the way,' he said. 'Have you got a quartermaster yet?'

La Salle shook his head.

'Mr Higgins has been handling our provisioning and so on,' he said. 'But I suppose we will need someone.'

'I've got just the man,' Oliver said. 'Jack White.' Oliver lowered his voice and leaned forward. 'He was in the *Titanic*, you know.'

'Quartermaster?' La Salle asked.

'Well, not quite,' Oliver said, sniffing. 'He's very keen to join up.'

'Where is he?'

'Right here, in the Cove. He's staying with me and the missus.' Oliver assumed a look that defied any man to challenge his probity. 'He's my brother-in-law.'

'Ah,' La Salle said.

Higgins turned to face Oliver.

'Has he been in a merchantman recently?'

'Er, no. Not lately,' Oliver said, sniffing. 'He's, er, been away.'

'Ah,' Higgins murmured.

'If he knows his business I'd be prepared to give him a chance,' La Salle said.

Higgins gave Oliver a sly look.

'If your dear brother-in-law came aboard this ship you wouldn't want him to go without amenities, would you?' he said.

Oliver's face showed he was wary of a trap.

'What sort of amenities?'

'Gramophones, books, picture papers. That sort of thing,' Higgins said.

Oliver shot a glance at La Salle who appeared to have just discovered something fascinating in the mainmast rigging.

'I suppose not,' Oliver muttered. He knew Higgins had snared him.

La Salle smiled. 'Why don't you send Mr White along?'

Oliver relaxed a little.

'Right,' he said. Then, to Higgins: 'When do you want to come. To the stores?'

Higgins beamed and rubbed his hands together.

'No time like the present!'

Jack White signed on the next day as quartermaster and captain's servant. La Salle liked him instantly. He was a Londoner 'out of Hoxton' as he put it and he had indeed been aboard the *Titanic*, although he was vague about his job in her. White, who was immediately christened "Chalky" by the crew, had a chirpy manner and seemed to be unfailingly optimistic about everything, from the weather to the progress of the war. When they read the grim news from the Dardanelles, and deplored the deaths

141

of thousands upon thousands of allied troops at the Battle of Krithia, Chalky tapped his nose.

'Don't you worry,' he told the forecastle. 'The 52nd Division is on its way. They'll sort out the Pashas.'

Chalky tied a teddy bear to a grabrail in *Freya's* saloon, explaining it was "good joss" – good luck. A former shipmate had brought it back from the China station, he said, although he did not explain how he had acquired it.

Chalky formed a close working relationship with Briggs, the cook, but La Salle couldn't help noticing they seemed to detest each other. Briggs was from a place he called The Elephant, south of the Thames, a fact Chalky noted with disdain. La Salle occasionally heard them trading insults and was alarmed when he once overheard Briggs shouting: 'The next time you nick something out of my galley I'll chop your fucking bollocks off!'

To which Chalky replied cheerily: 'You and whose army?'

Curiously, their conversation then resumed as before. Briggs had worked in a hotel and La Salle considered himself lucky to have him. Especially since he knew how to produce an omelette with precisely the level of inner viscosity La Salle believed crucial to the success of the dish.

Their consignment of railway sleepers arrived and they used a dockyard crane to load them aboard. La Salle and Granger watched the waterline anxiously as the wood was packed tightly into the hold.

'The deeper she goes, the better,' Granger said, ever mindful of the weight they now carried on deck. *Freya* had assumed a slightly bows-down attitude after the concrete was poured into her forepart and they were gratified to see that the load of timber helped bring her back to her lines. When the sleepers were stowed they reckoned she'd gone down about a foot on the waterline.

'That should do it, don't you think?' La Salle asked his friend, a touch anxiously.

'I darn well hope so,' Granger replied.

Sailing trials were frustrated by persistently fine weather. The long, sunny days produced hardly a breeze and La Salle became irritated by the constant slatting of the sails and the limp feel of the rig. When they did manage to pick up a light air, *Freya* sailed bewitchingly and La Salle pronounced himself pleased with her. The Bolinder, in Granger's care, ran well and they were glad of it. On a day without a breath of wind they motored out to the west and launched a target made of oil drums, planks and tarpaulin. The gunners took down the target within five shots at a range of 400 yards using the aft twelve pounder. The forward gun, under Edwards' command, mopped up the debris with a series of unerring hits. Roberts had brought on his new gunlayers well, La Salle thought and told him so.

'Nice smooth sea,' Roberts said laconically. 'Be harder in a gale of wind.'

Higgins had procured a magnificent gramophone and collection of recordings on his visit to Mr Oliver's warehouse of gifts from the public. Chalky immediately took charge of the machine and suggested to La Salle, as he brought his morning tea, that a concert party would be a good idea. La Salle concurred, in a vague kind of way, but before the proposal could be properly discussed a messenger arrived from Admiralty House with a sealed pouch. La Salle took it to his cabin, closed the door behind him and took out the papers. He found sailing orders and details of intelligence received about a German U-boat attacking shipping in the sea lanes off Ushant. It appeared the submarine had just arrived in French waters and was harassing everything from steamers to fishing craft. The pouch also contained a docket for collecting a set of large scale charts of the area around the French coast and a note from Admiral Pettigrew. '*Your promotion confirmed,*' it read. '*Good luck and Godspeed.*'

143

CHAPTER SIX

The weather broke the day *Freya* sailed. Squally fronts rolled in from the west as if marching in a regular procession, darkening the sky and stirring an ugly chop in the Cove. The wind was accompanied by heavy rain and La Salle donned a waterproof cape and sou'wester as he conned the ship out into the open sea. As they cleared the Old Head of Kinsale the breeze seemed to increase and La Salle reckoned it was well above Admiral Beaufort's force six. The seas, unimpeded on their march across the ocean, grew in length and height and the taller wavetops broke aboard, sending spray as far aft as the helm. La Salle glanced aloft. She was carrying reefed main, mizzen and staysails and she seemed content, although he felt a twinge of concern at the time she was taking to come back after heeling to the more vicious gusts. Granger had just shut down the Bolinder and he came up on deck, wearing a shiny black oilskin.

'What do you make of it?' he asked, raising his voice above the deep moan in the rigging.

'The weather?' La Salle lifted his head towards the west where the clouds seemed to be intent on thickening into a solid mass. 'Dirty and getting dirtier.'

Granger grinned. 'Like the forecastle,' he said.

'What?'

'Every man in Higgins' watch, except Roberts and Edwards, is sick.'

'Oh, no.' La Salle was afraid of that. Few of his ratings were experienced seamen and *Freya*'s motion would test the hardiest stomach. Fisk's watch had coped well setting sail and the helmsman, a paid yacht hand before the war, was steering skilfully. But Higgins's watch was woefully short of men who could be trusted to steer in difficult conditions. What would happen if the weather worsened after the change of watch?

La Salle sent word for Higgins to join him on deck. Their complement was more than twice the number a ship like *Freya* would normally carry and he had issued standing orders that the off-watch had to remain below. The sight of a large number of men on deck would immediately alert a U-boat commander. Yet his crew had to get their sea legs quickly and they would do it far more quickly on deck than they would stuck below in a fetid forecastle.

Higgins reported five men seriously sick. La Salle decided to swap them for men in Fisk's watch who were generally faring better. The stricken five stumbled on deck, grey-faced and hollow-eyed. Two, he saw, were new gunlayers. He told Higgins to have them sit on the hatch coaming and stare at the horizon. The small group clustered on the hatch on the lee side, sullen and cowed by the cruelty of their own innards.

'A pretty sorry bunch I'm afraid,' Higgins said, joining La Salle near the helm.

'I suppose we have to expect that.'

'Most of them will be all right by evening,' Higgins offered.

La Salle smiled to himself, remembering the old saw that mal-de-mer passed off when the moon came up. He once told this to a very sick guest aboard *Adela* who replied drily: 'The moon? Is that going to come up, too?'

At that moment a gust forced *Freya* over in a sharp heel to port and three of the men on the coaming tumbled into the lee scuppers.

'My God,' Higgins muttered.

Two of the men crawled back to the hatch but the third lay on the deck, arching his back as he retched helplessly. La Salle turned away.

'Make sure he doesn't go over the side,' he said.

Freya continued her course to the south east, shrugging off the increasingly hard buffets from the breaking seas but not standing up to her canvas as well as La Salle would have liked. At the change of watch he ordered the main to be lowered and they handed the outer staysail. The wind had backed slightly into the south west and increased to near-gale force. She was reaching fast at better than nine knots but she was shipping a lot of water over the bow. La Salle had been tempted to bear away – he had searoom to the east – but he told himself *Freya* was, after all, a ship of war and he could not afford to handle her with the delicacy that might be appropriate in a vessel like *Adela*. It did occur to him, however, that *Adela* did not have five tons of concrete in her bows or several tons of guns and explosives on her deck.

At midnight Chalky brought him a mug of cocoa. The wind had drawn ahead and it was blowing a full gale. *Freya* was close-hauled and heeling far more than was comfortable, or even safe. La Salle called for the mizzen to be deep-reefed. They'd hang on to the heavy working staysail for now. Under the shortened sail *Freya* regained her feet a little, although the deck was almost constantly awash from water coming aboard. The helmsman was a young rating who'd impressed La Salle with his enthusiasm but La Salle watched him steer with growing concern. The lad was terrified. His sou'wester had long since blown away and his hair streamed water. He kept wiping the salt spray out of his face, now and then shooting a horrified look at the seas pounding *Freya's* starboard bow.

'Keep your mind on the breeze,' La Salle shouted in the boy's ear. The lad did not look round, but darted glances at the binnacle, then the mast-top, wide-eyed, gulping. A savage gust struck the ship like a slap. La Salle grabbed the handrail around the galley to keep upright as

Freya staggered in her stride. She began rounding up into the wind. The mizzen shivered, then cracked like a pistol shot as the sheet slackened and began flogging, whiplashing from side to side uncontrollably. The boy on the helm froze, eyes staring, unseeing. *Freya* was almost head to wind, moving towards the point of no return where she would be caught aback and spun around at the mercy of the breaking seas.

Higgins ran forward from his place on the lee side. La Salle, closer to the helm, pushed the boy away and grabbed the wheel. *Freya* still had a little way on and he spun the spokes back, watching the staysail. A slight shift favoured them. The sail trembled, then partially filled. It was enough. *Freya's* bow paid off slowly, the reefed mizzen took up with a mighty thwack and she was sailing again. The helmsman watched dully as La Salle coaxed her back into the groove; a little to weather, a little a-lee. La Salle beckoned him back to the wheel.

'Remember now,' he shouted in his ear. 'Mind the breeze!'

The lad took the spokes. He had not expected to be allowed to steer the ship ever again. He swallowed hard and concentrated on the feel of the wind on his cheek. La Salle nodded at him reassuringly and drew back to the galley where Higgins was clinging to the handrail.

'Can you trust him?' Higgins asked.

'Yes,' La Salle said. 'So long as we encourage him to trust himself.'

He thought the gale might blow itself out quickly, in the manner of most summer storms, but the ferocity of the wind intensified and the seas, La Salle noted, were becoming confused and even higher. Granger came up and joined him at the binnacle.

'Aren't you going below?' he yelled, cupping a hand around La Salle's ear to make himself heard.

La Salle shook his head. The ship ploughed headlong

into a steep sea and they were caught by a sheet of solid spray that gushed into every opening and crevice of their oilskins. La Salle felt cold water run down his bare back inside his clothes. Granger wriggled inside his own waterproof. He seemed to choke on a word and La Salle laughed, unable to hear anything above the shrieking of the wind. He had never heard Granger use even mildly coarse language. If ever there was a moment for it, however, it was now. It was hard not to imagine they had been singled out for this punishment. The waves reared up in the darkness and hammered the ship with blows that sent tremors through hull and deck. La Salle reminded himself of Mr Conrad's words: "The sea can be cruel, but never vindictive." Of course, this roaring monster was a mere unfeeling, uncaring, disinterested force of nature. Its power to murder was incidental, never intended. And yet there was something spiteful in its attack; he imagined a desire to hurt in the stinging spray and there was a meanness in the wind's howl.

Higgins stood by the galley, his face impassive, but strangely smug. *I have seen worse than this*, his expression seemed to say. La Salle's thoughts returned to something that had been nagging away at him for hours. The Scillies were somewhere away to the east and he had no real idea of how much leeway *Freya* was making. The course should have taken them well clear of the reefs to the west of the islands but how was it possible to calculate sideways drift in these conditions and in a vessel new to him? He had to look at the chart. A gnawing began in his stomach as he imagined being set down on to the granite teeth around the Scillies, graveyard of many a ship. He clawed his way to the companionway and felt his way down the steps. Fisk was leaning over his chart table bracing himself against the bulkhead.

'What a night!' he said as La Salle grappled his way across the cabin, from handhold to handhold.

'Where are we?'

Fisk pointed to a mark on the chart.

'There. I hope.'

La Salle felt the grip on his stomach relax slightly. Fisk's position showed the Scillies now lay to the north.

'I've a mind to heave-to,' he said.

'Right.'

La Salle climbed up to the deck to find Granger steering the ship.

'The youngster needed a spell,' he mouthed.

La Salle nodded. He watched as Granger flicked the spokes between his hands, feeling intuitively for any increase, or decrease, in the wind that would demand a correction. He was a natural helmsman, La Salle thought, his nerve endings tuned to the breeze, its strength and direction, and his hands responding almost without his knowing. He imagined Granger in his Canadian fishing schooner, among sailormen as good as any afloat. He felt a jab of that odd sensation again, a kind of fatherliness. He was proud of his particular friend.

Freya was still making progress but the seas were becoming impossibly high hills to climb. The extra weight in her forward end seemed to rob her of vivacity and she lifted listlessly as each wave gathered ahead, sending dark water cascading over the starboard bow.

'We'll heave-to,' La Salle yelled at Granger. He beckoned Higgins and shouted orders over the din of the wind and crashing sea. Higgins groped his way forward to where men of his watch were sheltering behind the forecastle companionway. He called them together and they took up on the sheets, watching La Salle as he waited for a lull to bring the ship's head through the wind. It dropped a notch or two at last, the shrieking became a low growl and La Salle threw out his arm. Granger turned the wheel to weather and *Freya's* bow lifted to face the seas head-on. She faltered for a moment and as the mizzen and the staysail flogged with a clamour that rose even above the wind, La Salle thought she would refuse to turn. Then the staysail filled aback with an explosive whack and she was jerked hard on to the new tack. Higgins' men trimmed the sheets, Granger threw the wheel over, as if to steer her once more into the wind. But the staysail kept her head down and she seemed suddenly placid, riding the huge black slopes quietly now, forereaching slowly into the darkness.

Granger lashed the wheel to a ringbolt in the deck and glanced aloft.

'That ought to do it,' he said.

Now La Salle could hear his voice. The world was a different place. The wind, though still screaming vengefully, seemed less intimately close. The seas were just as huge but now they were almost benign, slipping away under the port side.

The watch changed, La Salle and Granger went below with Higgins and Chalky brought coffee and bully beef sandwiches to the mess. The small saloon seemed a world away from the uproar outside and La Salle sipped his coffee gratefully.

'Unusual weather. This time of year,' he said.

Granger raised his head, as if trying to divine the intentions of the wind and sea.

'You know, I had a feeling it was backing,' he said.

La Salle rose from the leather bench and leaned over the chart, left pinned open by Fisk when he went on watch.

'If it does back into the south-south-west, that would make the Scillies a lee shore,' La Salle said slowly.

'Just a feeling,' Granger said, taking a mouthful of sandwich.

La Salle shot him a smile. Just then he caught sight of Higgins, sitting across the other side of the cabin with his plate and mug. He was watching them with an intensity

La Salle found odd. When Higgins felt La Salle's eyes on him his expression changed quickly but La Salle had registered it and it alarmed him. It was something close to hatred.

La Salle had intended to get some sleep. He and Granger did not stand watches and took time below when their duties allowed. Now he felt a crushing burden of fatigue. He had risen very early to prepare for sailing and he had been awake for almost twenty-four hours. But if the wind did back, as Granger feared, they could not remain hove-to with the Scilly Islands under their lee. He shuddered inwardly at the thought of being blown on to the reefs and rocky ledges of that dreaded archipelago.

'I'm going on deck,' he said.

It was remarkable, he thought as he stepped outside, how a few planks of decking could mask the savagery of the elements. Below, there was a measure of tranquillity, cosiness even. On deck the wind tore at his skin, ripped the tops off waves and pelted him with what seemed like an invisible hail of pebbles. All around dark shapes of angry sea loomed and reared, menacing and unpredictable. There was a glimmer of light in the east and the coming greyness gave a raw edge to the seas as it lit the marble-like patterns on the face of the waves. The air was wet with spindrift and La Salle knew the wind had increased. Fisk was at the binnacle with the helmsman, standing by the lashed wheel. They exchanged nods as La Salle peered at the compass and took a rough bearing. Granger was right. The wind was backing.

'It's getting up a bit,' Fisk said.

La Salle nodded again.

'It's backing into the south,' he said, standing close so Fisk could hear. 'I want to get well clear of the Scillies.'

Fisk signalled he understood. La Salle told him they'd bear away and run for Falmouth.

Fisk's watch handed the mizzen and brought *Freya's*

stern through the wind. As her bow pointed north east, almost directly downwind, she set off like a racehorse. They carried a scrap of staysail to steady her but she was being driven by the windage in her spars and rigging. La Salle was shocked by her speed. She careered crazily down the face of the seas as if hurtling downhill. The man on the wheel gave every impression of being engaged in mortal combat, fighting it this way and that, straining to turn it against some unseen elemental force. Fisk ordered a seaman to help him and the two stood together as one, bending and heaving and spinning in the lulls.

Granger came up.

'That's some breeze,' he said.

La Salle glanced astern. The seas were rushing up behind them, towering over the ship.

'We're going to run into Falmouth,' he said.

Granger pursed his lips, looked aloft. The sky was becoming paler, the clouds thinning, tearing across the sky like mad things. The weather front was moving. Their speed through the water took some of the sting out of the wind, but La Salle was becoming ever more nervous about the ship's headlong dash. The helmsmen were barely able to cope with the weight in the wheel. *Freya* was charging down into the troughs and threatening to bury her deadened bow in the solid mass of water on the other side. He ordered the helmsmen to steer to each sea, taking them slightly on the quarter so *Freya* descended the steep slopes in a more or less controlled manner, rather than crashing into the trough. It seemed to work and although it compromised their course La Salle judged the safety of the vessel and crew to be his paramount concern at that point.

She hurried on. His feeling of tiredness had faded. He felt alert. Granger kept the deck with him and they sat together on the small bench forward of the galley bulkhead. La Salle knew Falmouth harbour and the approaches and he guessed that once they passed The Manacles they would find calmer water. He was picturing the layout of the ship buoys in his mind when it suddenly seemed to grow dark again. He jerked his head around. A vast expanse of sky astern had gone, its place taken by a moving wall of water. La Salle refused to believe what his eyes told him. The sea was standing almost vertical. The wave was twice the size of anything that had gone before. *Freya's* stern began to lift violently. Suddenly, she was in the grip of the monster and it hurled her forward, down, down. La Salle had an impression of falling. He gripped the rail around the galley and hung on. Granger did the same. Then they were thrown against each other as *Freya* was dashed into the crest ahead. La Salle just glimpsed a mast level with the sea as the ship was swept along her length by a rolling mass of water. Stillness. Then, slowly at first, she began to rise. La Salle saw the port side bulwark emerge from the water as if surfacing. *Freya* seemed to shake herself. Tons of water poured down her deck, over the side. The two helmsmen were nowhere to be seen. Granger lunged towards the wheel. Freya was now broadside on to the seas, at her most vulnerable. Granger wrestled with the wheel, trying to get her head to bear away downwind. La Salle saw a long shape leaning crazily over the deck. The foremast had snapped about halfway along its length. The splintered top section, still tethered by its rigging and with the shredded staysail flapping madly, swayed back and forth, threatening further disaster. Granger had her back under control and she was making way downwind again. Fisk, dabbing his bare hand on a nasty cut above his eye, clambered across the deck to the helm. The two helmsmen had been thrown into the scuppers, but were none the worse for it. La Salle ordered a head count. No one had gone over the side. He murmured quiet thanks for that.

Fisk collected a work party to deal with the shattered

mast. Granger took charge of them and climbed to the damaged area with a saw to free the top part of the spar. They soon had it lowered and lashed to the side deck. One of the boats had shifted and a few planks had been stoved in, but otherwise there was no damage on deck. The constructions around the guns had escaped unscathed, a credit La Salle thought, to Sitters and his men.

They had sight of the Lizard by mid-morning. Fisk took a running fix off the light and they set a course to clear The Manacles. The sky had cleared and the wind was down to a fresh breeze. *Freya* was scudding along with her main and mizzen set, making good speed towards Falmouth. Despite the change in the weather, La Salle knew he had to put in there now to repair the foremast. It was an inauspicious start to their mission, but as Granger swiftly reminded him when he mourned the loss of time, it could have been a whole lot worse.

They brought her on to a buoy under motor and Fisk took the undamaged tender ashore to the harbourmaster's office. *Freya's* papers showed she was carrying a cargo of timber from Milford Haven to Morlaix. Nothing about her should arouse suspicion, La Salle thought. Indeed, the harbour was full of ships taking refuge from the weather and some, with bent stanchions, crushed boats and broken portlights seemed to have had difficulties of their own.

Granger applied himself to the problem of the broken mast and it quickly became apparent that as well as being a first class engineer, he had considerable skill as a shipwright and carpenter. The bottom part of the mast could be saved, he said, and the topmast was undamaged. But a long section of the main spar would have to be replaced. Where, La Salle asked no one in particular, were they going to find a forty foot length of timber to accomplish that? Fisk's inquiries ashore yielded a scathing response. *Didn't he know there was a war on?* Stocks of good boatbuilding timber were either exhausted or had been sold to the admiralty for a good price. La Salle did not want to fall back on the navy, or even involve the service. His orders were clear: assume and maintain his disguise. He had purser funds and if, as seemed likely, Granger and the crew could do the work it should not take long. But he needed a new mast.

'A decent pine log would do it,' Granger said.

That triggered something in La Salle's memory. A few years ago, when they brought the telephone to Combe Hall, a number of pine trees had been cut down to make poles for the wire. He seemed to remember they had not all been used.

'I have to go ashore,' he told Higgins.

Granger accompanied him and they left the jolly boat crew at the steps on the quay. In the town they found a hotel willing to give him use of the telephone. He was put through to Lord Burnage quickly and he explained what he needed and why. Burnage listened carefully. The afternoon newspapers were full of reports of shipwreck and casualties in what was being described as the worst summer storm in living memory. Burnage congratulated La Salle on coming through it with nothing worse than a sprung foremast. He made no attempt to hide the pride in his voice. Burnage said he believed several pines had been left over from the telephone installation. They had been stacked and left to season. He said he would instruct the agent.

La Salle arranged with the hotel to handle messages for him and he and Granger returned to the jolly boat. The breeze was still fresh, but it favoured them as *Freya's* men laid on their pull across the harbour. The little boat flew across the water and as they neared the ship on her buoy, La Salle marvelled again at her lovely lines and attractive presence on the water, despite the ugly stump of foremast. Granger seemed to read his thoughts.

'Pretty, ain't she?' he said.

La Salle spoke without taking his eyes off his ship.

'Yes,' he replied, 'and there is something distressingly perverse in creating such a thing, with art and skill, then corrupting it to a vile purpose.'

Granger fell silent for a moment.

'Seems like the vileness has been inflicted on us by others,' he said at last.

'Yes, that's true,' his friend said. 'And I suppose you could argue that *Freya* is not a poisonous thing, but an antidote to poison.'

He slipped his hand into his jacket pocket, felt for his notebook and pencil. He caught Granger's eye. The other had turned down the corners of his mouth. Granger shook his head slowly. La Salle understood. He withdrew his hand from his jacket, left the notebook where it was. They simultaneously burst into laughter.

Higgins suggested the crew might like a run ashore. It could be done in two shifts, he said, so as not to arouse suspicions about the size of *Freya's* complement. La Salle readily agreed. Once their repair was complete there would be scant opportunity for jollies.

Higgins took the first boat and went ashore with a half dozen men. He left them at the waterfront and walked up the hill into the main street, turned into an alley and entered a tavern he remembered from some previous visit. He ordered a pint of bitter and carried it to a small table. He took a deep draught, set down the glass and stared at it intently. So La Salle was using his fancy connections to get a mast. He overheard him discussing with Granger a plan for doing the repair if, as he hoped, they could get the timber from his guardian's estate. Higgins swallowed another mouthful of beer. Estate! Nearly a quarter of a century in the service, to be outranked by a ... a popinjay. Higgins' face began working, the muscles in his cheeks twitched and his mouth took on a silent snarl. Him and Granger. No time for anyone else, locked in their little world of chess and talk. Even Fisk left them alone to their late-night discussions. What about? Bloody poetry! Omar Khayam and all that bollocks. What was that one Granger was always going on about? Whiteman? Whitman? Who'd ever heard of him? Couple of schoolboys, they were, playing at sailors. Taking jobs that belonged to better men. He emptied his glass and went to the counter. The girl went down to the cellar to draw off another pint when an unfamiliar voice seemed to address him. He turned to see three young men waiting to be served.

'Hi,' one of them said. 'Didn't I see you on that little sailing ship out there? Busted mast?'

Higgins sniffed. The man sounded like an American.

'I'm the mate,' he said, rather pleased with his easy mastery of the deception.

'Pleased to meet you,' the American said. He introduced himself and his shipmates. Swann was his name. They were in a US-owned freighter and were awaiting orders after unloading. Higgins accompanied them to a table when their drinks came up and Swann's face took on a quizzical expression.

'You know, Fred, I'm glad I've met you. When we came past your ship in the tender I saw a guy on your deck I thought I recognised. It was a while ago now, but then I remembered. Olsen. Merrick Olsen. Helluva good guy. Well, until he got himself into trouble, anyway.'

Higgins became suddenly alert. *Merrick Olsen*? Had Granger changed his name?

'What trouble?' he asked.

Swann shook his head. 'I don't know, Fred. It was a bad business.'

'I'm the mate. I have to know if any of my crew have secrets.'

'Well, it was almost a year ago now, in New York. Olsen went ashore with a couple of guys from the ship and, well, you know. They kind of got into some heavy drinking, or so we heard.' Swann sipped his beer.

Higgins leaned forward, listening.

'Then it seems they go to this place in Harlem.' Swann paused. 'One of those clubs. You know?'

Higgins did not know.

'A sissies club,' Swann said flatly. 'Anyway. They picked the wrong night. The cops raided the place and Olsen was arrested. With a guy.'

'I see,' Higgins said, with evident satisfaction.

'He got six months in the penitentiary. We all said that whatever he'd been up to couldn't have been that bad because you can get five years for a crime against nature in New York. Anyway. He went to jail and disappeared. Now he's on your ship.' Swann drained his glass. 'You know what, Fred? I think I'd feel funny about seeing him again. Don't tell him you've met me. OK?'

Higgins nodded. He had already decided that the information with which he was now equipped would require careful management.

'Let's have another drink,' he said cheerfully.

Late the following day, a forty-five foot long pine log arrived at the waterfront on a motor lorry and trailer. Fisk found a bargemaster who agreed to bring the log out to *Freya* on his deck and use his sprit to hoist it aboard and then raise it on the foremast stump. Granger had prepared a long scarph joint on the remaining length of spar and he made a number of steel bands to clamp and bolt the two pieces together. It took nearly two days to cut, plane and drill the new length of spar and Granger rubbed in two coats of Stockholm Tar, mixed with a little linseed oil, before they dressed it. Most of the old rigging was useable and the new piece, lifted into place on the barge sprit, fitted perfectly. The topmast went on and Granger eyed up the new mast from the deck, calling for alterations in rigging tension at the deadeyes as he went. At the end of their fourth day in Falmouth, *Freya* was declared ready for sea. Higgins asked if La Salle intended to sail first thing in the morning.

'No,' came the reply. 'We'll go on tonight's tide.'

CHAPTER SEVEN

The long dark outline of a cruiser crossed ahead as *Freya* sailed south. La Salle watched as the warship steamed down Channel, following the lane swept clear of mines. There was a confident purposefulness in the cruiser's swift progress he found reassuring. The threat from mines laid by German U-boats haunted him and the sight of a great ship trusting the efforts of the minesweeping trawlers was heartening. He and Fisk had worked out a course to take them through the channels declared safe, but the German UC class minelaying submarines had been assiduous in their efforts to make Britain's home waters unnavigable. Royal Navy men called the Channel minefield "The Rose Garden". La Salle liked the name. It said a lot about the courage of the men who steamed into it, not knowing whether there was a deadly surprise in their path. In many ways, he thought, the Germans deserved to win the war at sea, if only for the thoroughness of their preparations. In the years before hostilities began the British Admiralty dismissed submarines as fanciful contraptions, too small and with insufficient endurance to be effective. Even the men who served in them were looked down upon. Submariners were said to follow "The Trade", and more than most they felt the keen edge of the service's enduring snobbery. The Kaiser's Kriegsmarine and its Austrian counterpart had no such reservations about fighting from below the sea. Between them they assembled a sizeable fleet of U-boats, designed and engineered to a level that surpassed anything being built in the British yards. It was the same with mines, La Salle thought. The German Hertz horn mine was a device of great cunning, unmatched by anything in the Royal Navy's arsenal. Its anchor held it to a pre-set depth, tethered to the bottom. It lay in silent wait, just below the surface, and if a passing vessel struck one of the glass horns protruding from its casing it was detonated instantly. La Salle suppressed a shudder. *Freya's* comparatively shallow draught might carry her over most moored mines, but not all of them held the depth to which they were set. Some floated free, the most terrifying prospect of all. Yet the sight of a warty black sphere on the surface was not uncommon. La Salle thought of the awful, tingling dread that could seize one in the middle of a black night. The mind's eye roved over the sea ahead and saw a bobbing shape. Every muscle tensed at the thought of the explosion, rushing water, screams of men and a lost ship and her crew. The darkest nights fired the imagination and more than once La Salle had started from a half-sleep convinced he had been blundering through a minefield. Sometimes the sensation of being on the brink of catastrophe became a belief he was walking along a clifftop, blindfolded. German mines, now being copied by the admiralty, had already inflicted massive losses. Some ships had simply disappeared, a fate that struck La Salle as especially cruel. There was something in volunteering to fight for one's country that begged for recognition. In the trenches, he thought moodily, men at least went to their death in full view of their comrades who were witnesses to their heroism. Sliding out of sight forever, unseen, unexplained, seemed unfair. To be sunk by a mine was the most dud of all dud shows, La Salle thought.

'Let it not happen to us,' he murmured into the darkness.

'What?'

Higgins had crossed unnoticed to his side of the deck.

'Oh, nothing.' La Salle turned to face him. 'Did Greene get the signal away?'

He had asked for a short signal to be sent to

Queenstown reporting their forced stop for repairs. They expected to begin the patrol off Ushant before noon the next day.

'All gone,' Higgins said. 'Confirmation, no reply.'

La Salle looked out to sea. The breeze, now in the east, favoured them and they were making six knots with all sail set. The new foremast was standing well and La Salle guessed that if *Freya* had not been so weighed down in the bow and on deck she would be giving an even more creditable account of herself. No matter. He and Granger had decided she needed permanent ballast in the after end of the hold to restore her stability. At the end of the patrol they would shift some of the rail sleepers and put in twenty tons of iron pigs as low down as they could get them. *We should have done it before we sailed*, La Salle thought. He wondered whether Commander Campbell would have insisted on redressing *Freya's* ballast deficit. *Probably*, he thought, with a jolt of self-doubt.

'Eight bells,' Higgins said. 'Mr Fisk's watch.'

La Salle felt a flicker of annoyance. He had asked Higgins to drop naval terms. The crews of small merchant vessels like *Freya* operated without formality and La Salle had stressed the importance of outwardly appearing rather slack and relaxed. During their sailing trials Higgins had persisted in speaking of shackles of anchor chain, in the navy manner, rather than fathoms, as was the custom aboard merchant ships. La Salle had gently suggested their disguise was their prime weapon and it should be all-embracing, even to the extent of abandoning the language of the service. It seemed to him then that Higgins had accepted the point.

'Eight bells,' Higgins intoned again.

'Let's not forget we're supposed to be an easygoing merchant ship,' La Salle said, smiling.

Higgins' face twisted into a mask of wonderment. He put a hand to his ear mockingly.

'I'd be surprised if the U-boats could hear me,' he said.

La Salle turned to face him. There was something about Higgins' demeanour he had not previously remarked. The man was bumped up.

'I can hear you,' La Salle said icily and turned back to the ocean.

A few men from Fisk's watch came up, discreetly changing into the coats and sweaters of those going below, a measure La Salle considered necessary because even at night, they had to give every indication of being a shorthanded coasting vessel. The main duty was to keep a lookout. La Salle followed the same strict procedure as Commander Campbell with a man posted on each side of the ship with a field of view from the bow to the stern. Anything that even looked like the periscope of a submarine was to be reported immediately. They had frequent false alarms, but they were not allowed to let that deter them. Orders were clear: everything had to be relayed back to the officer of the watch. The lookout duty was conducted carefully. Each spell lasted no more than an hour and when a man was relieved he and his relief spent at least several minutes surveying the same stretch of ocean together to make sure there was no interruption in their scrutiny.

The breeze dropped just before dawn and *Freya's* progress slowed. La Salle was below taking a breakfast of toast and coffee with Granger when the lookout's cry signalled land in sight. A warm haze reduced visibility but a long dark shape, almost like low cloud, lay ahead. La Salle thought he could see the slim needle of the Ile Vierge lighthouse, marking the corner of Finistère and the meeting of the Channel and the Atlantic.

'Tallest lighthouse in the world, they say,' he said, handing his binoculars to Granger who had joined him on deck. 'Nearly 300 feet, according to the pilot book.'

Granger took a long look.

'Where is Ushant?' he asked.

'It's there,' La Salle replied. 'We won't see it until it stands out from the land behind. It has some impressive lights, too.' He took back the glasses and studied the land ahead. 'Need those lights. In these waters.'

Granger leaned on the capping rail and took a deep breath of warm, pure air. The swell was little more than a rhythmic ripple, the sea a deep cobalt, the surface glittering in the sun.

'Looks pretty now,' he said.

La Salle laughed. 'In a gale of wind it's a devil's cauldron. The stories the oldtimers tell about this coast are enough to make you want to swallow the anchor.'

'Sure, it's a big headland. But what makes it so bad?' Granger asked, not unreasonably.

La Salle swept his arm from the Ile Vierge to the indistinct haze to the south.

'Reefs,' he said. 'Reefs, ledges, islets and lots of rocks in between.' He turned to face Granger. 'Then, there are the tides, the tidal streams and the currents. A vessel can find itself making six knots over the ground, carried by the stream.' A thought struck him: 'Would our motor be any good if we were becalmed in a tidal stream like that?

Granger rubbed his chin.

'It would probably gives us steerage way.'

La Salle considered Granger's reply.

'Well, on a big spring tide the set among the reefs is very strong. Luckily, you'd be unlikely to find a U-boat in among the worst bits between the island and the coast. We'll make our patrol outside Ushant, following the coast around towards Morlaix. There's another island to the south, Ile de Sein. From the intelligence reports it seems our U-boat captain operates between there and north of Ushant, the most commonly used sea lane.' La Salle looked at his watch. 'We'll have a briefing in the wardroom … er, saloon, in fifteen minutes.'

He went below, slightly annoyed with himself for using the naval term for the officers' mess. Although, he reasoned, that was a slip. With Higgins there seemed to be a determination to make a point. Indeed, La Salle thought he perceived a change in the senior lieutenant. He had noticed, more than once, that Higgins tended to observe him. If their eyes met Higgins would quickly turn away, yet La Salle was left with an impression the man was looking for something, trying to seek out an answer to a puzzle he couldn't quite fathom. Their relations had been cordial enough and Higgins was a good officer. His efforts during the period of fitting out had been valuable. But a persistent feeling nagged at La Salle. Something had changed. It seemed to date from around the time they stepped the new mast. Higgins, never a cheerful man, had become sullen and, in his remarks, rather contemptuous. Granger seemed to be a frequent target. La Salle thought he overheard Higgins, in a discussion with Edwards, the gunlayer, refer to Granger as "Jane". Nicknames were common aboard ships, but they were usually confined to exchanges between men of equal or near-equal rank. And, La Salle wondered, what was "Jane" all about?

He walked through the narrow passage between his cabin and the saloon to find Higgins, Fisk and Granger waiting for him. He gathered them around the chart.

'As you know, gentlemen,' he began, 'we have had reports of a U-boat operating in this area.' He made a sweep with his hand, outside Ushant around the jutting corner of Finistère.

'The intelligence suggests he is a clever cove. He's been spotted from the air, but he always manages to get away. He has already sunk a lot of tonnage and seems intent on sinking a lot more.' La Salle paused. 'We, of course, must have no contact with the French navy. Our mission, as always, is a secret one. To the French, or any

British warship in these waters, we are what we seem to be, a sailing vessel in the Channel trade.'

Fisk nodded, as did Granger. Higgins continued to stare at the chart.

La Salle resumed. 'Our U-boat is probably out of the Zeebrugge flotilla and he seems to be fuelled and armed for a long patrol. One of his tricks is to stop French fishing boats to obtain fresh food, wine and fish. This suggests he intends to stay on station for some time.' He looked up and smiled. 'As do we.'

'What is his method of attack?' Fisk asked.

'So far he has torpedoed a 2,000 ton ship ...' La Salle pointed to a spot around twenty miles offshore. 'About here. But he has engaged smaller ships with his gun.' He glanced at them in turn. 'He has tended to fire a disabling shot as a way of introducing himself. No warning. Then he takes the ship's papers and sinks her.' He added darkly: 'My brief says more than a dozen casualties, so far.'

'Dead?' Fisk asked. La Salle nodded.

'What flag do we fly?' Granger asked.

'We stay with our Danish colours.'

'Had you worried, did it?' Higgins interjected, towards Granger. 'Did you think we'd be abusing the great American flag?'

'No flag is safe in these waters,' La Salle said. 'We show false colours because that is the nature of our work. When the time comes, as you gentlemen know, the white ensign will be raised.'

The briefing ended and Chalky brought tea. La Salle couldn't help noticing he seemed unusually out of temper.

'All well?' he asked as he took his cup.

'Yes, sir. That is to say, well, sir. Briggs is out of order. Fair gives me the fantals.'

La Salle made a face. 'What?'

'Briggs says Marie Lloyd was born in Lambeth. I know

166

it's not true, sir. She's out of Hoxton like me, bless her. He keeps going on about it. Drives me mad, sir.'

La Salle frowned. 'Hoxton and Lambeth are not that far apart, are they? I mean, in a city like London?'

Chalky gave him a horrified look.

'Lambeth,' he hissed, 'is south of the river!'

'Oh,' La Salle said. 'I see.'

The breeze filled in from the south west towards noon and *Freya*, all her canvas set, shaped a course for the north coast of Brittany. The tide turned as she approached the rocky corner of the land and despite making a good seven knots through the water, Fisk reported her progress at little more than four knots over the ground. Fine, La Salle said. They were in no hurry. Once they had cleared the northwest tip of the coast they would sail on towards Morlaix and then wear ship on to a reciprocal course. Greene sent a wireless signal to Queenstown reporting they had taken up station and a coded reply, wishing them good hunting, came back.

The day slipped by, night fell and the tide reversed its flow, hastening *Freya* towards the east. When she turned back on her course, close-hauled now with the wind and tidal stream both against her, she seemed to creep past the faraway dark shapes and lights ashore.

La Salle ordered double lookouts. The men on each side were joined by one in the bow and one at the stern. The weather was settled and there was little work to be done on the rig. *Freya* practically sailed herself as she polished Cape Finistère, back and forth, tide after tide.

After three days in French waters they had seen only a few fishing vessels, one large steamer and a few coasters, plying much the same route as *Freya*. The breeze died on the third night as the temperature climbed steadily. The day was uncomfortably hot and *Freya* wallowed in the swell, her sails slatting and deck rolling. La Salle ordered the fore and mizzen sails to be lowered to save the canvas from the constant chafe. They held on to the jib and tried to keep it full with the zephyrs created by her own slow progress on a favourable tide.

Granger raised the possibility of using the motor, but La Salle decided against it because *Freya's* reserve of fuel was not large and the prospect of a long patrol seemed more likely than ever. The Bolinder had been fitted with a dynamo to charge the batteries for the Marconi set and La Salle was unwilling to use precious fuel heading for a destination they did not even care to reach.

'With a cargo of wood a ship like this would probably wait for a breeze,' he said. 'Nothing unusual in it.'

So they rocked and dipped gently on a smooth sea, the watch below cursing the heat in the forecastle and the men on deck watching for a flicker of movement on the swell, a catspaw to signal the first sign of a coming breeze.

Granger found La Salle at the binnacle where the helmsman had reported an unusual stiffness in the steering.

'What do you think, Merrick?' La Salle said, pointing at the helm. 'Seems heavy.'

Granger took over the wheel and tried to turn the spokes back and forth, at first gently and then, when the wheel refused to move, with a tug in each direction.

'Something wrong,' he said. 'I need to get down into the lazarette.'

They lowered the sails and allowed her to drift as Granger took a bag of tools and a lamp below into the space under the after deck, above the rudder. He felt his way along the linkages until he reached the quadrant, the steel forging at the rudder head which took the turning force from the helm. When he reached the joint at the rudder arm the lamp revealed small pieces of bronze lying on the hull planking across the arc taken by the end of the steering arm. The bushing in the joint had disintegrated and the link was seizing up. Granger felt the bolt holding the linkage together. It was secure, but grinding against the steel around it. He muttered to himself, about the night in the western approaches, the battering *Freya* had taken and the shocks the steering had suffered. But mostly, as he crawled out of the lazarette towards the trap-hatch in the deck, he cursed himself quietly for not replacing this most crucial link in the steering chain when the ship was safely tied up alongside on Haulbowline Island.

'We are going to have to lash the rudder,' he said, reaching the binnacle. Then, turning to La Salle. 'I'm sorry. The darn linkage is shot.'

Higgins inclined his head.

'Shot?' he said. 'Shot? Have we been attacked then, without me noticing?'

Granger faced him. 'I mean there's a part I need to replace. We'll have to lash the rudder. And there'll be no steering for a few hours.'

'No steering!' Higgins coloured. 'No steering! We've spent less than a week at sea and we've no steering!' Higgins pointed at Granger's chest. 'That's your responsibility. You have let this ship go into action with faulty steering. Now we're a sitting duck!' He turned to La Salle. 'This requires a report. Dereliction.'

La Salle smiled. 'I hear every word you say,' he said quietly. Then: 'We shall lash the helm and heave-to until the steering is repaired.' He turned to Granger. 'Are you confident you can mend it?'

'I can fix it,' Granger replied, staring at the deck.

'So we are going to disable the vessel while in pursuit of the enemy!' Higgins spluttered. 'Reckless! That's what it is. Reckless and … foolhardy.' He wiped the back of his hand across his mouth. 'Or worse.'

'Worse?' La Salle said.

'We are on active service,' Higgins said.

'I know it is part of your duty to remind me about

things I may have forgotten, Mr Mate, but I'm beginning to find your assistance irksome.'

Out of the corner of his eye La Salle saw the helmsman, holding the wheel to weather, grinning. Two men in the waist were watching the small group at the helm. La Salle lowered his voice: 'We shall heave to and repair the steering and I want no more discussion on the matter.'

He went below, disturbed by the fact he was shaking slightly. Chalky seemed unusually subdued when he brought tea, offering neither his personal prophecy for the weather or a grouse about Briggs. La Salle interpreted this as confirmation the exchanges on deck had been instantly relayed around the ship.

Fisk took over the deck and Higgins disappeared into his cabin. La Salle went up and stood on the windward side. He watched as a shoal of sardines weaved at great speed close to the surface, pursued by some unseen predator. The fish made the sea boil as they turned and leaped as if joined together in one glittering mass. He turned inboard. Granger was climbing into the lazarette with the lamp, holding a metal part La Salle could not identify. Granger had not spoken since the business with Higgins. He had worked on drilling and reaming a new bronze bush at his tiny bench in the forepeak, disturbed only by Chalky who had taken him coffee and sandwiches made with freshly baked bread. Briggs, at Chalky's suggestion, also made Granger a small tart of tinned plums and Barbados sugar.

La Salle felt a pang of regret as Granger's head vanished below deck. It was unfortunate that an engineering weakness had manifested itself so early in the patrol. But Higgins had ridden him too hard. Things break down. Yet Higgins seemed determined to hammer him. Why? It was clear something was gnawing away at Higgins. Jealousy? There was something in his animus-laden stare that spoke of it, but he could not be jealous of Granger, the lowliest

170

officer in the ship. La Salle tapped the capping on *Freya's* bulwark, trying to clear his thoughts. Granger had become his friend; they spent time in each other's company. They shared an easygoing intimacy. Was this a mistake? Of course it was! With a dispiriting lurch of guilt he realised he had allowed his friend to become a target of Higgins' venom, simply through a failure to disguise their friendship aboard ship. Granger had travelled 3,000 miles to volunteer for the war and had already escaped disaster. He deserved better, La Salle thought.

The watch changed again, the lookouts reported nothing of interest and the day wore on. Granger emerged from the lazarette to get a blowlamp, then disappeared again. Fisk had the deck when he climbed out of the hatch at last.

'I'll just feel the helm,' Granger said, loosening the lashing. The wheel spun between his hands. 'That ought to do it,' he said.

Fisk put *Freya* back on course, although the sea breeze that had been blowing towards the land had begun to falter. Granger went below and reported the steering in good working order. *Freya* crept towards Cape Finistère during the darkness. The tidal stream carried her around its bulk but she was barely making steerage way when La Salle came up shortly after daybreak.

'Anything?' he asked.

'Not a thing,' Fisk replied. 'A few fishing boats during the night. No ships and no U-boat.'

La Salle nodded and turned to the helmsman.

'How does the steering feel?'

'Very smooth. Very light,' the man replied.

'Good. Mr Granger knows his business.'

At that moment Higgins appeared at the top of the companion. His face revealed only too clearly that he had heard what La Salle said.

'My watch below,' Fisk said, giving them both a strange look as he left the deck.

La Salle nodded to Higgins. 'Good morning, Mr Mate,' he said pleasantly.

Higgins grunted a reply and checked the course over the helmsman's shoulder. He straightened, put his hands behind his back and walked to the windward side of the deck. La Salle glanced aloft. The sails were drawing in the first of a light breeze and the ship was beginning to make way. He crossed to the companionway and went below. Fisk had turned in but Granger was in the saloon with Chalky.

'Some coffee?' La Salle asked.

'I was just explaining to Mr Granger,' Chalky said, 'about Marie Lloyd.'

He sniffed, adding a touch witheringly: 'He's never heard of her. Fair to say, there's some as finds her numbers a little bit on the naughty side. Can't say I see any harm in it myself.' He leaned back, stared at some imagined object in the heavens, placed a hand on his chest and sang: 'Oh, Mr Porter what shall I do …'

'Chalky. Some coffee please?'

Chalky assumed an expression of having been deeply offended.

'All right. All right,' he muttered. He chucked his Good Joss teddy bear under the chin, as if it alone understood, and stalked off to the galley. They could hear him resuming his song as he went.

'Did you ever find out what he did on the *Titanic*?' Granger asked.

La Salle raised his eyebrows: 'Lookout, probably.'

There was a burst of boyish laughter. La Salle moved over to the chart desk. He picked up a pencil and moved the blunt end across the paper, tracing their course.

'I remember when I first joined *Farnham*,' he said. 'The first few patrols were an agony of boredom. When you first sail you think a U-boat is going to pop up right away. That's what you're there for, after all. Then day after day, crossing the same bit of ocean, seeing nothing.' He looked at Granger. 'I hope this won't be one of those dud outings, Merrick.'

'Seems to me we've only just started,' Granger said.

'I know.' La Salle crossed to the table and sat down. His voice became a whisper. 'It's just that I feel this tremendous burden of expectation. Promotion, getting this ship. If I can't show anything in return I'll feel like a fraud.'

Granger stared hard at his cup. He seemed about to speak when Chalky entered with a pot of coffee. He was humming softly, a touch defiantly.

'Will you be taking breakfast?' he asked, putting a mug on the table.

'Yes, please.' La Salle poured himself coffee, raised the pot towards Granger inquiringly. Granger advanced his own mug for a refill. They sat together in silence, each with his own thoughts.

Greene, the wireless operator, put his head around the saloon door.

'*SOS*!' He pushed a piece of paper towards La Salle, unsure whether he was allowed into the saloon.

'Come in, man!'

Greene entered, extending his hand with a slip of paper in it. La Salle took it, glanced at the pencilled words and figures and dashed to the chart table.

'Steamship. U-boat attack. Just about …' he traced a finger down and then horizontally across the chart '…here.' He tracked the dividers to the spot.

'About twelve miles.' He eyed Granger. 'Twelve miles. No breeze. How long if we motor?'

'Couple of hours, maybe.'

'Right. Let's get her steaming.'

La Salle hurried to the deck and quickly briefed Higgins: Dutch ship attacked by a submarine off Cape Finistère. Crew abandoning. No further message. Position given close to *Freya's* usual route. La Salle reasoned they would not be suspected of having a radio if they steamed in the sea lane and appeared to come upon the scene by chance.

Freya picked up speed as her engine powered her over the swell. The day was already hot and the breeze had died to nothing. They lowered her sails, leaving the reefed mizzen to steady her. The sky was clear, a limpid blue but the heat haze restricted visibility to a few miles. La Salle had Fisk roused from his cabin. The tidal stream was running in their favour and Fisk made some calculations. He reckoned it would take less than two hours to reach the stricken ship's position. Roberts and the gunlayers brought up twenty rounds apiece for the twelve pounders. There was no room to store shells in the enclosures around the guns and, in any case, if they had not accomplished their task in twenty rounds, a lack of ammunition was unlikely to be their biggest problem.

The men worked in silence, each with his own thoughts. Roberts checked both guns, elevation and traverse. He exchanged a few words with Edwards, in command of the forward gun, and they both went towards the bow. La Salle saw them open the locker covering the Maxim gun. They raised it slightly, easing it up on its steel frame, but did not expose it. They closed the locker lid.

'Guns ready,' Roberts said, reaching the after deck.

La Salle nodded. Roberts walked over to the main hatch and sat next to Edwards, lighting a cigarette. La Salle watched them discreetly. The Welshmen were friends, enthusiastic smokers who enjoyed the freedom to light up on deck, one of the benefits of mystery ship duty and its pretence of lax discipline. If there was action to come, much would depend on the skill and coolness of those two, La Salle thought. He had no anxieties about them. Indeed, he felt he owed Roberts a debt he could never repay, or even acknowledge. Roberts's sinking of the U-boat aboard *Farnham* had created his own success.

The inevitable guilt stirred briefly. At least he had made sure Roberts and his men had been properly rewarded. All had been decorated.

La Salle went forward and was training his binoculars on the sea ahead when he had an impression *Freya* was falling back. He glanced over the side. She was gliding more and more slowly through the water. The distant throb of the Bolinder had stopped. Granger was already in the engine room when he reached the binnacle. Fisk gave him a look of mystified exasperation. Higgins stood near the helmsman, arms folded. His face wore an insolent half-smile. La Salle said nothing. He glanced at his watch. Granger appeared, rubbing his hands with a rag.

'Seems like a blockage,' he said. 'I'll have to take the fuel lines apart.'

No one spoke. La Salle nodded, then Higgins took a step towards them.

'What?' he said, his voice excited to a high-pitched whine. 'I seem to remember you spent a lot of the navy's money replacing all that.'

'Shut up about the navy,' La Salle said quietly.

'I will not shut up!' Higgins moved to within a few feet of Granger who continued to rub his hands slowly, watching him. Higgins pointed a finger, trembling slightly. 'Yet again this man's incompetence has brought the ship to a standstill. Why was he given a job he can't do? Why?'

'That's enough, Mr Mate,' La Salle said. Heads had begun to appear at the top of the forecastle companion.

'I'll say it's enough! This man was given a commission, but nobody mentioned his past, did they?'

Granger had stopped wiping his hands and had rolled the rag into a tight ball in his right fist.

'Whatever it is you're talking about will not be discussed here,' La Salle hissed.

'Well it should be discussed,' Higgins went on, shrilly. 'Because he has put the ship in danger. Again.' He paused.

'I have information about this man.' He pointed at Granger
– 'He is not only a –' he groped for a word ' – Uranian …
he's served time for it!'

La Salle resisted an impulse to turn towards Granger.
What was Higgins talking about? Uranian?

'Mr Mate, if you will, please.' He held out an arm, inviting
Higgins to join him at the rail on the starboard quarter. La
Salle's face wore a pleasant, almost smiling expression as
he spoke, out of the hearing of the others on deck.

'You and I will talk when we have dealt with the SOS,'
he said, growling out the words viciously. 'Until then I
want no more of this! Is that clear?'

Higgins made as if to speak, La Salle cut him off.

'You heard me. Shut up!'

Higgins sneered his assent and walked towards the
companionway. La Salle glanced aloft, a mechanical
impulse driven by a sudden craving for normality. The
mizzen, still set to steady her, bellied back and forth on
the swell. The air was eerily still. La Salle had rarely felt so
desolate. He seemed to feel the old gnawing of childhood
insecurity, a profound loneliness. Granger remained in his
place on the deck, his tanned face a murky beige. He had
unfolded the rag. It hung limp in his hand. La Salle walked
back to the binnacle.

'Mr Granger. I'd be obliged if you'd get the ship
steaming again. As soon as possible, please.'

Granger looked up. La Salle couldn't bear to hold his
gaze. His eyes were dark.

'Yes,' Granger said. He walked to the hatch and
disappeared below. Fisk had brought his sextant on deck
and was taking a sun sight.

'When Mr Granger gets the motor working again,' La
Salle said, 'We shall carry on towards the position given
by the Dutch ship.'

Fisk murmured something to acknowledge the order.
La Salle crossed to the bulwark and trained his binoculars

on an empty ocean, swung around to the land and just stared, thinking. What was Higgins talking about? Uranian? La Salle was not sure but he thought that was what homosexuals called each other. Had Granger been imprisoned for homosexuality? They had never discussed sex, a subject La Salle found hard to reconcile with his fastidious nature. He may have conveyed some of his admiration for Miss Vaizey during a conversation about the effort to help victims of the *Lusitania*, but that was all. An unwelcome thought occurred. If there were a problem in Granger's past it would reflect on him. That's why Higgins had made the allegations against Granger so others could hear. He wanted it talked about, deplored so that when *Freya* made her next patrol he, Higgins, the passed-over officer, would at last be in command. La Salle thought of Lord Burnage, Miss Vaizey. The admiral. What would they make of him now? After all, what did he really know about Granger? He had found much to admire the American for, his heroism apart. Yet their friendship was based on little more than a feeling of enjoying each other's company, a sense of oneness. *Hang it all*, he thought. *Wasn't all friendship like that?* He let the glasses fall on their lanyard and shook his head to try to clear it of a sense of shame. To try to rationalise his feelings for Granger now, to try to find a justification for liking the man seemed an act of betrayal. Whatever difficulty there was, if it presented a problem they would face it together. And despite what Higgins said, Granger was still the same man he knew and had come to think of in a sense of brotherliness. They would see Higgins off.

He turned his back to the sea. Tried to blank his mind. *Freya* was still lolling on the long swell. The lookouts were in their places, a couple of men were putting a coat of paint on the whaler. Fisk was talking to the helmsman. There was no sign of Higgins. That, at least, was a blessing.

Chalky was in the saloon when Higgins stalked in. He

177

made straight for the chart and glowered at it. Chalky moved sideways, trying to reach the door.

Higgins rounded on him.

'You and Briggs want to be careful who you're so pally with,' he said. Then in a dangerous voice: 'I'm watching everyone in this ship.'

Chalky made his most impudent face and moved to open the door. Higgins stared at him, then pointed at his toy bear tied to the grabrail.

'Good luck, is it?' Higgins spat, pulling his folding knife from a pocket. He drew the blade hard across the bear's throat.

Chalky started forward, then stopped. A trickle of sawdust ran down the bear's front. Then its head flopped over its chest, conveying a ghastly sense of lifelessness. Higgins folded his knife, pocketed it and pushed past Chalky to the door.

The Londoner watched him go, then addressed the bear in a calm voice: 'I'd say he's just earned himself some very Bad Joss, wouldn't you, Teddy?' He walked out of the saloon, to get his ditty bag and sewing kit.

It was stinking hot in the engine space. Granger stripped off his shirt, tied his electric lantern to a beam and rifled through a box of spanners. He found one to fit the nipple at the end of the fuel line, loosened it carefully and held a rag under the free end to catch the spurt of diesel. There wasn't one. He leaned forward, put the pipe in his mouth and sucked hard. Nothing. He could draw nothing through the fuel line, even sucking until his cheeks ached. Granger wiped his mouth with the rag, straightened and moved aft to the tank. He selected another spanner and quickly undid the nuts holding the removeable plate he'd asked them to fit at the dockyard. He plunged his bare arm into the diesel and felt for the fuel intake. His fingers closed on a gritty sludge. He took a pinchful and held it under the battery light. *Goddam*. It looked like mud.

Granger rocked back on his heels. The tank was in new condition when they sailed. He had scrupulously cleaned it himself and the new top fitted at the dockyard was fine; not a trace of rust. He lowered his arm into the diesel again, took a good handful of the muck at the bottom then sieved it through the rag. It was mud. Had they taken on contaminated fuel? Granger took some more cloth from his small sack of rags and slowly wiped the diesel from his bare arm. He thought carefully. The filler on the bunkering barge had a filter on it. He was sure of it. So whatever that was at the bottom of the tank got there after they took on fuel. He whistled softly. *Sabotage.* Someone had tried to wreck the motor. Granger felt a prickling sensation on his arm. The diesel was irritating his skin. He sat on one of the engine bearers, leaned against the bulkhead, rubbing absently at his skin with a clean rag. *Sabotage.* He moved to get up. He would have to tell Julian and – he sank back against the bulkhead, paralysed by a single, appalling thought. What if it were Higgins? What if Higgins had sabotaged the motor, as part of his evident campaign to discredit and dislodge Julian? Granger's thoughts ran riot in his head. Was it possible? Certainly, Higgins had opportunity. And, yes, he was probably crazy enough. Yet how could he voice these suspicions to Julian? Granger saw it all too clearly. He, Granger, was the conduit for Higgins's mad jealousy. If Julian became aware that Higgins was a possible threat to the ship how did that leave him, Granger?

He took some more rag, wiped at the sweat on his neck and shoulders. Of course, Julian would have to view him, Granger, as part of that threat. And now he knew his past. A bubble of anger rose in his throat. He had come within an ace of striking Higgins. It would have been so easy to smash his fist into that ugly, curled mouth and silence it. Only thought for his friend stopped him. He could not do that to Julian. They were on active service.

He could not blight Julian's first command with an affair that might end with a court martial, even a firing squad. He tied the rag around his head to stop the sweat stinging his eyes. He would have to get the engine going somehow. It meant decanting the fuel into tins, filtering it and cleaning out the dirty stuff at the bottom. It would take hours.

A deep gloom possessed him as he worked. He thought of the letter his father had written him when he was in jail. And the one Anders, his brother, sent. He shuddered inwardly. His dear brother, his best friend. No more. The letter made that clear all right. Now Julian. Was he to lose him, too?

Granger rigged a rubber hose to siphon off the fuel, finding a deep place in the bilge to place the cans. He worked quickly, but it took four hours to get *Freya* motoring again. He eased his stiff limbs out of the engine space, stood on the deck and stretched. He called to Fisk who still had the deck.

'The engine is running,' he said.

They set off again towards the position given by the stricken steamship. La Salle asked Chalky to bring tea to his cabin. He sat at his tiny desk and began writing in his notebook everything that had happened since the motor broke down. Later he would decide how much of this account would be consigned to the log. His eye fell on a few lines he had scribbled late in a middle watch:

Dripping shades of men I've killed came again last night
Crooking fingers scoured of flesh they ringed my sleepless bed
Come, they sighed, to where we lay, below, beyond the light
We've saved a place for you down there, among the fish-picked dead.

Chalky knocked and pushed open the door. He had a

small tray with tea and a slice of the plum tart Briggs had made for Granger.

'Begging your pardon, sir,' he said.

La Salle slammed his journal shut. Chalky held out a piece of paper.

'Roberts asked me to give you this.'

La Salle took the folded page, opened it and read.

'Lieutenant Higgins had it in for Mr Granger ever since we sailed. We will give evidence.' It was signed by Roberts, Edwards, the rest of the gunlayers and Greene, the Marconi operator.

La Salle waved the sheet of paper at Chalky.

'Have you read this?'

Chalky shrugged and examined the deckhead.

'I have seen things myself,' he said.

'What sort of things?'

'Well, Mr Higgins has been rubbing Mr Granger up the wrong way. He calls him "Jane", you know. He's always saying he's not fit to be aboard one of His Majesty's ships. That sort of thing.' Chalky drew closer, became conspiratorial. 'Mr Higgins asked me if I knew what you and Mr Granger talk about.'

'What did you say?'

Chalky drew himself upright.

'I'm sorry you had to ask me that, sir!' He sniffed. Then: 'Mr Higgins cut my bear open.'

'What?'

'He slashed my bear. Good Joss Teddy.'

La Salle shook his head in wonderment. His command was turning into a ship of fools.

'All right, Chalky. Tell Roberts I have his note, please, and tell him it will be dealt with when the time comes.'

La Salle turned to his tea, glancing at his watch. It was gratifying to learn the ship didn't want Granger to suffer. Higgins had clearly offended the crew's sense of fair play.

'We might be seeing some action soon, mightn't we?'

Chalky asked as he turned to leave.

'I hope so,' La Salle replied grimly. 'I really hope so.'

The gunlayers crept into their dummy structures as *Freya* neared the position given in the wireless SOS. The ship's progress was helped by a light breeze from the south west but as they approached the cross on Fisk's chart all they could see was an empty ocean. There was nothing to suggest a ship, men or boats had ever occupied that stretch of sea. The lookouts reported a slick of oil to the eastward, but nothing more.

Higgins appeared on deck to take his watch and stood sullenly behind the helm. For the hundredth time La Salle scoured the same expanse of ocean, but saw nothing.

'Someone must have picked them up,' he said, addressing no one. They had seen fishing craft but none of them appeared to have a large number of men aboard, or boats in tow. *Must have been a passing steamer*, he thought. They would have to continue their course now. Hanging around an empty stretch of ocean would look strange and in the mind of a U-boat commander, knowing what had happened there, it would excite suspicion.

'Periscope! Periscope!'

The starboard lookout was waving wildly towards a point between the ship and the land. La Salle swung his glasses. It was a periscope all right.

'Continue the course!' He crossed to the binnacle. 'Mr Mate, I want everything to appear as normal. If he engages us you will take the panic party away in the boat. I'll remain hidden aboard with the gunlayers.' He paused, adding: 'And Mr Granger.'

Higgins shuffled slightly. 'Aye aye,' he said.

La Salle estimated the periscope to be about 2,000 yards away, probably too far for the U-boat commander to see *Freya* in detail. But he could not be sure. He ducked to the U-boat's blind side and called to Roberts through the dummy hen coop around the after gun.

'Periscope in sight, Roberts. It looks as if he'll come up on the starboard side if he goes for us.'

There was a muffled reply and La Salle heard Roberts talking into the voice pipe connecting the two gun positions, alerting Edwards to the probability of action on the starboard side. Fractions of seconds counted when the guns went into action and knowing more or less where to shoot saved time.

La Salle took off his brightly-checked shirt and handed it to Higgins.

'I shall keep out of sight now,' he said. 'Carry on as normal. Don't let him know we've spotted him.'

La Salle went below to change his clothes. Chalky brought him a working shirt with buttons at the cuffs. He dressed quickly and told Chalky to pass the word for Granger and Fisk.

Fisk could not mask his excitement. He seemed to shift his weight from one leg to the other as La Salle spoke of their fighting the ship while Higgins went away with the panic party to persuade the Germans the ship had been abandoned and was no threat. Granger, by contrast was subdued. He merely nodded when La Salle wished them both luck.

La Salle added a last instruction: 'From now on we keep out of sight. We'll …' He was cut off by shouts from the deck. Fisk started for the door, La Salle and Granger followed him up the narrow companion ladder.

'What's going on?' Fisk cried, sticking his head out of the opening on to the deck.

Freya was turning hard to port. La Salle squeezed past Granger and thrust his head out of the companion hatch. He glimpsed the starboard lookout pointing at the sea, not at something in the distance, but something much closer. Then the man scrambled away from the rail and the word T-O-R-P-E-D-O formed in La Salle's head, a moment before

Freya was borne upwards, lifted as if she had sailed over a volcano. There was a rush of heat and then the noise. It shook them like a mouse in a cat's jaws, with an almighty crash and simultaneous punch of the percussion wave. Fisk was hurled backwards, piling into La Salle and Granger on the ladder. La Salle staggered and fell, dazed. He felt Granger propping him against a bulkhead. Fisk lay on the sole, blood oozing from one ear.

'You all right?' Granger asked.

'I think so.' La Salle pointed to Fisk. 'What about Gordon?'

'Just unconscious. Maybe.'

Freya was listing to starboard and even in his groggy state La Salle knew she was settling fast. He tried to get up. Granger lifted him and held him until he was able to trust his legs. He climbed slowly to deck level and crawled out. A long section of the starboard bulwark and deck had gone. The foremast and mainmast had collapsed, crushing the house concealing the forward twelve pounder and trapping the men inside. The hen coop, where Roberts and his men were hiding with the aft gun, seemed undamaged. *Freya* was not on fire, La Salle thought. The torpedo had struck the starboard side as the ship took her turn hard a'port and it seemed it had exploded upwards, through the deck near the mainmast.

'Higgins! Higgins!'

La Salle eased himself towards the binnacle on his stomach. He saw Higgins sitting against the galley. He was dazed and bleeding from a cut on the head.

'Higgins! Get the boat away!'

Higgins pulled himself upright. Of the five men who had been on deck only three could be seen, including the helmsman. La Salle's hearing began to return. He became aware of a crying sound. Then sobs and a voice, speaking urgently, incoherently. It was coming from the shattered house around the forward gun. He crawled along the deck. The fallen mainsail was draped over the gun and the splintered remains of its disguise. A wide rivulet of blood ran from beneath an impenetrable tangle of wreckage.

'Are you hurt?'

There was silence then a stream of gurgling noises.

'Are you hurt?'

The sound stopped. La Salle saw Higgins and two men hauling out the tender. They seemed to launch it successfully. Granger rolled towards him along the deck, below bulwark height so he would not be seen by the men in the U-boat. La Salle caught sight of Chalky hovering at the top of the companionway. He was wearing a mouldy lifebelt marked *RMS TITANIC*. La Salle crept along the deck aft and peeped through a gap in the undamaged bulwark. Higgins and the three men, and two others La Salle had not seen, including Briggs, were in the boat, pulling away from the ship. Acting out the role of a panic party was probably easier after being torpedoed, La Salle thought grimly. Beyond them, less than a thousand yards away, he could see the U-boat clearly. It had surfaced and there were men on deck, at the guns. La Salle willed it to come closer, just a little closer. He turned towards the dummy hen coop where Roberts and his men were waiting with the aft twelve pounder. Just as he raised himself to run doubled across the deck, he heard the distant lazy chatter of a machine-gun. He dived back to the bulwark. The men in *Freya's* tender were being jerked around as if on strings. One tried to leap out of the boat. La Salle saw his check shirt, the one he had given to Higgins. The man in it was scrambling over the side of the tender. The machine gun clattered again and he fell back. Pieces of wood from the boat flew through the air. There was no longer any sign of movement aboard. Still the machine gun fired, creating angry little splashes around the sinking tender. There was a dark shape or two in the sea and the firing stopped.

La Salle leaped up and ran to the aft twelve pounder.

'Roberts! Let Go! Let Go!'

The sides of the hen coop clattered down and the barrel of the twelve pounder swung outboard, just as the whine of a shell passed close over *Freya's* deck. La Salle hardly noticed the explosion, in the sea, close by. The twelve pounder fired. As the smoke cleared La Salle saw a plume of water rise just in front of the U-boat. Roberts's men were ramming a new charge in the gun. La Salle thought abstractedly of the white ensign, bundled at the foot of the shattered mainmast. How to raise it? Another screaming shell, this time much closer. *Freya's* gun fired again. La Salle leaned through the smoke, trying to spot the shot. Then everything stopped. He was aware of a flash, a searing blast of heat, things rising into the air, a feeling of being lifted by unseen hands, then darkness and silence washed over him.

CHAPTER EIGHT

So sweet; sounds from his childhood. Not his mother's voice, but the language they spoke together, rising and falling in a long unbroken swell. Words that conjured home, the first happiness. Ignorance of pain. Whispers, to comfort him. Light, barely audible whispers.

'Vous m'entendez, monsieur?'

La Salle opened his eyes. A woman in a man's cap.

'Can you hear me?' she repeated.

La Salle tried to move his arms. They felt as if they were weighed down and impossibly heavy at his side. His legs, too, felt leaden, immovable. A dark shape moved swiftly towards him.

'Julian. Julian. It's me. Merrick.'

He felt a gentle hand slide behind his head and lift him slightly. He could see now. A boat. Spars, rigging. Faces. Granger.

'He's alive,' the woman said.

Granger raised him a little more and tilted a metal cup towards his lips. La Salle drank. He became aware of pain. A deep throbbing pain in his right side. Where? His leg? He tried to feel for his leg. His arm trembled, but he couldn't raise it. Granger lifted the cup again and he sipped some water. Then Granger seemed to twist something. Around his thigh. The pain increased, then ebbed. The light faded and he glimpsed the woman's lips moving and those sounds again, accompanying him into the darkness.

Towards nightfall he woke again. He was being carried. He saw the tops of houses as he swayed on a piece of canvas held by two men. Slate roofs. Was that Granger?

He saw the back of his head, the blond hair, his wide shoulders. Yes. Granger. He slipped back. Deeper. Deeper.

It was the same woman, without her cap. She was holding a glass, looking at him.

'Du lait,' she said gently.

He sipped the milk. It was warm. He saw daylight coming through some thin curtains. He was in a bed. Something stirred in the corner of the room, someone loomed out of a chair, came closer.

'Are you awake?'

It was Granger. La Salle closed his eyes, re-opened them. Now he could see.

'Yes.'

He tried his arms. They moved. His left leg moved. His right leg felt numb, though it ached.

'Where are we?'

'In this lady's house.'

The woman smiled at him. La Salle turned back to Granger.

'What happened?'

'He got us with his third shot. You were blown clean over the side. Roberts and I got away with Chalky. Over the port side. We got you on to some timber. This lady – ' he glanced at the woman, still holding the glass '– picked us up. On a fishing boat.'

'The ship?'

'She didn't go down, but she looked as if she was heading that way. She capsized after she was hit. There wasn't much standing on the deck. Even if the wood in her hold keeps her afloat, she's a wreck.'

La Salle sank back on the pillow. So he had lost his ship and most of his crew. The sight of Higgins and the others being machine-gunned in the tender suddenly filled his head. He turned to the woman.

'Parlez-vous Anglais, Madame?'

She looked at Granger, then him.

'Non, monsieur.' She tossed her head slightly. 'Mademoiselle.'

La Salle raised himself on the pillow.

'Pardon,' he said. He tried a smile but feared the result might have been disturbing. She made a curious expression, a sidelong glance and her large eyes widened even more. She put the milk on a small table then exchanged a few words with Granger. La Salle experienced a slight shock to hear his friend speak French, fluently but heavily accented. The woman left the room. La Salle gestured after her with a look.

'What does she know?'

'Nothing. I told them we were carrying wood to Morlaix, just as we always said. By the time they picked us up *Freya* was out of sight. Probably on the bottom.'

'Chalky, Roberts. Are they wounded?'

'Chalky hasn't got a scratch. Roberts was shielded by the gun. Bit of concussion.' Granger lowered his voice. 'The gun crews were wiped out.'

La Salle heard in his head the awful human sounds from the destroyed forward gun housing.

'My leg?'

'It's still there. Looks like you caught a splinter. Big one. Just above the knee. I had a tourniquet on it. Monsieur di Fario – he's Mademoiselle's father – called in a physician. He cleaned it up and stitched it.' He pointed to a small bottle on a table next to the bed. 'Those pills are for the pain. It's going to start hurting bad, he says. But you'll be fine in a week or two, if there's no infection.'

La Salle did not need to ask what would occur if the leg was infected.

'What happened to Gordon?'

'Dunno. I never saw him on deck after the action started.'

La Salle imagined Fisk lying unconscious below the

companion hatch as *Freya* was shelled to oblivion. Granger pulled his chair over to the bedside.

'You know, something's been worrying me. Why did that guy torpedo us? Didn't you tell me they never use torpedoes on small ships?'

La Salle wriggled more upright.

'That thought occurred to me the moment we were hit,' he said. 'Why waste a valuable torpedo? And why didn't he get our papers? And –' he paused '– why did they kill the men in the boat? It doesn't make sense. Unless –'

'Unless what?'

'Unless he knew we were an armed ship. Then he wouldn't risk a surface attack.'

'What do you mean? How could he know that?'

La Salle slumped back.

'I don't know, Merrick. But nothing else makes sense. If he had somehow bowled us out he would do exactly what he did: disable us from periscope depth then surface to finish us off.'

'Monsieur di Fario – the guy who owns the house – says the fishermen think this U-boat has been prowling these waters since the spring, on and off. Some of them have been stopped more than once, he says. With the small fishing craft he just takes their wine and food and some of the catch then lets them go.'

'Who is this di Fario?'

Granger glanced at the door. His voice became almost a whisper.

'Funny old guy. He owns the boatyard –' he gestured out of the window. 'His daughter does a bit of crewing on one of the local fishing boats. They picked us up. They've got plenty of room here and I've arranged lodging for the four of us until you can travel.' He paused. 'You do have French money, don't you? Apart from anything else I have to pay the doctor.'

La Salle sighed. 'On the ship.'

'Mmmm. I've got some English paper money. Maybe he'll take that.'

'Don't worry about money,' La Salle said. 'There's someone in Paris. We can get French money.'

Granger looked relieved.

'They seem good folk, these people here. Di Fario and his daughter …' he swallowed, glanced at the door again. 'But I get a feeling they're … well. I don't know, Julian.'

'What do you mean?'

'I think they are just a little crazy,' Granger said flatly.

'Crazy?'

There was a sound of heavy footsteps on the stairs.

'You'll see what I mean,' Granger said, just as the door flew open.

A man stood on the threshold, glaring into the room. La Salle saw a leonine head, a mass of grey curls. The face looked as if it had been beaten out of copper. The nose, aquiline and not quite straight, seemed to quiver. The top lip, clean-shaven, trembled.

'The Prussians!'

The man strode into the room, took La Salle's hand between two huge fists and squeezed mightily.

'The Prussians! Here, at our door. Murdering. Again!'

La Salle smiled. Nodded. The man became grave, his voice almost a whisper.

'But you will live.' He sought La Salle's gaze and held it. His eyes clear, unblinking. 'There is no feeling like it! You are shot at and when it's over you have survived. Never are you more alive! What a feeling!'

This man is too old for the war, La Salle thought. *How does he know what it's like to be shot at?*

Di Fario straightened and turned to Granger.

'How many of your crew did they kill?'

Granger threw an anxious look at the bed. *Freya* carried more than twice the complement of a merchant vessel her size.

'Three,' La Salle said quickly.

'Ah,' di Fario murmured, turning back towards him. 'And you are their captain?'

'Yes.'

Di Fario nodded slowly. 'Well, you can stay here as long as you like. We can send a telegram, if you wish. To your owners. Family.'

'No. No telegrams,' La Salle said swiftly. 'For now.'

'Well,' di Fario said. 'Well.' He looked at them both. He held La Salle's eye for a moment, then nodded and left the room.

La Salle and Granger exchanged meaningful looks.

'He does seem an odd sort,' La Salle said.

'The place is full of books,' Granger whispered.

'What is this boatyard you mentioned?'

'Seems like a small ship repair outfit. For the fishing boats, I'd say. We're only a few miles from Douarnenez here. Big fishing fleet. Mademoiselle di Fario goes out on one of the boats sometimes. Seems they're shorthanded. With the war and all. That's what she was doing when they picked us up.'

La Salle sank back on the bolster. Di Fario had given him a penetrating look. Did he think it strange four men of military service age should be aboard a merchant ship? If it came to it he could probably persuade him they were somehow involved in the war effort. Carrying vital cargo. It was imperative their true mission remain secret. He had to get a signal to Queenstown. How? The French military – and especially the navy – had to be avoided. And he couldn't send a telegram in service code because the codebooks were still aboard the ship. Probably at the bottom of the sea by now. He felt suddenly very tired. If di Fario was right about the exhilaration of surviving hostile fire he certainly wasn't feeling it yet.

Granger had returned his chair to the corner of the room. It seemed he had one of di Fario's books. La Salle closed his eyes. They would have to get home, all four of them. Together. When he could travel.

The pain came on slowly at first, a mere edge to the throb that never went away. Then it struck like a knife thrust. La Salle cried out. Granger leapt from his chair, fumbled with the pills. It was dark. He swallowed two, three tablets in a gulp of water. The knife twisted, boring deeper, hacking back and forth against every nerve ending. La Salle mumbled, shook his head. He felt sweat run into his eyes, stinging. Another stab. He couldn't suppress a scream. Now the pain was his entire being. It engulfed him, the world swam in front of his eyes. He twisted the sheet between his teeth, groaned into the cloth, rocking. Light. Suddenly there was light in the room. Held by a tall man, pushing Granger gently aside. He saw him toss away the water in the glass and pour something. The back of his head was in a strong grip, pulling him towards the glass. Burning his mouth, sweet, the smell rising like a vapour, filling his head. A creeping numbness. He swallowed more. The drink was building something between him and the pain. The hurt was still there, but it wasn't reaching him like it did before. He took another greedy mouthful. It burned his throat and he felt its fiery path all the way to his guts. The barrier was stronger now. He was beginning to float on one side, the pain on the other. It was bearable. Di Fario still held his head in his huge hand. He tilted the glass again. La Salle thought he heard him say 'comrade'. The hotness slipped down again. Now he was aglow, warm and safe on his side of the barricade.

Granger made him a crutch. It was Sunday and the boatyard was deserted. Di Fario gave him a piece of elm and some tools and Granger carefully sawed and planed the wood to a circular section. Then he made a cut about two feet down its length, put a tight whipping where the cut ended and opened up the top, wide enough to receive a gently curved crook he found among a pile of grown oak in the workshop. He chose another short end of oak, in a slightly hollow bend, to make the handhold. He ran a razor-sharp scraper over the wood, polishing it to a sheen.

'You are accustomed to working with wood,' a voice behind him said.

He turned from the bench. Mademoiselle di Fario was smiling at him.

Granger set down the scraper.

'I guess I've always done it. Since I was a kid.'

'Is he coming down today?'

'Yes. Well, he wants to.' He eyed the crutch. 'It's a bit too soon for this, though.'

She ran her fingers along the smooth wood.

'So you are the carpenter?'

Granger shuffled. 'Yes. Well, engineer really.' He hesitated. Was he trying to impress her?

'You have escaped the war?'

Granger ran his thumb along the edge of the scraper, testing its keenness.

'So far,' he said.

'Like me!' She laughed. 'I am a woman so they deny me the chance to kill Prussians!'

Granger looked up from the tool in his hand. Had he understood her correctly?

'I would know how to deal with them!' she added fiercely.

Granger smiled at her. What was this? Was she serious? Then, before he could find an answer, the strange darkness in her eyes vanished. She smiled. It illuminated her face and he felt his own cheeks flush.

'Thomas has made some lunch,' she said in a quite different voice.

Granger thought: *Thomas? That was her father's name.*

194

'Perhaps your friend could sit with us. At the table. If he wants to.'

'Yes,' Granger said.

He rinsed his hands at the pump in the yard and followed her into the house. Di Fario, in his shirtsleeves and unbuttoned waistcoat, was stirring a large pot on the range. The smell of the food seized Granger with a rush of nostalgia. Fish, fresh onion, tomato, garlic and white wine; the stew he had first tasted with boyish delight aboard the Canadian fishing schooner.

'That smells good,' he murmured.

Di Fario turned, waved his spoon in the air.

'If I were not a devout atheist I would thank God for the gift of food from the sea,' he said. Then, grinning: 'And wine!'

Granger noticed three bottles of wine already opened on the table. It was set for seven. He could hear Chalky and Roberts moving around upstairs, in La Salle's room.

'Shall I bring him down?' he asked, glancing upwards.

'It is ready,' the old man pronounced.

Granger went up the narrow staircase, puzzling over how they would get La Salle down. He found Chalky sitting on the bed, talking in subdued tones about Briggs and what he said was his "murder". Roberts, at the window, looked round as he entered. Granger sensed Roberts wanted to say something, but he remained silent. La Salle did not look well, he thought. His face was sallow and his cheeks hollow, although he wondered whether that was caused by his wound. It was more likely, he thought, to be the effect of the absinthe di Fario was giving him for the pain. Indeed, he had spent the past two days in a state of grogginess.

'Now how are we going to do this?' he asked, standing over his friend.

'I don't care. But I must get up,' La Salle said. 'I could probably hop down if I tried it.'

Granger laughed. 'I don't think so,' he said. He pulled back the bed cover. La Salle was still fully clothed, apart from his right trouser leg which had been cut away. In its place was a fresh dressing and a tight bandage that ran from his thigh to his calf.

'You don't look that heavy to me,' Granger said. He bent down, slipped his arms around La Salle's shoulders and lifted him bodily. 'You want to try to put some weight on that good leg?'

La Salle leaned on his left leg as Granger held him. The leg buckled instantly.

Granger bent down and put an arm under him.

'Up we go.'

Granger lifted him easily, tenderly. He crossed to the door, holding him like a baby. Turning sideways, he descended the stairs, resting both feet on each step as he went down. Chalky and Roberts followed them.

Di Fario asked for La Salle to sit next to him. He was unsteady at first and they found a chair with arms that allowed him to better arrange his weight. At the other end of the long table, opposite the old man, a place was set and a plate, with a small helping of food, stood waiting. Granger, next to Mademoiselle di Fario, inquired about this seventh person.

'My mother,' she said simply.

Di Fario ladled out portions of stew, brimming with langoustines, mussels and chunks of fish. There was freshly-baked bread and the men fell upon the food eagerly.

La Salle asked where he might use a telephone, to call Paris to arrange funds to be transferred to him. Di Fario said the doctor had a telephone and he would doubtless allow it to be used if it expedited payment of his bill. La Salle and Granger smiled; Chalky and Roberts ate in silence, apart from Chalky's occasional observation about the delicious stew and a desire to treat di Fario to a plate of jellied eels, should he ever find himself in the Kingsland Road.

La Salle said they would try to get to Brest when his agent in Paris sent money, to arrange their passage home. It should not be more than two or three days, he said, as if trying to assure the di Farios he and his companions would not be a burden for very much longer.

'You are at home here,' di Fario said in a serious voice. 'All. Stay as long as you wish.'

La Salle shifted in his chair. His wound, though less painful than it had been, was beginning to hurt again.

'You have been a Good Samaritan to us,' he said. 'We thank you.'

Di Fario threw back his handsome head in an expression of mock outrage.

'Never have I wished to be taken for a character from priests' tales!' he roared, downing half his glass.

La Salle blushed, confused. Mademoiselle di Fario smiled.

'The church is not universally followed in France,' she said.

La Salle's sense of awkwardness was relieved by the sound of someone tapping at the door. It was ajar and the knocking was followed by a low whistle and a shout, calling di Fario. The old man looked mystified. He rose from his chair and went out. They heard his voice, and one other, in what seemed to be a serious discussion. Then he bade someone goodbye and re-entered the room. He waved his hand in the direction of the door.

'Interesting visit, that,' he said, resuming his seat. He sipped his wine thoughtfully, turned squarely towards La Salle. 'You are not what you seem, are you, my captain?'

La Salle felt his face redden. He sensed Granger shifting uneasily next to him. Chalky and Roberts, too, while not understanding di Fario's words, seemed to know something was wrong.

'What do you mean?'

Di Fario waved towards the door again.

'That was Jules Bahuon. Fisherman. An old friend. He came here to tell me your ship has been found.'

La Salle started in his chair, prompting a fresh jab of pain in his leg. He rubbed his thigh gingerly.

'Where?'

'In a place called Vann Ar Gall. Some rocks off the Ile de Sein.'

La Salle felt Granger's eyes on him. He glanced towards him, then turned back to di Fario.

'Normally such a find would be welcomed,' di Fario went on. 'But your ship has made the fishermen afraid.' He paused. 'It is an armed vessel, is it not?'

La Salle studied his plate and a langoustine he had been on the point of dismembering. He looked up.

'Yes,' he said.

Granger made a barely audible noise. Chalky and Roberts were watching the two men at the top of the table.

'What is this about?' Mademoiselle di Fario cried. She stood up, moved to her father's chair. 'What did Jules say?'

Di Fario continued to look at La Salle.

'The English ship did not sink. She is waterlogged and on her side, but she stayed afloat. She drifted on the tide and is now wedged in the rocks at Vann Ar Gall.'

'Who knows this?' La Salle interrupted.

'Bahuon and his brother found her this morning. They were fishing on the reef. She cannot be seen unless you get in among the rocks, Jules said.'

La Salle felt a surge of relief at this.

'Who have they told?'

'No one. They knew you were in my house. Bahuon has told only me. I have asked him to remain silent, for now.'

'It would be very difficult for me –' La Salle began.

Then: 'If the authorities are involved … the French navy. Well, it would cause problems.'

'Without doubt,' di Fario murmured. He put a hand on La Salle's shoulder. 'You owe me nothing, my friend. Nothing. Stay here as long as you need. I shall not ask you about things you may wish to keep secret.'

'I shall!'

Mademoiselle di Fario thrust herself between her father and La Salle.

'I brought you here because I thought you were honest seamen, victims of the Prussians. So what are you – pirates?'

La Salle sighed. His leg was on fire.

'In a way, yes.' He looked down the table. Chalky and Roberts were staring at him. He addressed them in English. 'Our ship has been found. In some rocks. They know she is not a merchantman.'

Roberts lowered his eyes. Chalky treated di Fario and his daughter to his cheekiest grin.

'Now what?' Roberts said.

La Salle thought quickly, trying to blot out the agony in his right leg. He had to get to *Freya*. Orders, ship's log and codebooks had to be retrieved. The French navy was not privy to the Special Service's operations and it would be a disaster if *Freya's* secret was exposed. Yet what could they do? They were helpless in their present state. Only di Fario could help them.

'What do you mean, "in a way pirates"?' Mademoiselle di Fario demanded angrily. She gave Granger an odd look. La Salle thought he saw a suggestion of a smile on her father's lips.

'I am going to explain everything,' he said. 'Because I need your help.'

'We will not help pirates!' She was pointing now, one hand menacing some distant abomination.

'I am a British naval officer,' La Salle said calmly.

'Monsieur Granger is my engineering officer.' He gestured down the table. 'These gentlemen are Royal Navy volunteers.'

Di Fario threw back his head and laughed.

'Leave him, Laurentine,' he cried gaily to his daughter, pulling her on to his lap. 'I knew he was an officer from the moment he opened his eyes!'

She gave her father an impatient look.

'Do you believe him?'

'Well, let us hear his story,' di Fario said. He persuaded her to make coffee, although her manner remained cold. She did not return to her seat, next to Granger, but sat rather stiffly in an old chair near the stove. As La Salle's account of *Freya's* mission unfolded she seemed to relax a little. When he said he had been blown off the deck and pulled on to some wreckage she shot Granger a glance, then she got up and asked if anyone wanted more coffee. She took Granger's cup and re-filled it, before he could reply, then turned to the others. La Salle said he had to get to the ship, to recover her papers.

'One of my officers may still be aboard,' he said. 'I should like to find him, if he's there. Bury him properly.'

Di Fario listened in silence. When La Salle mentioned Fisk he nodded agreement.

'We have a small tug,' he said. 'She draws very little. We could get her in among the rocks.'

He left the room and returned with a chart, cleared an end of the table and unrolled it, holding it down with glasses. Vann Ar Gall, they saw, was a cluster of rocks off the north west tip of the Ile de Sein.

'We will need sufficient rise of tide to get in there,' di Fario said. 'But it would be better to examine the ship at low water, depending on how she lies.'

La Salle agreed. 'What time is high water tomorrow? When could we leave?'

'What do you mean?' Granger said, in English. 'You're not thinking of going? With that leg?'

'I'll be fine.'

Granger pointed at the chart.

'That place has to be twenty-five miles from here. I've seen the tug. It will take four, five hours just to get there.'

Di Fario understood. 'It is a bad wound,' he said. 'We shall have to cross the Raz de Sein. It can be difficult.'

La Salle knew the Raz's reputation as one of the most dangerous stretches of water on the Atlantic coast. In bad weather a small vessel would be lucky to survive its steep, breaking seas.

'I have to go,' he said. The pain returned in a wave. He felt sweat running down his face. He desperately needed some absinthe. He looked at di Fario. The old man smiled.

'The green fairy,' he murmured and turned towards a cupboard on the wall.

'Well I'm going anyway,' Granger said.

'Fine.' La Salle said. Di Fario handed him a glass. He sipped the pale green liquid gratefully.

'So am I,' said a firm voice behind him. La Salle twisted in his chair. Laurentine di Fario was looking at him, arms folded on her chest. La Salle took another drink and straightened in his chair. The liquor coursed through him, warming, numbing.

'Fine,' he said.

CHAPTER NINE

Di Fario said they would need to cross the Raz near slack water, when its fierce tidal stream was at its most weak. From what Jules Bahuon had told him about *Freya's* position, the best time to approach would be close to the top of the tide. It meant a departure at 4 am. Di Fario left a note for the boatyard foreman and when Granger carried La Salle downstairs, an hour before dawn, di Fario was already aboard the tug making steam. The vessel was barely thirty feet long and most of the space below deck was taken up by its triple expansion steam engine which, di Fario told Granger, they had recently fitted with an oil-fired boiler. The screw was geared to provide towing power, not speed, he explained almost apologetically. Granger glanced around the tiny ship. She was probably twenty years old, wooden built; straight stem. A steam winch and towing post occupied most of the after part. There was a small wheelhouse with seats and La Salle braced himself in the corner of a bench.

They cast off a little later than planned and there was already a glimmer in the eastern sky as they chugged slowly away from the yard's jetty, out into the Baie de Douarnenez. The breeze was in the north, quite fresh and a few whitecaps slapped the tug's starboard side as she steamed west. Di Fario glanced at La Salle from time to time as he steered. Laurentine and Granger stood on deck, on the lee side of the wheelhouse. She was pointing out shoremarks as the land slipped by and Granger listened attentively as she spoke words the men in the wheelhouse could not hear over the gurgle and hiss of the old engine. *It's almost as if she is teaching him the way back home*, La Salle thought as Laurentine waved her arm towards a tall spire on a cliff.

He had been thinking about her in the night. The absinthe wore off, as it always did, leaving him trapped in a state of fatigue and wakefulness. The pain in his leg relented a little and he found he could conjure an almost perfectly detailed image of Mademoiselle di Fario – Laurentine – in his head. In Paris, or London, she would be a pretty girl, her hair gathered in a luxuriant chignon de cou. It was a rich dark brown, but she wore it cut short. Pity, La Salle thought. She had worn a cotton dress for their lunch *en famille*. It revealed nothing of her figure, being rather shapeless, but he had seen the way she moved, occasionally standing with a hand on her hip, or brushing back a wisp of hair. He imagined her without the dress. And she had looked at him. Quite boldly, he thought. Her large eyes, unblinking, deliberately held his. Probing. Exploring. It excited him in a way he had not known before. Yet when he thought of her in the long hours before Granger came to take him down, he imagined again and again one expression. It was a glance, a sideways flick of the head, an oblique look that suggested something hidden very deep. It was thrilling, yet strangely alarming. Then she would assume her quiet confidence again. A young woman secure in her ability to cope in a man's world.

She was laughing. Granger had said something that made her laugh. La Salle turned from the wheelhouse side window, looked out ahead, irritated. She had preferred his friend from the beginning. That much was clear.

Di Fario jabbed a finger at the folded chart next to the helm.

'The breeze will kick up an ugly sea against the flood,' he said. 'We'll go north of this little island here to avoid the worst of the Raz.'

La Salle saw an islet with a light marked on the chart.

The place they were heading for was about five miles to the south west of there.

'How long, do you think?' he asked.

Di Fario took out his pocket watch.

'Just over an hour. Then we have to find what we are looking for.'

La Salle nodded. He had taken a couple of the doctor's pills before leaving and he carried the rest of them in his pocket. If the pain came on hard they would be useless, but for now they kept it to a manageable ache. The tug was beginning to roll violently as her port beam caught the surge of the flood-tide rushing north. Granger opened the wheelhouse door, bundled Laurentine inside and followed her in.

'Quelle houle!' Granger exclaimed, meaning the rough swell. La Salle felt an unreasonable jab of bad temper. Granger's accent had improved enormously in the past few days.

'We'll use the light at the west of the Ile de Sein as our mark,' di Fario said. They were steaming south west now and the lighthouse was clearly visible ahead. The land was low-lying and surrounded by drying rocks and reefs. La Salle saw from the chart that there was some deep water around the place they were making for. The fisherman had said Freya was barely visible and the tug, with its low freeboard, offered a poor platform for scanning the sea.

'Bahuon said she bears west-northwest from the light,' di Fario said. 'So we'll go beyond, turn and approach on a reciprocal bearing.'

La Salle nodded.

'She lies in what the Bretons call a yoc'h,' di Fario added. 'A group of rocks.'

Bretons, La Salle thought.

'Are you not a Breton, Thomas?' he asked.

Di Fario laughed. 'I cannot claim that honour,' he said.

'I am from the south. Nice. Laurentine's mother is Bretonne.' His face clouded slightly.

La Salle smiled and nodded. Yet he did not understand. Di Fario spoke of Laurentine's mother as if she were still alive. Her place was set at the opposite end of the table and a small helping of food was left on a plate which, at the end of the meal, was cleared away with the rest of the dishes. Was she away, and expected back at any time? Something told him it would be unwise to seek this information before it was offered.

As they closed the island's west coast, the swell dropped and the sea took up a strange swirling pattern, eddying back and forth, sometimes in circles. Laurentine went into the bow to act as lookout. Granger followed her out on deck. He glanced over the side. And froze. The deep grey-green of the water was patched with vivid turquoise and near-white. He could see fingers of weed moving, curving below, as if beckoning. They were over rocks.

Laurentine held out an arm to indicate to her father, at the helm, where to steer. Closer to the island shore the rocks were only just below the surface and on some shiny black peaks ahead the sea was breaking viciously. Granger swallowed hard. This was a sailor's horror. He glanced back at the wheelhouse. Di Fario was staring out, unmoved, watching his daughter's directions. A flash of white ahead revealed an ugly broken tooth of granite, exposed by a crashing sea. Laurentine held out her right arm and her father steered the tug to leave the danger to port. *These people are risking their lives to do this*, Granger thought. The chart had shown hazards – lots of them – but the reality of half-hidden, ship-killing rocks and baffling, malign currents had to be seen to truly appreciate the terror. Yet di Fario and his daughter must have known. And still they came. *There was more than kindness in this*, Granger thought as he watched Laurentine conning the tug.

The wind was picking at her canvas smock, flattening it against her slim back. She held out a steady arm. Steer to port. Then she took off her cap, shook her hair, put the cap on again, never taking her eyes off the course ahead. It was dangerous work and she did not have to do it. The thought made him strangely uneasy.

The rocks at Vann Ar Gall were awash and they were almost upon them before *Freya's* stern, just visible between two larger pinnacles, could be seen. Laurentine threw open the door of the wheelhouse.

'The ship is ahead,' she said.

'I see it,' di Fario muttered. 'Can I get there?'

She shrugged. 'How slowly can we go?'

La Salle realised di Fario was unable to steam at dead slow because the currents were setting the vessel sideways. He had to keep way on to maintain control. Yet to approach at speed invited disaster. He hauled on a handhold above his head and tried to struggle to his feet.

'Attention!' Laurentine ran forward and held him under one arm.

'I must see the ship,' La Salle said, between gritted teeth.

She steadied him in the corner, opened the door and shouted.

'Merrick! Merrick!'

The sound of her calling out Granger's Christian name came as a mild shock. La Salle pulled himself up on his left leg. He would not be carried, now.

Granger took him immediately under the arms, but La Salle shook his head.

'No. Just take the weight. Here.'

He put his right arm around Granger's shoulder and hobbled out on to the deck. *Freya's* black-painted counter was seven or eight feet above the surface of the sea. From any distance it would look like another rock. A few shapes could be seen bobbing and circling in the currents: baulks

206

of timber. Her cargo, the wood that had kept her afloat, was floating away through her torn hull. She was on the bottom now and awash like a half-tide rock.

Di Fario was trying to hold the tug on station, but the vessel was being swept to the west. He waved through the wheelhouse window, calling La Salle inside.

'I cannot get alongside safely. Too much sea running. We'll wait for low water,' di Fario said. Since most of *Freya's* hull seemed to be submerged there was little point trying to examine her before the tide dropped, he reasoned.

La Salle listened carefully as di Fario outlined his plan for getting alongside the wreck. Di Fario may not be a Breton, he thought, but he had learned well the ways of that race of seafarers. His strategy for manoeuvring the tug so they could get to the ship seemed impeccable.

It was clear to La Salle that he would not be able to climb aboard *Freya*, but Granger could and he wanted him to search the ship, recover the papers and codebooks and – an image of Gordon Fisk crowded his head. They would do what was necessary.

Di Fario let the tug fall away on the westgoing stream until she was in clear water about 150 feet from the ship. He handed the helm to his daughter and dropped a heavy anchor from a roller-fairlead at the stern. He paid out the chain by hand around the towing post, as Laurentine steered the tug slowly back towards *Freya*. The tug weaved and yawed but the weight of the chain hanging from the stern steadied her, and by turning the rudder into the tide it was possible to keep on course. Within thirty feet of *Freya's* overhanging counter he called for dead slow. He had transferred the chain to a windlass and he was using it to control the tug's progress, hauling to stop her, relieving to let her gather way. Thus they edged towards the ship. The current was weakening but it was still strong enough to enable Laurentine to take a sheer with the rudder when the tug stopped and her bow threatened to fall away. Granger, in the bow, threw a grapnel anchor attached to a line over *Freya's* taffrail. He tugged on the rope and the hook bit hard around the sturdy teak. Then di Fario turned the windlass, bringing in the chain at the stern as Granger paid out the grapnel line, keeping it taut with a turn around the samson post. With her screw stopped, the tug moved astern pulled by the raising of the chain, her bow held steady as Granger released a corresponding length of line on the grapnel.

Di Fario sounded the depth and he reckoned the tug would float safely at low water. What lay elsewhere around the rest of the wreck was impossible to know and, in any case he said, not worth the risk of trying to find out. He explained that as the depth dropped with the ebb, the stream would push the tug towards the ship. The anchor would hold her and they would drift slowly back to *Freya* by letting out the chain again with the line at the bow keeping her on station.

'When?' La Salle asked.

Di Fario glanced at some pencil marks he had made on the chart.

'The ebb is starting now,' he said. 'Low water here in five to six hours. We could probably get aboard before that. Say four hours.'

La Salle glanced at Granger.

'You'll have to go,' he said.

'Sure.'

'The code books are with the other papers in a sealskin bag, locked in that little desk in my cabin. You'll have to break it open. God knows where the key is.'

Granger looked at di Fario.

'Do you have any tools aboard. A hatchet, maybe? Not just for the desk. I don't know what I'm going to find up there.'

Di Fario crossed to a locker under the bench and raised the lid. La Salle noticed a large pouch of fine old leather lying in the locker. It was about three feet long, like an envelope, beautifully made and out of place among tools aboard a workboat. It looked like a rifle case. Di Fario caught him looking at it, pulled a small hatchet from the locker and quickly closed the lid. He handed the axe to Granger.

'Will that serve?'

Granger weighed it in his hand. 'Fine,' he said.

They settled down to wait for the tide. Laurentine unpacked her basket and handed out bread, cheese and slices of ham on thin wooden plates. Di Fario opened a small trap door in the cabin sole, reached down into the bilge and pulled out a bottle of wine. They ate and drank in silence. La Salle watched the old man out of the corner of his eye. He ate slowly, pensively, occasionally turning to smile at his child. La Salle coughed slightly.

'Forgive me, Thomas,' he said in a good-humoured tone, 'but I'm curious as to how you, a Southerner, find yourself here at the top of the Bay of Biscay?'

Di Fario emitted a short laugh.

'I suppose we have to blame the war,' he said.

La Salle frowned. The war was less than one year old, yet di Fario had clearly been in the Bay of Douarnenez for many years.

'War?'

'Not this one. The last Prussian war.'

'Of course.' La Salle faltered. 'But you would have been too young to fight? It was 1870, no?'

'I was too young to join the army, but not too young to fight,' di Fario replied.

La Salle noted a slight edge to his voice.

'Tell them,' his daughter said.

'It was a long time ago.'

'I should be glad to hear, sir,' Granger put in.

Di Fario looked at him, then La Salle.

'We are not so different, you and I,' he said. He struck

a match and held it to the bowl of his pipe, puffing gently. 'I, too, have fought Germans without the benefit of uniform or a cap with a badge. Disguised as a civilian.' He leaned back and fixed his eyes on the deckhead.

'My father was notaire, in Nice. It was an Italian city when I was born, a lot of families from Sicily, like us. At that time shooting clubs were very popular and my father was a famous marksman. Rifles were becoming more sophisticated, more accurate. We had some of the best guns in France at our club. On my sixteenth birthday my father gave me a Spencer repeating rifle, imported from the United States. Do you know it, Merrick?'

Granger nodded. 'I've heard of it. It was considered a fine weapon in the Civil War, I believe.'

'Yes. Rimfire cartridge; .52 calibre. Seven round magazine, held in a tube in the stock. My rifle is not the carbine version, with the slightly shorter barrel. My gun has a full-length barrel. Accurate up to around 500 yards. In the right hands.' He shook his head, spoke almost to himself. 'My hands are steady enough, but you need a sharp eye. Young eyes.'

La Salle thought: *Does he still have it, then, nearly half a century on? Is that it, in the locker?*

Di Fario returned his gaze to the overhead.

'In the summer of 1870, not long after my birthday, Louis-Napoleon declared war on the Prussians.' He looked at the two men and smiled. 'A foolish decision, as it turned out, but it filled young men like me with joy! War! It's in our blood and bones, isn't it? You have felt it, haven't you? That feeling that makes you throb to your very core. Action! We crave it as young men, don't we?'

He gave out a short, bitter laugh. 'I did. So did the others. Many of the men from the rifle clubs joined the regiments they were hastily putting together and I longed to go with them. But I was too young. Another option offered itself, however.'

210

He drew deeply on his pipe, exhaling slowly.

'A few of the older men – too old for the army – formed a band of irregulars. I left a letter for my father, packed a small bag with a few clothes, spare boots and my Spencer rifle and before dawn one morning I slipped away to join them.'

'Francs tireurs?' La Salle asked.

'Yes. That's what we were called, although the Prussians called us "terrorists". Our small band linked up with men from rifle clubs in Cannes and, later that summer, Nantes. We didn't see much of the Prussians until the fighting moved to the west and south of Paris. By late September, Paris was under siege and the Prussians were marching on Orléans. We were deployed in the forests, harrying the Prussian patrols, ambushing. Cutting their telegraph wires. By October they were running trains down there and we attacked those, too. Stopped a few. Then we were ordered to Châteaudun.'

'Châteaudun?' La Salle tilted his head, struck by a thought. 'I've read about that. At school. In Paris.'

'Yes,' di Fario smiled. 'It is still considered French history.'

'There was a battle and a famous woman, a kind of Jeanne d'Arc, wasn't there?'

'Mademoiselle Proust,' di Fario said. He beamed at his daughter. 'Laurentine Proust: the bravest woman in France!'

He coaxed his pipe back to life and resumed his tale: 'Châteaudun was taken by the Prussians – in fact they were mostly Bavarians – at the beginning of October. Then a lot of their troops were withdrawn to reinforce the investment around Paris. We, the irregulars, were placed under the command of a Colonel Lipowski who had a small force of national guards and gendarmes. Lipowski ordered a surprise attack on Châteaudun and we took the town, killing rather a lot of Bavarians; taking some prisoner. The Prussians were outraged. They came back. General Von Wittich brought up a force of cavalry, infantry and artillery. On the 18th of October, a bright, sunny autumn day, they attacked.'

Di Fario rose from his seat and looked out of the wheelhouse window. *Freya's* stern loomed higher now.

'The ebb is well away,' he murmured, returning to his seat. Then: 'Lipowski reinforced the town with barricades and I was posted at a point on one of the roads leading to the west. The Prussians had their guns drawn up out of our range and they started shelling. I had never experienced anything like that. I thought my bones would turn to jelly. The shells were falling among the houses, the barricades. Fires started. People were being blown to pieces. We could see men gathering outside a wood. What were they waiting for? In the late afternoon they began to advance and we realised why they had waited. The setting sun was now in our eyes. We fired as best we could, but it was almost impossible to see properly. They came on quickly and we were forced back from the barricades to a second line of defence in the town itself. Lipowski was everywhere. So was Mademoiselle Proust. She had a small basket –' he pointed at the picnic hamper '– like that. In it she carried water and ammunition. From barricade to barricade. Smiling, calm. So beautiful, so serene amid the smoke and the noise and the whistle of the bullets and splinters of shell.'

He paused. 'She was eighteen, you know. A little older than me. I was ashamed to feel afraid in her presence and the sight of her, her grace and courage, inspired us.' He sighed mightily, gave up the pipe and tapped it against the heel of his boot.

'We were forced to fall back into the town and little by little they took it, house by house. Out of nine in my group, three of us were left. Lipowski commanded a fighting retreat and we reached the forest in the darkness.'

'Tell them about Fontenay,' Laurentine whispered fiercely.

'Yes. I should tell you about that. Perhaps you don't know what happened there?'

La Salle sensed something dreadful. 'I remember hostages being taken,' he said. 'Some shot out of hand. A lot of looting.'

'That was everywhere,' di Fario said. 'But what happened in Fontenay was worse, although it was not an isolated case. The difference, for me, is that I was there. I saw for myself.'

He fell silent, gazed out at the clearly visible wreck, then continued: 'After Châteaudun we were ordered to Paris, to reinforce the National Guards. We moved by night and soon after we set off we saw the glow of fire in the distance. Two of us were sent to investigate. The village of Fontenay was ablaze. We crept through some fields. We could see the church and a lot of smoke. There was no one in the square and we ran to the door. There was a stink of paraffin everywhere. The door had been locked but it was half burned through and we kicked it open. The fire had almost burned out and it was dark and we couldn't see very well. But at the other end of the church, near a side door, we made out a smouldering black mound. The pews were burned and most of the roof had fallen in, but this pile was not debris. It was people.'

Di Fario looked at them in turn. 'They had been locked in, doused in paraffin and set alight. Perhaps thirty or forty people. Most of the village.' He stopped. 'But not all.

'We shouldered our rifles as we left the church, desperate to see a Prussian, desperate to make someone pay for this crime. There were none. They had gone. We checked whatever houses we could, those not burning. They had been looted, of course. Not one of them had a clock in it.' He seemed to ponder some intriguing enigma: 'Prussians are especially fond of clocks.' Another pause.

'We found an old man in one house, lying next to a sword, one of those curved cavalry sabres from the time of the Grande Armée. He had been shot and bayoneted, perhaps a dozen times. In the next room we found a young woman half-lying, half-sitting in a chair, a baby in her arms. Both had been stabbed many times, probably by more than one bayonet.'

Granger shifted uneasily. Di Fario stared at him.

'Do you find it hard to believe, Merrick?' he said gently. 'Well, so do I. But I have to believe it because I saw it with my own eyes. And Fontenay was not the worst. The Prussians openly declared a policy of hostage-taking and reprisals among the population. They repeated Fontenay many times. Whole communities were burned out; "eingeaschert", as they called it in their ugly tongue. Reduced to cinders. They were trying to stop us, of course, the francs tireurs. And, for my part, I was glad to be heading for Paris because I believed there I would have the opportunity to slaughter, yes, slaughter, the human beasts who could do such things.'

Di Fario smiled. 'Do you know what it is to crave blood? Have you felt it? You have seen action, I suppose? Have you felt the agony of hatred that can only be eased by taking life?'

La Salle felt uncomfortable. Di Fario spoke quietly, almost reasonably, but there was a terrifying sense of menace about him. He was clearly an educated man, yet a malign barbarity radiated from him like heat. He thought of something Granger had said, at the beginning. *The father and daughter. Both a little crazy.*

'Were the Prussians very different from Napoleon's armies? Or the English in the Hundred Years War?' La Salle asked.

'Yes,' di Fario said emphatically. 'For one thing there was an organised, I would say, scientific approach to their cruelty. It was not just the sporadic evil-doing found

214

among soldiers everywhere. No, this was very much part of the Prussian method of war. And we should not forget. It was happening in a supposedly enlightened age, when we could reasonably expect a civilised nation to conduct itself without unnecessary cruelty, even in war.'

'Surely you don't blame an entire nation for the sins of their soldiers?' La Salle asked. 'Is that fair?'

'Yes!' di Fario replied fiercely. 'Yes I do!'

His daughter laid a hand on his arm which, La Salle saw, stirred restlessly. Di Fario took a deep breath, relaxed a little. She was squeezing his forearm tightly, La Salle observed. Her knuckles were quite pale.

Di Fario continued: 'After the war I returned to Nice, carried on with my studies and joined my father's legal practice. Of course, I read all the memoirs. I consumed every book, every article about the war. One referred to something Bismarck's wife said after some incident or another: "Shoot and stab all the French, down to the little babies." Those were her precise words, never denied. How many babies have they killed in England already, Julian? With their naval guns and airships? There were many in Belgium, you know, at the beginning, when they invaded. How many babies and children died on the *Lusitania*?'

La Salle shifted on the bench, bending his wounded leg slightly. The dead infant in *Lusitania's* lifeboat, the one he had picked up out of the swamped bilge, flashed into his thoughts.

'Merrick was on the *Lusitania*,' he said. He wanted to add, with pride, that his friend had saved the life of a child, but he did not. Granger had never talked about it and was not aware La Salle knew.

'Ah,' di Fario breathed. 'Then he, too, has seen how the Germans make war against women and children.'

Granger shuffled and eyed the floor. He seemed about to speak when a loud crack and groaning noise came from the wreck. There was a sharp jerk as the line to *Freya's* stern pulled taut. Granger threw open the wheelhouse door and he, di Fario and Laurentine rushed on to the tug's foredeck. La Salle pulled himself up and looked out of the windshield. *Freya* had collapsed amidships with the falling tide, raising the stern and burying the hull forward. The after sections had twisted to an almost even keel. He glanced at his watch; more than three hours before low water. Would his cabin, and the papers, be submerged, even then?

Laurentine stepped into the wheelhouse. 'It will be dangerous going aboard that wreck,' she said.

La Salle nodded. She was thinking of Granger, of course.

'He'll be all right,' he said. 'He's the most resourceful man I've ever met.'

She smiled. 'He is your great friend, isn't he?'

'Yes. He is. There is something rather special about Merrick.'

She dropped next to him on the bench, pressed her hands together on her knees and leaned towards him earnestly.

'I sense that,' she said. 'He –'

Di Fario and Granger came in. Di Fario resumed his seat on the bench. His daughter straightened and brushed back her hair.

'We can only wait for the ebb,' di Fario said. He stooped to open the trap into the bilge, felt around inside and withdrew another bottle of wine. As he pulled the cork, Granger spoke.

'Terrible things were done during our civil war. But it seems to me we should blame war itself.'

Di Fario nodded energetically. 'I agree with you. Now, have you read that book I gave you?'

'Well, sir. I have. But I can't say my French is up to taking it all in.'

Di Fario waved his hand. 'No matter. It is relevant to what we are discussing here. I shall explain.'

'What book is this?' La Salle asked.

'It's called *Germany and the Next War*. It was written by a Prussian general, Friedrich Von Bernhardi,' di Fario said. 'I got my copy shortly after it was published in France, two years ago.'

'The year before the war started? In 1913?'

'Precisely. And this book, apparently written with the compliance of the German high command, is a detailed, carefully reasoned exposition of Germany's aims. They are, put simply, to crush France and England and transcend them as the world's greatest power. War, Von Bernhardi tells us, is the method by which Germany will civilise the world.'

'We all knew a war was coming,' La Salle murmured.

'Yes. But the significance of this book is that it explains why. Not to defend territory, not to right a wrong but to achieve domination.'

La Salle shook his head. 'I doubt the German people share that view.'

'Perhaps not. But they are the ones we are fighting. History teaches us, by and large, that people get the governments they deserve. The Germans, for whatever reason, have a government that considers war a suitable instrument of policy. Or so it seems.'

Di Fario raised his head. La Salle was reminded of the image on a Roman coin.

'I console myself with the thought,' di Fario said gravely, 'that nations tend to slip on the blood they have shed.'

La Salle looked covertly at Laurentine. She seemed entirely serene about her father's lawyer-like delivery of a judgment on an entire people. It occurred to him that she somehow shared his views. It was a troubling thought.

Granger wanted to change the subject.

'Excuse me, sir. But how did you come to be running a shipyard here, in Brittany, with your family and business and all in the south?'

Di Fario sipped his wine. He seemed lost in his own thoughts for a moment. 'Well, as I told you, we were ordered to Paris. We slipped through the Prussian lines to reinforce the National Guard and the regiments of Mobiles who, at that time, were preparing to break the siege to link up with what was left of the army. It was a disaster, of course. The siege went on, month after month, through the winter, to its awful conclusion; the Commune and the murder of so many.' He fell silent. Then, offering a refill of wine and topping up his own glass he brightened. 'You know, the one thing that never ran out in Paris during ten months of siege was the wine. Salut!'

'Tell them about Uncle Eric,' Laurentine urged.

'Ah. Eric. Eric Audrin was the best man who ever lived! My friend, my brother.'

Mlle di Fario slipped an arm around her father's shoulders.

'My uncle Eric was in the Breton Gardes Mobiles,' she said. 'A little older than Thomas. They met in strange circumstances.'

'The siege had been going on for months,' di Fario said. 'Food was short, although in my small band we always had bread and we'd load our rifles with shot to bag pigeons in the Bois. I, myself, never ate rat, as far as I know. But many did, and were glad of it. There was a chap with a stall near the Hôtel de Ville. He had live rats in cages and you could buy one for two francs. They caught them by dangling baited fish hooks in the sewers. Brewery rats were rarer, and more expensive. In any case, the rat butcher sold his rats live but he offered his clients a free service. He kept an English bulldog in a box without a top. If the rat-buyer wished it – and most did – he would tip their rat into the box and the bulldog would despatch it with a bite to the head.'

'What about those who could not afford even a rat. Did they starve?' Granger asked.

Di Fario faced him. 'Despite the best efforts of the Prussians outside the walls, few people actually starved. Those that died from want were almost all babies. There was no milk towards the end. Every cow was killed for its meat. Mothers couldn't provide because their diet was so poor. So the babies died of hunger.' His voice became soft. 'In Belleville, around Christmas, I remember walking along one of the poor streets and hearing the cries of infants from almost every house. At the end of the winter, just before the Commune, those houses were silent.'

'The Prussians!' Laurentine whispered fiercely. 'They killed children with their shells, too. They tried to force Paris to surrender by bombarding the people. Homes, schools, hospitals. Everything was a target.'

La Salle lowered his eyes. She was right. The Prussians killed civilians with their artillery during the siege. It could not be denied. The world was outraged yet the newly-proclaimed Kaiser and Bismarck ignored the protests. They made war their own way. Even so, La Salle thought, the sense of hatred harboured by this father and child was unsettling.

'You've forgotten about Uncle Eric,' the girl said.

'Yes. Well, one day we heard they were planning to shoot the elephants at the zoo. For their meat. I went along out of curiosity. There were a number of young men there, National Guards and Mobiles. I fell into conversation with a Breton, Eric, as they prepared to kill the elephants. There were two of them, young males, called Castor and Pollux. They shot Castor first, with an exploding bullet. It entered at the shoulder, seemed to be deflected into the animal's guts, then exploded. I can hear the screams of that beast to this day. It lay dying in agony while the zoo officials argued over what to do. Imagine! This creature had been accustomed to giving children rides on its back! They would feed him chocolate croissants! I couldn't help myself. Tears came to my eyes. I was fighting, yes, killing men, but

I had the heart of a boy. Eric, my new acquaintance, put his arm around me. He walked with me back to my lodging. He had a small flask of Calvados and we sat at the kitchen table in silence, sipping the brandy. From that time, December 1870, we were separated only by duty. We spent hours walking in the Bois, or exploring Paris. I survived the slaughter of the Commune thanks to Eric. We left Paris together, after the civil war, and we returned to our homes. But we vowed never to let our friendship die.

'Eric's father owned the shipyard in those days and every summer I would travel up from Nice and spend a holiday with the Audrin family. Eric would teach me about the sea. And –' di Fario broke off. He rose to look out of the wheelhouse, at *Freya's* stern.

'It may be time,' he said. His voice was thick and he did not face them. He crossed to the door and went on deck, forward.

'It's because of my mother,' Laurentine whispered. 'She is Uncle Eric's baby sister. When she was nineteen she married Thomas. That's how he came here, to Britanny.' She stood up, glanced outside. 'You can get aboard your ship now, I think.'

With the fall of the tide they saw that *Freya's* back was broken. She lay in a crevasse of rock, her timber cargo and buoyancy gone, her steel hull firmly wedged. Di Fario let the tug creep forward, held by the stern anchor until the ship's counter was almost above them. The stream was sluicing wickedly around her sides and they could see the rocky bottom only a few feet below the surface. Di Fario used a boathook to thread lines around the taffrail and he made fast a rope ladder with wooden treads. Granger stuck the small hatchet into his belt and climbed. He swung a leg over the stern and stepped on to *Freya's* aft deck. It sloped down to starboard and it was still wet, but he found he could keep a footing on the planks. He made his way gingerly towards the after gun. It had partly collapsed through the deck and as he came close he saw a blackened hole left by a direct hit. Amid the torn metal and splintered timber he saw a boot and lower leg; its ripped flesh bleached white, jammed in a steel bracket. There was no other sign of the gunlayers who had manned the twelve pounder. Granger swallowed hard and moved forward to the other gun. It had fallen into the hull and was partly submerged. The dummy house around it had been washed away and there was nothing left of the men he knew had died there. He crept slowly towards the companionway. It seemed clear of the water and he started down the steps. It was almost dark at the bottom and he cursed himself for not bringing a lamp. He stopped in mid-step. Something was moving. He strained his eyes and slowly became accustomed to the near-darkness. He could see water at the bottom of the companion. It was disturbed, rippling with small splashes. Granger felt a trickle of sweat run down the back of his neck. He pulled the hatchet from his belt, slowly and noiselessly. Something was down there. He stepped on to the last tread above the water, bent down and stared hard. There was a strange clicking noise. He saw the shape of a man lying in the narrow passageway. All over the shape, moving forms, digging, jerking this way and that, scurrying in the shallow water made it seem alive. Granger felt something rise in his guts. Crabs were devouring what was left of Gordon Fisk. He leaned forward, swung the small axe at a huge crab squatting on the dead man's face. It flew away with a crack, revealing a sight that made Granger retch. He stepped down, avoiding Fisk's legs, kicking at the creatures in the water. It was no more than a foot deep. He turned and made his way aft, towards La Salle's cabin. The passageway climbed slightly and the water had drained away leaving puddles and a sodden mass of bedding piled on the sole. He found the desk, smashed it open and withdrew the sealskin bag, tucking it into his jacket. At the foot of the companion he looked down at Fisk. There would be little left soon. He stepped over the seething crabs and climbed up, breathing deeply as he emerged on deck. He paused for a moment, then crossed back to the stern. As he was about to climb over to the ladder he saw two barrels still in their lashings on the counter. There had been six, he remembered. The depth bombs, concealed in fake kegs. The other four must have been washed over the side. He put a leg over the taffrail and felt for the ladder.

Di Fario, his daughter and La Salle were on the deck of the tug, watching him climb down. He reached the deck and handed the pouch to La Salle.

'Gordon?' La Salle asked.

Granger shook his head. 'Bad. He's dead. Crabs everywhere.'

La Salle said nothing. He opened the pouch and felt inside, then withdrew a small money bag. He weighed it in his hand and replaced it, placing the pouch under his arm.

'Thomas,' he said. 'I want to charter this vessel. I want to take care of one of my officers who is dead aboard the ship. I have money now. Gold.'

Di Fario took out his watch and frowned.

'The flood has already started,' he said. 'It would be foolish to go back aboard now.'

'I understand that. I want to come back tomorrow. With my men.'

Di Fario glanced up at Freya's stern.

'She probably won't move much. Now.' He stooped slightly to bring his eyes level with La Salle's face. 'Don't talk to me about money, Julian,' he said softly. 'We shall come back tomorrow. I'll get some canvas sewn. Some iron weights.'

'Yes. We could do it in the deep water west of the island.' La Salle paused. 'I would need a bible.' A thought occurred to him. He added quickly: 'It's not something you'd have, I suppose.'

222

Di Fario snorted. 'I am an atheist, not a heathen! Of course I have a bible!'

La Salle smiled apologetically. Granger hadn't quite understood and looked bemused. Laurentine gave La Salle a hard look.

They hauled in the ladder and cast off from *Freya's* stern. Di Fario showed Granger how to work the windlass and he drew the tug away from the wreck, towards the anchor. They weighed easily and steamed north-east, towards the islet of Tevennec and the course they would take back into the bay. No one spoke as the tug puffed slowly over the swells, stretching like endless dunes into the wilderness of the Atlantic. The wind had dropped but the sky was still overcast and the rock-bound coast loomed even more forbidding in the greyness.

'Something I ought to mention,' Granger said suddenly, in English. 'Two of the depth bombs are still lashed to the stern. Maybe we should do something about them. They'll get loose sooner or later and those things could sink a ship.'

La Salle looked up. He ran a hand over his chin, held Granger's eye.

'Or a submarine,' he murmured.

'What?'

La Salle glanced at di Fario. He and his daughter were looking ahead, staring at the sea.

'Were they secure?' La Salle whispered. 'Will they still be there tomorrow?'

'Well ... I don't – say, what are you thinking?'

'Not now. Let's talk later. When we get ashore.'

Di Fario altered course and the tug rolled and ploughed its way to the eastward. La Salle hunched himself into the corner of the small cabin and stretched out his wounded leg, stroking his chin. The leg throbbed, but he thought the worst of the pain was over. He became aware of something and looked up. Laurentine was watching him.

CHAPTER TEN

By the time they reached the boatyard, La Salle had a plan. It was vague and dependent on many unknowns but it was, nonetheless, a plan worthy of the name. And he thought, a touch grimly, it was no more desperate than a lot of what the Special Service was doing to try to sink U-boats. He insisted on hobbling to the house, leaning on Granger's shoulder and, despite the aching that didn't go away, he felt the outing on the tug had helped his recovery. He told Roberts and Chalky he'd talk to them in his room at six o'clock, but first he wanted to see Granger alone.

'I have an idea for getting that U-boat,' he said as his friend helped him into the chair.

Granger straightened. 'I guessed that,' he said quietly.

'Don't you see, Merrick? We have everything we need!'

Granger laughed softly. 'Sure we do. Why, we'll get the old ship sailing again in no time.'

'No. Not *Freya*.' La Salle drew his fingers through his hair, shaking his head slightly. 'Listen …'

There was an attractive simplicity in La Salle's idea, Granger had to acknowledge. They would acquire a French fishing boat, arm it with the depth charges aboard *Freya* and lure the U-boat into a trap. From what di Fario had told them the submarine made a practice of stopping fishing vessels and taking their food, fish and wine. Getting close might be easily accomplished. Yes, Granger agreed, that part was feasible. But they had never used depth bombs. Even Roberts, who had been trained before they sailed from Queenstown, had never actually fired one. And if they failed they would be at the mercy of a captain who had already demonstrated his readiness to kill out of hand. They could not shoot back; *Freya's* guns were lost and even if they could somehow get to the Maxim machine gun in the submerged forward locker, it would probably be useless. Q-Ship warfare was always high-risk but Granger felt his friend's plan approached the suicidal. He told him so.

La Salle went silent. Then he raised his head.

'Not for all of us,' he said.

'What do you mean?'

'I realise it would be hopeless to try to drop two charges in the way they are usually delivered. On top of a submerged U-boat. But I'm not suggesting that. I propose using the depth bombs in a way that makes it virtually certain the U-boat won't survive.'

Granger tilted his head. 'And just how do you mean to do that?'

'By fastening them to his hull.'

Granger stood up and walked to the window. The breeze had returned and the gusts were whipping some stray wood shavings into little vortexes in the yard below. He turned back into the room.

'Tell me more,' he said.

La Salle explained his idea for concealing the depth bombs inside a small launch or tender. This boat would be used to transfer the food demanded by the Germans from the fishing vessel to the submarine. He reminded Granger that di Fario said the U-boat, ever cautious, never approached the fishing vessels closer than about 100 feet.

'So when we are stopped,' La Salle said, affecting his most reasonable voice, 'I row over with the fish or whatever; as they are taking it aboard I trigger a time fuse and jump over the side. Before they realise what is going on – Bang! Up she goes!'

Granger smiled. 'And you with it.'

'No. Not necessarily. It's all a question of timing. I reckon I would need to be about sixty, perhaps seventy-five, feet away. Men in the water have survived shell blasts closer than that. So I need to know how long it will take me to swim that far.'

'All day, with that leg,' Granger said.

La Salle shook his head. 'No. It's getting better by the day. By the time we've got a boat and sorted out the explosives, I'll be fit as a fiddle.'

Granger whistled softly.

'You really mean to do this, don't you?'

'As soon as we've buried poor Gordon I want to secure those depth bombs. There should be smoke canisters in *Freya's* magazine. A smokescreen would give the rest of you a chance to get away if I fail. As soon as I know we can recover what we need I'll go to Brest. I've got the codes now. I can send a signal informing Admiral Pettigrew about *Freya* and the crew. Then I'm going to say I have a plan for attacking the U-boat and request permission to try it.'

Granger was staring at the floor. He looked up.

'What about a boat? You can't charter a vessel for what you're planning. You'd need to buy one. Do you have that much money?'

'I do,' La Salle said. 'My mother's lawyer in Paris has charge of my funds. He can wire a bank draft to me here. We don't need the admiralty's money. Anyway. The cash aboard *Freya* would hardly be enough.'

Granger stared. 'I've heard of officers at the front buying their own kit, weapons – even horses. But a boat?'

La Salle laughed. 'I happen to know that a retired admiral was so keen to join the war he offered the navy a fully-equipped patrol vessel, bought from his own funds, if they allowed him to skipper it. The admiralty accepted gratefully. As far as I know, he's out there now, aboard his own ship.'

'What about Thomas?' Granger almost added: 'and Laurentine,' but he didn't.

'I've been thinking about that. We need him. He has the contacts we'll need to get a boat and he has the perfect place to do the work. But I just don't see how I can ask a civilian – a foreign civilian at that – to get involved in something like this.'

'I have a feeling he would want to help.'

'Really? I thought that too. Do you think I should talk to him?'

'Yes.'

La Salle paused. 'What did you make of that story he told us, about the last war?'

Granger moved to the bed, sitting opposite him.

'It's been bothering me. He's been nursing this hate all these years. Like it's a wound. Don't you think? He seems a different person when he gets on about the Germans. The Prussians, as he calls them. When I first met him I felt he was a little crazy, but eccentric crazy. Now. I don't know.'

'You think he might be … well, mad?'

'I hope not,' Granger said, half whispering.

'We need him.'

'I see that.' Granger tugged at the coverlet absently. Then: 'Do you think he's infected her with it?' He tried to smile when he spoke but there was a trace of agony in his eyes.

La Salle felt flushed with shame. The thoughts he'd been having about Laurentine. While his mind had ranged indulgently over the erotic possibilities, Granger clearly had a real affection for her. They always sat together now, whether at the table or in the large, whitewashed room filled with old chairs and a couple of sofas, the place where di Fario kept most of his books. There was nothing improper about the way either of them behaved, although it seemed clear to him that Laurentine was setting the pace. He came across them in the yard once and she had her arm around Granger's shoulder, something his friend appeared not to mind until he saw him. Then he had gently shaken himself free.

Granger drew closer; earnest.

'Did you see her when he was telling us about that place, you know. The village.'

'Fontenay.'

'Yes. That was it.'

Granger ran his fingers through his hair. He needed a haircut now, La Salle thought.

'Well, I saw something that kind of troubled me. Her eyes were very wide, did you see that? Like she was staring at something she wanted to …'

'Hurt,' La Salle said. 'Yes. I saw that.'

'Then when he talked about that other girl, Laurentine. With the basket. Helping the fighters. Well, she seemed to swell up.' He looked up. 'And she's such a lovely girl, Julian. I don't know …'

His voice trailed away. He stood and moved to the window. Neither had shaved that morning and the window lit a nascent golden beard on his face. It made him look boyish, La Salle thought. Granger's open, generous smile stirred a feeling of tenderness. Not for the first time, he was seized by a kind of nostalgic yearning. He wished they had grown up together. Almost since they met he had found himself imagining Granger in his own childhood, becoming that secret sharer of his lonely adventures and fantasies, a companion who alone knew him, but who existed only in his head. And heart, probably. He did not reproach himself for this and he did not feel he had allowed himself to fall victim to unmanly thoughts. So far he had lived his life without forming a meaningful human bond with anyone, outside the Burnage household. On the school ship he had fumbled with friendships but found himself unable to hold on to one. As a young adult he had thought deeply about this and concluded it may have had something to do with his unusual origins. He accepted it with a philosophical shrug. Now he had someone. The young American, with his auric looks and quiet strength was his friend, his officer-brother.

'What happened in New York, Merrick?' Asking the question surprised him, although he had been wanting to ask it ever since the business with Higgins.

Granger shrugged. 'Oh that,' he said. 'It wasn't much.'

'If you don't want to tell me –'

'No! No. It isn't that.'

La Salle said nothing, an invitation for him to continue. Granger stayed at the window, looking out.

'I was on a freighter, 5,000 tons; good ship. Good skipper. We were berthed on the Hudson, just in from Chile. Round the Horn. Couple of the guys said let's go up to Harlem. We drank a lot of whisky.' He paused. 'Can't say I've got much of a head for it. Well, we ended up in one of those clubs. I didn't know it at the time. Place was full of sissies.'

He laughed. 'Darn it, I was so drunk I didn't know anything by then! Anyway, when the cops came in this guy I'd never seen before was sitting on my knee. I was arrested and they charged me: "Lewd behaviour". I got a lawyer, of course. He said plead guilty. Heck, as the law stands I was guilty! So I did six months in jail. Other guys who were in the place got five years.'

He turned, spreading his hands expressively.

'That's all there is to it. When I came out I bought a ticket on the *Lusitania*.' He chuckled, without humour. 'Thought I'd come over here and redeem myself.'

He was looking out of the window again. A jumble of questions crowded La Salle's head. He knew he couldn't ask them, especially the one for which he most wanted an answer. Neither spoke for a moment. La Salle thought: *redeem? Did he consider himself a sinner, for whom redemption would be needed?*

'So you came over here to risk your life,' he said at last.

'Seems a bit of an extreme reaction. To something so trivial.'

Granger turned into the room. He had relaxed a little. He waved a hand carelessly.

'It wasn't just that,' he said. 'I guess Thomas was right when he said there's something in us that makes us want war. It excited me.' He lowered his voice. 'It still does.'

'We have our duty,' La Salle said.

'Yes. Whenever we feel guilty about wanting action we can always tell ourselves we're just doing our duty.'

'We mustn't treat it like a game, Merrick.'

'But it is, isn't it? We handle war like a game and we play games as if they were war. I'm not criticising anybody. That's just the way I see it.'

La Salle raised himself in the chair and leaned on an arm. His leg really did feel better. He glanced at the small clock on the table.

'I must see Roberts and Chalky. They'll be here in a minute. There's really no point in pursuing it if they're not with us. I can't order them to go on a stunt like that.'

Granger noted the "us". So he had already volunteered, then. Well, there was never really any doubt about it.

Roberts and Chalky sat quietly on the bed as La Salle outlined his plan. When he had finished Roberts coughed.

'It seems to me there's a problem,' he said. 'How do you detonate the explosives? The fuses on the depth charges are hydrostatic. They work on sensing the pressure of the water. At forty feet, or more if you want, the detonator kicks in. You want to set it off at the surface.'

La Salle pursed his lips. 'Well, couldn't we rig some sort of timer? Get a fuse out of a twelve pounder shell?'

Roberts made a face. 'They're percussion fuses. They go off when they hit something.' He thought for a moment. 'There are timers in the smoke shells. If I could get a fuse out of one of them and rig it to the depth bomb, then maybe set it off with a wire.'

'Look,' La Salle said, 'I won't order you to do this. If you feel it's beyond what you volunteered for we'll pack up and try to get home. But I think it will work.'

Roberts sucked in his thin cheeks. 'I'd like to get the bastards who killed Edwards,' he said.

'And Briggs,' Chalky put in. He added quickly: 'It's a bit like do-or-die, though, isn't it?'

'Wasn't it always like that?' La Salle said. 'Even when we had the ship?' He shifted awkwardly on the arm of his chair. Granger, at the window, saw his precarious perch, started towards him, then paused.

'Let me ask you something,' La Salle said, looking directly at the two men. 'Would you feel more confident of getting away with it if you were in the trenches, going over the top, charging straight at machine guns? I reckon you'd have a better chance joining me on this little enterprise.'

There was silence for a moment, then Roberts spoke.

'I always knew it was kill or be killed,' he said. 'If I can get smoke shells off the ship I reckon I can make the timer you want.'

'We'd need smoke as a cover, too,' La Salle said. 'If we could envelop the U-boat in smoke from the tender it would offer some protection to a man in the water. Before the charges exploded.'

Roberts nodded.

'Gawd love us!' Chalky exclaimed. 'When do we start then?'

La Salle grinned. 'As soon as we can. I have to talk to Monsieur di Fario because we'll need his help.'

Roberts and Chalky left La Salle alone with Granger. When they had gone La Salle turned to his friend.

'I haven't actually asked you, have I, old man?'

Granger was looking out of the window, watching something below in the yard. La Salle guessed Laurentine was drawing water from the pump.

'Oh,' Granger said. 'You don't need to.' He turned into the room, nodded at La Salle's tenuous position on the armchair. 'Is that your way of telling me you can swim a hundred feet in sixty seconds?'

La Salle grinned. 'I'm getting better. Really.'

Granger crossed to the bed and sat opposite him.

'It could take weeks for that wound to heal properly. You know that.'

La Salle shook his head vigorously. 'No I don't. I feel it improving quickly now. Really.' He waved an arm towards the door, lowering his voice. 'What do you think Thomas will make of our plan? You don't think he'd report us to the French authorities, do you?'

Granger looked up sharply. 'Not after the risks he and Laurentine took to get us to the ship! My guess is he'll do what he can to help us. He's an unusual guy. In another war he did what we are doing now.'

'That's true,' La Salle mused. 'Do you want to get him up here?'

'OK.' Granger walked to the door, then turned back: 'Don't fall off that chair!'

It became apparent to La Salle, as he talked about his idea for an attack on the U-boat, that di Fario assumed he would be part of the scheme. This was at once gratifying and disturbing. He wanted his help in getting back to *Freya*, then acquiring and fitting out a vessel and tender. He didn't want a civilian volunteer. But since di Fario seemed enthusiastic – even suggesting a fishing boat he knew was for sale – La Salle decided against laying down the limits of his role at that stage. It was agreed they would return to *Freya* on the next morning's tide; di Fario, Granger, Roberts and he. Di Fario said he had a canvas bag with iron weights at the foot 'for the brave officer'. When he rose to leave the room he took something from his jacket pocket and handed it to La Salle.

'The bible,' he said.

Alone in the room, La Salle opened the book. Inside the cover, written in faded ink, he saw: "Antonio di Fario. 1864." So Thomas was a nom de guerre, a practice common among the francs tireurs. Like the long-ago war itself, he thought, the name had stayed with him.

He felt under the bed for the bottle Laurentine had bought for him. He poured a measure of absinthe, scrutinised the level and added more. He tipped in some water from the glass on the small table and lay back on the bolster, sipping greedily. He reached for the bible, opened it and leafed through, found Corinthians Chapter 13, verse 4. He read to himself in a soft voice:

> *'Love is patient, love is kind. It does not envy, it does not boast, it is not proud. It does not dishonour others, it is not self-seeking, it is not easily angered, it keeps no record of wrongs. Love does not delight in evil but rejoices with the truth. It always protects, always trusts, always hopes, always perseveres.'*

He paused, laid down the book and reached for his glass.

The timing of the tide allowed a later start for the passage back to *Freya* and the sun was already visible over the hills on the Crozon peninsula as di Fario steered the tug on to its course. They congratulated themselves on the fine weather. The glass was steady, the breeze slight and the sea shone blue and benign. Di Fario had memorised the dangers around the wreck of the Q-Ship and manoeuvred the tug with confidence to a position off her stern. The hull had settled even more and there was no sign of the baulks of timber that had kept her afloat. La Salle guessed they had washed away and it would not be long before the ship sank deeper behind the screen of rocks.

Roberts climbed aboard with Granger, carrying the canvas bag. Fisk was in a foot of water left by the outgoing tide and as they kicked away the crabs, a slender eel darted from under the body. The two men emerged on *Freya's* after deck, carrying the canvas sack between them, their faces grey. They gently lowered the bundle on a line parbuckled to *Freya's* stern.

The hatch into the magazine was damaged and it took all their strength to force it open. Below, the steel casing of the ammunition store was split and water had penetrated almost to the top. The twelve pounder rounds had shifted from the racks and lay in a glistening pile. Roberts sorted carefully through the heavy shells until he found what he was looking for.

'This is smoke,' he said, gently pulling a round free. Granger could see the shell was soaking wet.

'Is that any good?' he asked, doubtfully.

'They're supposed to be watertight,' Roberts said, holding the round towards the light coming in through the hatch. 'But I don't like the idea of them being submerged.'

He laid the shell down on the soaking sole of the magazine, leaned into the space and felt around at the top of the pile.

'Look you!' he cried. 'There's one here that didn't get wet.'

He retrieved the shell. It did indeed look as if it had escaped the seawater.

'That's smoke, all right.' Roberts leaned deeper into the magazine. 'Here's another.'

He found three smoke shells which, he was sure, had not been underwater.

'That will have to do us,' he said.

They carried the shells up and Roberts took them one by one, in his arm, cradled like a baby, as he descended the rope ladder hanging from the ship's stern.

'Are three enough?' La Salle asked, unable to disguise the anxiety in his voice.

'For a fuse, yes,' Roberts said. 'And there should be

enough smoke in there to give us a good screen.' He hardened his lip over his teeth. 'There's more down there, but I just don't see how we can trust ordnance that's been underwater all this time.'

'You're right,' La Salle said. 'We have to play safe.' For some reason La Salle couldn't fathom, Granger laughed out loud at this.

They returned to the wreck and loosened the barrels holding the depth bombs. Each was lowered carefully on to the deck of the tug in a net attached to the tackle at *Freya's* stern. They made the charges fast, covered them with a tarpaulin and hauled in the tug's stern anchor.

La Salle looked back at his ship as di Fario steered the tug through the rocks with Granger conning her from the bow. *Freya* looked ungainly with her bottom sticking up like that, he thought. Ugly, even. There was nothing now of her beauty, her sweetness of line and harmony of detail. Soon the sea would claim her completely and, as she disintegrated, her component parts would be carried away by the sea to invisibly rot. La Salle tried to suppress anger, directed against himself. She was his failure. He did not even know how he had failed. But he had. His men had been lost and his ship was dead. He turned towards the canvas bundle lying on the deck. Fisk. He thought of the new Rudge Multi motorcycle, ordered before they sailed, waiting for his dead shipmate in Queenstown. Roberts and Chalky talked of avenging the deaths of their friends. Did he want revenge for Fisk? He glanced back at the vanishing black shape of his broken ship. No. It was less honourable than that. He wanted something for himself. If they could kill the U-boat there would be an end to the gnawing questions. If he, weakened as he was, could still destroy the enemy he would acquire something that had, thus far, eluded him. He would not wonder about his fitness for the war, nor shrink in the presence of heroes, even those from the trenches. He would be able to face any man. A face flashed across his mind's eye. Or woman.

They steamed towards the deep water west of the Ile de Sein. Di Fario leaned out of the wheelhouse, called aft.

'We are in a hundred metres depth,' he said.

La Salle limped forward, took bearings from two lighthouses and a headland, noted the position on di Fario's chart and wrote out the coordinates on a piece of paper, then slipped it into his pocket. Roberts and Granger lifted the canvas sack, holding its weighted end first over the tug's starboard side. La Salle took out the bible. Poor Fisk. He would have to go to the bottom accompanied by sacred words spoken in a foreign tongue. He read the psalm quickly, murmured a private prayer for his friend and nodded. They let the bag slip over the side. As the foot hit the water the bundle bent double, floated like that for a moment then sank swiftly. There was a flash of pale green and then it was gone.

No one talked as the tug steamed back into the bay. They tied her up in silence and La Salle, walking without the crutch for the first time but leaning on a stick, made his way into the house alone. He managed to negotiate the stairs, resting often, although he was relieved to reach his room and fell, half-lying, on the bed. It had already been a long day and he was tired. There was an agreeable sensation of weightlessness as he felt his body float towards a cosy hinterland, remote from the troubling thoughts at the front of his mind. He suddenly jerked up his head and shook himself awake. There was a lot to be done and no time to lose.

Di Fario had no motor of his own. He used an old dray to move lumber and machinery and on the occasions when they needed to go to Douarnenez they travelled round the short stretch of coast in the boatyard's launch. There was a transport company in the town, he said, and La Salle would have no difficulty arranging a motor to travel to Brest.

La Salle counted the gold coins from *Freya's* ship's

funds. There was enough to pay for transport, lodging, the doctor and – if need be – passage for four back to England.

'Let that not be necessary,' he whispered fiercely. He heard Granger's knock at the door.

'Come in!'

Granger was smiling broadly. La Salle raised his eyebrows, tacitly requesting some explanation for his good humour.

'He's a hell of a guy, that Thomas,' Granger said, shaking his head. 'We almost lost one of the depth bombs over the side. He didn't turn a hair.'

'Are they off now?'

'Yes. Roberts has them stowed in an old smelting pit. He says they'll be stable for at least another six or seven weeks. After that we'd have to take the detonators out and dump them at sea.'

'We'll use them long before then,' La Salle said.

'You think so?'

'Yes. If the admiral is offered the least chance of accounting for a U-boat he'll take it. I don't have to tell him my plan; I'll just say there's an opportunity.'

'When are you going to Brest?'

'First thing tomorrow. Thomas is taking me to Douarnenez in his tender. To introduce me to the people with the motors.'

Granger sat on the edge of the bed, his voice suddenly earnest.

'He's pretty keen, you know. He's been telling me about this fishing boat he thinks we should get.' He paused. 'You know, Julian, sometimes I get the feeling Thomas is too keen.'

'What do you mean?'

'Well, have you noticed how he's changed? Since we went out to *Freya* that first time?'

La Salle had noticed. It made him feel faintly depressed

that Granger had, too. It meant he was not imagining it. Yes, di Fario had changed. The dangerous passage through the rocks, the wrecked ship of war, a plan to strike back at his old enemy; all these things had brought about a difference in the old man's demeanour. He seemed even taller; straighter and there was a lively look in his eyes that made him appear almost young.

Granger shrugged. 'I hope we can shake him off. When we have to.'

'We will. When the time comes,' La Salle said. And yet, as he and Granger fell to discussing the fishing boat di Fario had talked about, a nagging voice at the back of his mind told him the old franc tireur was now part of his crew.

Granger was woken by voices. He could hear movement and men talking, below his window. His attic room overlooked the jetty and, dressed only in his drawers, he crept out of bed and glanced down. Di Fario was casting off the launch with Julian aboard. He watched them motor slowly out on the fairway that led to the bay and Douarnenez. Granger yawned. It was still early. Roberts and Chalky would probably be asleep. He slipped back into bed, stretching luxuriously beneath the covers. The indolence of recent days was not entirely unpleasant, he had to admit, although he hankered for something to occupy himself. Watching two of di Fario's men fitting new garboards to a wooden tuna boat had made him want to pitch in and help. It was work at which he could acquit himself well and it seemed right he should try to earn his keep. But Julian was adamant. They had to keep out of the way as much as possible. Working with di Fario's men was simply not on, he had said. They had been lucky so far. Their presence had attracted no attention and the Bahuon brothers, who found *Freya*, had kept their word and had said nothing. Inevitably, Julian said, mixing with di Fario's men would involve personal exchanges, questions. All di Fario's people knew was that they were English seamen awaiting funds to get passage home. And his friend wanted to keep it that way.

Granger yawned again and nuzzled into the pillow. Well, it could be a whole lot worse and – he suddenly became very awake, nerves taut. Someone was opening the door to his room. He pulled the bedclothes up to his chin, peeping over. Laurentine was closing the door, turning towards the bed.

'Qu'est -' he started, but she silenced him with a finger at her lips. She was wearing her mackintosh and looking at him strangely. There was a half smile on her mouth. Granger sat up, pulled the sheet around his chest. She was barefoot.

'What's going on?' he whispered. She stood by the bed, pulled back her raincoat and let it slip from her shoulders. She was naked. Granger stared at her face, unwilling to lower his eyes. She murmured something and slipped under the covers, feeling for him with her bare legs and arms. With a sense of shock he realised she was wearing a perfume. He remained quite still, arms folded across his chest. She was whispering into his neck, words he could not understand. Then she pulled his head towards her and Granger felt her mouth searching for his. She stabbed him with her tongue. The sensation was at once nauseating and dizzingly thrilling. He opened his arms, held her, but not tightly. Her legs were working against his thighs and she half spoke, half moaned indecipherable sounds as her open mouth moved relentlessly over his.

Granger felt a rush of panic. He raised a hand, patted the back of her head gently, as if consoling her.

'Merrick!'

They froze. Quite still. It was Roberts' voice.

'Merrick! Chalky's making some coffee. Do you want a cup?'

239

Granger sat up. 'Oh? Yes. I'll be right with you.'

He turned to her. She was staring at him. She understood what he had said. He took her head between his hands and kissed her on the forehead. Lightly.

'Méchante!' He whispered. Indulgently. She continued to stare, eyes wide. He thought she might cry and he prayed she wouldn't. He swung his legs out of bed and crossed to the chair where his clothes lay in a neat pile. He pulled on his trousers first, then faced her, smiling. She lowered her head, ransacked her hair with her fingers. He moved to the bed, picked up her coat, handed it to her. She slipped it on dumbly and tied the belt. He raised a finger to his lips and tip-toed exaggeratedly to the door, opened it and glanced towards the landing.

'OK,' he said.

She paused at the door and looked at him in that odd way. He bent down and kissed her forehead again. She reached up and pulled his head fiercely, kissing his lips, which he allowed. She smiled at him with a kind of defiance in her eyes, then skipped to the staircase. He closed the door, walked to the chair and picked up his shirt. He saw his hands were trembling.

He dressed slowly. Her scent clung to his skin. He poured some water into the basin and soaped his hands, rubbing them hard over his face and neck. An act of elimination. Yet part of him wished she'd come back. This part of his deep self may not have been dominant, or even identifiable, but it was determined to be heard, nonetheless. And it said: give me another chance.

The car broke down twice on the way back from Brest. La Salle sat impatiently in the back as Maurice, the driver, stripped down the carburettor, cleaned it and cranked the engine back to life.

'It's the petrol,' Maurice explained over his shoulder. 'We get all the dregs. The rest goes to the Front.'

Maurice was about twenty-five. As they drove south, passing Daoulas, La Salle wondered why he, an apparently fit young man, was not at the Front. He asked him. Maurice twisted in his seat and made a mournful expression.

'A cause de ma vue,' he said. 'I've got terrible eyesight.'

Ah, La Salle thought, feeling at the side of the banquette for something secure to hold on to. His other hand ran over the packages lying next to him on the seat. He had bought fishermens' clothes, caps and, in one smartly wrapped bundle, a French tricolour. He tapped the parcel thoughtfully. There was also a package containing two bottles of absinthe. One had been opened and used to fill the new hip flask he now carried in the pocket of the jacket he'd borrowed. He had asked for just one bottle but the shopkeeper remarked that the government was on the point of declaring the drink illegal, to preserve public morals in time of war. When La Salle said he'd take two in that case, they both laughed. He was fighting down an urge to try out the new flask, more or less successfully. The leg troubled him little now, but he'd grown to like the company of the green fairy.

Maurice appeared to see the road well enough, although the journey back felt as if it were taking far longer, breakdowns apart, than the drive to Brest. *Perhaps it's my impatience*, La Salle thought. Certainly, he could hardly wait to tell Granger and the others he'd received a signal to go ahead: *'PERMISSION GRANTED. DO NOT INVOLVE OUR FRIENDS. GOOD LUCK'*.

"Our friends", of course, were the French. His orders had always been to avoid the French navy. The two nations were allies and their armies fought together, but the Royal Navy kept its secrets to itself. Indeed, it was not unusual to hear long-serving officers describe the French navy as "the old enemy". La Salle was struck by a sudden disconcerting thought. What would Admiral Pettigrew think of his having acquired an ancient franc tireur?

Maurice dropped him at the boatyard. La Salle found he could walk well enough with the stick now and he stumped briskly towards the door. As he approached, it opened and Laurentine stepped out. La Salle smiled at her. She closed the door behind her and motioned with her hand, directing him to follow her to the side of the house.

'Did you get your permission?' she asked.

La Salle sank down on to the low wall that ran along the side of the kitchen garden. So she knew.

'I can't talk about it,' he said.

She stood over him. 'But yes! I insist that you talk about it!' She pointed towards the house. 'My father wants to risk his life! You will tell me. But yes, monsieur.' She had one hand on her hip now, leaning forward slightly.

'Or I will tell the police,' she breathed.

He looked up at her. Her face was a mask of resolve. Not quite as pretty as he remembered it. The eyes seemed rather hard, almost cruel.

'You would be doing your country a disservice if you did that,' he said.

'What do I care? I care about my father.' She turned and sat next to him on the wall, staring.

'Did he tell you?'

She laughed sharply. 'He didn't need to say much. I see what's going on. And I know him.'

'Thomas may want to risk his life, Laurentine. But I won't let him. Once we have prepared everything the task will be for us. Navy men.'

'And you will leave?'

'Yes. If we succeed I plan to use the new vessel to return to England.'

'And if you don't?'

'I'm not considering that possibility.'

She nodded slowly, seemed to swallow hard. La Salle remained still. Silent. *Her father is only part of it*, he thought.

She was facing up to the idea that, whatever happened, she was unlikely to see Granger again. In some ways this came as an enormous relief, almost as if he had suddenly shed a difficult burden. The attraction he had felt (still felt, if he was honest with himself) and the thoughts he had allowed into his head, no longer mattered. While not entirely free of those strange yearnings, he felt he soon would be.

'The war will end, Laurentine. People will have normal lives again.'

She looked up, then lowered her eyes.

'It is not so far, England,' she whispered.

A lamp went on inside the house. She got up, turned to him.

'I would never have denounced you,' she said.

He smiled, pulled himself up, leaning on the stick.

'I didn't think you would. Not for a moment did I think that.'

She walked slowly with him into the yard and they entered by the back door. Thomas was in the kitchen, sitting at the table with Granger, Roberts and Chalky. A chart was spread across the tabletop. The men looked up as La Salle entered, each one held his eye. He nodded. Laurentine pulled over the chair with the arms and La Salle lowered himself into it.

'We can proceed,' he said in English.

There was silence, no one moved. Then Di Fario, who had understood perfectly, stood, crossed to the dresser and picked up some glasses and a bottle of cognac. He set the glasses on the chart and poured, including one for Granger who took his glass, twirled the pale liquid and stared at it.

Di Fario raised his drink. 'To us!' he said, beaming.

They lifted their glasses. La Salle and Granger exchanged a brief look, each noting the other's unease. Di Fario was leaning over the men at the table, a smile spreading over his face. He seemed to want to embrace them, La Salle thought. He suppressed a shudder. He knew what the old man was thinking: *'Mes francs tireurs!'* Well, maybe they were. He felt Laurentine's eyes on him. *Not now*, he thought. *Now is not the time for worrying about Thomas. Now we have work to do.*

'Thomas has been showing us where the U-boat likes to prey on the fishing fleet,' Granger said, inclining his head towards the chart.

'Yes,' di Fario said. 'The ones he has stopped were all coming back to Douarnenez. He seems to lie in wait –' he placed a finger on the deep water to the north west of the Chenal Du Four '– around here.'

La Salle studied the chart. The area indicated by di Fario was close to the shipping lanes around Ushant. The submarine commander could easily break off from raiding a fishing boat if a more substantial target offered itself.

'What kind of boats has he robbed?' La Salle asked.

Di Fario shrugged, spreading his hands.

'Around here, there are only two kinds; sardine boats and tunamen. From what I have heard, the submarine has only stopped chaloupes returning with a haul of sardines.' He glanced at the men at the table. 'Not because the Prussians are especially fond of sardines, I think. The chaloupes pick up other fish; bass, sole and sometimes a lobster or two. These are what the Germans like. And the wine, coffee and bread they have on board.' Di Fario smiled. 'And he doesn't rob. It seems that in each case he pays for what he takes and gets the skipper to sign a receipt.'

La Salle's surprise at this communicated itself to Chalky and Roberts. He explained what di Fario had told them.

'Blimey,' Chalky said. 'Do you mean the murdering swine tries to pass himself off as a gentleman?'

Di Fario waved his hand. 'It was the same the last time. They took everything, but usually they paid for it.

Apart from the looting, of course.'

La Salle translated for Chalky and Roberts.

'They'll pay for it, all right,' Roberts said.

'We have to move fast to try to catch him before his patrol ends,' La Salle said. 'We need to get a boat and refine the plan for delivering the explosives.'

He turned to di Fario. 'Thomas, what is this craft you hear was for sale?'

'It is a chaloupe, exactly like the ones we have been talking about. There are many of them in this bay.'

'I'm not familiar with this type of vessel. How big is it?'

'For a chaloupe, it is big. More than fifteen metres. It has the usual two-masted rig and we fitted a paraffin engine, here in the yard, last year. Just after the war began. The boat is one of a number owned by the Le Goff family. They have a house near the Vieux Port.'

'Why are they selling?'

Di Fario shook his head. 'The war. There are few men to crew the boats and Jean Le Goff does not want to see a good boat rot at its mooring.' He lowered his voice. 'Both his sons are in the trenches.'

La Salle rubbed his chin. 'How can we do the transaction without arousing suspicion?'

'Very simple. I act as your agent. I acquire the vessel for a Monsieur J. La Salle. You have an address in France?'

'I have an apartment in Paris. But it is leased.'

'No matter. An address will suffice for the paperwork. Leave it to me.'

La Salle felt his sense of unease return at this. Di Fario was becoming more than just a helpful friend. The plan was beginning to depend on him. Yet what choice did he have?

That afternoon he called on the doctor, received a satisfactory report on his leg and paid his bill. Then he used the doctor's telephone to call Paris. A banker's draft would be with him in two days, he was assured.

The chaloupe sardinière *Telenn Mor* was delivered to di Fario's yard by Le Goff himself, accompanied by two elderly men. They sailed the vessel on to the small quay, either unable or disinclined to use the motor, and as La Salle watched them arrive from his window overlooking the yard, his seaman's heart sang at their insouciant display of skill. The fairway to the quay was narrow and there was just enough room to turn the chaloupe into the wind and bring her to a shivering halt, neatly alongside the jetty. A mistake would have seen the vessel blown on to the slipway further in but the ease with which the three men handled the boat suggested a lifetime of familiarity and a certain handiness in the chaloupe's rig. She had two masts of near-equal length, both carrying lugsails. The sails were loose-footed, without booms, tacked down forward of the masts and clewed to big wooden blocks holding the sheets. As di Fario's launch took Le Goff and his men back to Douarnenez, La Salle saw one of the elderly sailors glance back, giving the chaloupe one last look.

He found the others waiting for him at the kitchen table.

'Shall we inspect our new ship?' he said brightly.

They crossed the yard to the quay where di Fario was adjusting the chaloupe's lines. He stood and extended a hand towards the boat.

'Eh, voilà!' he said gaily.

'Blimey!' Chalky emitted a low whistle. 'Is that it?'

La Salle had to admit the chaloupe was a small ship. She was a little over fifty feet in length but her low freeboard, overhanging stern and a complete lack of superstructure made her seem tiny.

'She's big enough for what we want,' Roberts said stoutly. He glanced over her foredeck and long counter.

There was little decking and most of the space inboard was piled with nets and gear. 'But where do we stow the tender?'

La Salle put the question to di Fario.

'The tender is towed astern,' he said.

La Salle translated for Roberts and Chalky. Roberts looked thoughtful.

'That makes my job a bit more tricky,' he said, nibbling at his lower lip.

'But not impossible?' La Salle shot back anxiously.

'No more impossible than everything else about this caper,' Roberts growled. 'I'll just have to make sure it doesn't get bumped about too much.'

'What does the name mean?' Granger asked, pointing to *Telenn Mor* painted in white lettering on the bow.

'It's Breton for *Harp of the Sea*,' di Fario replied.

La Salle relayed the name of their new ship to Chalky and Roberts.

'Let's hope it's the Huns and not us who'll be hearing harps,' Chalky muttered.

Aboard the chaloupe they found benches outboard with locker space below and enough shelter under the foredeck for two people to sleep. But, as di Fario explained, the sardinières were essentially day boats. They would hunt the shoals of fish offshore, net as many as they could, and return. Below the deck on which they stood they found a deep well for storing the catch. It had been scrubbed clean but there was a lingering odour of fish that La Salle found not unpleasant. He glanced around the boat's fittings. Everything was as simple as it could be. The sails were trimmed to belaying boards, hauled in by hand without any concession to machinery. On the gunwale he saw two sets of thole pins on each side to take sweeps. Two pairs of oars were lashed to the frames and it made him think of the motor di Fario said he'd fitted last summer, at the outbreak of the war. Apparently Le Goff hoped the engine would make up for men who had marched away to fight, but even with a motor the chaloupe took at least four or five pairs of hands to manage the rig and the nets when she was fishing. As the war took its toll a big boat like *Telenn Mor* became unviable. Di Fario had suggested to him that Le Goff might accept a low offer, given the circumstances.

'I can pay him what he asks,' La Salle replied.

At this di Fario paused, threw out a huge arm and seized the younger man's shoulder. He squeezed hard, all the while staring into La Salle's confused and embarrassed face.

'I like you well, my captain,' he said, and let go at last.

Granger found the engine. It was tucked under boards at the after end and when La Salle peered over his shoulder into the space he felt a pang of disappointment. The motor was tiny.

'What do you think?' he asked.

Granger was feeling around the green-painted metal with his right hand, like a doctor with a patient.

'Paraffin,' he said. 'If it works, it'll be fine.'

Di Fario understood. 'It is a good machine,' he said. 'But it hasn't been used. The men on this coast dislike them.' His face broke into a wide grin, displaying his remarkably white teeth. 'They think using a motor says something suspect about their manhood!'

'I'll get some tools,' Granger said. 'Check it over.'

'So what do you think, Julian?' Di Fario asked, guiding him to one of the benches. La Salle sat down slowly, stretching out his wounded leg.

'I think she will serve us well,' he said. 'I want to get her to sea as soon as Roberts has sorted out the explosives.'

Di Fario nodded, a serious expression on his face. 'Yes,' he said. 'We mustn't waste time.'

CHAPTER ELEVEN

Elwyn Roberts stepped back from the rough bench they had built against the side of the smelting pit and felt inside the unfamiliar folds of his new fisherman's smock. He found the pocket at last and withdrew a packet of the cigarettes La Salle had brought back from Brest. Without taking his eyes off the pieces of metal and dark substance on the bench, he lit one of the stubby yellow tubes, cupping the cigarette in one hand, the match in the other. Grimacing slightly, he inhaled. He let the smoke go slowly, suppressing a cough. Every fibre in his body yearned for a Woodbine. He ran his tongue over a thumb and forefinger and doused the match, dropping it absently. He turned; Granger was stepping down into the pit.

'Pretty easy on the fire regulations, aren't we?' Granger said pleasantly.

Roberts flattened his top lip over his teeth, gestured at the bench with the cupped hand holding his cigarette.

'That stuff's a lot harder to set off than you might think,' he said, adding, almost below his breath: 'That's the problem.' Roberts dropped the alien cigarette on the bare earth with a flicker of contempt, grinding it hard with his heel. 'Look at this,' he said.

Granger followed him to the bench. He saw the dismantled head of a smoke shell, a spring, detonator and what looked like compacted powder.

'In our line of work,' Roberts said, 'rounds with a time fuse are not used often. We load with good old percussion shells; they go off when they hit something nice and hard. Like a submarine. These timed fuses, look, are used in the trenches, mostly. To explode in the air. We only use them

249

in these new smoke shells. I've only ever fired one in training.'

He pointed to the bench. 'This fuse can be set to different times, but from the markings it seems the longest it will burn is about thirty seconds.'

'We need longer than that,' Granger said.

'Right.' Roberts pressed his thin nose between finger and thumb, staring at the bench. 'So all I can do is to put two fuses together. That would give you your sixty seconds, give or take a second or two.'

Granger peered at the pieces on the bench.

'So how does it work?'

Roberts picked up a small metal object.

'This is the cap,' he said. 'It has a small charge that's set off by the explosion of the propellant that fires the shell. The cap ignites this stuff –' he lifted the dark, cement-like substance '– which burns at a known rate. When it's burnt through it releases the spring that fires the detonator into the main charge.'

'So you are suggesting using two lots of the powder?'

'Composition, it's called. Yes. We'll need to make a metal cylinder to take the composition and hold the detonator. At the top we'll rig something simple to fire the cap.'

Granger imagined a submarine crew hearing a sudden explosive crack coming from a fisherman's tender tied alongside.

'How loud is the cap?' he asked.

'Not very. You never actually hear it because it comes right after a very big bang, but from the size of it I'd say it's little more than a click.'

Granger nodded. 'So how do you want to set it off?'

Roberts shrugged. 'Something like a pistol hammer to fire the cap. Triggered by a wire or small piece of line. We need to make a safety pin to hold the detonator spring. You wouldn't want that going off by surprise.'

Granger glanced at the two depth charges, covered by a tarpaulin in a corner of the pit.

'How powerful are they, do you think?'

Roberts turned towards the covered barrels.

'There's 200 pounds of high explosive in there. If that went off next to a U-boat – any vessel, armoured or not – it's going to make a very big hole.'

'What about a man in the water?'

'I can't speak of that,' Roberts replied slowly. 'Obviously, the further away he is the better. Men swimming do survive heavy shellbursts. Surprising, really, but –'

Granger cut him off. 'What about the percussion wave?'

'It goes up as it goes out. That's why a man lying prone, on the deck, can survive a burst that kills the man standing up.'

'So swimming at the surface would offer some protection?'

'I think so.' Roberts thought for a moment. 'But if the explosion is underwater and he's near it he wouldn't have a hope. The percussion is lethal underwater. Within about thirty feet. That's how those things work.'

'But we are setting ours off at the surface.'

'Well,' Roberts said, rubbing his hands on the front of his smock, 'that's the plan.'

Granger was struck by an uncomfortable thought. What about the fuses that were already in the depth bombs? How was Roberts going to deal with the hydrostatic fuses? Would they have to be removed to get at the detonators? He put the question to him and Roberts made a face.

'I'm not looking forward to that bit,' he said. 'They're tricky little buggers. These –' he gestured at the tarpaulin '- are set to go off at forty feet. That's standard. You can change that to eighty feet if you think the U-boat's gone deeper.' He paused, seemed to weigh a thought. 'I only need to get one of the hydrostatic fuses out. The timer only needs to be rigged to one of the charges, see. Exploding one will set off the other, so I'll leave one just as it is.' He ran the back of his hand across his mouth. 'So long as it's not submerged it will be all right.'

Granger nodded. He saw quite clearly the benefit of not interfering with a second hydrostatic fuse if it were not necessary. The pit was some way from the house but if the depth bombs went off by accident who knows what could happen? An image of Laurentine flashed through his mind. Roberts was explaining how he thought the smoke shells could be set off, also using a spring trigger and trip wire. There would be no fuse on the smoke, he said. The wire would go straight to the detonator. Lieutenant La Salle wanted it that way so the man in the water would have cover from the moment he dived over the side.

Granger noted that Roberts always gave La Salle the rank he'd had aboard *Farnham*, the ship in which they had served together. A stranger might interpret this as carelessness, or disrespect even. Yet between them, in their tight little group, using his friend's former rank seemed almost an expression of supreme loyalty. *We go back*, it seemed to say.

Granger thought he detected a sense of unease in Roberts when he talked about the fusing arrangements.

'Are you sure it will all work?' he asked.

Roberts looked him in the eye.

'Bugger it, Merrick. You're an engineer. You know as well as I do. This is a bloody experiment, man. I wouldn't put it any higher than that.'

Granger shrugged. Roberts was right. In theory, it should all work. In theory.

They returned to the house and sketched out a design for a metal cylinder to house the timer and detonators.

Granger showed it to di Fario, who suggested a minor change in the spring arrangement for firing the fuse cap.

'Can you weld?' he asked Granger.

'Oh yes,' Granger replied with a grin.

By evening, the device was ready. They gathered in di Fario's workshop where Granger had the firing mechanism fixed in a vice. He pulled the cord and the metal hammer snapped downwards with a satisfying click, on the place where the cap would be.

'So how long after that do we have?' La Salle asked.

'About a minute,' Granger replied, then looking at Roberts: 'Right?'

Roberts looked at each man in turn.

'I have put two, thirty second fuses on top of each other. Together they should make about a minute's worth.' He twisted a foot on the workshop floor. 'I would have liked to fire it,' he said, 'to test the cap, the detonator and the timing.'

'We'll have to manage with what we've got,' La Salle said.

'I wish to Christ I had a few more of the buggers,' Roberts muttered. 'To experiment a bit.'

'It'll work, old man,' La Salle said. 'And if it doesn't go off we should be safe behind our smokescreen before the Huns guess what's happening.'

Granger glanced at him. That, he thought, was a highly optimistic take on the situation.

That afternoon La Salle and Granger were at the kitchen table, going over di Fario's charts. Laurentine came in with two folded sacks.

'I'm going to check the creels,' she said lightly. 'I could use a strong man. To pull them up.'

Granger glanced across the table, noting a weary raising of eyebrows.

'It won't take long,' he said reasonably, rising from his chair. 'We'll be back before you know it.'

La Salle waved a hand as if to say *please; take as long as you like*. Granger grinned and followed Laurentine out into the yard. She took his arm naughtily.

'I feel like we've escaped from school,' she said, giggling.

'He just wants to make sure everything is as ready as it can be,' Granger replied loyally. 'But we'd pretty much finished for today.'

He gently unclasped her arm from his and steered her towards the launch, tied up on the small quay. Since that morning in his room she had behaved differently, even in the presence of the others. It was as if they had an understanding. At supper she brought him a plate and, pausing behind his chair, she squeezed his shoulders in a brazen expression of affection that made him colour. Granger found Laurentine's recent proprietorial manner embarrassing, yet thrilling. He had felt attracted to women before, but somewhere along the path to intimacy he had always stumbled and retreated. Lack of conviction, he thought and resigned himself to it. Yet Laurentine appeared to have enough resolve for both of them.

They boarded the launch and she threw the sacks on to the duckboard. Granger started the motor and slipped the lines. The sun was behind them as they motored out, heading north east into the bay.

'Do you have a chart?' he asked her.

She shook her head. 'I know where the creels are,' she said. 'We use transits and landmarks. They are all quite close inshore.'

Granger nodded. He knew Laurentine and her father set lobster traps around the bay but he had yet to see how successful they were.

The weather refused to break. It was hot, with just a few feathers of cirrus blurring the edges of an otherwise pristine blue. Granger leaned back as Laurentine steered the boat. He closed his eyes, felt the sun warm his hair to the roots as the boat's movement through the water created a zephyr that brushed his skin. It had been a long time since he had felt that good. What lay ahead seemed almost insignificant against the quiet joy of that moment. As a child he had experienced entire happiness, but only rarely it seemed now. Perhaps he had forgotten. He remembered best a strange encounter with something he still was unable to define. It was a day in spring and he was walking in the woods where, a little older, he would wander with his sketchbook. But on that day, alone and with no aim in mind, he had walked between the trees until he came to a small clearing. The sun filtered through the canopy overhead and drew a perfume from the grass and earth and fallen leaves. It rose in his nostrils, elemental and intoxicating. Just then he began to sense what seemed to be a growing clamour, although there was no identifiable sound. Rather, it was an omnipresent tingling, a throbbing of the life surrounding him, from the ground at his feet to the treetops. It was terrifying and enthralling. The sensation subsided, leaving him trembling and weak and with a feeling the forest had wanted to take him in for its own. It was the thing he remembered most about his childhood. It was his most cherished memory.

He looked out over the bow of the launch, across the bay to the high ground on the far shore.

'Have you ever felt like the world wanted to gobble you up?' he asked suddenly, adding quickly: 'In, well, a good way.' He searched for words. 'A bit like going home.'

'The world?' Laurentine's brow furrowed.

'I mean the earth, the sea.' Granger sat up, looking directly at her. 'Nature, maybe.'

Laurentine bit her lip. 'Please,' she said. 'Never say this to my father.'

Her voice frightened him. He stood, gripped the back of the seat.

'Well, I wouldn't. But why?'

Laurentine shot him a smile wreathed in pain.

'My mother was lost to the sea.' She turned away. 'And my uncle Eric.'

Granger felt unnerved. Her father never said what happened to his great friend Eric, his comrade at the siege of Paris. And he never spoke about her mother. He had blundered, quite innocently, into something deeply hurtful.

'I'm sorry,' he began. 'I had no –'

She pressed a finger to his lips. 'I will tell you everything,' she whispered.

She turned the launch into a small cove and asked him to drop the anchor. Granger could see a sandy bottom and reckoned they were in ten feet of water. He let go the hook with about thirty feet of chain, made it off on the bollard in the bow. He moved aft. She beckoned him to sit next to her. As he did so she curved into his shoulder, gripped his arm above the elbow. She spoke in a low voice, almost a whisper.

'My mother was uncle Eric's little sister, much younger than he. She grew up knowing my father. He was her big brother's close friend and I think she always loved him. He had his legal practice in Nice in those days, but he spent his summers here and he would always travel up for the Christmas holidays. Uncle Eric had a beautiful cutter. She was called *Elodie*, after my mother. They built her here in the shipyard. My father says she was one of the loveliest sailing boats in this part of France. Uncle Eric loved that boat – you know, the way men do. So did my father. Every summer when my father came up on the train they would take the boat on a cruise, sometimes to England. My mother was nineteen when she married and naturally she moved to Nice with my father. But they came back twice a year as he had always done and even after I was born they all went on the summer cruise. When I was three years old we sailed to the Odet River.'

Her voice darkened and Granger felt her fingers dig into the muscle of his arm.

'Of course, I can't remember it but my father told me we spent a very happy week there and on the way home they planned to put into Audierne to let me have a few days playing on the beach.' She gave out a short laugh, almost a cry. 'Audierne!' She pulled herself nearer to him and their heads were close to touching.

'I was asleep below, apparently, when it happened. It was raining and my father was preparing some food.' She smiled up at him. 'You have seen, haven't you, how my father loves to cook?'

Granger thought of the delight di Fario took in serving up his simple, irresistible food. He nodded.

She continued: 'My mother and uncle Eric were on deck. There was a fresh breeze and we were sailing fast before it. My uncle called my father to look at a steamer sailing on an opposite course. It was close inshore, too close to the dangers around the Pointe de Penmarc'h. My father told me Eric decided to run up a signal to try to warn the ship. Then they altered course to close with it. So they could see our warning.'

Granger thought of the flag they would have raised; red triangles spelling the letter *U* – *YOU ARE STANDING INTO DANGER*.

Laurentine was almost whispering into his ear now.

'As we came close to the ship they saw our signal.' She drew a deep breath. 'The ship turned sharply away from the shore. Towards deep water. Towards us.' She was shaking her head gently. 'My uncle was on the tiller. He could do nothing. My father dived below at the last moment to get me out of my cot. The steamer ploughed into us. My mother and Eric were thrown over the side by the impact. The boat broke up as it bounced down the ship's side.'

Granger felt her head twist as she swallowed hard.

'The boat was sinking. The tender was still lashed astern and my father managed to get me into it. He cast it off just before the cutter went down. Then he began shouting. I seem to remember it. I don't know whether it is really a memory. I was only three years old. Perhaps what my father told me has formed such a powerful image in my head I think I witnessed it.'

She shifted her hand from his arm to his neck, the better to hold him close. He put his arm around her shoulders. The launch rocked gently on the slight swell creating a rhythm intent on welding them together.

'First, he called their names. He rowed, around and around. In the rain and the wind. Calling out. Nothing. Then he called to God. He pleaded with God. He begged God. It got dark.' She paused, swallowed hard again. 'And then he cursed God!'

She was embracing him and he held her like a child holds a doll; with affection, if not commitment.

'So we managed to get into Audierne, thanks to the following breeze. He chartered a boat and crew that night. They were out for three days and nights. Nothing. A few small pieces of wreckage, but –' she stopped. Granger tightened his grip on her shoulder a little. She sat up suddenly and looked at him directly in her penetrating way.

'Have you lost someone? Someone you love?' she demanded.

Granger thought of his father, mother and brother. Separated from him by a gulf of Christian dogma, created by a supposition he could not disprove.

'I guess I have,' he said. 'Not in that way, but – yes.'

She nestled back into his chest. 'I sensed it,' she said, satisfied. 'I knew.'

He stroked her hair, conscious of a growing turmoil. It seemed to communicate with her and she twisted her head upwards, found his lips. She pulled him on to the duckboard, snatching feverishly at his clothes. She touched him then seized him, forcing a gasp from his throat. Granger glimpsed the deepening blue of the sky as they rocked and turned on the hard wood and he remembered again the pull of the forest, drawing him in.

They weighed and motored to the first creel, then picked up half a dozen more. They had six fine lobster and she said it was enough. He steered the launch back along the coast as she dipped the sacks in seawater and a relaxed silence overtook them. Granger tried to blot out, for now, the chaos in his thoughts and concentrated instead on what she had told him, about her mother and uncle. He imagined the scene on the bridge of the steamer when her captain saw the warning, hastily checked his chart and position and realised he was heading directly into the rocks that extend a long way offshore on that coast. Panic. A hard turn to starboard to run clear. Regardless of the small craft in their path, the people who had come to warn them.

'Didn't he stop?' he asked suddenly, a note of anger in his voice.

'What?' Laurentine looked up from the lobster sacks.

'Didn't the steamer stop? I mean they must have seen what happened.'

Laurentine brushed back her hair, straightened.

'They saw what happened, but they didn't stop. My father tried to see the ship's name, or port of registry. But even then his eyesight was poor and all he could make out was her ensign.'

She exhaled slowly through pursed lips.

'It was a German flag.'

Laurentine entered the kitchen with a dainty step, carrying her dripping sacks and smiling as if concealing some private triumph. She tipped the sacks into the sink and the men saw large, lumbering lobster, wriggling and climbing lazily over each other.

'Our dinner!' Laurentine laughed. 'To be cooked by

259

the master chef – my father!' She did a little skip and made a theatrical sweep of her arm.

La Salle moved over for a closer look. They were magnificent specimens, creatures that would cost rather a lot anywhere. He became uneasy.

'I should pay you for these,' he said quietly. 'This is too generous of you.'

She tapped his arm gaily. 'Oh, you worry too much about paying! Vous êtes chez vous ici!'

La Salle responded with a courtly nod, almost a bow. *Chez vous*, he thought. He noticed that when she spoke to Granger now she always used "tu".

Di Fario took charge of the lobster. La Salle was surprised to see him lift each one carefully and place it on its back, almost tenderly, on the board around the sink, its legs in the air. Then he dispatched the animal with the curved blade of a large knife, slicing the head in two with a swift thrust.

'Don't you boil them?' La Salle asked.

'I do,' di Fario said, washing the knife in a basin of water. 'But if the roles were reversed, I myself would prefer the knife first.' He turned to face the younger man, a teasing look on his face. 'It is a question of courtesy to the vanquished, no?'

La Salle smiled as di Fario turned back to the board. He began to sing in a low voice, some strange and sad melody La Salle could not identify, then he realised the words were not French, but Italian. Laurentine brought in onions and her father sliced them into a wide pan that almost covered the top of the stove. As the onions fried in hot oil, di Fario opened a jar and tipped the contents over the onions. Almost immediately, La Salle was hit by an intense smell, a delicious, salty pungency that could have been the very presence of the sea.

Di Fario breathed in deeply. 'Anchovies,' he said, stirring the conserved fillets of fish into the onions.

La Salle rose and crossed to the stove. He, too, took a deep breath, nodded approvingly.

Di Fario was slicing tomatoes into the pan. He mashed them into the onion-anchovy mix with a wooden mallet, pressing down with the heel of his hand. Soon he had a viscous, golden-red liquid. He threw in a handful of herbs, a mound of crushed green garlic and some dried chilli then poured in a bottle of white wine. Into this liquid he placed the newly-dead lobster. He covered the pan, gave it a shake and resumed his song. He remained there, bent over the range, stirring and shaking the pan occasionally, until the room was filled with a smell – no, La Salle thought. It was more than that. It was the very taste, the concentrated essence of the opulence of the sea.

Di Fario served the lobster in its thick red sauce on beds of spaghetti with a bowl of green salad in the centre of the table. He had spent a little time in his cellar choosing the wine and brought up four bottles of a Loire white. The spaghetti baffled everyone except him and his daughter, but soon they were all twirling their forks successfully and digging out the lobster flesh, making appreciative murmuring sounds.

La Salle glanced around the table. Roberts and Chalky were scorning each other's attempts to master the spaghetti; Granger and Laurentine, in their customary positions next to each other, were talking in low voices and, next to him at the head of the table, di Fario was eating slowly, raising his lion's head from time to time to beam at his daughter and their guests. La Salle felt a stab of anguish. The deed they were contemplating could not be reconciled with this scene. Yet from the moment the idea of attacking the U-boat occurred to him it seemed the only course he could possibly take. He could not shirk it. He had volunteered for warfare by deception. They all had. That was what they would do.

'Have you read anything of Helmuth Von Moltke?' di Fario asked suddenly.

La Salle paused.

'Von Moltke, commander of the German military?'

'No. That's Helmuth's nephew. I'm talking about the uncle, Bismarck's great strategist. Some think he invented the modern way of making war. Certainly, to us, the French, it seemed like that in 1870. With his lightning advances, long-range canon and skirmishing attacks, we felt we were facing a different kind of enemy. Von Moltke was a meticulous planner, but he once said something very interesting.' Di Fario waved a finger in the air magisterially: 'No plan survives contact with the enemy!'

He smiled, speared a piece of lettuce with his fork, deftly crumpled it into a parcel and popped it into his mouth. He chewed, then: 'I say this not to deter you, my captain, but to encourage you to make a plan that has the best possible chance of working.' He pointed his fork at La Salle's chest. 'Apart from anything else, I would dearly love to prove Von Moltke wrong.'

'You think the plan is inadequate?'

'In some ways, yes.'

'Tell me, then.'

Di Fario smiled again. 'I am telling you,' he said gently. 'Now, as I understand it, you and your men intend to pose as fishermen. No?'

La Salle nodded.

'Have you – any of you – ever fished?'

'Merrick has,' La Salle replied stoutly.

'Ah, yes. But he fished from a dory with a long line. In a chaloupe one uses nets.'

La Salle felt his face redden. Di Fario was right. None of them had the slightest idea about how to cast a net for sardines. Their U-boat commander would certainly bowl out a bunch of fumbling amateurs.

'Perhaps you could instruct us,' he said coolly.

'Perhaps.' Di Fario sipped his wine, then pursed his lips. 'There is something else.'

La Salle tilted his head inquiringly.

Di Fario leaned towards him, suddenly very earnest.

'The attack depends on you attaching the tender to the submarine, setting a short fuse and then swimming away, no?'

La Salle nodded.

'I can see a difficulty,' di Fario said quietly.

'What?'

'Well, the men on the submarine will realise something is wrong when you dive in and swim for your ship. No? They might well think the tender is a danger. So. What would you do, in their place?'

La Salle rotated a strand of spaghetti on his fork moodily.

'Cast it off,' he said.

'Yes.' Di Fario held up a hand. 'Let us say it takes them what? – ten, perhaps fifteen seconds to realise something is wrong and untie the tender? Let's say thirty seconds, to be generous. You have been working on the basis that a sixty second fuse will give you time to get clear, no? So the tender now has thirty seconds to drift away from the U-boat before the charges go off. In that time it could move far enough away for even your depth bombs to fail in their purpose.'

La Salle felt a jolt in his leg. He shifted painfully. Di Fario was right. The U-boat crew might well shove off the tender. And if the U-boat survived the depth charges, *Telenn Mor* would have only smoke shells to cover an attempted escape. He sighed.

'What do you suggest?' he said, his voice taking on a mocking tone. 'If we tried to attach the tender with a lock and chain they might get a little suspicious, don't you think?'

Di Fario did not answer. He rose from his seat, went

out into the porch and returned with a length of rope. La Salle recognised it as a light hemp, untarred; the sort of line that might be used as a tender's painter. Di Fario returned to his place and, with a slightly theatrical flourish that attracted the attention of everyone at the table, tied the rope to the top rail of his chair. La Salle watched as his fingers moved quickly over a familiar knot, a round turn and two half hitches, it seemed, with a tight twist at the end.

'Voilà!' Di Fario said. 'I have secured the tender.' He handed the standing part of the rope to La Salle. 'Now cast it off.'

La Salle stood, took the rope, noting a slight stiffness. The others were watching. Di Fario held out a hand expressively and smiled. He nodded meaningfully at his knot. La Salle felt for the end and started to work the knot loose. The hitch would not move. He tried to pull the end of the line through but it refused to budge. He tried pushing with the fingers of one hand and pulling with his other thumb and forefinger. It was solid. He could not unbend di Fario's knot. Granger jumped from his seat, grinned at di Fario and set about the knot. He could not loosen the last hitch, let alone undo it.

'So cut it,' di Fario urged.

Granger pulled out his pocket knife and sliced at the rope. The blade cut easily through the strands, but it held. The feel of the blade reminded him of the *Lusitania's* copper wireless cable which he had, ultimately, managed to cut. Granger cocked his head quizzically, then cut down again, harder. He could not sever this. La Salle held out his hand, requesting the knife. He, too, cut hard, without parting the line. He glanced at di Fario and bent back towards the rope and separated the strands, cutting with Granger's knife. He straightened and smiled, pulled back the fibres and showed them to Granger. Spliced into the lay of the rope was a bright steel wire.

Di Fario pointed at the bight of cut rope and wire in La Salle's hands.

'It's rigging steel,' he said. 'It took very little time to weave it into the line. It will work. By the time they bring out wire cutters it will be too late.'

La Salle sat down. Granger, who understood immediately what had been under discussion, returned to his seat. The two men exchanged a glance across Laurentine's back. Granger's expression prompted a wave of misery. It said what La Salle felt; di Fario was taking charge.

La Salle declined cognac with his coffee. He felt di Fario had not quite finished with him and his plan. Sure enough, as Laurentine re-filled their cups, the old man leaned towards him.

'So how is your leg?' he asked.

La Salle sniffed. 'Fine.'

'Can you swim with it?'

'Of course.'

Di Fario turned back to his coffee. 'And if you can't?' he said softly.

La Salle squirmed slightly. 'I'll be all right.'

Di Fario faced him.

'Why not spend a few hours training. Tomorrow. This weather is set to last; the sea is warm.' He lowered his head. 'See how fast you can swim. Take a watch. Time yourself.'

Granger heard him. He looked past Laurentine. 'That's a good idea, Julian,' he said.

La Salle glanced at them in turn. Of course it was a good idea.

'Where do you suggest?' he asked, a touch wearily. 'Without arousing suspicion?'

'Morgat,' di Fario said. 'Across the bay. At this time of year the beach is full of people. Even with the war. Swimmers will not arouse anyone's curiosity.'

'You know, something's been bothering me,' Granger said. 'You are going to be swimming in pants and shirt. That's going to slow you down.'

La Salle groaned inwardly. Why was everyone so intent on finding flaws in his plan as precious time slipped away?

'Yes,' he said. 'Yes. So?'

'Thomas is right. We should try to see just how far you can get in sixty seconds, in your clothes.'

La Salle sighed. 'All right,' he said, then, irritably: 'Where am I to get a spare pair of trousers?'

Annoyingly, Granger seemed to find this funny.

Di Fario was called away to look over a damaged tuna boat and Laurentine was appointed skipper of the launch to take them on the swimming trial. La Salle watched as she packed her picnic basket in the after end and Granger helped her with a bag of towels. Their casual intimacy piqued him. He felt like an outsider.

'Come on, you two. This isn't a holiday outing you know,' he grumbled.

Granger grinned. 'We might as well make the most of it,' he said.

La Salle frowned, did not reply. He settled on a thwart as Laurentine used a length of line to deftly spring the launch away from the jetty. She was dressed in trousers and shirt, and although she was not wearing her fisherman's smock or cap, she looked just as La Salle had first seen her when he drifted in and out of consciousness aboard the boat that rescued them. She was lovely, he had to admit. He just wished he could feel more generous about the bond that seemed to be growing between her and his friend. Was it jealousy? Certainly, he felt attracted to Laurentine. Her casual grace, that twist of the head, the quizzical sidelong glance, inflamed him. In his secret thoughts he possessed her, pulled her slim hips against him, pressed against her mouth. Then he would see her and Granger together and he'd feel grubby. Sometimes she laid a hand lightly on Granger's shoulder and she had acquired a habit of arranging his long hair in a motherly way.

They were chatting now, as she steered towards the land across the bay. He heard Granger's Canadian-accented French rise and fall with newly-acquired fluency. At first, he found Granger's growing mastery of the language irksome, because of the Laurentine connection, of course. Now, as his friend demonstrated an unsuspected linguistic skill, he felt an inexplicable stirring of pride.

She was pointing ahead. La Salle shaded his eyes and saw a small sandy cove. Someone was walking at the water's edge, otherwise it was deserted. On the starboard side lay Morgat's pleasure beach which he was anxious to avoid. It was still early but he could see a number of swimmers and groups of children playing on the sand. Laurentine's cove, he thought, was admirably suited to their purpose.

'Not much tide in there, is there?' La Salle asked.

She shook her head, gesturing from one side to the other.

'It would be better to swim across the entrance. No current,' she said.

As they closed the land, she pointed to the hills behind the coast.

'There is a wood over there. Full of pheasants.' She smiled at Granger. 'Perhaps we can get some. Another day. Thomas roasts them.' She gathered the fingers of one hand to her puckered lips, made a kissing noise and opened the hand towards heaven. 'Delicious!'

'Does Thomas shoot?' La Salle asked, thinking of the gun case aboard the tug.

She shook her head. 'Not any more. His eyes are weak.' She tossed her head slightly. 'But he taught me. Since I was a child.' She gave La Salle a look he found disconcerting.

'I shoot,' she said.

Granger turned towards her.

'You shoot?' What with?'

She shrugged. 'My father's old gun. We have bullets for it but we don't use them. It is a big bullet, no?' She held up a finger and thumb, about half an inch apart to show the size of the rifle's round.

'If a bullet that big hits you, even in the arm, it can kill you. My father says so. He has seen it. Shock.' She sniffed. 'For hunting we load with shot. It's fine for small game. Birds. Rabbits.'

Granger sucked in his cheeks. Shooting creatures for food was OK, although unlike his brother he could take no pleasure in it. And he had never been able to think of fishing as sport. Now he felt disquiet at the idea of her killing things. And with a gun that had taken down men. He looked away from them, at the woods she had pointed out. Why not use a shotgun? The big bore of the Spencer rifle would allow a moderate load of shot, but it was far from an ideal weapon for pheasant shooting. He remembered di Fario said he had used shot to kill pigeons during the siege of Paris. Did Laurentine want to relive her father's experience? Did she want to live up to Laurentine Proust, the heroine of Châteaudun whose name she bore? There was something in this, he felt. Her look, her demeanour, during the telling of di Fario's tale suggested she felt very much part of her father's adventures in war. Without doubt, she shared its aftermath of hatred. Granger felt a creeping sense of gloom. Psychic traces would linger on di Fario's gun. Of course they would. Granger found himself haunted by a word, a French word: *malsain*. Unhealthy.

They had brought a couple of fishing floats and Granger dropped them about 200 feet apart. He looked at the space between the bobbing glass spheres. It didn't seem like much distance on water. Far less than he had imagined. They anchored the launch close to the float on the south side of the cove.

'Right, then,' La Salle said.

He kicked off his shoes and climbed on to the thwart. The launch rocked a little and he had to fight for his balance. Granger thought he detected a flash of pain cross his face as he tensed his legs to jump. Granger looked at the watch di Fario had loaned him, then La Salle. He was in the water now, swimming awkwardly.

After covering half the distance to the float, Granger thought La Salle's action was becoming smoother, but it was clear his leg was refusing to co-ordinate properly. Granger bit his lip. La Salle reached the float, swam around it and trod water for a moment, looking back at the launch. He started swimming towards them, much more slowly than before. Granger looked at the watch. It had taken La Salle nearly two minutes to swim the 200 feet.

Granger experienced a sensation of utter clarity, like sailing out of a fog on the Grand Banks. He saw the way ahead as he stood there in the boat, watching his friend approach. He did not want to die. More than at any time in his life he felt he had so much to live for. In his secret heart he yearned for a future, perhaps with Laurentine or someone like her who would help him understand himself, answer some difficult questions. It was a future in which he would travel, perhaps aboard his own ship, to places where he would see and paint the wondrous creatures he had seen only in ornithology books. In this dreamed-of life Julian, too, had a part. No, he did not want to die. But the life he wanted to live had to include Julian.

Granger reached down and helped La Salle climb back aboard the launch. He sat on a thwart, panting.

'Well?' he said.

Granger made a face. 'One minute, fifty seconds,' he said.

La Salle looked at Laurentine. Then Granger.

'Are you sure?'

Granger nodded. La Salle dropped his head, making a swift calculation. If he had been swimming away from a charge on a sixty second fuse he would have been little more than a hundred feet away from it when it went up.

'Let me try,' Granger said. He spoke in English but Laurentine recognised instantly the meaning of his words. La Salle looked up. She was gripping Granger's arm tightly, a look of fear in her eyes.

La Salle shook his head. 'I have to do it,' he said. He saw Granger was barefoot. He had taken off his shoes.

'Why?' Granger gently shook Laurentine's arm free, dropped down on to his haunches, looked into La Salle's face.

'Why you? It should be the one best suited to the job, shouldn't it?' He stood up, handed the watch to Laurentine and dived noiselessly into the sea.

La Salle got to his feet. Granger was almost at the float. Then he disappeared. Laurentine gasped, but Granger's head appeared on the far side of the mark as he turned and struck out strongly for the launch.

'How long?' La Salle asked her as Granger pulled himself aboard.

'Fifty-five seconds,' she whispered.

La Salle sank down on to the seat. Granger was grinning, tossing his head like a dog.

'I'm kind of getting used to swimming in my clothes,' he said.

Laurentine gave him a towel and turned away as he shucked off his shirt. La Salle had never seen Granger without clothes. He watched as his friend rubbed the towel over his chest and shoulders, the contours of his heavily muscled frame sharpening as he moved.

'You're not going to get dry?' Granger asked.

'I'm all right,' La Salle said, thinking of his own spare torso. 'The sun's drying me already.'

'I was always pretty good at swimming,' Granger said, by way of apology.

'I knew that.'

Laurentine brought out her basket and arranged a cloth on the launch's bench. She did not speak; her mood had changed, the holiday air had vanished. La Salle watched discreetly as she spread the bread with tuna rillettes. She understood perfectly the change that had just been made to the plan. She had not been involved in the discussion, such as it was, but she was perfectly aware that it would be Granger and not he who would be exposed to the greatest risk. He tried to discern the thoughts behind her rather stern face. He could not. All he detected, for sure, was a hardness around the mouth. It was a look of resolve.

'So I'll take the tender. When it comes to it,' Granger said.

'All right,' La Salle replied. Granger was right. He was the better man for the task. They ate in silence. It was hot, a flawless day in high summer. The beach at Morgat was becoming busy and La Salle watched as a small yacht sailed into the bay on a light south-westerly breeze. The boat brought up smartly into the wind and he saw a woman at the tiller as a man dropped an anchor from the bow and tugged down the sails. *Normal life,* he thought. Someone on leave from the war, no doubt. Snatching what happiness they could. He felt a stirring in his guts. What was his happiness? A part of him yearned to be on that small boat, with someone. Someone. To light a small oil stove and make tea and cook food that always tastes better afloat than it can ever taste ashore. To feel the oneness he knew existed but which, thus far, had eluded him. He longed for this yet the greater part of him hungered for something else, something just as deeply rooted in his elemental self. He wanted, most of all, to prove he, La Salle – scorned by people like the Bathwells – could match any pedigree.

'We should take the chaloupe out as soon as we can,' he said. 'Tomorrow. We'll need Thomas to show us how to handle the nets.'

'Yes,' Granger said, chewing thoughtfully.

Laurentine understood. 'You will need me,' she said quietly. Granger sat up.

'What are you saying?' he asked sharply.

'You will need me,' she repeated. 'My father has never used a net. He is a lawyer and a boatbuilder, but he is not a fisherman.'

La Salle tossed the last of his bread into the sea.

'Well...' he said, in English.

'I don't like the idea of taking her out in the new boat,' Granger said quietly.

'Do you think I do?' La Salle ran his fingers through his drying hair. 'What choice do we have? You've seen the gear on that boat. Unless we get someone to show us how it all works we'll look like a gang of chumps or –' he paused, 'a crew of men up to mischief. From a U-boat's point of view.'

Granger thought for a moment.

'Couldn't we just sail out, spend a little time and come back. That's when we hope to be stopped, isn't it?'

La Salle shook his head. It was no good. Everything had to be done the way it would be done in the service. Their disguise had to be perfect. *Telenn Mor* was now a Q-Ship and she would be operated like one. Nothing could be left to chance.

'It won't work, Merrick. You know the lengths we go to with our deceptions. We can't relax that discipline now.'

Laurentine was leaning back against the gunwale, her eyes closed, face bathed in the sun.

La Salle turned to her. 'It will help us. If you show us how to work the gear,' he said.

She opened one eye, looked at him, then Granger.

'Whenever you like,' she breathed.

'But when we begin our mission, it will only be us.'

'Naturally,' she said, breaking into a smile which, for some inexplicable reason, La Salle found eerily unsettling.

They recovered the floats, weighed the launch's grapnel and motored steadily back across the bay. The swim had benefitted his leg, La Salle thought as they walked to the house. It felt better than ever and he was moving with barely a limp. He asked Chalky to come to his room.

'Is everything all right, sir?' the Londoner asked anxiously, as he closed the door behind him.

'Oh, fine.'

La Salle opened a drawer in the clothes chest and took out a parcel. He laid it on the bed and unwrapped it. Inside was the large French tricolour. Chalky's eyes widened.

'We're not going to fly that, are we?' he asked.

La Salle smiled. 'No. Well, not in its present form.' He shook the flag, arranged it tidily on the counterpane. 'I got this in Brest. We only want the bunting. Look.'

He took a piece of paper out of his pocket, unfolded it and handed it to Chalky. It was a design he had drawn of the Royal Navy's white ensign, with RED, BLUE and WHITE written into their respective places.

'Could you sew one of these, using material from the tricolour?'

Chalky studied the drawing.

'I reckon so,' he said. 'The thin red lines are a bit fiddly, but if I can get some decent scissors and needle and thread, I reckon I can make that all right.'

La Salle ran a finger over the narrow red bands.

'They have to be exactly like that, Chalky or it will be upside down.'

'Oh, I know that, sir. Like a little union flag in there, isn't it?'

'Precisely. You'll see I've put some measurements along

the edges. They are what they call centimetres. The tape's in here.' He handed Chalky a small bag which, from the bulges, clearly contained a large pair of scissors.

Chalky looked at the bag, smiled and tapped his nose.

'You want me to do this quietly, like. I won't show the old man or the girl?'

'There's no need for them to know. We've had a relaxed time recently, but we're going back into action now. You remember your orders for raising the ensign?'

'It goes up when we start shooting.'

'Usually, yes. In this case I want it raised exactly forty-five seconds after I jump out of the tender.' He waved a hand. 'Sorry, Chalky. I forgot to tell you. Mr Granger will be doing that.'

Chalky did not seem surprised.

'He's a crack swimmer, isn't he?'

'Yes he is. Now, can you do that flag for me tonight?'

'I reckon I can.' Chalky frowned. 'Does that mean we start tomorrow?'

'We're going out, yes. But just to get the hang of the fishing gear. It'll be a dry run, so to speak. We'll go in earnest the day after. Could you ask Roberts to pop up?'

Chalky left with the bundle under his arm. Roberts appeared a few minutes later and confirmed the charges and the timers were ready. The space they'd made in the tender's bow was ready to be sealed with a dummy bulkhead once the explosives and smoke composition were loaded aboard.

Roberts turned to leave, La Salle called after him.

'By the way. Miss di Fario will be coming with us tomorrow. To show us the ropes.'

Roberts rubbed his thumb on his lower lip, nodded and left the room.

The southwesterly breeze was freshening as they motored the chaloupe into the bay heading almost due west.

Laurentine had wanted to sail *Telenn Mor* out of the yard, but Granger had insisted on running up the motor to familiarise himself with it. It ran well, La Salle thought, although the cloud of white smoke emitted by the burning paraffin was unfamiliar and, at first, alarming. They were making about four or five knots and Granger said she might do even better in a calm. Laurentine was teasing Granger, affecting a pouting scorn over his desire to use the engine. She knew boats, La Salle had to admit. And in his sailor's heart he, too, would have liked to sail *Telenn Mor* out of her berth, the way she had arrived. But Granger was right. They might need the motor. They had to know its capabilities and flaws.

After a mile or so Granger pronounced himself satisfied and they hoisted the sails. La Salle was surprised at how easily the big lugsails went up and, when they trimmed the sheets, how well the chaloupe footed, close reaching at six or seven knots. He looked astern. The tender was towing well, not yawing much, apparently quite happy in the slight turbulence of the wake. They had not loaded the charges for this training outing and La Salle wondered how the tender would tow with the extra weight in its bow. Well, tomorrow they would find out. He took the tiller from Laurentine, felt the pull. There was a slight tug to weather, otherwise the helm was wonderfully light.

'If we lashed it she'd sail herself,' he said.

Laurentine nodded. 'We do that all the time. Downwind can be more difficult, but with the breeze like this, these boats take care of themselves.'

'Having a good time back here?' Granger grinned, joining them aft.

'Lovely balance,' La Salle said. 'Here. Try her yourself.'

Granger took the tiller, glancing instinctively aloft.

'Reminds me of the catboats back home,' he said. 'Good boat.'

They sailed on, south of the Pierres Noires, bearing

away slightly towards Ushant. They were reaching fast, helped by the north-going stream. Soon Ushant was abeam, then on the starboard quarter.

'We should start looking for fish,' Laurentine said. 'You will see a disturbance on the sea. Like melted silver. And the birds: the gulls always spot them first. When we – '

She stopped and raised a hand to shade her eyes.

'What is that?'

La Salle followed her stare. There was something in the sea, fine on their port bow.

'Merrick, can you make that out?'

Granger changed hands on the tiller, moved to the port side. 'It's a periscope,' he said quietly.

'See that! U-boat!' Chalky, standing amidships, was jumping up and down, pointing.

'Stop it! Chalky! Stop pointing. No English!' La Salle bit his lip. 'What is he doing down here? He should be miles to the north.'

'Looks like you'll get a chance to ask him,' Granger drawled. 'He's coming up.'

The submarine did indeed appear to be climbing out of the sea, less than a mile away, steaming directly towards them.

'Right. Everyone. No English.' La Salle hissed. 'I'll talk to them.'

He felt a pounding in his ears. Why hadn't they loaded the depth bombs? It had been his decision to make this a dry run and he knew why. He did not want Laurentine on the boat when it was towing a potentially lethal cargo which, in safety terms, they could not guarantee. Yet, he reasoned, they could never have imagined they would see the U-boat in these waters, so far from its hunting ground further north.

'Chalky, get our lunch out. And that tinned food, the bread and wine in the locker.'

They had stocked *Telenn Mor* with stores, as the fishing

276

crews did. Armed or not, they would act out their part.

The U-boat steamed slowly towards their port side, fully surfaced, its shark-grey hull glistening. *Telenn Mor* was still sailing close hauled. A figure appeared in the conning tower, then another. The taller of them was flapping his arms, ordering them to lower their sails.

'Drop the sails,' La Salle said. 'Chalky, Roberts. Keep out of the way.'

Laurentine and Granger dropped the sails quickly and bundled the canvas on to the lugs. One of the men in the conning tower had a megaphone. The submarine was almost abeam now, about 200 feet away. The megaphone man was waving them back, shouting in German; 'keep your distance', he seemed to be saying. La Salle thought he was the first officer. The man at his side was the commander, he was sure. Then they saw two seamen emerge from a hatch aft, carrying a tiny boat. One of the men climbed the conning tower, took something from the captain, returned to the deck and, with the other rating, launched the dinghy. He rowed it furiously towards *Telenn Mor*. They took his painter as he came alongside and secured the little boat amidships. The sailor bobbed to his feet, holding the chaloupe's gunwale. He saluted unsteadily as his boat slapped against the hull.

'Je suis Hirsch,' he said. 'Please take.'

He handed over a small package in waterproof canvas. La Salle took it, glancing at the submarine. The officer he believed was the captain was pointing, nodding. *Open it*, he seemed to say. La Salle unwrapped the package, his eye immediately fell on a sizeable wad of French banknotes. There was a letter. He unfolded the paper, reading quickly.

'If you are reading this message you are at my discretion. I propose to spare your ship, on condition. You will use the money to purchase as many items listed overleaf as possible. They are arranged in order

of preference. You will bring the goods to this position twenty-four hours after receiving this message. In the meantime I shall entertain aboard my ship one of your crew. He will be returned to you when we receive our purchases. If you do not agree I shall sink your ship immediately. If you agree, your man can accompany my crewman and he will be kept safe, provided there is no intervention from your navy. Wave this letter three times from your bow to show you intend to comply. Yours, Kapitanleutnant Heinrich Falk.'

La Salle turned the paper over. His eye fell on "six cases Bordeaux" and "one dozen large cheeses". He turned to Hirsch, still gripping the gunwale.

'Vous parlez Français?' he asked in a friendly tone.

'Un peu,' Hirsch replied, grinning at Laurentine.

La Salle gestured to the shopping list.

'You cannot carry all this in your little boat.'

Hirsch pointed aft, to *Telenn Mor's* tender.

'Use that,' he said.

La Salle nodded. He turned inboard. Granger had been trying to read over his shoulder. La Salle lowered his head, whispered to him: 'Come with me to the bow.'

They walked around the chaloupe's masts and La Salle revealed the contents of the German commander's note.

Granger whistled softly, hunched his shoulders.

'What choice do we have?'

La Salle glanced over his shoulder at the submarine, holding station on the port side.

'None.' He bent his head. 'Don't you see? This is more than we could have hoped for. I'll go on board of the U-boat. You bring the food. Then we carry out the attack as planned.'

'Why don't I go?'

La Salle waved the note. 'Whoever wrote this has excellent French. You are becoming fluent, but your accent

278

would give you away to anyone with a good command of the language.'

Granger sniffed. 'You've got an accent, too.'

'I know. But I can disguise it.' La Salle made an impatient gesture. 'Hang it all, Merrick. Don't make me remind you that you are under my command.'

His friend shrugged, turned a toe on the deck.

'Good. Now I'll signal I agree. You take the boat back and get Thomas to help you put this list together. I'll mark this position on the chart. You return tomorrow.' He whispered. 'Just you, Roberts and Chalky.'

'I know.'

'Then you come over with the tender, as we planned. Armed. As soon as I can I'll jump over the side. Then you can trigger the charge and do the same.' He lowered his head. 'But if I am unable to get clear and you see your chance, take it.'

Granger glanced aloft.

La Salle gripped his arm. 'We are on active service, Merrick. Remember that. There are no choices, no alternatives, no half measures. We were bowled out; our people were killed. Now we fight back.'

Granger held out his hand. La Salle brushed it aside and took him into his arms. They embraced for a moment and La Salle thought he heard Granger murmur something, but it was nothing he could hear properly. He climbed into the chaloupe's bow, turned to the U-boat and waved the German's note three times over his head. The smaller of the two men in the conning tower waved back, once. He and Granger made their way aft.

'I shall be going with the German gentleman for a while,' he said to Laurentine. Roberts, entirely mystified, nodded. Chalky looked as if he were about to speak, then grinned amiably at Hirsch. La Salle climbed over the side and lowered himself into the U-boat's dinghy, smothering the discomfort in his leg.

'A demain,' he said, waving cheerfully back at *Telenn Mor*. Hirsch began to pull towards the U-boat. She had been kept accurately in position, La Salle noted. Never more than about 200 feet closer to the chaloupe. *Good*.

'Where did you learn French?' he asked the young seaman.

'A l'école.' Hirsch grinned back.

La Salle smiled. *And not that long ago*, he thought. Hirsch was probably in his late teens, an athlete from the look of him. He rowed the dinghy with muscular grace. Yet the note and the shopping list had been written by someone with better French than this youngster. The thought prompted a spurt of unease. He hoped the U-boat's linguist was not sufficiently skilled to detect his own accent. Before arriving in the Bay of Douarnenez he had not spoken French on a daily basis since he was ten. He glanced back at *Telenn Mor*. Granger and Laurentine were making sail. The tender was bobbing astern. It looked a little large, he thought, to serve a vessel like the chaloupe, but otherwise everything about his ship seemed perfect. God knows, it would have to be.

He turned and saw the submarine's ugly shape ahead. A few men were standing on the foredeck watching him. The two officers in the conning platform had not moved. The taller one was scanning the sea all around with glasses. The dinghy bumped against the rounded hull and Hirsch threw a line to a man on deck. La Salle saw him take a turn on a rail running a few inches above the hull casing. *Please*, he whispered in his head, *let Merrick be watching this. Let him see where they take the lines of small craft coming alongside.*

Hirsch urged him up on to the U-boat. Some metalwork projected from the deck-at-side and he grabbed it, hauling himself up. Hirsch climbed out of the tender and they pulled it aboard. Then he took La Salle's arm, leading him in a friendly fashion to a steel ladder attached to the tower.

'Allez!' he said, grinning and pointing upwards.

La Salle gripped the ladder and climbed. He emerged on to a steel grating. The tall officer watched him. He had a huge red beard and an expression La Salle took to be of faint disgust. As he mounted the platform the man gave a snort and pointedly turned his back, resuming his search of the horizon. The other officer leaned forward.

'I am Kapitanleutnant Falk,' he said. 'Welcome to my ship.'

Unlike his companion, Falk had a thin beard and a wispy moustache. His face was a curious mixture of young and old. Pre-aged, perhaps. He gestured towards the other: 'This is my first officer, Humke.'

The redbeard turned, stared at La Salle and nodded curtly.

La Salle gave them his family name. The two officers spoke together for a moment.

'Come below,' Falk said.

He pointed to a hatchway. La Salle lowered his body through the opening, felt for the rungs of a ladder and climbed down. As his upper body and head descended into the gloom he faltered, hit by the most appalling stench. It was unlike anything he had ever encountered, a mix of urine, diesel, body odours and filthy bilge water. He gagged, reached the bottom of the ladder and covered his face with a hand.

'You'll get used to it,' Falk said.

He spoke in near-perfect French. La Salle thought he detected an eastern accent; Lorraine, perhaps. Falk waved to a rating. It was Hirsch, he saw, who had entered the interior of the U-boat by another hatch. Falk spoke to him and although La Salle could not understand what he was saying he was struck by the informality of the commander's tone. Indeed, all the men he had seen apart from redbeard seemed relaxed.

'Hirsch will take care of you,' Falk said. 'We shall talk later.'

281

Then he disappeared into some recess screened by a heavy green curtain. Hirsch tugged his arm.

'Come with me,' he said amiably.

La Salle followed, moving forward along a narrow passage between winding pipes, racks holding cables and complexes of metalwork he found bewildering. They passed through a bulkhead with a watertight door held open with a piece of small stuff. Beyond was a long corridor, gloomy and almost dark, lit by a weak electric bulb.

'Here is your bedroom,' Hirsch pronounced grandly, gesturing into the space with a flourish.

La Salle saw long steel casings, shelves and a few pieces of bedding. It was the torpedo room. Hirsch pointed to a wooden shelf over one of the long metal tubes.

'Your bed,' he said.

La Salle nodded. In the Royal Navy submariners were generally thought of as a sub-species for whom comforts were not at all necessary. Was it the same in the German navy?

'Thank you,' he said.

Hirsch grinned, pointed to another shelf over an empty space forward where, it seemed, a torpedo had been stowed.

'My bed,' Hirsch said.

La Salle nodded again. As his eyes became accustomed to the near-darkness he saw there were six torpedo racks. Four were empty. Which one had accounted for his ship, he wondered? His bunk seemed to be a spare; unlike the others it was not hung around with clothes, duffel bag and odd pieces of kit. La Salle marvelled at the squalor. The smell from the bilge jammed in his throat and the pale paint on the metalwork was smeared with grime. He poked the thin mattress behind the leeboard of the bunk. Nothing alive in there, as far as he could see. The passageway seemed to be the only living area in the ship.

282

A folding metal table near Hirsch's bed looked like it served as a mess. The thought of food, in that stink, propelled his guts towards his throat. He swallowed hard and was about to ask Hirsch where he would find the head, when the engine noise increased. As the revolutions rose he felt a trembling in the steel shell around him. They were steaming; quite fast, he guessed, from the pitch of the diesels. He gripped the edge of the bunk, but the ship was steady. A klaxon noise made him jump. The diesels came to a clattering stop. A whirring noise came from somewhere aft. Suddenly there was the sound of rushing feet, clanging bulkhead doors. Hirsch was pulling his arm.

'Forward! Forward! Schnell!'

La Salle followed him forward to a steel bulkhead. In moments they were surrounded by men, all edging as close to the metal wall as they could. Hirsch gestured towards him, pointing a hand downwards at a sharp angle. They were diving. La Salle felt the sole dip under his feet. Then they were all pressed together, hard up against the bulkhead, a mass of men adding living ballast to the bow as the vessel tilted sharply towards the bottom. The men were hanging off pieces of tubing, clinging to the submarine's innards as it dived. To La Salle's immense relief they ignored him. They seemed to be listening. For what? Shifting the weight of the crew into the bow was obviously a measure taken to speed up the dive. Why the hurry? La Salle tried to visualise the chart in his head. The French navy would be unlikely to hunt U-boats in that location. And they were far from the shipping routes and the submarine's favoured targets. Were they running away?

He did not wait long for an answer. A mighty tremor gripped the submarine, shook it, just as the crash of a deafening explosion filled the interior. The vessel seemed to groan as the shock passed through it. The light bulbs shattered. La Salle had never known such darkness. Utter darkness. He felt his stomach heave, his pulse throbbed in his head. He fought to keep down the surge of fear. One of the men shouted something; the others laughed. They were still plummeting towards the ocean floor. In control? Damaged? There was another explosion, frightening, but less close than the first.

'Flugzeug!' someone called out.

La Salle recognised the word: aeroplane. So they were under attack from the air. *It could even be a British aircraft*, he thought. The Royal Naval Air Service had a number of machines in that part of France.

The U-boat seemed to be levelling out. Men around him were finding their feet on the sole, regaining balance. An electric torch flickered. Then another. He saw Hirsch a couple of feet away. He was grinning.

'They only have two bombs,' he said gleefully.

The U-boat was returning to an even keel. The whirring noise increased slightly and La Salle guessed they were motoring at her submerged speed. The lights were restored. He felt the chill of cold sweat inside his shirt. He put an arm behind his back and rubbed. Just then something touched his leg. A hot trickle ran down into his shoe. He jerked his head down, concentrating his eyes in the gloom. An enormously fat cocker spaniel was looking up at him, having just piddled on his foot. Hirsch glanced around, saw the dog and emitted a loud guffaw. He slapped his thigh a few times.

'Fritz! Komm!'

The dog ambled over to Hirsch. The boy picked it up, nuzzled it, apparently unconcerned by its behaviour.

'English dog,' he said. 'From an English freighter. We picked him up out of the sea. He loves wurst. We are teaching him German.' He kissed the dog's nose, beaming. 'Soon he will be a German dog.'

La Salle imagined a sinking steamer, men in the water. He shook his wet foot.

'With German manners?' he said.

'Oh? Ja!'

Hirsch set the dog on to the floor and it waddled aft, apparently quite at home in that stinking tube of steel. A man leaned through the bulkhead opening and gestured to Hirsch. They exchanged a few words.

'The captain will see you,' Hirsch said. He held out at a friendly arm to usher La Salle aft.

Kapitanleutnant Falk was standing at a massive steel structure, surrounded by dials, levers, metal wheels and cables clipped to bulkheads. Men were at various stations nearby. La Salle guessed it was the command centre of the ship. Falk looked up, waved Hirsch away and led the way towards the curtained recess off the control room. It was the smallest cabin La Salle had ever seen aboard any craft. The bunk disappeared halfway along its length into a locker, with just enough room for a man's legs. There was a desk attached to the bulkhead and a metal stool secured by a hinge. Falk gestured him to sit at the stool, his back to the desk, while he sat on the bunk. There was barely two feet between them.

'We are at the end of our patrol,' Falk said baldly. 'We want food to take back to our families.'

He was chewing a pencil. The end was feathered from continual nibbling.

'The English are trying to starve us,' he continued, almost as if he were talking to himself. His eyes roamed the unlined deckhead, festooned with cables. Then he faced La Salle, fixed him with a hard look.

'They won't succeed!' he rasped. He tugged at the strands of his sparse beard thoughtfully. Then, more gently: 'Are you a fisherman, La Salle?'

La Salle felt his heart pound. Falk was still looking into his face.

'Not really,' he said. 'My family own a boatyard. A few boats. It is hard to get sailors.'

Falk nodded. 'I knew you weren't a fisherman. And is your family rich enough to buy you out of the war?'

La Salle smiled. Falk was talking about substitution, the appalling French practice of paying someone to take a conscript's place.

'Oh, they finished with that some years ago,' he said. 'I was refused service. My eyesight is very bad.' La Salle made a silent vote of thanks to Maurice, the short-sighted driver who had taken him to Brest.

Falk laughed, showing a set of small stained teeth.

'It's strange how little failings can save a man's life, isn't it?' he grinned. He resumed his serious air.

'The war will not be won in the trenches. The victor will be the side that manages to starve the other. The Spartans, great warriors though they were, could not defeat the Athenians. But what brought that long war to end? How did Sparta triumph? Hunger! They used their ships to block the grain route into Piraeus. The Athenians had to ask for terms. The English will do the same when our U-boats subdue them. You, the French, won't starve. But the English will. They must be supplied from the sea and we shall control it. When everything runs out, when the English are eating grass, they will stop trying to fight us. And we shall return to Paris. This time, we shall stay.'

La Salle shrugged. 'I have lived in Paris,' he said. 'I like it as a French city.'

'You will like it as a German city,' Falk said quietly. 'You'll see.'

'How many more civilians will have to die before that happens?'

Falk turned his head sharply.

'Civilians? What civilians? The men supplying Britain with food are the enemy, as far as I'm concerned.'

La Salle could not help himself.

'I was thinking of the *Lusitania*.'

Falk slid off the bunk and pushed past him to a

286

bookshelf over the desk. He removed a large book, opened it, searched for a page and pushed it under La Salle's nose.

'There!' he said. 'Read!'

It was *Brassey's Naval Annual, 1913*. La Salle looked down at the English text and made a face.

'I can't read that,' he said.

Falk snatched the book away.

'Lusitania,' he read, then translating directly into French: *'Built under special Admiralty subvention for the Cunard line. Armament: eight 6-inch guns. Permitted to fly the Blue Ensign.'* He snapped the book closed.

'Do you know what the Blue Ensign is?'

La Salle shook his head.

'It is the flag of the British navy reserve. *Lusitania* was an armoured cruiser. What do you say now of your allies? Who use women and children to shield their warships?'

La Salle knew *Lusitania* and her sistership, *Mauretania*, had been built with an admiralty grant and it was known both were on the reserve list. But neither had been called into service and he was sure neither had been armed. Yet he could see how, to Falk, the evidence of *Brassey's Annual* would be enough to judge them ships of war.

'I was in Germany when Schweiger sank the *Lusitania*,' Falk said. 'I read the newspapers, the comments from around the world. No one mentioned this!' He shook the *Brassey's* violently over his head. 'No one!' He relaxed a little and his voice took on a schoolmasterly tone.

'In war, La Salle, atrocity is a matter of interpretation.' He handed him the book. 'Replace that for me, please.'

La Salle took the volume and turned, for the first time, towards the bookshelf. His eye fell on a few grainy photographs pinned to the shelf. One was of a three-masted schooner. In the background was the familiar shape of Haulbowline Island. The ship was *Freya*. Across the bottom of the print someone had written "Spurlos Versunkt" then, in English: "Devils sent to Hell!"

He pushed the *Brassey's* back into its place, trying to suppress the trembling in his hand. So they had been betrayed. Some spy had circulated a photograph of *Freya* to German naval intelligence. Were the other photographs pinned to the shelf also of Q-Ships? He paused, unwilling to look around before he could compose himself. He noted Falk's small collection of books. The spines were mostly written in Greek. He thought he recognised Plato. He turned, resumed his seat on the stool.

'Sparta's victory was followed by an age of tyranny, I seem to recall,' La Salle said evenly.

'You are wrong. The Thirty Tyrants were men of wisdom. Their title has been misinterpreted.'

'Excuse me,' La Salle said calmly. Then: 'My people will bring your goods tomorrow.'

'Good. You can go then.'

La Salle stood, sensing the interview was over. Falk was chewing his pencil thoughtfully.

'You may feel you have been treated unjustly,' he said. 'But in war one should try to remember the words of Thucydides: "Justice exists only between equals in power, while the strong do what they can and the weak suffer what they must." We are the strong, La Salle. You see that, don't you?'

La Salle smiled. 'Thucydides? Wasn't it he who said of all the manifestations of power, nothing impresses more than restraint?'

Falk showed his unusually small teeth; a half-grin.

'Don't let me think you are a classics scholar, Frenchman. I might be reluctant to let you go!'

La Salle nodded and brushed past into the control area. Hirsch was waiting. He conducted him forward.

The U-boat motored onward, the electric engines making little more than a soughing whine. La Salle stretched out on his bunk, aware that the dog had returned. It was lying on the sole nearby.

'Fritz likes you,' Hirsch said, returning from some task aft.

'What does he do to those he dislikes?' La Salle said, thinking of his wet foot. Hirsch did not fully understand. La Salle spared him discomfort.

'I like dogs,' he said simply. Hirsch nodded enthusiastically.

The ship remained submerged. La Salle became aware of a tightness in his chest, a slight pounding in the ears. His throat was dry. His breathing cycle seemed to have changed. Falk was right about the smell. He was getting used to it. But there was something else in the fetid atmosphere of the U-boat, something noisome. He became afraid. It was not the sharp fright that accompanies sudden danger, or the giddy sensation of fear he'd known in action. This was different. It was a gathering sense that he was suffocating. The thought struck hard and for an instant he was seized by an urge to run, to escape. Air. He needed air. There seemed to be a casual watch system aboard the submarine and Hirsch was lying on his bunk over the torpedo. La Salle lowered himself to the floor. The spaniel did not stir as he stepped over him, groping his way forward. He became aware of a ringing in his ears. His movements seemed ponderous. Hirsch was asleep. He shook his shoulder gently.

'There's no oxygen,' La Salle said. 'No air. No air down here.'

Hirsch blinked and sat up. He felt in his trouser pocket, pulled out a watch, opened it.

'We're going up soon.' He pointed a finger upwards. 'It will be dark now.'

La Salle felt his way back to his bunk. The dog stirred as he climbed over it, but there was no other sign of life in the forward part of the ship. He could hear muffled voices from the after end of the long passageway and there was light there. He lay down, felt a wave of drowsiness. *God, how he longed for the green fairy.*

He was jolted awake by a long, deep gasping noise. The machine seemed to be exhaling. Then he detected a change of trim. The boat was rising forward. There was another blast of breath, from somewhere outside. She was surfacing. He lay quite still. He could hear men moving around quickly. The voices were louder. The trim seemed to change again. She was level. There was a clanging noise, then the throb of pumps. A draught of air. He sucked it in greedily. Hirsch came over to his bunk.

'Dinner time,' he said.

La Salle counted nine men, including himself, around the tiny steel table. They ate a thin pea soup in which floated a meat-like substance that reminded him of the Royal Navy's Harris's pre-cooked bacon. There was also a plate of tinned sausage which he declined to try, to the delight of Fritz. A couple of the men asked him questions, with Hirsch revelling in the role of interpreter. They seemed obsessed with the notion that France was stuffed full of wonderful things to eat and drink, overflowing with an abundance they had not known since the English blockade began. One of the German sailors sought reassurance that the chaloupe's crew would bring the things their captain had ordered.

' Yes,' La Salle said. 'My men will bring the food.'

'Good,' the German replied. 'My wife has not tasted chicken for six months.'

They drank a brackish coffee then Hirsch and the rest went aft, to be replaced by the other watch. La Salle returned to his bunk. From what he could gather the U-boat was at least partly surfaced and in hunting trim. He fell into an uneven sleep, repeating in his head a short prayer: *let no one sink her before I do.*

CHAPTER TWELVE

Di Fario was waiting when they docked the chaloupe. He listened as Laurentine briefly described the encounter with the U-boat then, without saying anything, he ushered them into the house. He stood in front of the range in the big kitchen, a finger pressed against pursed lips.

'Of course, we shall do everything they ask," he murmured.

They were gathered around him. Like children, Granger thought miserably. Di Fario's shoulders were square, his back straight. His eyes gleamed.

'Show me the list,' he said.

Granger handed over the piece of paper. The old man scanned it quickly.

'This will take some time to put together.' He turned to his daughter: 'Laurentine, the market is today, isn't it?'

She nodded.

'Good. That will help us.' He ran a finger down the page, stopped at 'two dozen live hens', continued. He turned to Granger.

'How much money did he give you?'

Granger felt in his pocket for the wad of notes and handed it over. Di Fario flicked through the money.

'I'd say there is more than enough here.' He waved Falk's list. 'Laurentine and I will attend to this.' He looked at Roberts. 'Is everything ready? With the charges?'

Granger stepped forward.

'The charges are my concern, Thomas,' he said evenly.

Di Fario's face took on an expression Granger had not seen before. The eyes that laughed and always seemed to suggest a droll thought was never far away, hardened to a cold stare. Di Fario stood over him, his powerful frame quite tense. Granger resisted an idiotic urge to square up.

'And mine,' di Fario said, 'because we go together.'

Granger felt Roberts and Chalky staring at him. They understood all right.

'Oh no. We don't. This is a navy job now.' Granger added lightly: 'Why would you want to get into something like this anyhow?'

The older man shrugged.

'Fate, perhaps.' He waved an arm distractedly. 'Whatever it is, none of you leave here in the chaloupe unless I go with you.'

Granger emitted a short laugh.

'Thomas, how could you stop us?' he asked in his most affable way. He tried to think of the French to add, in a joking sense, something about the disadvantages of being outnumbered, when di Fario took a half-step towards him. Granger experienced a shiver of shock. Di Fario's entire body radiated menace, danger. His eyes seemed fixed on something deep inside Granger's head. Granger shifted his weight and leaned back.

'Thomas …' he began. But the man in front of him was no longer the father-like character he had come to like so much. He was now dealing with someone who had shot down men, lived among and fought with killers who inspired terror in their enemies. He knew di Fario had been damaged by his war. He had not suspected he carried murder in his soul. Now he saw it.

'I will stop you,' di Fario said softly.

Granger became aware of his own fists being tightly clenched. He relaxed self-consciously, searched desperately for some solution to this. Found nothing.

'I have to talk to my men,' he said finally.

Di Fario nodded, backed away. Granger signalled Roberts and Chalky to follow him out into the yard.

'Thomas wants to come with us,' he said flatly.

'Blimey,' Chalky said. 'I thought something was up.'

Roberts ran the back of his hand over his mouth.

'Why does he want to do that?' he growled.

'I don't know. He seems to have some reason of his own.'

Granger made a gesture with his hands. Too late, he realised it might have been taken as a sign of helplessness. The sense of wretchedness deepened.

'If we don't take him he could scupper the whole plan,' he said.

Roberts thought for a moment.

'I say take him. The plan wouldn't be much cop without him anyway.'

Granger glanced over to the quay and their newly-acquired ship. Roberts was right. Di Fario had been crucial to everything they had done. Salvaging the depth bombs, getting the boat – even the secret wire in the tender's painter was a masterstroke that had not occurred to any of them apart from him.

'All right,' he said.

It was early evening when di Fario and his daughter returned in the launch. The boat was down on its marks and Granger, waiting to take their lines, noted with apprehension the crates of squawking hens lashed to the afterpart.

'Did you get it all?' he asked.

'Everything,' Laurentine said.

They transferred the goods to the chaloupe's tender, packing the cases of wine down low alongside the tinned meat and vegetables, with the hams, cheeses and boxes of biscuits and chocolates on top. The hens were packed in the stern and di Fario brought out light tarpaulins to cover the piles of food. Space was left around the thwart for Granger to row. It would be slow work, he reckoned, with that much weight in the boat. The others went inside and he and di Fario made a last check of the chaloupe. Satisfied, they stepped down on to the jetty and, as one, glanced at the sky. The heavens seemed entirely settled and di Fario forecast fine weather with little wind.

'Just what we want,' he said.

The day broke as he predicted. There was a light sea breeze and the mist revealed by the dawn soon gave way to warm sunshine. They checked the stowage in silence. The bulkhead they had built around the depth bombs was obscured by the food and wine, but the three lines leading to the triggering mechanisms for the smoke and the charges were clear of the packages. Roberts had the cords secured to three small cleats on the starboard gunwale, inboard. He and Granger went over the drill one last time; the forward line pulled the safety pin in the timer, arming the charges. The middle cord set off the smoke. The aftermost cleat held the line that started the sixty second timer on the explosives.

Granger looked for Laurentine as they brought the tender astern of the chaloupe and made it fast. He hadn't seen her for an hour or more. Di Fario was boarding the chaloupe, carrying a long leather case.

'Have you seen Laurentine?' Granger asked him.

Di Fario shrugged and shook his head. He tucked the long satchel in behind the sweeps and went forward where Roberts was preparing to cast off the bow line. Granger felt suddenly desolate. He could not leave like this, without seeing her, without saying goodbye. He checked an impulse to call out her name. Too late now.

Chalky called 'all clear' on the stern line, the bow was free and Granger steered the chaloupe into the channel with the boat's paraffin engine puffing out a healthy cloud of white smoke. He glanced back at the quay. It was deserted.

Di Fario had the chart on his knee and was plotting their course, back to the position La Salle had marked.

There were a few fishing boats in the Raz, but they could see no ships. *Good*, Granger thought. Roberts was watching the tender. It pulled steadily at the line made fast to the chaloupe's stern and seemed to cope well with the load it was carrying. The rope with the wire in it was coiled innocently on top of the tarpaulin covering the hens, although Granger noted a certain untidiness about it he had not previously remarked. Roberts lit a cigarette.

'Everything all right back there?' Granger asked.

'Seems to be,' Roberts said.

After three hours motoring they reached a point di Fario judged to be within two miles of the rendezvous. They were ahead of time. Granger was reluctant to stop the engine. There was no wind and he wanted to reach the meeting place and circle rather than risk being caught without power if the motor refused to re-start.

'If something goes wrong, you'll have to run for it,' he said.

Di Fario smiled. 'We cannot outrun a U-boat. Even submerged it would catch this vessel easily.' He pointed to a feature on the chart, southeast of Ushant.

'I would try to head for here. Ile de Molène.'

Granger saw a mass of rocks and shoals around several small islands.

'He could not follow us in there,' di Fario said. 'It would just be a question of whether we could get there before he disposed of us.'

Granger decided not to relay this to Roberts and Chalky.

'You have the smoke,' he said.

Di Fario nodded, expressionless. Granger felt a wrenching in his guts. Was di Fario forgetting it was he, Granger, who was taking the greatest risk? And La Salle?

Di Fario seemed absorbed by something about the tender, tugging hard at the line fastened to the chaloupe.

'Did you re-pack the goods?' he asked.

Granger shook his head.

'Well, someone has,' di Fario muttered. 'Let's get it alongside.'

Granger eased back on the motor, mystified. Di Fario was hanging over the side, pulling the tender up to the port quarter.

'What's going on?' Roberts asked, shuffling aft. Granger shrugged and was about to say he was unable to divine the actions of a madman when Laurentine's head appeared at the gunwale.

'Bloody hell,' Roberts said.

Chalky started from his place near the mast.

'What the devil –' he began, then Laurentine was aboard, holding Granger's stare with a defiant triumph in her eyes.

Di Fario let the tender drop back into its position astern. He turned towards his daughter. His face had acquired a paleness and his features appeared slack. He spoke quickly and quietly to the girl. Granger was unable to follow what he said but he understood perfectly her reply.

'I will not be denied,' she said, forming the words around an angry hiss.

Di Fario seemed about to speak again when Laurentine's eye fell upon the gun case lashed to the frames amidships. She turned to her father.

'Did you hope to be able to use that?' she said, almost mockingly. She crossed the deck, dropped to her knees, untied the case and opened it. She slid out the Spencer rifle, looked down the barrel, checked the sight and moved the trigger guard to load the first round. Di Fario spoke again but she ignored him, felt inside the case and removed two more tubes of ammunition, slipping them into the pocket of her fisherman's smock.

Granger felt his mouth go dry. The way she handled the gun was upsetting. There was something in the practised, familiar movements he found shocking. As if it were some treasured plaything from childhood. He swapped hands on the chaloupe's tiller, moved closer to di Fario.

'Now what?' he asked accusingly.

Di Fario shook his head, faced him.

'What would you have me do? Throw her overboard?' He paused, seemed to stumble on a secret thought. 'She wants to kill Germans.' His voice cracked. 'Like I did.'

Granger glanced at Roberts. The Welshman shifted his gaze from di Fario to Laurentine, still kneeling with the rifle in her hands, back to Granger. Roberts made a slight movement of his head. *You can do nothing*, it seemed to say.

Di Fario laid a hand on Granger's arm.

'Don't worry about us,' he said, recovering his poise. 'The plan is a good one. We carry on as agreed.'

'Here we go,' Chalky said suddenly. He was pulling something out of a bundle he'd been carrying. Granger saw it was the lifevest he'd been wearing when they were picked up. His *Titanic* lifevest.

Roberts was pointing. They followed his outstretched arm. A periscope, trailing a white feather of wake, was moving off their starboard side. Granger slowed the motor and pulled the lever to disengage the shaft.

'Don't turn it off,' he said. He handed the tiller to di Fario and took off his shoes. The U-boat was closing with them, surfacing slowly. They watched, not moving. At a few hundred feet it shook off the last cascades of water and sat motionless on the sea. They saw figures; the officers of the day before emerged in the conning tower then men appeared on deck. Granger recognised the seaman who had rowed away with La Salle. He thought he saw his friend's blue shirt. Yes. It was him. Just forward of the conning tower. There was something at his feet. Granger squinted. It looked like a dog. Goddamn. Then his eye fell on two men working aft. They were setting up a Maxim gun. A mast had been raised from the conning platform.

Granger saw two flags run up: *QN; COME TO MY STARBOARD SIDE.*

'Let's get the boat alongside,' Granger said, with a manly effort to keep the turmoil in his chest out of his voice.

They pulled the tender forward, held it amidships. He swung a leg over the chaloupe's gunwale and turned back.

'Well,' he whispered in English. 'Good luck.'

He climbed into the boat, pulled in the painter, lifted the coil of line on the chicken coops, laid it down carefully and pushed off. The boat was sluggish to row. He strained at the oars, trying to get a little momentum going. The U-boat was more than 200 feet away, he guessed. Not as close as the previous day. The two men at the Maxim gun were watching him. He saw a rail at the edge of the submarine's deck and rowed towards it. He glanced down at the three cords fastened to the cleats on the gunwale. *Try not to think about anything,* he told himself. *Just do what has to be done.* The tender's starboard bow bumped gently against the U-boat's side. He threw the forward painter to a rating leaning down from the deck. As casually as he could, he picked up the line aft, lying in a stiff coil on the tarpaulin and executed a swift bend on the steel rail, securing the boat's stern. The hidden wire tightened hard on the U-boat's metalwork. *Yes,* Granger thought. *It would be impossible to release that without cutters.* He looked up. No one seemed to notice the stiffness in the line. The men on the submarine's deck were all looking at the packages in the boat. Where was La Salle? He had been right there, now he had disappeared. Granger pulled back the tarpaulin. The sudden clamour from the hens startled him. 'Steady,' he said under his breath. 'Steady.'

One of the men on deck started climbing into the boat. Granger watched helplessly as the man brushed past him, reached into one of the cages, pulled out a squawking bird and held it over his head like a trophy. The men on the U-boat laughed. Some clapped.

Then he saw La Salle. He had edged forward, to a clear space at the deck edge. La Salle waved and made a crooking gesture with his finger, as if pulling a trigger. Granger looked up at the man with the hen, smiled and reached for the cleated cords. He loosened them, pulled out the safety pin. He took a deep breath, then yanked on the line to start the timer. He glanced back at La Salle, nodded and stood on the tender's thwart. Then he triggered the smoke. Nothing happened. The German sailor was saying something, asking him something. Granger saw La Salle jump clear into the sea. He mumbled at the sailor, twisted on the thwart, dived deep over the side.

Never had he swum so fast. Granger surfaced far from the boat, striking hard back to *Telenn Mor*. He flipped on his back, tried to locate La Salle. He saw him in the water, swimming in his direction. Still no smoke. Just then the red-bearded officer shouted and pointed and a sailor on the U-boat dived into the sea. It was the boy in the dinghy. The one who had rowed La Salle to the U-boat. The German boy began swimming powerfully towards La Salle. Granger saw the dog. It jumped in after the sailor.

Granger ducked his head, sliced hard with his arms, kicked fiercely and turned towards his friend. The German had almost caught him. Granger flew through the water, vaguely aware of men moving around the boat tied fast to the submarine. No smoke. Nothing.

The boy had La Salle by the foot. Then he crooked an arm around his neck.

'Komm! Come back!' Hirsch shouted.

Granger dived. He came up, reached between the swimmer's legs and gripped his balls. Granger closed his fist like a vice. Twisted. Hard. The knees came up in a quick jerk, almost catching his head. He surfaced.

La Salle had broken free. The German was gasping. Granger smashed a fist into his face. Then again. His hand came back running with watery blood. He turned. Shouted to his friend.

'Swim! Go!'

They were less than a hundred feet from the submarine. No smoke. No smoke from the tender. Granger turned to look at the men on the Maxim gun. One was aiming the weapon straight at them, the other held a belt of ammunition. Then he heard something. A crack. One of the gunners clapped a hand to his forehead. Another crack. The man with the ammunition pitched forward, lay still. Granger rolled on to his belly, swam face down, six strokes to a breath. He raised his head. La Salle was close to the chaloupe. He saw Laurentine standing in the stern, aiming her father's rifle. There was a shot. A rhythmic movement of her hand. Reload. Another shot. Granger was close enough to see her face, tucked into the stock of the ancient gun, calm, aiming with expert care. Chalky and Roberts were pulling La Salle aboard. He reached them, took a hand lowered from the boat, pulled upwards. *Well*, he thought. *It seems a lot more than a minute.* Another shot. Granger looked back. There were inert shapes around the Maxim gun. A man had slumped to his knees on the conning platform; an officer's cap had fallen over his face. The deck was empty. Granger raised himself to get a leg over the gunwale.

'He's diving!' Chalky, wearing his *Titanic* lifevest, was pointing at the U-boat. It had taken on a bows-down angle. Granger took Roberts's hand and heaved himself aboard the chaloupe. La Salle was watching the U-boat.

'Yes. She's going down,' he said, breathless, his chest heaving.

Laurentine dropped an empty ammunition tube to the deck, slid another out of her pocket. There was nothing to fire at now. No living thing on the fast-disappearing submarine's deck.

'What's he doing?' Chalky cried, not taking his eyes

off the U-boat's mast, all that could be seen of the vessel.

'The captain is dead. Perhaps the first officer, too,' di Fario said softly. 'They are panicking.'

'Looks that way,' Granger said, staring at what was now an empty patch of sea. 'He left his mast up. Gun on the deck.' It occurred to him that there were probably no volunteers to recover the Maxim gun, given the deadly sniper fire that had accounted for its crew.

La Salle turned to Laurentine.

'Did you shoot the commander?' Unaccountably, he addressed her in English and was about to repeat the question when Chalky broke in excitedly.

'Did she?' he babbled. 'Got him in the head. One shot! And the other one! Wounded him, anyway. And the gunners!'

'God in heaven,' La Salle breathed, shaking his head. 'God in heaven.'

The chaloupe was gathering way, but slowly.

'What's he going to do?' Chalky asked, still staring at the patch of sea vacated by the U-boat.

La Salle tried to think, clear his head.

'Well, he can't be sure about what we've got here, in the way of weaponry,' he said. 'The crew know all about Q-Ships so he'll play safe, go down to a comfortable depth and get out of range of anything we might carry on a boat this size. That's my guess.'

'Then what?' Chalky said nervously. 'Torpedo?'

'Possibly,' La Salle replied. 'More likely he'll try to blow us out of the water with his gun. From a safe distance.'

'What's that?' Chalky pointed to something in the water, off the boat's bow. They followed his arm. There were two shapes in the sea, swimming.

'It's Hirsch,' La Salle said. 'And Fritz.'

'Whoever it is, they're heading this way,' Granger said. 'One looks like a dog.'

He became aware of a movement. Laurentine had the rifle to her shoulder.

'No!' Granger leaped at her, swung an arm at the gun. Di Fario was quicker. He snatched the barrel of the rifle upward as she fired. He pulled the gun away and at first she resisted, then dropped her hands to her sides. She started to cry quietly and di Fario put an arm around her. Granger gently took the rifle out of di Fario's hand, kneeled on the deck and replaced it in its case.

As he straightened La Salle caught his eye. The devastated expression on Granger's face appalled him. He looked as if he had just been thrashed. *Yes*, La Salle thought, *he does love her*.

'We have to pick up those men,' di Fario said gruffly, apparently unable to discern, with his poor eyesight, that Fritz was a dog.

Seeing them approach, Hirsch gathered up Fritz and they were both hauled into the chaloupe. La Salle nodded at the boy. He was sniffing badly, his nose broken. He stared, said nothing, just hugged the fat, dripping spaniel closer to his chest.

La Salle ranged his eyes over the sea. The breeze was beginning to fill in from the southwest and he thought he saw a sail far to the westward. Miles away. Another fishing vessel, probably. There may have been another just astern of it. Well, whatever was going to happen would happen long before they came anywhere near them.

'How fast will she go?' La Salle asked no one in particular, trying to mask any trace of anxiety in his voice.

Di Fario shrugged. 'Six knots, perhaps. With this much weight.'

La Salle glanced astern. Even submerged, the U-boat could do better than that. He felt suddenly chill. The wind was working its way into his wet clothes. He shivered, ran his fingers through his matted hair.

'We should make for Ile de Molène,' di Fario said. He

sniffed the air. 'The breeze is strengthening. She'll sail faster than she'll motor.'

La Salle nodded. Granger had torn a piece off the bottom of his shirt and passed it to Hirsch, who gingerly dabbed at his nose. *My dear Hirsch*, La Salle thought grimly, *a broken nose may be the least of your troubles when your comrades get themselves organised. Well, Chalky might be able to do something for you.*

'Right,' he began. 'Let's get the sails up. Merrick, you steer and –'

If La Salle said any more than that, no one heard it. The noise of the explosion split the air around them, came up from the sea itself, a deep booming throb that, for a moment, wiped out even conscious thought. La Salle jerked his head around. A white plume streaked with black smoke was climbing out of the depths, not a mile away. It rose then tumbled around a crater of water which spread, then ebbed and in moments, was calm again.

'What was that?' Chalky cried, eyes wide.

La Salle looked at Roberts. The Welshman was standing, staring at the flattening sea.

'The hydrostatic!' Roberts shouted. Then, turning towards them and thumping a fist on his thigh: 'The bloody hydrostatic! I left the hydrostatic detonator on the second depth charge. He must have gone down more than forty feet!'

Di Fario did not understand. 'What happened? What's he saying?'

La Salle explained that Roberts had left one of the depth bombs with its original detonator, set to go off at a certain depth. There was no point taking extra risk in dismantling it. He had expected his homemade timer to set off both charges. Except the timer hadn't worked. But taking the tender, securely lashed with its steel reinforced line, down to forty feet must have triggered the hydrostatic fuse.

Di Fario looked hard at the sea, then back, holding La Salle's eye.

'So you have killed your submarine,' he murmured.

They motored towards the spot. Soon they were passing through a slick of oil, slivers of wood and a great quantity of bloodied feathers. There was a steady eruption of bubbles near the centre of the slick. They came up in a stream popping angrily through the surface then, as they watched, the bubbles became smaller until there was just a slight ripple beneath the oil and then, nothing.

Hirsch started to sob. He was standing, rocking back and forth with Fritz in his arms. Granger gently pushed him down on to a bench. The boy sat there, cradling the dog. Granger stood at La Salle's shoulder.

'Is that it?' he said.

La Salle turned away from the oily sea, facing his friend.

'Yes,' he said. 'That's it.'

La Salle looked towards di Fario, glanced away at the sky, then back, avoiding the old man's gaze.

'We'll try to sail home,' he said. 'We'll take you back. Then leave tonight.'

Di Fario nodded. La Salle was struck by the thought that di Fario had shrivelled. His rock-like features seemed to have crumbled. Laurentine was staring out over the side.

'There's no need to take us home,' she said quietly. 'Look.'

She lifted her head towards the west. La Salle saw the fishing boat he spotted earlier, sailing fast before the wind, closing with them swiftly. The people aboard would have heard and possibly seen the explosion, he thought.

'That is a Douarnenez boat,' Laurentine said.

She had somewhat recovered herself, La Salle saw, but she seemed strangely slight, drained of vivacity.

'Let's try to close with that vessel,' he said, in English.

Then, to di Fario: 'It would be better, Thomas – for everyone – if what happened here is not disclosed.'

Di Fario nodded.

'There are many things I should say. About what is owed to you,' La Salle continued. He turned towards Laurentine. 'Both of you.'

Di Fario raised his head. His lips seemed to move, but he said nothing, looked away. La Salle felt a surge of pity. So this is where his obsession had taken him. He had triumphed, finally, over his old enemy at the cost of living out the rest of his life with a hideous secret. And Laurentine, driven by a frightening mix of love and hatred, saving her man from almost certain death in a way that made her abominable in his eyes.

It was half an hour before they came alongside the fishing craft, a chaloupe a little smaller than *Telenn Mor*. Di Fario knew the boat and spoke quickly to the skipper, promising an explanation later. They rigged lines to hold the boats together and Laurentine climbed aboard, looking back, searching, waiting. Granger was engrossed in re-arranging the ties holding a folded sail. At last she turned away.

La Salle looked skyward as di Fario stepped up.

'The breeze is freshening. If it holds, we'll make Falmouth before morning,' he said.

Di Fario nodded, sucked in his cheeks. La Salle remembered something. He bent down, picked up the gun case and handed it to the old man. Their eyes met. Di Fario took the leather satchel and, without shifting his gaze, held it over the side and dropped it into the sea.

'Eh voilà,' he said, a film of tears on his cheeks. 'Adieu.'

He stepped stiffly aboard the Douarnenez boat as the crew watched in silent amazement, impatient for his story. They freed the lines and the wooden hulls bumped together for a moment before the sails filled with a crack and a widening stretch of sea opened between them. Granger took the helm and *Telenn Mor* galloped gaily to the north with the breeze on her port quarter. La Salle glanced at Hirsch, still cradling Fritz. No one spoke. He looked aloft. Their homemade white ensign fluttered boldly at the top of the foremast. *That will have to come down*, he thought, although he allowed himself a secret moment of joy. A bit of England created from a French flag. *Not unlike me.* Well, it would have to be lowered. For now. But in the future, in the war that lay ahead, it would be their battle flag. For him, Merrick and, if they wanted it, Roberts and Chalky.

He glanced at Granger, tweaking the tiller in his right hand, eyes focused on an empty sea ahead. La Salle wanted to reach out to him, smother his sadness the way a father engulfs in his loving arms a hurt child. Not now. The Channel lay ahead and a night of uncertainty. He caught sight of Chalky looking astern, staring. La Salle thought he had seen something and snapped his head around anxiously. But there was nothing. Just the fading shape of the Douarnenez chaloupe, aboard which two familiar figures could still be discerned, rising and falling on the abiding rhythm of the sea.